THE
APOSTLE'S
SISTER

JERUSALEM ROAD • BOOK FOUR

THE
APOSTLE'S
SISTER

ANGELA HUNT

BETHANYHOUSE
a division of Baker Publishing Group
Minneapolis, Minnesota

Published by Bethany House Publishers
11400 Hampshire Avenue South
Minneapolis, Minnesota 55438
www.bethanyhouse.com

Bethany House Publishers is a division of
Baker Publishing Group, Grand Rapids, Michigan

Printed in the United States of America

Library of Congress Cataloging-in-Publication Data
Names: Hunt, Angela Elwell, author.
Title: The apostle's sister / Angela Hunt.
Description: Minneapolis, Minnesota : Bethany House, a division of Baker
Publishing Group, [2022] | Series: Jerusalem road ; book 4
Identifiers: LCCN 2021061898 | ISBN 9780764233876 (paperback) | ISBN
9780764240065 (casebound) | ISBN 9781493437214 (ebook)
Classification: LCC PS3558.U46747 A66 2022 | DDC 813/.54—dc23
LC record available at https://lccn.loc.gov/2021061898

Unless otherwise indicated, Scripture quotations are from the Tree of Life Version. © 2015 by the Messianic Jewish Family Bible Society. Used by permission of the Messianic Jewish Family Bible Society.

Scripture quotations labeled NLT are from the Holy Bible, New Living Translation, copyright © 1996, 2004, 2015 by Tyndale House Foundation. Used by permission of Tyndale House Publishers, Inc., Carol Stream, Illinois 60188. All rights reserved.

This is a work of historical reconstruction; the appearances of certain historical figures are therefore inevitable. All other characters, however, are products of the author's imagination, and any resemblance to actual persons, living or dead, is coincidental.

Maps are copyright © Baker Publishing Group.

Cover design by LOOK Design Studio
Cover photography by Aimee Christenson
Cover architectural photography by Roman Robroek / Arcangel

Author is represented by Browne & Miller Literary Associates.

Baker Publishing Group publications use paper produced from sustainable forestry practices and post-consumer waste whenever possible.

22 23 24 25 26 27 28   7 6 5 4 3 2 1

The Old and New Testaments are filled with stories of daring men and noticeably few courageous women. This is not surprising, for the inspired writers could not recount every story of each man, woman, and child who experienced God. But even though few women's stories are recorded, they are still worthy of consideration. The JERUSALEM ROAD novels are fictional accounts of real women who met Jesus, were part of His family, or whose lives entwined with the men who followed Him.

Ancient Near East and Its Road Systems

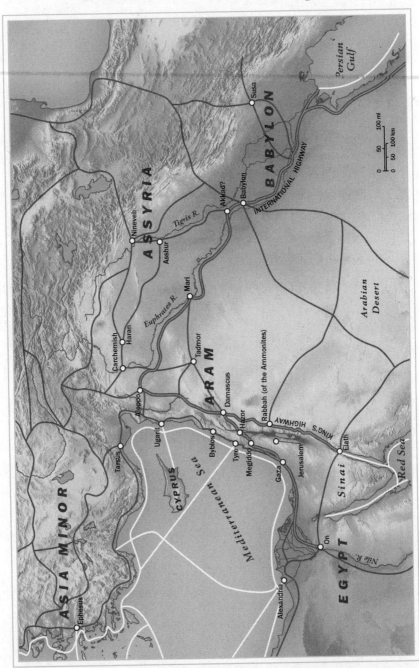

Jerusalem at the Time of the New Testament

Herod's Temple Complex

Daughter

AD 30

Only the love of God is capable of placing the one it loves on the altar.

Julia Blum, *If You Are the Son of God*

ONE

Aya

At thirteen, I carried a secret that would have broken my mother's heart and devastated my father. My rabbi would have scolded me had he known it, and the other girls at synagogue would have been horrified.

I did not want to marry.

At fourteen, I prayed HaShem would afflict my family with scandal or poverty to make me less attractive to a suitor, but my parents kept hinting about suitable matches. Whenever I tried to broach my concerns, my parents promised that I was destined to be as blessed as Sarah, Rachel, and Leah, the mothers of Israel.

At fifteen, I began to notice an eager light in the eyes of prospective fathers-in-law. After all, my father was a leader in Tarsus, as comfortable in the governor's palace as he was in our synagogue. We were Roman citizens, we owned a successful tent-making business, and I had been educated by the finest tutors in the city.

At sixteen, I could not understand why HaShem had showered our family with more blessings than others. Our wealth, our high standing in a Gentile city, our Roman citizenship—

why did we deserve them? And why were other families so desperate to join themselves to us?

When Abba came home wearing his best tunic and an ear-to-ear smile, I feared the worst had happened. The sight of our Torah teacher, smiling like a crazy man, confirmed my suspicion.

Abba spotted me in the atrium. "Ah, my Aya," he said, his lips the color of wine. "You are such a fortunate girl."

"Indeed." Gabor, the administrator of our synagogue, staggered beneath the weight of my father's arm. "Everything has been arranged for your future happiness."

I bit my lower lip to suppress the wail rising in my throat.

Ima must have been anticipating my reaction because she gripped my shoulders. "Is it—?"

"Avidan." Abba lifted his chin. "A fine young man and a serious scholar. Aya will make him a fine wife."

"Young?" Somehow the word slipped through my tight throat. "He is *old*."

"He is but twenty and six," Ima corrected, her grip tightening. "Only two years older than your brother."

"But Sha'ul is also old!"

When Abba squinted, I knew I should have kept quiet. Ima kept talking, eager to repair my social gaffe. "You will be grateful for a husband who has ten years more experience. Avidan will be wiser than a youth, and better equipped to take care of you and your children."

I bit my lip until I tasted blood, then slipped from Ima's grip and darted down a hallway, tears blurring my vision. In my bedchamber, I threw myself upon the bed and wept, though I knew my tears could not change my future.

My parents believed in three things: HaShem, the Law, and diplomacy, but they reserved diplomacy for their interactions with Gentiles. HaShem, on the other hand, was unchangeable and eternally direct, as was His Law. So I would do as I was told and marry a man I had only glimpsed from across the synagogue. I would be an obedient wife, I would bear my husband's children, and my own desires would not matter unless my husband was kind enough to care about them. This was the role of Jewish women, and I had been born to it.

The realization filled me with fresh despair.

"Aya." The door creaked as my mother entered the room. Her silk tunic rustled as she sank onto the bed. "I do not understand why you are so distressed. I was fifteen when I married your father, and he was twelve years older than I. I was always grateful to him for being more experienced."

"You are not me, Ima."

"How can you say that? You are my daughter. You are heart of my heart, flesh of my flesh—"

"But we are different. You have never wanted to do anything but marry and raise children."

Her brows flickered. "What else could a woman want? HaShem created us for those purposes. We are the guardians of our homes, our husbands' encouragers, and those who fill the earth with new life. We lead the celebration of Shabbat and educate our sons and daughters. Without us, men would be unable to provide and study and fulfill all the commands of the Law."

I slammed my face into my pillow. Ima would never understand.

"Aya? I do not know what else you think you could do, but you cannot remain an unmarried woman. Eventually your father and I will leave this world, and then what would happen to you?"

"I never said I wanted to live in your home forever."

"Then what do you want?"

"I . . . I don't know!"

The pillow muffled my words, but it didn't matter. In truth, I was not sure I understood my feelings. My parents had arranged a good marriage for me, so why did I long for something else?

13

"Aya? I am waiting for an answer."

Exasperated, I rolled onto my back and stared at the ceiling. "I do not know how to explain. It is only . . ." I shrugged.

"What, daughter?"

Ima was struggling to understand, and I knew she loved me. She also knew I possessed a gift, but she had never understood the pleasure I felt while exercising it. How could she when she did not share my love of music? When she opened her mouth to praise HaShem, a sound as deep and rough as my father's voice emerged. But when I sang, the melody soared up and out, like birdsong on a breeze . . .

I sat up and wiped my tears, hoping to make her understand. "Ima, I know you and Abba are trying to do the right things for me. But HaShem has given me the gift of music, just as He gifted Jubal. All I have ever wanted to do was play and sing."

"Have I not encouraged you? Did I not find students for you to teach?" Her hand rose to pat her elaborately curled hair. "You speak as though I am ignorant of your desires, yet you are blind to everything your father and I have done to please you. I suppose that is typical of young girls."

"I do not take you for granted, and I *do* appreciate what you have done." I exhaled slowly, forcing my emotions to calm. "But if I marry, my husband may not allow me to teach. He may not allow me to sing at the synagogue."

"Has Avidan not already heard you? Why would he forbid you to sing?"

"He is a scholar. Scholars build walls around the Law to restrain us."

"The Law does not forbid singing."

"Perhaps not, but the Pharisees certainly will. Give them time, and they will find a dozen reasons why a woman should not sing in public."

"Now you are being foolish." Ima folded her hands. "Yes, once you are married, you may have to abandon certain activities. You will have a household to run and a husband to please. Avidan may allow you to sing at home, but I do not think he will allow you to teach Gentiles. As for singing in public places—" she drew a deep breath—"your father and I have allowed you to sing at the occasional city festival because we did not want to offend the governor. You have been allowed unusual freedom, Aya, but things will change once you are married. You cannot know the same freedom you have in your father's house."

"You call this *freedom*?" I gaped in bewilderment. "I go where you tell me to go; I eat what you tell me to eat. I did not decide to sing for the governor; you arranged it to gain favor with him. I did not decide to give music lessons; you arranged them and chose my students. You and Abba have planned everything in my life since the day of my birth."

"And what sixteen-year-old has the authority to make her own decisions? None, not even the daughters of Gentiles."

"You could have asked what I wanted!"

"Why? If you wanted something inappropriate, we could not let you proceed. And have we not allowed you to do everything permissible?" Ima's conciliatory tone vanished, replaced by barely bridled irritation. "You are under our authority, Aya, and will be until the day you marry. We have protected you because you do not realize who and what you are. You are a daughter of Israel, living in an idolatrous and pagan city. If we had allowed you to go where you wanted, when you wanted . . ." She looked away, her chin trembling, and I knew I had pushed her too far.

After a long moment, she took my hand and encased it between hers. "One day"—she gentled her voice—"you will have children, and you will do anything in your power to keep them from harm or shame. You will forbid them to travel alone. You will shield them from people who could sully their reputations. You will choose their teachers and companions, forbidding them to associate with anyone who might poison their minds or lead them from the worship of HaShem. And one day, HaShem willing, you will choose a suitable bride or groom for your precious child."

I swallowed hard. "Ima, you gave yourself an impossible task. How could I not be exposed to pagans when I see idols on every street corner? How could I not meet idolaters when we attend banquets at the governor's palace? Even though we dine at a separate table, you cannot shield my eyes from the unclean foods, from the immodest dancers, from the slaves who wink at me as they carry trays past our table."

"Your father and I have not always been successful, but we have done our best." Ima closed her eyes. "Tarsus is not the Holy City; it is a Gentile capital. HaShem placed us here for His reasons, and we trust the Creator of the universe to guide and direct us. But we have taken precautions—why do you think we sent Sha'ul to Jerusalem as soon as he was old enough to study at a Temple yeshiva?"

"Because he was brilliant?"

"Because we did not want him to be overly influenced by the Gentiles in Tarsus. Yes, your brother is brilliant, thanks be to HaShem, because if he had been ordinary, he could never have obtained a place in a renowned yeshiva. But HaShem heard our prayers and Gamaliel accepted him. That is why your father and I are happy for you to marry Avidan. Under his protection, we know you will be safe."

I exhaled a long breath. Ima's voice overflowed with sincerity, so she believed her explanation. But what she had *not* said was equally true: they had sent Sha'ul to Jerusalem because he was the beloved firstborn. They sent him away because they wanted my brother to be an esteemed Pharisee, as was my father, to be another link in a holy chain of the *Hasidim*, the set apart.

I was neither brilliant, firstborn, nor male, and I could never be a Pharisee. Even though I had been a toddling child when Sha'ul left for Jerusalem, from an early age I realized my parents would never regard me with the same affection they gave my brother.

But then I discovered my gift. A voice was nothing unusual—every human had one, and many had voices more nimble than mine. But Sha'ul could not sing, a fact frequently confirmed on visits to the Holy City. Because I possessed something Sha'ul did not, I treasured my gift and honed it as best I could.

My parents had planned a traditional life for their second-born, but their refusal to acknowledge that I might be meant for more than marriage chafed like a chain around my wrists.

"Ima." I lowered my voice. "What harm would be done if I remained unmarried? I could continue to teach my students and sing at the synagogue. Does HaShem not rejoice in music and praise? Do I not bring you joy as a daughter? If Adonai intends for me to be married, perhaps a wedding can be arranged later."

"When you are no longer a fresh flower?" Sorrow mingled with love in my mother's eyes. "You bring me joy, daughter," she said. "You also bring me gray hairs because you do not know the world. The unmarried life is not for you. In time you would long for a home and children, and you would hate me for allowing you to follow your own inclination. You would yearn for a loving husband, but only widowers and old men would consider you. No, Aya, we will not let you follow your heart. You will obey us and follow HaShem's will."

I would have protested again, but Ima stood, settled her himation more firmly about her shoulders, and strode out of the room. She had listened to my protestations, but she had not heard the cries of my heart.

I cradled my head and wept over my frustrated desires. Did no other girls object to a planned marriage? Some of my friends had expressed reservations about their betrothed husbands, yet they did not utter a negative word after their weddings. Did they change their minds, or fear being disloyal to their husbands?

Surely some women discovered that marriage did not bring happiness or contentment.

My thoughts turned to my brother. My parents had arranged a betrothal for Sha'ul as well, and soon he would come from Jerusalem to claim his bride. My parents seemed relieved to have settled the future for both their children, but I wondered about my brother's state of mind. He had always been ambitious and focused on his studies, so could he be even less excited about the prospect of marriage than I?

TWO

Sha'ul

Ever eager to renew the bond between Jews and the Roman ruler of Cilicia, my father visited Cossutianus Capito, governor of the province, and asked if he would be willing to provide me with safe transportation from Jerusalem to Tarsus. I am certain Abba offered to pay, and equally certain that Capito, who wanted to retain his influence with my father, agreed to send a conveyance without charge. So instead of walking the dusty furlongs or riding a mule, I spent the journey in a closed carriage, frequently lulled into a shallow doze by the rhythmic creaking of wooden wheels.

From Jerusalem to Caesarea, I shared the conveyance with three Gentile merchants, who eyed my tallit with suspicion and spoke to each other in low whispers. They did not speak to me, for I was clearly a being whose mindset differed from their own.

The merchants departed in Caesarea and headed toward the port. A grizzled Roman army veteran replaced the carriage driver and climbed to his seat without a single glance inside.

From Caesarea we traveled to Tyre, and I had only my thoughts for company. Abba had insisted I come home, because twenty-four, he wrote, was long past the proper age for marriage and I had kept my bride waiting long enough.

He was correct, for my betrothal ceremony had taken place years before. I vaguely recalled meeting Bettina and her family in Jerusalem. To seal the marriage contract, I had presented her with a gold necklace my father purchased. I could not recall its design, only that her eyes lit with pleasure when she beheld it.

For two years I had been married in all but deed, but soon I would take possession of my wife and escort her back to Jerusalem. In his last letter, Abba mentioned that my sister had also been betrothed. In the spirit of economy that had made Abba a wealthy man, he planned to celebrate the two weddings within a few days of each other.

I did not know if Aya's betrothed wanted to be married so soon, but perhaps he burned with passion that should be assuaged. Though I saw my sister every year during Pesach and noticed that she had become a lovely young woman, I did not know her well. During the hectic celebrations of Pesach and Sukkot, when Jerusalem overflowed and tens of thousands visited the Temple, I had little time to converse with family members.

The situation would be different in Tarsus. How would I fill the hours in my father's house? He would not be interested in debating the Law, and I had no need to hear about his business. Ima would want to know about life in Jerusalem, and Aya—who knew what filled her girlish head?

When we arrived in Tyre at dusk, I climbed out of the carriage. The driver grunted in my direction, then unhitched the horses and led them to a barn, where he would probably bed down in the straw. I wrapped my cloak around me and went to the inn, where a large room had been furnished with a table and several flimsy cots. The air smelled of smoke, charred meat, and unwashed bodies. Three men had already stretched out on beds, and a fourth sat at a table, his head bowed and his hand wrapped around a clay mug.

I nodded at the woman, who looked up when I entered. "How much for dinner and a bed?"

"Two assarion."

I gave her the bronze coins and moved to the table, which offered a meal of bread, goat cheese, and grapes. I glanced around to see if anyone had not yet eaten his fill, but the figures on the beds did not stir, nor did the other man lift his head. I took the grapes, a solid chunk of crusty bread, and cut a slice of cheese. After pouring wine from a brass pitcher into a cup, I picked up my meager meal and sat cross-legged on a bed against the wall.

My mind filled with sour thoughts as I nibbled at the goat cheese. I did not want to be in Tyre, a city of unscrupulous merchants, religious idolatry, and brazen sexual immorality. Ezekiel had prophesied against Tyre, and the city's destruction could not come soon enough.

Nor did I want to eat and sleep in a Gentile inn. I would have to purify myself after this journey—I was in a building where Gentiles slept, among them shepherds and tanners and those who routinely worked with dead things. The air in this place was certain to be contaminated with substances that rendered a man unclean, so when I finally arrived at Tarsus, I would need to go immediately to a mikveh and wash the filth away.

I was also unhappy to be leaving Jerusalem. My fellow yeshiva students had mocked me, saying I was more devoted to the pleasures of women than to the study of Torah. Though I knew they were joking, their barbs stung. Nothing, not even a wife, could be more important than HaShem's holy Law. If I were free to do as I pleased, I would still be in Jerusalem, studying by lamplight as the words of holy men filled my head and heart.

My father had been wise to send me away. Though at the time I experienced loneliness and confusion—what boy of ten would not?—time and Torah taught me that I could not rely on anyone but HaShem. I was stronger on my own.

I briefly considered refusing my father's summons, but Gamaliel, my teacher and head of my yeshiva, echoed my father's opinion that a righteous man was required to marry and bear children. "A man with no wife is not a proper man; for it is said, 'Male and female created He them,'" Gamaliel reminded me, "and 'It is not good for man to be alone.' HaShem also said you should honor your father and mother. So go to Tarsus and fetch your bride. When you return, you will understand why Solomon wrote, 'Whoever finds a wife finds good, and receives favor from Adonai.'"

I was not yet convinced that a wife would be good—surely my duties to a woman would be a distraction—but I respected my teacher above all men and would walk through fire to obey him.

I finished eating and stretched out on the bed, covering my chest with my prayer shawl, careful not to allow the long fringes to touch the filthy floor.

I closed my eyes and slammed the door on my frustrating thoughts. Later, after I had cleansed my body and soul, perhaps I would understand why Gamaliel considered a wife a blessing and not a curse.

Until then, I would have to bear the frustration as best I could.

To cleanse my mind for the night, I recited the evening prayer:

"Hear, O Israel: the Lord our God, the Lord is One.

"Help us, our Father, to lie down in peace; and awaken us to life again, our King. Spread over us Your shelter of peace, guide us with Your good counsel. Save us because of Your mercy. Shield us from enemies and pestilence, from starvation, sword, and sorrow. Remove the evil forces that surround us, shelter us in the shadow of Your wings. You, O God, guard us and deliver us. You are a

gracious and merciful King. Guard our coming and our going, grant us life and peace, now and always. Amen."

My outlook brightened when I joined the driver the next morning. As I waited for him to break his fast, another Pharisee appeared on the road. I identified him as a brother at once, for his tunic, like mine, featured long blue fringes, a symbol of personal piety. His dark eyes gleamed from bony caves above his white beard. Probably thirty years older than I, he wore broad leather phylacteries that covered most of his forehead. I wore the phylacteries only when praying, but some wore them every waking hour—a practice I never wanted to adopt. People would know I was righteous due to my actions, so why advertise my piety?

As he entered the coach, the Pharisee gathered up the bulk of his garment to prevent his fringe from touching the wooden floor.

"Shalom," I greeted him.

He settled back on the seat, his eyes brightening when his gaze met mine. "*Shalom aleichem.*" He released the folds of his garment and crossed his hands in his lap. "Are you traveling far, brother?"

"As far as Tarsus."

"Tarsus." The man grimaced. "For what reason would a Pharisee journey to a Gentile capital?"

I forced a smile. "You forget that Tarsus is home to hundreds of righteous Jews. My family belongs to a community in that city—the provincial governor has even praised my father for his leadership. We live peacefully alongside the Romans, and they have always demonstrated their appreciation for my family's support."

The man snorted softly.

A sharp remark sprang to my lips, but then I decided to forgive his lack of manners. He was an elder and deserved respect.

I cleared my throat. "Where is HaShem leading you?"

"Sidon," he said. "I have business with an affiliated chaburah in that city. I must arrange for the transport of wine to our community."

I nodded. No Jew would drink wine from a Gentile vineyard, and no Pharisee would buy wine from a Jew who was not a member of the fraternity. We Pharisees were sworn to separate ourselves from the heathen and the unclean.

My companion propped his elbow on an armrest and stroked his untrimmed beard. "You must be visiting your parents."

I gave him a reluctant smile. "Indeed, I left Jerusalem only because my father insisted. I am going home to marry my betrothed. Then my wife and I will return to Jerusalem so I can continue my studies."

"A wedding!" Some of the sourness went out of the old man's features. "You are a blessed man. I have such fond memories of my wedding. I had met my bride only once, but, may HaShem be praised, she proved to be a beautiful and gentle woman. She has made me a happy man for many years."

"May it be so," I murmured, averting my gaze.

"You are not thrilled to celebrate your marriage?"

As the coach began to roll forward, I looked out the window. "My situation is similar to yours—at this point, I do not know my betrothed. I have met her twice."

"Is she not beautiful?"

I shrugged. "Are not all young girls attractive?"

The man snorted. "Ask a man who knows; they are not. If your bride is beautiful, why are you not thrilled? HaShem created Eve to be the perfect companion for Adam, and your wife will be the perfect companion for you. You will fit together like a tree and its bark, and she will bring joy to your eye and liveliness to your step. A righteous wife will do you good and not evil—"

"How do I know if she will be a righteous wife? Some women only pretend to be righteous."

My companion gaped. "Surely your father would not betroth you to a woman who was unsuitable. Does she observe the Sabbath? Does she honor her parents?"

"Do those acts prove what lies in the heart? Observing Shabbat, obeying one's parents—those are outward signs. I want a wife who is completely devoted to HaShem, and that sort of devotion is not always evident. I want a woman who loves HaShem with her heart, soul, and mind, and how can a man measure devotion in a woman he barely knows? I want a woman who can study with me, challenge me to learn more, and refine my behavior so I do not stray one breath from the Law I love more than anything."

"You do not want a wife," the man interrupted, his teeth gleaming above his white beard. "You want a Torah teacher. Trust me—among all the women of Israel, you will not find such a one."

I drew a breath and released it slowly. Perhaps this fellow saw my situation more clearly than I did. Elders often had such a gift.

"You imply that I am not fond of women, but I am. I love my mother and my younger sister. I appreciate the female form. Like most men, my pulse quickens at the thought of lying with a woman. I understand that HaShem established marriage to fill the earth and to prevent immorality among His people."

"But living with a woman . . ." The old man shook his finger at me. "Speak the truth—the idea terrifies you."

I stared out the window and considered his charge. Could I be terrified by the idea of living with a woman? I was not afraid of my mother or sister. I did not have a single female friend among my acquaintances, but he could not possibly be correct.

"Why would you say that?" I asked.

"When a man does not want to be married," the old man said, "he is either a eunuch or he is afraid his wife will not love him."

"I am not a eunuch," I said. "And I am not afraid."

But was I? The thought of *living* with a woman—of dealing with a home and children, of providing food and drink and clothing, of being responsible for others' lives as well as my own—the thought *was* daunting. What if I could not manage it? What if I failed?

What if my wife found nothing in me to love?

All I wanted—all I had ever wanted since beginning to study—was to obey the Law and reap the rewards of living a righteous life. Ever since coming to Jerusalem and seeing the rulers and chief priests at the Temple, I had dreamed of becoming such an esteemed scholar that I could earn a seat on the Sanhedrin. If HaShem willed, one day I might even rise to the highest position in Israel . . .

"A pity," I finally said, "that HaShem requires a righteous man to eat and drink and sleep and beget children."

"Why would you say so?"

"Because those distractions prevent us from studying Torah."

The older man's mouth twisted. "Perhaps man was not meant to study Torah without ceasing. The man who eats nothing but honey soon becomes sickened by sweetness. But the man who eats honey in moderation will always find it delightful."

I understood what he was trying to say, but this Pharisee was a merchant, not a Torah scholar.

"Let us hope for a safe journey," I said, propping my elbow on the windowsill. "And a quiet one, because I need to sleep."

THREE

Aya

"Aya! Shalom!"

I turned at the sound of a familiar voice and saw my best friend hailing me. I looked at my handmaid. "You may go home without me, Lyris."

"But your mother will be angry."

"I will be only a few minutes behind you. I would like to walk home with Moselle."

Lyris gave me a dubious look, then turned and started walking. I watched Moselle squirrel her way through the marketplace until she grabbed my hands. "I'm so glad to see you. Are you excited?"

I lifted a brow. "About what?"

Moselle scoffed. "Surely you jest. Even I have heard the rumors, and my father makes certain I am the last to know such news."

"What news is that?"

She laughed and squeezed my arm. "Silly girl. Surely you know Avidan is coming for you after Shabbat! His father has

27

completed the arrangements for your wedding—you *must* have heard. I am sure your parents have known for weeks because they sent for Sha'ul. My father says he and Bettina are to marry the week after you and Avidan are joined."

My heart jumped in my chest. If she was right, why hadn't my parents told me?

"Your father is such a wise man," Moselle continued, oblivious to my panic. "Having Sha'ul come to Tarsus is brilliant. He can be part of your wedding, and you can be part of his."

I turned away, unwilling to let her see the emotions that had to be rampaging across my face. I would be married so soon? Of course my parents would not warn me—they would save the news until the last moment so I would not have time to whine or complain. But they would inform the leader of our synagogue, the baker, the servants, and even Sha'ul, who must have left Jerusalem days ago.

I gritted my teeth and leaned toward my friend. "So I am to be married—what of it? Tell me, what have you heard about *your* wedding? Surely it cannot be far away."

Moselle's cheeks went crimson, and I felt guilty for my sharp words. Her betrothed, the son of a butcher, was renowned for his laziness. He had a tendency to sleep while others worked, yet his father always made excuses for him. I used to wonder why the administrator of our synagogue would betroth his daughter to a slothful man, but then I overheard my mother telling a friend that the butcher had promised Moselle's father an unusually large dowry.

Even at sixteen, I knew money was the answer to many mysteries.

Moselle sighed. "I have heard nothing from my betrothed. But the wedding will surely happen soon."

"I hope so. Then I will not be alone in my misery."

"Listen to you!" Moselle swatted my arm. "You cannot be serious!"

"Why shouldn't I be? When I marry, my life will change forever. I will lose my parents and my best friend."

"You will not lose me. I shall visit you every day, if Avidan will allow it."

"How would he know? He will spend most of his time studying at the yeshiva. You may visit anytime you like."

Moselle drew her lips into a tight smile. "If you do not want to marry, why did you accept the betrothal contract?"

I snorted. "How could an obedient daughter refuse?"

"If memory serves, you have not always been perfectly obedient."

"I signed because Abba said he would find another scholar if I did not accept Avidan. If he found another scholar, I might find myself living in Jerusalem, and I would rather die than leave Tarsus."

Moselle linked her arm through mine. "Do I mean so much to you?"

"You do. I do not want to lose you, my parents, or . . ." I hesitated, trying to find the words to describe my feelings about the city of my birth. "Jerusalem is rigid and forbidding. I can breathe in Tarsus." I tugged on Moselle's arm. "Come, we should go. My mother will send the servants for me if I am not home soon."

"Where is your handmaid? I thought I saw her—"

"I sent her home."

Moselle released a nervous laugh. "Your mother will be furious to know you are in the marketplace alone."

"I am not alone; I am with you."

"Still." Moselle cast an anxious glance around, where Jews mingled freely with Gentiles of every tribe. "My mother would say the marketplace holds too many Gentiles, too many ungodly men."

"I have done nothing wrong. I shopped with my handmaid by my side. I spoke to no one except the women who work in the booths."

Moselle's fretful look eased into a smile. "What did you buy?" She peeked into my shopping basket. "Fruit and linen? You should have been buying aromatic oils for your wedding night. Like Esther, you should be preparing for your king."

"I see no need to anoint myself like a sacrificial lamb. Avidan will take me as he finds me."

"Aya." Moselle halted, her arm an anchor impeding my progress. "I cannot believe what I am hearing. You are marrying one of the finest men in our community, and you should be grateful. Your father did not choose a lazy butcher's boy, but a serious scholar."

"You sound like your father."

"Perhaps. I think I am growing up. We are no longer carefree girls. We are brides, soon to be united with our husbands."

The chiding note in her voice made my blood run thick with guilt. Abba had done his best for me, and I could not find fault in my future husband. But I did not object to Abba's choice as much as I objected to what marriage would mean for my future. Why couldn't anyone understand?

"Dear friend." I softened my voice, hoping I could make her see things from my perspective. "I have no objection to Avidan. He seems nice."

"So why are you not excited about your wedding?"

"Because I will not be free to do what I want." I bit my lip, afraid I had been too blunt. I had told the truth, but the words, spoken aloud, made me seem selfish. "I spoke too quickly. I do not want to do horrible things. I simply want to continue teaching music and singing in the synagogue. Ima says that as a married woman I will have to keep a house, take care of my husband, and obey him in all things. I am not ready to surrender the things I enjoy."

Moselle eyed me with a critical squint. As a Torah teacher's daughter, she had been born and bred to observe the Law, but, like me, she possessed a daring spirit. She had never been openly disobedient, but whenever she saw a way to express her over-sized personality, she did not refrain from speaking her mind . . . with me, at least. Her honesty was one of the things I admired most about her.

"By the way"—I smiled—"what are *you* doing on the street without an escort?"

"Because I came to find you." She gave me a sidelong look. "You know I can slip through the marketplace like a mouse. No one could catch me, much less harm me."

I patted her hand as we began to walk again. "It is only by HaShem's grace we have not encountered trouble on our adventures together."

"I have never made you do anything you did not want to do." She sighed. "I will miss sneaking out to see you after you are married. And I do not think you will mind being under your husband's authority. Avidan may be more lenient than your parents. You may find he is a doting and generous husband."

I shrugged. "Even if that is true, I doubt I will have more freedom. We will be living with his parents, so they will be watching me."

"Your parents watch you now, so what will change?"

"My parents love me. His parents do not know me."

She bit her lip. "If you could have one night, even one hour, to do anything you wanted, what would you do?"

"What kind of question is that?"

"An honest one."

"I do not know how to answer."

She shrugged. "Perhaps you should think about it. And once you decide what your answer is, you should fulfill your desire the night before your wedding. If you want to slip out and go dancing, let us do it together. We could splash in the fountain outside the temple of Hebe, goddess of youth. We could go to the marketplace and eat anything we like, even forbidden foods. We could—"

"I want to sing." The words slipped from my lips like mischievous children.

Moselle's brows drew into a knot. "But you sing every week at the synagogue."

"I want to sing for people I do not know. I want to sing something other than the psalms of David. I want to sing a lament at a funeral. I want to sing a love song at a banquet."

Moselle gasped. "You want to sing for *Gentiles*?"

"I know I should not want to sing anything but sacred songs, but if a Gentile hears my song and is pleased with what he hears, is that a sin? My father says the governor often hires singers for his banquets—"

"Even I would not suggest you sing for the governor. Your father—and my father—would never condone it."

"But I have sung for a citywide festival. And Abba frequently visits the governor's house."

"He does not eat at the governor's table, does he? We have limits, Aya. We observe boundaries."

I pressed my lips together, conceding her point. My father allowed himself liberties Jerusalem Pharisees would never take, but there were certain lines he would never cross. He would never eat at the same table as a Gentile. He would never eat food forbidden by the Torah. And he would never allow his daughter to sing for an audience composed only of Gentiles. *That*, I could almost hear him saying, *would be like eating bread made only of leaven.*

If I married a non-Pharisee, perhaps the situation would be different, but Avidan had been inducted into his father's chaburah as soon as he became of age. He would be a Pharisee for as long as he lived, and I would soon be a Pharisee's wife, as set apart as my husband.

"No righteous husband would want his wife to sing before an audience of Gentiles," Moselle said, lowering her voice. "Your father would be astonished if he knew you were thinking of such things. Your mother would say the idea was in-decent."

"Then let us speak no more of it." My words silenced her, and we walked on.

But a few minutes later, Moselle spoke again. "Help me understand why you would want to risk incurring the wrath of your parents and your husband. What is so great about sing-ing? I like to sing, but not as much as I like talking to you or haggling in the marketplace."

I blew out a breath. "My mother sings around the house, even though she doesn't sing well. She must enjoy it because she does it often."

"So why are *you* not content to sing around the house? Surely Avidan would not object to you singing at home. He might even enjoy listening, so why is that not enough?"

I searched for words that would be true but not boastful. "I enjoy singing because when I sing, people see who I am." I gripped her arm as a flood of words spilled from my heart. "I read a story the other day, written in Greek. A girl was pray-ing to one of her gods and said she was happy to be obedient and gentle, soft-spoken and genteel, but she would rather be a twirling, leaping dancer, someone who could command the attention of kings and warriors—"

"Now you want to be a *dancer*?"

I sighed. "I don't want to be a dancer, but I understood that girl's feelings. I am surprised you do not." I peered into her eyes. "Have you, a Torah teacher's daughter, never wished you did not have to be the girl people *expect* you to be?"

Moselle snorted softly. "I wish it every day."

"Exactly. When Hagar fled into the wilderness and Adonai called to her, she said, 'You are the God who sees me.' To Him, she wasn't only a slave . . . He *saw* her and called her by name. I want people to *see* me. You don't want to be just another Torah teacher's daughter; you want to be the girl who dreams of dancing. I don't want to be a tentmaker's dutiful daughter; I want to be a singer . . . because that's what makes me unique."

I fell silent, suddenly exhausted. I had never verbalized these thoughts, and if Moselle hadn't pressed me, I might never have put my feelings into words. But there they were, and I couldn't deny them.

When I finally caught my breath, I squeezed Moselle's arm. "When HaShem bestows a gift, does He not expect us to use it? He instructed craftsmen to use their gifts in the building of the Tabernacle and the Temple. He gave David the gift of music to soothe King Sha'ul. He enabled Judah Maccabee to use his strength to create an army from unskilled farmers."

"They were men," Moselle pointed out. "Leaders."

"HaShem has also gifted women," I countered. "He gave Esther such beauty that a pagan king allowed her to save our people. He gave Moses' mother the courage to set her baby afloat on the Nile, and He gave Deborah the wisdom to put Barak over our army and defeat the Canaanites."

"And you expect HaShem to use your music . . . to do what? Set the Romans to flight?"

"I do not know," I admitted. "But I feel, and I do not feel like being married."

We walked on without speaking. The babble of foreign tongues and the whine of flies on a garbage heap flowed into the space our conversation had made.

"I do not know what to tell you," Moselle finally said. "My father appointed you leader of the women's choir, so you *are* using your gift to bless our community. And I do not know why I am marrying a butcher's son. But I trust my father, and I trust HaShem.

"I understand the yearning to live a different life, but how can we defy HaShem's plan? We cannot live apart from our families any more than we can live apart from the Law. 'In His book were written the days that were formed—'"

"'When not one of them had come to be.'" I finished the psalm and lowered my head. "You are right, of course. I know HaShem has written His plan for our lives, though I cannot see what that is. And that is—"

"Frustrating," Moselle finished.

I nodded. My friend understood the fire in my heart, but, like me, she was powerless to do anything but let it burn.

While Moselle would have been happy to walk me home, once we entered the Jewish district, there was no need. I insisted that she go home at once, and perhaps she would not get into trouble. With seven siblings, her mother might not realize her daughter had been away, but she would definitely notice if Moselle arrived too late to help prepare dinner.

I quickened my steps, anxious to shorten the time between my handmaid's arrival and my own. Ima would not be happy that I came home without Lyris, but I could bear Ima's displeasure better than my father's. Abba's disapproving countenance always held more sorrow than anger, and something in me shriveled whenever I disappointed him.

Every night, just before going to bed, I knelt for his blessing. Abba would place his hands on my head and pray:

"May you be like Sarah and Rebecca, Rachel and Leah.
In the name of Adonai the God of Israel:
may the angel Michael be at your right,
and the angel Gabriel be at your left;
and in front of you the angel Uriel,
and behind you the angel Raphael,
and above your head the Shekinah."

As I listened to his rumbling voice, every particle of my being yearned to please him by being a good daughter and, *someday*, a good wife and mother.

But why must I deny my desires in order to be blessed? If Ima was correct about my voice being a gift, would HaShem be pleased if I never sang again? Yet I was about to marry a Pharisee who might forbid me to sing outside our home. He might not allow me to sing at the synagogue. He had undoubtedly heard me sing there; perhaps that is why he noticed me. Once we were married, however, he might not want other men to take note of me . . .

My eyes were downcast, and my thoughts so focused I did not realize someone stood in my path. When I nearly collided with a masculine figure, I looked up and saw Avidan. My cheeks began to burn.

"Aya." His voice brimmed with pleasure. "Shalom."

"I am sorry, Avidan. I did not see you."

"A fortunate accident, then." His smile deepened. "I hope your father has shared my news. Everything is arranged, so we will wed on the first day of the week. I am looking forward to our wedding."

I swallowed hard. We had scarcely spoken to each other, yet soon we would be entwined in the most intimate of all personal relationships. This marriage, I had been assured countless times, was what HaShem intended. A man should leave his mother and father and cleave to his wife, and they would be one. I would be a blessing, my father frequently reminded me, because "It is not good for man to be alone."

What about a woman?

"The sages"—Avidan folded his arms—"say that forty days before a child is born, a voice from heaven announces, 'The daughter of this person is destined for so-and-so.' I am certain that when your father was born, heaven announced that you were intended for me. You are my *bashert*, my destined partner."

I tried to smile, but my lips only wobbled. I had no skill for pretending.

"Even so," I replied, meeting his gaze, "do the sages not teach that a father is forbidden to give his daughter in marriage while she is yet a minor? He must wait until she is grown and says 'I want so-and-so.'"

I hoped he would catch my implication—that although I was no longer a minor, I was not eager to rush the marriage—but Avidan's smile broadened. "You have studied the sages? Then what do you think about the sage who said that to teach a woman Torah was to teach her lewdness?"

I drew a slow breath to temper my rising irritation. "My father has taught me Torah since I was old enough to hold a stylus. My brother was such a devoted student that he was sent to Jerusalem as a youth, where he now studies under the esteemed Gamaliel."

Avidan nodded. "I know about your brother. I have great respect for your father. But most women, including my sister, spend their time learning to keep a home. They do not read Torah."

"I have learned those things as well," I answered, both embarrassed and emboldened by my defensiveness. "I apologize for my outburst, but I do not want you to think you are marrying an ignorant woman."

"I never thought I would." The gleam in his eyes brightened. "Indeed, I need no encouragement to honor you. My father has repeatedly told me that a man should love and honor his wife more than himself."

I looked up, searching his face for any trace of dominance or arrogance, but saw nothing but honesty. Perhaps he meant what he said. And if he was sincere, perhaps I had nothing to fear.

"If you abide by your father's wisdom," I said, giving him a tentative smile, "we should be happy together."

Ima came running when I entered the house. Excitement shone in her eyes as I sat on the courtyard bench and slipped out of my sandals. To my astonishment, she did not scold me for sending my handmaid ahead.

"Imagine my surprise when this morning I looked out and saw Avidan's father coming through the gate," she said, her hands fluttering in the space between us. "He came to tell me the wedding date has been set."

I forced a smile. "Moselle gave me the same news a few moments ago, and so did Avidan when I met him outside."

Ima pressed her hand to her throat. "You spoke to him? I hope you did not say anything to discourage him. But why would you, and how could you? Even if you insulted him, Avidan is a man of honor. He would not divorce you, not at this late hour."

"I would not insult him, Ima." I lowered my feet into the washbasin we kept beneath the bench. "And I found him . . . pleasant."

Ima clapped in delight. "I am so happy to hear it. I know you are anxious about your future, but Avidan will be a good husband. Everyone speaks highly of him."

"He seemed surprised to learn that I have studied Torah. Apparently, he thought women should take little interest in the Scriptures."

"He is not so well acquainted with your father, or he would know our family often reads the Tanakh together. How unfortunate that Sha'ul has lived so long in Jerusalem! If he came home more often, Sha'ul and Avidan would be fast friends."

"Avidan knows about Sha'ul," I pointed out. "He may even be a little envious."

"Whatever for?"

I shrugged. "Perhaps he wishes he could study under a great Torah teacher like Gamaliel. He must not be as gifted as Sha'ul, or he would have gone to Jerusalem long before this. Then again"—I couldn't stop a wry smile—"few men are as brilliant as my brother."

"Bless you, Aya, for reminding me. Sha'ul should arrive in a few days, and there is still so much to be done for his wedding. We have hired the musicians and caterers, we have spoken to the wine merchant, and your father has engaged Gabor to recite the vows and the blessings."

She had hired musicians . . . For a moment I considered asking if I could sing a love song for my brother and his wife, but my father's booming laugh scattered my thoughts.

"Where is my wife? My *aishet khayyil?*"

Ima blushed at the compliment, for an aishet khayyil was a woman of valor, a descriptor I could not imagine ever being applied to me. I would try to be a good wife, but I also wanted to be a woman who could exercise the gifts HaShem had given her.

Ima turned to Abba and asked if he had heard anything about Sha'ul's arrival.

"Excuse me, Ima and Abba, but it is time for me to join my students." I left them in the vestibule and hurried to the garden where my class would be waiting.

I found my three students waiting for me: Pontus, a Greek boy from outside the Jewish community; Ilana, the daughter of one of Abba's friends; and Baruch, our neighbor's son. Ordinarily I would not be allowed to teach a Gentile, but because Pontus was only six and clearly gifted, my father agreed to let me teach him as long as he remained outside the house. Though he had been playing the flute less than six months, his skill had already surpassed Ilana's, who had been playing three years.

HaShem had clearly gifted Pontus. I suspected Ilana's father encouraged her to play because flautists were often employed at banquets and funerals, but she had yet to produce a lovely tune.

The ten-year-old, however, had a talent for creating squeaks and squawks I had never heard from the delicate instrument.

Nine-year-old Baruch wanted to blow the shofar. The ram's horn was not the most melodious of instruments, but as long as the Temple rituals required its use for Rosh Hashanah, Yom Kippur, and Sukkot, we would need skilled young men to blow the horn. Baruch's small shofar had been designed for beginners, yet even a short instrument required a great deal of breath to produce the proper sound.

My students bowed respectfully and sat, holding their instruments. Pontus held his flute on his lap while Ilana twirled hers. Baruch cradled his ram's horn like a baby.

"Shalom." I shelved all thoughts of weddings and gave my students a smile. "Before we begin, I have an announcement. In less than a week, I will be married. I do not know if I will be able to teach you after I have moved to my husband's house."

Baruch's forehead knit with concern. "Will we never take lessons again?"

"I do not know. But if I cannot teach, I am certain you can find someone else to teach you to blow the shofar. Perhaps someone from the synagogue will do that." I turned the break in my voice into a cough and went on. "One day, when you are older, I hope to go to the Temple and see you blowing the shofar. You will be the *ba'al tekiah*."

I spoke with more confidence than I felt. I did not know if Baruch would keep up his efforts, but I could not worry about situations I could not help.

"Now, Baruch, shall we begin with you?" I smiled at the youngster while Pontus and Ilana looked on. "Before you blow your horn, have you memorized the different sounds a shofar makes?"

He nodded.

"Tell me about them."

Baruch's eyes narrowed to slits. "The first one is the *tekiah gedolah*."

"Quite right, the long blast we hear at the end of Yom Kippur. It reminds us to seek HaShem's forgiveness. And the others?"

He opened one eye and peered at me. "The *teruah*?"

"Yes, that is the short, choppy sound. And the other?"

He closed his eyes again, then shook his head. "I cannot remember."

Pontus waved his arm. "I know."

I hesitated, wondering what his Greek parents would say if they knew he was learning Hebrew. "What is it?"

"The *shevarim* is the alarm call, the warning."

"Yes—it is the sound we hear when we must stand for HaShem. It reminds us of Abraham's willingness to sacrifice his son—and Isaac's willingness to sacrifice himself—to do HaShem's will. Very good, Pontus."

I turned back to Baruch. "Remember, the shofar is only a ram's horn, so you must teach it what to sing. Before you can teach your horn, you must know the songs yourself. The same applies to you, Pontus and Ilana. You must know a song in your heart before you can play it on your instrument. But before you learn to blow, you must learn to breathe. Ready? Take the biggest breath you can."

My young students inhaled, lifting their shoulders. I raised my hand, urging them to hold that breath, and when I dropped my arm, the three of them collapsed into giggles.

"You took baby breaths," I told them. "But if you would play an instrument, you must breathe like a musician. Come closer, each of you."

They approached with wide-eyed eagerness. I tied a linen belt loosely around each child's rib cage. "Now," I said, watching as each belt fell to its wearer's waistline, "I want you to lift your belt until it fits snugly over your ribs."

Ilana protested when her belt dropped back to her belly. "It won't stay in place."

"You must make it stay in place. I want each of you to take

41

a big breath, not by lifting your shoulders, but by filling your rib cage. Breathe deeply, hold your breath, and make your belt stay in place. Ready? Breathe."

Baruch failed immediately, his belt dropping, but Ilana managed to keep her belt around her ribs for a moment, then she gasped for air. Pontus outlasted them all.

I applauded when he finally relaxed, allowing the belt to drop. "That is not easy," he said, grinning. "But I did it."

"Indeed you did." I looked at the others. "Take your belt with you and practice at home. You can practice while you work, while you study, and while you eat with your families. Without bothering anyone, position your belt, take a big breath, and see how long you can keep the belt around your ribs. This is the kind of breathing you must master if you want to be a good musician or singer. If you want to play the flute without running out of air. If you want to blow the shofar at the end of the Yom Kippur service. Do you understand?"

My mother stepped onto the portico, her face twisted in frustration. "Aya, the class must end now."

"Is something wrong?"

"Your father calls you," she said, regarding the children as if they were diminutive devils. "You must tell them to go."

I turned to my students and smiled, though inwardly my heart ached. I had worked with them for weeks and we had yet to play a complete song. Who would teach them when I was married?

"Thank you for working so hard," I said. "I hope you will find another teacher and continue to make music."

"I don't know anyone who will teach a girl," Ilana said. "Everyone wants me to sing, but I want to play the flute."

"Then you must teach yourself." I hugged each child in turn. "The next time we meet, I expect each of you to be a champion breather."

"I will be," Baruch said, clutching his belt.

"Me too!" Ilana echoed.

Pontus clutched his belt as well, but then he turned to bow before leaving. "May the gods bless your wedding!"

I waved good-bye, though I felt a pang of sorrow at his ignorance of the one true God. How unfortunate that he was not born a Jew.

FOUR

Sha'ul

The coach deposited me at a watering station just inside the ornate gates of Tarsus. Grateful to be out of the rolling box, I grabbed my bag from the top of the carriage and set out, eager to stretch my legs.

I had scarcely taken ten steps when I heard the sound of my name above the noise of the busy street. "Sha'ul, son of Zebulun!"

I turned and saw a youth with dark hair shouldering his way through the travelers waiting to water their beasts. He wore a short white tunic, the attire of a slave, and when he drew closer, I spotted the piercing in his ear. Whoever he was, he had chosen to be a slave for life.

"Sha'ul." The youth gave me a breathless smile. "I have been sent to escort you to your home—or to my master's home, if you prefer."

"And who is your master?"

He bowed. "I serve Ezra, father to your bride."

I considered my options. Since I barely knew Ezra, it hardly seemed appropriate to visit his home first.

"By what name are you known?"

"I am Adrastos. I have served the family since my youth."

"Ah." I nodded. "How did you know I would arrive today? It was a long journey."

The young man flushed. "I have been waiting in this spot every day for a week. I have examined the occupants of every arriving carriage."

I chuckled. "You are dutiful, Adrastos."

"I am obedient, for I willingly serve my master's family."

"Very well. If you will allow me, I must first visit a mikveh to cleanse myself from the journey. After that, I must visit my father and mother. I am sure they have also been anxiously awaiting my arrival."

"We have all been waiting." He bowed again, causing me to wonder how I had been portrayed in Bettina's house. Judging from this enthusiastic welcome, they looked forward to welcoming a promising student into their family.

I nodded toward the street. "Shall we be on our way?"

He pointed to my bag. "May I carry that for you?"

"No need. But please lead on."

Since two men could not walk abreast in the crowd, Adrastos walked ahead of me, leaving me to follow in his wake. I smiled at his eagerness and remained two steps behind, thoughts of the journey fading as the sights, sounds, and odors of my birthplace filled my senses. No city in the world compared to Tarsus of Cilicia.

My home city stood in stark contrast to Jerusalem, for while every brick in the Holy City was regarded as ancient and precious, in Tarsus the sacred and sacrilegious collided in full view. Pagan temples stood near the governor's palace, while a gilded statue of the current emperor towered over the paved street. At the statue's golden feet, lowly street vendors sold barley cakes and cups of toasted grain.

The city had changed since my last visit, but the notable

landmarks remained, bearing witness to periods of rule by the Hittites, Persians, Greeks, and Seleucids. Julius Caesar once rode through the same gates I passed through, and later Mark Antony declared Tarsus a free city. Now, due to an order from the late Pompey the Great, Tarsus served as capital of the Roman province of Cilicia. The city no longer had a king, only a provincial governor.

I settled my bag on my shoulder and followed Adrastos past carved stones from the time of the Hittites, weathered statues from the Greek occupation, and elaborate Assyrian columns. To my left stood a Persian fountain decorated with colorful mosaics; to my right, etchings in a crumbling wall praised Antiochus Epiphanes, the Assyrian king who had defiled the Jerusalem Temple and ignited the passion of the Maccabees. Near the river, from the time of the Babylonians, stood the tomb of the prophet Daniel.

I lifted my eyes to the horizon, where the setting sun warned of the dying day. Beneath the blazing horizon lay the river Cydnus, where Cleopatra had sailed in on her barge, eager to host a banquet for Mark Antony. On that occasion she had dressed as Aphrodite, the goddess of love and passion, so how could Antony resist her?

I shook my head, bemused as ever by the antics of pagans.

"Does something confuse you, Sha'ul?"

"Nothing that need concern you," I said, waving the slave's question away. "I was thinking of Mark Antony, and how he lacked a religious Law that would have protected him from Cleopatra's machinations. He was fond of making sacrifices, but none of his gods could protect him from the disaster the Egyptian queen brought upon him."

Adrastos's wide mouth curved in a smile. "Yet your invisible God requires the same sacrifices, does he not? I have never been to your Temple in Jerusalem, but my master has always encouraged me to ask questions."

Not wanting to discuss sacred matters in a public place, I gestured to a niche at the side of the street. When we reached it, I pinned the slave with a serious look. "I am glad Ezra answers your questions, but let me explain a difference between Jews and pagans. The pagans offer sacrifices to bribe their gods—they spill blood in order to bend the gods to *their* will. Our God requires sacrifices because they effect a change in *us*. Our God is unchangeable, but we are prone to sin. Sacrifices enable us to feel the pain of wrongdoing so we do not commit that sin again."

Adrastos rubbed his chin. "Then why did my master's wife have to sacrifice a lamb when she bore her last child? Is childbirth a sin?"

I snorted softly. The slave was more intelligent than I realized, and I could not answer his question while distracted on a busy street.

"Adrastos," I said, sighing, "the Guardian of Israel is a jealous God, One whose ways cannot be fully understood by men, but whose wishes have been precisely spelled out in a Law we will cherish until the end of time. Our forefathers neglected that Law and paid the price with seventy years of exile from our Promised Land. We have vowed never to neglect the Law of Moses again. If HaShem says a woman who gives birth must offer a sacrifice, then so be it."

The slave nodded. "My master would agree. But he also says it can be difficult to live as a Jew in Tarsus, so he is happy to know his daughter will be living in Jerusalem."

"In Jerusalem, even under the Romans, we can live as Jews and worship freely. Our religious leaders are determined to ensure that Jerusalem remains inviolate until the end of the age."

A pair of giggling girls breezed past us, their feet eager to meet some mischief. Greek girls, from the look of them, and another example of the degeneracy that pervaded Tarsus.

"Shall we continue?" I gestured to the street. "I want to reach my father's house before the day ends."

"Of course."

"You know where the mikveh is?"

"Close to the entrance to the Jewish Quarter. There is a bath for men, another for women."

"Lead the way, then."

Adrastos plunged back into the bustling crowd, and I followed.

FIVE

Aya

The servants had just brought out a steaming platter of roasted peacock when I heard unexpected sounds from the vestibule.

Ima turned to Abba. "Who could that be?" she asked, her voice sharp. "What sort of fool would come calling at the dinner hour?"

I rose from my dining couch. "I will see."

"Let a servant tend to the visitor," Abba called, but I barely heard him over the pounding of my heart. Avidan could have come. He said the wedding would not take place until after Shabbat, but what if he had changed his mind?

I turned the corner in time to see Hulpa, my mother's maidservant, kneel to wash a visitor's feet. The bearded man looked up as I approached, and for a moment surprise stole my breath.

"Sha'ul!" As Hulpa stepped back, I hurried forward and threw my arms around my brother. "We did not know when to expect you."

He returned my hug and released me. "You have grown, little

sister. Now I can see why your betrothed is so eager. You will be a beautiful bride."

I ignored his compliment, though my heart warmed to hear it. "And you!" I pressed my hand to my chest, intimidated by the thickness of his beard and the distinguished lines around his eyes. "You look much older."

"Study ages a man," he quipped, sitting to have his feet washed. "An inevitable consequence of trying to read in dim light."

I was no scholar, so I changed the subject. "They say Bettina is happy to know you will soon be married."

"Is she?"

He spoke not to me but to the slave who arrived with him, and for a moment I was confused. Then the slave said, "My lady Bettina does not share her feelings with me. I spend most of my time with my master."

"As is proper," Sha'ul said, patiently waiting for Hulpa to finish. "You must thank Ezra for me. If you had not been available, I might not have found my way home."

The slave bowed and left the house.

Hulpa dried Sha'ul's feet and departed.

"Clearly you have written Bettina," I said, taking my brother's arm, "or her father would not have sent a slave—"

"I wrote Ezra," he interrupted, "and I told him I would be coming to Tarsus for your wedding, so my father suggested that I marry soon afterward."

"You did not write her?"

Sha'ul shrugged. "I will speak to her soon enough."

Spoken exactly like a man. Sighing, I led him toward the triclinium. "Well," I said, "I see your betrothed at synagogue every week, and she certainly seems eager to be married. I am sure she will miss her family, but she frequently speaks of how much she looks forward to living in Jerusalem. Many of the other girls envy her. Living in Jerusalem, they say, is an honor and a blessing."

"Would you feel the same way?"

My smile froze. "Why would it matter?" I looked away from his inquisitive gaze. "I have no plans to live in Jerusalem."

"You are betrothed to a scholar," Sha'ul pointed out. "And any scholar with ambition yearns to study in Jerusalem. Has Avidan considered studying in one of the Temple yeshivas?"

"No," I replied, hoping I spoke the truth. "I am sure he is happy in Tarsus. His family lives here. He can serve HaShem here as a teacher or a synagogue administrator."

"You should ask him about Jerusalem," Sha'ul said. "If he wants to study in a Temple yeshiva, I could pave his way."

His voice brightened as we entered the triclinium. "Abba! Ima! Your lost son has returned!"

I went back to my dining couch, freeing my parents to greet their firstborn without tripping over me. Abba hurried to embrace his son, nearly upsetting a dining tray on his way. Ima followed, embracing Sha'ul for a long moment as tears spilled over her cheeks. "It has been too long," she murmured, finally releasing him. "But we are eager to celebrate this joyous occasion with you. It is long past the time for you to be married."

"Sit, eat," Abba commanded, sliding over to make room on his couch. "Livius! Bring more food, for Sha'ul is certain to be hungry. Bring wine, the best we have. Water too."

Sha'ul lifted his hand and offered a blessing for the meal— a serious, detailed, and extremely *long* blessing, it seemed to me. Finally he began to eat, answering my parents' questions between bites.

"Was the journey pleasant?" Ima asked. "Was the coach comfortable?"

"Comfortable enough," Sha'ul said, winking at me. "I had good company on some days, tiresome companions on others. The best days were those when I had the coach to myself. I spent many hours memorizing the oral traditions."

"That coach was a personal favor from Capito," Abba

reminded us as he tugged on the end of his beard. "You should go to the governor's palace and thank him."

Sha'ul lifted a brow. "Is it not enough that I have to walk through a pagan city to reach my home? How can I enter the house of a Gentile?"

"You can stand in the courtyard and call out a blessing, can you not?" Abba's brows pulled into an affronted frown. "I am not asking you to disobey the Law; I am asking you to be polite. The man did you a tremendous favor and you should be grateful."

Sha'ul dipped his bread in the tahini sauce, then turned to our mother. "How is your health, Ima?"

"Good." Ima's cheeks went pink. "Though I am heavier than I want to be, the physician says it is good for a woman of my age to carry a little extra flesh."

"Are you heavier? I had not noticed. You are as lovely as ever."

I brought my hand to my mouth, smothering a smile. Sha'ul may not have spent much time with us over the years, but he certainly knew how to please our mother.

"I saw Bettina the other day," Ima added. "She is looking lovely, as well."

"Ah." Sha'ul dipped his fingers into a water bowl. "How is my bride? Is she ready for the wedding?"

"She has been ready for months." Ima's smile deepened. "Bettina would have married you long ago if you had been able to come home. Only her great respect for you prevented her from growing impatient. I was afraid some other man might try to win her away, but—"

"I would not have minded." Sha'ul shrugged. "I am marrying because it is the right thing to do, but I would not have grieved if she had married another. I would be content if I never married at all."

"You must not say such a thing." Abba's face darkened. "HaShem said, 'It is not good for man to be alone.'"

"I know what HaShem and the sages have said," Sha'ul countered, his voice calm. "But exceptions have been made for those who wish to devote their lives to study. I love the Law. I eat it and drink it; I wear it on my forehead and hand. I want nothing more than to study Torah and see where it leads me."

Abba looked at my mother, his face deepening to the color of a pomegranate. "Is this what the yeshiva has done to our son? Given him an exception for every Law? Turned him against his parents?"

"Sha'ul has not turned against you, Abba," I said, hoping to cool my father's temper. "But, like me, he would like to do something other than what is expected."

"Be silent, Aya, for you know nothing of these things." Abba batted away my opinion as if it were a noisome fly, then returned his attention to Sha'ul. "How can you expect to become a member of the Great Sanhedrin if you do not marry? If you are to become a man of authority, you must obey *all* the Law, especially the command to marry and beget children. Study if you will, but those who do nothing but study never amount to anything. Itinerant teachers, the lot of them. If you ask me, they are too lazy to undertake the disciplines of family life. So you, my son, *will* marry, and you will marry the woman I have chosen for you. Is that understood?"

Sha'ul folded his hands. "You are right. It is only because I *do* wish to join the Great Sanhedrin that I am willing to marry. So I will, willingly and reluctantly."

I listened with growing interest. Though Sha'ul had never spoken of such things to me, I knew his nature. He was like our father and wanted to be the best at everything he undertook. Ima said that even as a child, Sha'ul had to be the fastest, smartest, and most excellent in any group, so of course he would want to sit on the highest court in Israel.

Abba drank deeply from his cup. When he lowered it, his face had returned to its customary hue. "I know you," he said, fixing his gaze upon my brother. "I do not understand why you wish to argue, but I know you want to be numbered among the great religious rulers of Israel. I long for you to take your place in Jerusalem—did I not send you to Gamaliel's yeshiva when you were only a boy?"

Sha'ul dipped his head in a respectful bow. "Forgive me, Abba, for being argumentative. I am weary from the journey or I would not have dared voice my opposition. Name the day, and I will marry according to your wishes."

Abba's smile flashed in the depths of his beard. "Let us drink to the coming weddings," he said, lifting his cup. "To Aya, who will soon wed Avidan, and to Sha'ul, who will soon wed Bettina. May HaShem bless them and make them fruitful. May they live long and prosper in Israel!"

I raised my cup with the others, and for a rare moment my family was united.

SIX

Sha'ul

I was not surprised when my sister found me after Abba and Ima had gone to bed. Though she had not yet been weaned when I left Tarsus, my favorite memories of Pesach, Pentecost, and Sukkot were tinged with Aya's high-spirited laughter, my mother's indulgent smile, and my father's effusive pride in our family. Every year, when the pilgrimage feasts united us in Jerusalem, I marveled at how quickly Aya had grown. She had been a chubby baby when I left home, but at sixteen her beauty was enough to create a crisis in a poet's vocabulary.

Avidan would be envied by his fellow yeshiva students.

Though I did not often lose control of my eyes, I did have an appreciation for female beauty. I felt no pangs of passion for my sister, for such feelings were perverse, but I could understand why more than one young man had begged our father to accept a betrothal contract for my sister. Abba had told me about many such offers, and each time he beamed with pleasure, as if Aya's beauty were a credit to him and not HaShem.

I was walking on the rooftop of my father's house, admiring a city tinted by the golden glow of torchlight, when Aya crept up the stairs and whispered my name. I turned, smiled to assure her that she was not interrupting my prayers, and gestured to the stone bench near the balustrade. "Sister! Come and tell me what you really think about your upcoming marriage."

She smiled. "Abba would say I have said too much already."

"Even more reason for you to confide in me. I would like to hear what you did not say to our parents."

We sat, but she remained quiet for several minutes. When she finally spoke, she did not seem inclined to talk about her betrothed.

"Look at the lights in those windows." She leaned forward as if she would dive into the darkness and swim away. "Have you ever wondered about what happens in those houses? About the people who live inside? Are the husband and wife happy? Are their children?"

"In a few days you will be lighting lamps in your own home." I tugged at the long braid resting on her back like twisted silk. "And a few days after that, I will watch my wife do the same."

"Why can't a man light lamps?" she asked, a teasing light in her eyes. "Why must Bettina light the lamps, sweep the floor, and cook while you sit and read?"

My thoughts veered suddenly toward my bride, whom I had not seen in nearly a year. Had she changed? Had she grown weary with waiting? We signed our betrothal contract when she was fourteen and I twenty-two. In the intervening two years, we had seen each other only briefly when her family visited Jerusalem. We had exchanged greetings and spoken carefully of topics that neither enlightened nor offended . . .

"Sha'ul—" Aya's tone sharpened.

"Hmm?"

"You are not as young as I, so surely you have considered your life's purpose. What do you desire more than anything?"

I gave her a skeptical look. "Who is asking—you or Ima?"

"Me. Only me."

I relaxed. "That is not a difficult question. My chief desire is to love the Lord Adonai with all my heart, soul, and strength." I tilted my head to see her better. "Does my answer meet with your approval?"

"That is half an answer. The heart can love, but what will you do with your mind? I know you have ambitions."

I nodded. "True. I want to finish my studies and become ordained as a Torah teacher."

"And after that?"

"I would like to earn a seat on the Sanhedrin."

"And after that?"

"Only HaShem knows what comes after that. But if He wants to take me higher . . ."

She narrowed her gaze. "The high priest no longer has to be a Levite, true?"

"We haven't had a son of Aaron as high priest since before the time of the Maccabees."

"So . . . ?"

"I do not expect to become high priest, Aya. The best way to avoid disappointment is to maintain reasonable expectations."

She made a face, then propped her elbow on her knees. "Everyone tells me marriage is HaShem's plan for women, but I want to do other things—should I lower my expectations? If being married is my purpose, why do I desire to do more?"

I stared, stunned. "What's this? You desire something more than a husband and children?"

"Don't look at me as though I have lost my mind. My friends—all but Moselle—think I am peculiar. They obey their parents and expect nothing but life as a wife and mother. None of them seems willing to consider other choices."

"Except Moselle."

"Yes."

"What does she want?"

Aya laughed. "She is daughter to our synagogue's administrator, so she delights in scandalous talk. She dreams of splashing in the fountain outside the temple of Diana, eating forbidden foods in the marketplace, and dancing like a slave girl. But she will never do any of those things because she respects her father. Instead, she will marry the butcher's lazy son and raise his children."

"So she is all talk."

"Yes."

"And what daring thing do you yearn to do?"

Aya blew out a breath and looked out over the city. "I would become a singer."

I blinked. "A singer? Why would you want to do that?"

She turned, her eyes shining. "Do you not know that I have a gift? I sing in our synagogue, but I would like to sing for other people, as well. HaShem has given me a voice, so why shouldn't I use it wherever I can?"

I leaned back, stunned to discover a new aspect to my younger sister. "I have never heard you sing."

"How could you? When we visit Jerusalem, everything is about you. You are the one destined to be a religious ruler; you are the brilliant student. I cannot compare to you, so I have never even tried to study. But—" she leaned closer, her eyes blazing like stars—"the other night I walked by a Gentile house near the marketplace. Inside, a woman was singing. I assume she had been hired for a banquet, because every voice went silent when she began to sing. I stood outside the garden, listening, and when she finished, I knew I could have sung the same song in the same way. I am not saying this to boast, but you asked what was in my heart."

"I did . . . and I believe you are sincere." I smiled at the passion in her eyes. "But before I can render judgment on the wisdom of your desire, I need to hear you sing."

She pulled away, a blush shadowing her cheek. "I cannot. I am embarrassed."

"A hired singer cannot afford to be embarrassed."

"Hired singers perform for strangers. You are not a stranger."

"I am the brother who loves you. If you are good, I will affirm your gift."

"And if I am not?"

"I will say HaShem wants you to marry and have a dozen children."

She laughed again. "I am still embarrassed."

"Go to the balustrade, face the street, and pretend I am not here. Sing as you would if you were singing at a banquet."

She hesitated, and for a moment I was certain she would refuse. But in one fluid movement she stood, walked to the railing, and pressed her hands together. Facing the street, she drew a deep breath and sent a melody winging through the night. I sat, speechless, as the sound mingled with the hush of evening and the churring of insects in the trees.

I recognized her song immediately—the lyrics came from one of our father's favorite psalms:

> The Torah of Adonai is perfect,
> Restoring the inner person.
> The instruction of Adonai is sure,
> Making wise the thoughtless.
> The precepts of Adonai are right,
> Rejoicing the heart.
> The mitzvah of Adonai is pure,
> Enlightening the eyes . . .

I had heard the song many times, but never had I heard it sung by a woman. The melody, even with occasional vocal embellishments, had never sounded so pure and lofty. My sister's slender throat and voice produced a song that left me astonished.

When she had finished, she remained at the balustrade, facing the street. I sensed she was too self-conscious to turn, so I broke the silence: "Aya . . . that was beautiful."

She swiveled, her eyes shining with hope, and knelt in front of me. "Did you really think so? Or are you being a supportive brother?"

"I have never heard anything so lovely and unexpected. I will never hear a Temple choir sing that song without remembering that you sang it better."

"The Temple singers are men. A woman's voice is more . . . ethereal."

"I have to agree."

A dimple appeared in her cheek. "Now you see why I want to sing. Abba allows me to sing in the women's choir at synagogue, and twice he has allowed me to sing for a city festival, but on both occasions the crowd was filled with Jews. He would never allow me to sing at a banquet for Gentiles."

I tugged on my beard, wanting to encourage her, but not wanting to promise the impossible. "How would Avidan feel about it?"

"I do not know what he will allow me to do. I have determined not to say anything for a while. I will serve him as best I can and hope he will love me enough to allow me to sing."

I exhaled slowly. Would I want my future wife to sing outside our synagogue? To sing for *Gentiles*?

I shook my head. "You have a gift, but you ask too much, Aya. Sing at home if allowed or sing when women gather. But it would be highly improper—and immodest—for a married woman to sing before other men. I cannot imagine any husband allowing such a thing. If our mother could sing, Abba would never allow her to do so at another man's house. The idea is unthinkable."

"You agreed I have a gift."

"A gift, yes, but from whom did it come? Your voice came

from HaShem; it is not your own. I cannot believe you would place your love of your voice above your love of Adonai. As it is written, 'Thus says Adonai: "Let not the wise boast in his wisdom nor the mighty boast in his might nor the rich glory in his riches. But let one who boasts boast in this: that he understands and knows Me."'"

In Aya's eyes the torchlight reflected as two small flames. "If HaShem does not delight in my singing, why did He give me a voice?"

"He gave you a voice for His reasons, whatever they may be. If you cannot see them, wait for His plan to be revealed. As for what you should do now, I will remind you that Sarah was blessed because she called her husband 'Lord.' In the same way, you will be blessed if you marry and obey Avidan in this area and all others."

My sister stood and nodded. "Good night, Sha'ul," she said, walking toward the stairs. "For your bride's sake, I hope HaShem never sends Bettina a special gift."

SEVEN

Aya

As Ima lit the Shabbat candles and blessed my last dinner as an unmarried woman, I bit the inside of my lip and tried not to cry. Abba must have noticed my forlorn expression because his disapproving grumble shivered the sprigs of holly on the table. He would not otherwise express his feelings, however, because we had guests.

On the left side of the triclinium, Avidan occupied a couch between his parents. At the right side of the chamber, Bettina and her parents reclined on couches as well, and all of them looked as uncomfortable as I felt. My parents held sway, naturally, at the center of the room, while Sha'ul and I shared a wide couch across from them.

When a servant brought out the bread, Abba stood to recite the ha-Motzi: "Blessed are you, Adonai our God, Ruler of the universe, who brings forth bread from the earth."

Another servant appeared with a pitcher of wine, so Abba made kiddush, reciting the blessing over the wine. When he had finished, I glanced at Sha'ul, knowing this would be our last meal as unmarried siblings. He did not look at me, but stared into the empty space at the center of the chamber.

We ate with stiff, self-conscious movements. We both felt awkward, and neither of us knew what to say to our guests. Sha'ul, being older and more experienced, should have been more relaxed, but since no one wanted to discuss Torah, he had little to say. I kept my gaze lowered while Sha'ul focused on eating.

Ima had hired servants to provide several baked delicacies in honor of the impending weddings. An abundant assortment of gazelle, chicken, and peacock had been roasted to moist perfection. Ima herself prepared the soup, a delicious broth featuring roasted locusts and chicken bones. The servants moved noiselessly from group to group, offering bowls of *globi*—bite-sized balls made from cheese, honey, and flour—and delicate wafers fashioned from almonds and eggs. Two other servants carried pitchers of wine sweetened with raisins.

The food was delicious and our surroundings beautiful, yet I had little appetite. As servants brought in bowls of Ima's soup and platters of stuffed grapevine leaves, I tucked a wayward wisp of hair beneath my head covering and prayed the evening would pass swiftly. The combined family feast must have been Ima's idea, for hospitality was not in my father's nature. Neither was mercy, for in his face I saw no sign of reluctance to give his only daughter to a man she did not love.

I nibbled on a mound of globi and glanced at Sha'ul, wondering if his thoughts mirrored mine. I found no clue in his face—he wore the benign expression of a son who was happy to be home after an extended time away. Ima had a server pass him the bread, allowing him to break off the largest piece. Abba sent him a plate of salted fish, offering him first choice.

And why wouldn't they favor him? He was the firstborn, the celebrated scholar, the one who had traveled for weeks to obey their wishes. Despite his personal desires, he would marry his betrothed and take Bettina to the Holy City. Once there, he would happily return to his books and study sessions and continue making a name for himself among the scribes and Torah teachers. He would be kind to Bettina, never cruel, but he would not love her as Jacob loved Rachel . . .

Sha'ul might not want to marry, but he would be obedient to Ima because he would obey the Law.

Was Avidan also marrying against his will? I had never considered the idea, but if he was, I could not help pitying him. Perhaps he had dreamed of building or traveling or farming. While he might have seen a girl he preferred over me, his father had made a bargain with my father instead.

When my children became of age, I would *not* force them to marry.

I swallowed the lump that had risen in my throat and tried to feign enthusiasm for the meal. As the others ate their fill, I nibbled on honey wafers and tried to avoid Avidan's gaze. I could not help feeling the pressure of his eyes on me, and that awareness made me even more uncomfortable.

When finally the evening ended, Sha'ul and I walked with our parents to wish our guests a good night's rest.

Avidan lingered a moment, and I knew he would stay until I acknowledged him, so I finally did. "Until the first day of the week," he said, giving me a smile that seemed to go straight through me. "Have a blessed rest."

I woke to the sight of my mother's face, an unusual beginning for a Sabbath. Then I remembered—as soon as three stars appeared in the night sky, this Shabbat would end and the first day of the week would begin. Avidan might come at night, or he might wait until daylight. Only he knew when he would arrive, so my duty was to be ready.

Ima patted my cheek. "Rise, my love," she called. "You and Lyris must still decide on how you will wear your hair."

I passed the rest of Shabbat in a teary mood while Ima flitted happily around the house and Abba pretended not to notice my despair. Sha'ul spent most of the day in the garden, engrossed in a scroll from Abba's library. "One thing I have always appreciated about Tarsus," I heard him tell Abba, "is the availability of Greek manuscripts. Such writings are difficult to find in Jerusalem."

I did not believe Sha'ul for a moment. He was reading, I suspected, to avoid having to meet with his future bride before their wedding.

As Shabbat drew to a close, Ima summoned me to her bedchamber and bade me sit on the edge of her bed. "Have you decided how you will arrange your hair for the wedding?" She raked her fingers through the strands around my face. "Would you like a simple braid or should it flow freely? Perhaps you would like to arrange your curls in the Grecian style with pearls for adornment."

I sighed. "I will be wearing a veil, so what does it matter?"

Ima refused to indulge my petulance. "You will not wear a veil the entire time, so I have instructed Lyris to arrange your hair as soon as you return from the mikveh, in case Avidan is overeager. I have also told your maids to arrive shortly after sunrise—we will break their fast with honey wafers and sweet cakes, and they will put you at ease. Moselle will be excited to help you, yes?"

"I suppose."

Ima drew me into an embrace. "Do not be nervous, little one. We have long awaited this day, and we are praying your marriage will be a blessed and happy one."

I pulled away. Did she ascribe my melancholy to anxiety? I was not nervous; I was *dismayed*. I had been spoiled in my father's house—I freely admitted it—but why should life have a glorious beginning and shift into drudgery once a woman married? I did not want to leave home and live with a stranger whose parents I barely knew.

Avidan's father, Matan, was also a Pharisee, but some Pharisees were stricter than others. Matan might be the sort who rarely allowed family members to leave the house because they might encounter an unclean object. Though several in our community believed we should not venture outside the Jewish district, my parents had taken a different approach. "Did Esther not live in a pagan palace?" Abba was fond of asking. "If she had refused to leave the Jewish Quarter, our people would have been eradicated."

I could not imagine living in Tarsus and never venturing beyond the Jewish Quarter. Tarsus offered Persian ruins that glimmered with shimmering mosaics, ornate Greek statues, and stately Roman architecture. Moselle and I often walked along the riverbank and marveled at the beauty of the merchant and military ships. When passengers disembarked, we quietly admired the elegant clothing and hairstyles of Greek and Roman women.

To boost their tent-making business, Abba fostered relationships with Gentile merchants, and Ima cultivated friendships with their women because they sold exquisite fabrics from faraway places. Those fabrics found their way into Abba's beautiful awnings, which adorned many fine homes and even the governor's palace.

Before he left for Jerusalem, Sha'ul had learned to write and speak Greek with the sons of Gentiles. To them he was known by his Latin name, Paulos, but among the Jews he was always Sha'ul. I had not been as fortunate, though my tutors taught me to read and write Hebrew and Aramaic. From watching my mother negotiate in the marketplace, I even learned a smattering of Greek. Would I ever have another chance to speak it? Or would Avidan keep me at home? I would not know until I lived with my new husband.

I met Ima's gaze. "Will any of Abba's merchant friends be at my wedding?"

She shook her head. "Avidan's family would never allow a Gentile to cross their threshold."

"What of Sha'ul's wedding? Will any of his childhood friends be invited?"

"We are not certain, but your father has invited the governor."

I groaned. Sha'ul would always be able to mingle freely in Tarsus, yet I would soon be locked into the Jewish enclave. Would my husband grant me grace, or would he forbid me to follow my interests? Avidan had seemed gentle and kind on the few occasions we met, but only time would reveal the real man.

I drew a deep breath and directed my thoughts toward heaven. God must want me to marry, because He was omniscient and all-powerful. So I would marry Avidan like a good daughter of Abraham, but I did not have to be happy about it. But sometimes, Ima said, when HaShem closed a door, He opened a window . . .

I leaned forward, kissed my mother on the cheek, and wished her a good night. She would probably sleep well, but I might not sleep at all. In a few hours the sun would rise as it always had, sending me out to follow a path I did not choose.

Wife

AD 30

EIGHT

Aya

When I was a young girl, I dreamed of what I would feel on my wedding day—excitement, anxiety, joy . . . I did not expect to feel numb.

The events of the day unfolded as they should. My friends, including Moselle, arrived after sunrise and greeted me with smiles and warm embraces. Together we went to the mikveh, where I immersed myself entirely in the flowing water. Then my maids applied fragrant oils to scent my skin and hair.

A few moments later, my mother entered with a wooden chest containing my bridal garments: a chiton of fine linen, a richly embroidered tunic, and two golden cords, the symbol of a virgin—one to be tied around the waist, the other beneath my breasts.

After helping me dress, Ima brought out jewelry, a wedding gift: a gold chain for my neck, pearl earrings, and several gold and silver bracelets. As a last-minute surprise, she pulled a gold diadem from a velvet bag. "You have always been our princess," she said, her eyes wet with tears. She set the crown on my head, then placed her hands on my shoulders:

"May HaShem bless you as you marry your groom.

May *El Shaddai* keep you under His wings.

May *Elohim Chayim*, the Living God, guard your life and grant you shalom.

May *K'dosh YIsra'el*, the Holy One of Israel, lead you in the path of righteousness.

May *El Elyon*, God Most High, overshadow you as you rest in Him.

May *Adonai Yishma*, the God Who Hears, answer your prayers."

I bowed my head so she would not see my tears—she had not mentioned *El Roi*, the God Who Sees. Would anyone see the real me on my wedding day?

Ima kissed me on both cheeks. I hugged her, tears streaming down my face, my heart too confused for words. Ima kissed me again, impulsively, and draped a delicate silk veil over the crown.

Surrounded by my friends, I walked home, purified, adorned with the gifts of my parents, and blessed. Lyris did not fuss with my hair—because it was still damp from the mikveh, she pulled it back into a braid and tied it with a gold ribbon. Then she stepped away and pressed her hands together. "You are so beautiful, mistress!"

"You are," Moselle agreed. "So where is your betrothed?"

I did not have to wait long.

Just before midday, Avidan and his companions arrived amid the pounding of drums and jubilant shouting. My friends led me to the courtyard, where Abba and Ima kissed me and sent me out to meet my groom. My friends scattered flower petals and mingled with Avidan's companions as we made our way through the narrow streets and finally entered the gate at Avidan's home. His parents greeted us, and behind them a crowd lifted their cups and drank to our happiness.

Guests showered us with flower petals as Avidan and I walked to the head table. We waved to the crowd and sat, and for the first time I met my bridegroom's gaze. His eyes were bright, open, and joyful, and in that instant my despair evaporated. I could not understand why he made me feel at peace, but then I realized . . . he *saw* me. Not as a daughter, not as a friend. No, he looked at me as if I were a priceless treasure.

My parents and Sha'ul arrived moments later. My brother joined the other unmarried men at a long table and began to sample the food spread on platters and dishes. Ima and Abba sat with Avidan's parents, Matan and Zara. Together they accepted compliments and congratulations from wedding guests.

Not knowing what to say to my husband, I looked out through the gauzy veil and noticed odd details—the gold threads running through Zara's tunic, the gray streak in the tambourine player's beard, the laughing woman with the missing front tooth. Was she a neighbor or one of Avidan's relatives? I did not ask.

Finally, as the sun dropped toward the western horizon, Gabor, the leader of our synagogue, gestured to me and Avidan. Trembling in every limb, I followed my husband to a canopy of woven branches and flowering vines. Gabor's voice seemed to come from far away as he recited the traditional *Sheva Brachot*, the seven blessings: he thanked HaShem for the fruit of the vine, the creation of earth, the creation of man, the creation of man in His image, and the blessing of children.

Then he finished with the most important blessing of all: "Blessed are You, Adonai, our God, Sovereign of the universe, who created joy and gladness, groom and bride, mirth, song, delight and rejoicing, love and harmony and peace and companionship. O Lord our God, let there be heard in the cities of Judah and in the courtyards of Jerusalem the voice of joy and the voice of gladness, the voice of groom and the voice of bride. Blessed are You, Adonai, gladdener of the groom with the bride."

Amid shouting and the lifting of cups, our marriage was consecrated. Avidan lifted my hand and smiled while I gazed at the cheering crowd. Matan must have invited every Jew in Tarsus, for all the men were bearded, and most wore prayer shawls edged with the elongated fringe favored by Pharisees. Like my father. Like my brother.

I was now a married woman. In the mikveh I had washed away my old life; I had put on new clothing, new jewelry, and a crown. My past was over, my new life beginning. I turned toward the parents' table and saw Abba and Ima applauding with Matan and Zara; all four had tears in their eyes.

I wept with them, though I could not say why.

⸻

As the sun painted the western sky in brilliant orange and purple, servants lit torches and the dancing stopped. Avidan took my hand and gave me a shy smile. For an instant I wondered why, then I realized the time had come for another important ritual: the consummation of our marriage.

My face heated as I followed Avidan to the bridal chamber he and his parents had prepared. As the wedding guests crowded behind us, Avidan's mother opened the door, revealing a bed covered with rose petals.

The fluttering in my rib cage intensified. My hands warmed as Avidan pulled me into the chamber and turned to face me.

Behind us, the door closed with a solid sound.

My husband reached out and lifted my veil, then studied my face as if he were seeing it for the first time. His smile trembled as his hand traced the shape of my face in the air, and then he removed my veil and let it fall.

"My queen." He lifted the diadem and set it aside. "I have waited for you with great anticipation," he said, a tremor in his voice. "I have longed for you as my soul longs for Jerusalem."

I attempted to smile, intuiting that for this moment he had

prepared the most beautiful phrase he could imagine. I wanted to respond with an apt reply but could think of nothing comparable.

So I gave him the gift of honesty. "I do not know how to be a wife," I confessed. "But Abba says HaShem wants me to marry and have children. I will obey you because a good wife should be obedient, but I am young, a little spoiled, and I do not know what I want from life. I was not certain I wanted marriage, so I beg you to be patient with me."

His brows lifted, and his voice brimmed with humor when he responded. "Your brother said you were unusual."

"You know Sha'ul?"

"I have met him twice. A few days ago, I spoke to him about the best yeshivot in Jerusalem. One day I hope to follow in his footsteps."

"If you want to be a Torah teacher," I said, realizing I was probably talking too much, "you could not choose a better man to emulate."

Avidan did not answer but pulled on the cord tied beneath my breasts. "You said you do not know what you want from life"—he loosened the cord at my waist—"but the sages say that if you do not know what you are living for, you have not begun to live."

My husband caught my hand and pressed it to his cheek, then turned his face into my palm and kissed it. Overcome by the warmth of his touch, I could barely draw breath to speak. "Perhaps . . . the sages are right."

A smile glimmered through his beard. "You are mine, Aya, and I am yours. Together we will seek the will of Adonai in all things. Together we will make a life, complete with children and the blessings of HaShem."

He drew me closer, and I pressed my hands to his chest, maintaining a measured distance between us. I don't know why—I knew what was supposed to happen next, and I was not afraid.

But neither was I ready, so I scrambled to find an interesting topic of conversation, anything to delay the inevitable.

"Do you believe," I asked, gently holding him at bay, "that HaShem has something special for each of us to do?"

His arms drew me closer. "Yes." He nuzzled my ear. "I do."

"Do you believe"—I caught my breath—"we can know what this thing is? That HaShem will reveal His will?"

His lips left a trail from my ear to the corner of my mouth. "I believe that, as well."

"And do you believe—?"

"Yes." His lips touched mine, scrambling my thoughts. "I believe a great many things, but at this moment I believe this is what I am supposed to do."

The hunger in his kiss shattered my reserve. His gentleness opened a hidden place within me, a well that had never been touched or even imagined. I slid my hands up his chest and locked them behind his neck as he carried me to our flower-bedecked bridal bed.

NINE

Sha'ul

When the agreed-upon day of my wedding arrived, I went downstairs and wondered if my parents had spent every drachma in their strongbox to impress their friends and neighbors. Servants had draped leafy garlands from pillar to pillar, and baskets of flowers scented the air. New carpets covered the tiled floors, and a score of unfamiliar servants hurried through the house, their arms filled with flowers or food.

I thought the expense a tremendous waste—surely the money could have been better spent on the purchase of scrolls for the synagogue's yeshiva—but Ima would not allow my wedding to be one tittle less impressive than Aya's.

"Good morning, son." Ima paused from her work to kiss my cheek. "I hope you slept well."

I gestured to the extravagance around us. "Must we do all this, Ima? I do not require it."

"Avidan's relatives will be among our guests," she said, lifting the hem of her tunic as she prepared to go upstairs. "We cannot allow ourselves to look stingy."

"But what would be the harm in appearing modest? Or being good stewards of what HaShem has provided?"

Ima waved the notion away. "You do not understand, Sha'ul, because you have never engaged in commerce. This knowledge cannot be found in books."

"I once spent a summer making tents. I learned plenty about commerce."

"One summer is nothing compared to your father's lifetime." She glanced around. "What was I doing before you distracted me?"

I laughed. "How could I know? But tell me—has Abba invited Gentiles to my wedding?"

Ima's mouth twitched. "Your wedding will be among the finest in Tarsus, so do not worry about anything."

"You did not answer. Will Gentiles attend my wedding?"

She sighed and met my gaze. "Yes, but they will not remain for the entire week, only the day. Your father invited several officials from the governor's palace. A man in his position is expected to extend hospitality."

"But the members of our chaburah will object—"

"Let the Pharisees object. By the sixth day, when they are deep in their cups, they will not even remember that Gentiles were present."

While she hurried up the stairs, I went to the study at the back of the house, one of the few rooms that would not be festooned with greenery and flowers. There I could read without distraction.

I sat on a bench by the window and picked up a scroll but could not seem to focus on the words. Frustrated, I crossed my arms and considered the necessity of what lay ahead. Abba had informed Bettina's father that we would celebrate my wedding soon after Aya's wedding banquet ended. My father exaggerated my importance when he added, "Sha'ul's master, the esteemed Gamaliel, does not want my son to be away more than a month, so the wedding should take place as soon as possible."

My patient bride had to be eager for marriage. A betrothal of two years was unusually long for a girl of marriageable age. If I made her wait any longer, people would wonder if something was wrong with one of us.

I heard commotion on the street and looked out the window. At the front of the house, Aya and Avidan were stepping out of a litter. Aya looked pretty in her matronly tunic and veil. She walked to the door and strode inside, leaving Avidan in the courtyard.

I chuckled. From the determined look on my sister's face, I suspected she was on her way to find me.

A moment later, her voice confirmed my suspicion. "Sha'ul? Sha'ul! Where are you?"

"In here."

She opened the door and glared, her face a mask of frustration. "Why are you hiding? And why are you not ready to fetch your bride?"

"The day is still young . . . and Ima is not ready for guests."

Aya frowned. "You do not seem nervous. Are you not even a little anxious?"

"Why should I be?" I shrugged and crossed my arms. "I knew I would have to marry, so why not now? I have nearly finished my course of study and hope to be ordained soon. The timing is convenient and logical."

She snorted softly. "By this time tomorrow, you will not be thinking about logic."

"Has marriage made you a prophetess?"

A furious blush spread over her cheeks. "What would you know? I have been married eight days, and—"

"You are happier than you have ever been."

She gaped at me, then sat on a low stool. "In truth, I am more confused than ever. I do not know who I am. I am Avidan's wife, a woman who did not exist before the wedding. I have no idea what she should think, what she should like, or what she should want. I used to like and think and want, but my old ways do not seem to suit Avidan's wife."

I lifted a brow. "If you can explain further, you might help me understand Bettina. She may experience the same feelings."

"If I could explain, we would not be having this conversation." Aya lifted her chin. "Have you asked Avidan to be one of your 'friends of the groom'? He does not feel comfortable asking for the honor."

"He should not worry. He is now my closest friend in Tarsus."

She snorted a laugh. "Pretend you are best friends, and all will be well. He is excited to be part of your wedding. I think he might be more excited about *your* wedding than he was about ours."

She continued chattering about her husband, but I heard no derision in her voice, only affection. For a girl who had not wanted to be married, she seemed content with the changes in her manner and appearance. She wore her hair up now, and the change made her look older than sixteen. A touch of red colored her lips, and her lashes appeared fuller and darker than I remembered. Her tunic, which had been ankle-length when she was unmarried, now touched the floor, covering her bare feet in voluminous folds.

"You have changed a great deal." I offered my opinion casually, but she swooped on my words like a raptor.

"You truly think so? Changed for the good or bad?"

"I cannot decide. You look more like Ima. Older."

"I look *older*?" Dismay and delight struggled on her face. "*Much* older, or only a little older?"

"I said *older*, not old. I would say marriage agrees with you."

"If—perhaps—oh, never mind!" She was turning to leave when I caught her arm.

"Do not rush off. This Avidan—is he good to you? He is not cruel, is he?"

A sudden rise of water filled her eyes. "He is not cruel. He is gentle and good."

"Then you must be happy—so why are you crying?"

She dashed away a tear that had slipped from her lower lashes. "I do not know, brother. I want to be happy, but when I think about leaving Ima and Abba and Moselle, happiness evades me."

"Who said you are leaving?"

"Avidan—and you, apparently. I know he asked you about the yeshivot in Jerusalem."

"He asked, but he did not say he wanted to move to the Holy City."

"He is thinking about it. I do not know when he wants to go, but your advice has awakened his ambition. Now he yearns to learn from Torah teachers in Jerusalem, and nothing else will satisfy."

I tugged on my beard. "You should be happy he wants to study with the best teachers. Many women would love to move to Jerusalem. The Holy City is the center of the world, the apple of HaShem's eye."

"I know Jerusalem, and I know Tarsus. And I know I am happier in Tarsus."

"Then perhaps you should redirect your thoughts. Instead of thinking about how much you will miss Tarsus, think about how wonderful it will be to live in Jerusalem."

"What you suggest is not easy." She lifted her head. "How can I have peace about the future when I do not know what it will bring? Only HaShem knows what will happen tomorrow."

"Aya." I caught her hand. "When we last spoke, you were convinced you would not be happy as a married woman. Yet here you are, looking beautiful and content. Marriage was not the end of your happiness, was it?"

"I have been married only eight days."

"You worry when you should be trusting HaShem. 'In all your ways acknowledge Him, and He will make your paths straight.' Your task is simply to walk in His way."

She lifted a brow. "And what about you? Do you have peace about marrying today? You did not have shalom a week ago."

I drew a deep breath. "I was not upset then and I am not upset today. I know what HaShem expects, and I am ready to follow His will."

"Then let us speak next week and measure our happiness again."

With a wry smile, she pulled her fingers out of my grasp and walked away.

A few hours later, Avidan and I went to the house of Ezra, father to Bettina, to fetch my sixteen-year-old bride. Avidan stood behind me, occasionally shouting and banging a drum, doing his best to produce the celebratory sounds usually supplied by the friends of the bridegroom.

After ringing the bell at Ezra's gate, I locked my hands behind my back and endured Avidan's pitiful pounding for as long as I could. Then I told him we had no further need for noise. "We will be merry in our hearts. Let the friends of the bride make the sounds of celebration."

From inside the house I heard muffled voices, then a veiled woman stepped into the courtyard. Behind her appeared a crowd of females, all dressed in colorful tunics and head coverings. At the bride's side, looking pleased and proud, stood her parents, Ezra and Noya.

"Sha'ul?" An uncertain note filled the bride's voice, but I extended my hand with a confident gesture. "Come, my bride. Everything has been prepared for our wedding."

Though I did my best to sound enthusiastic, my voice seemed

insubstantial without a few manly shouts to accompany it. Avidan whooped when Bettina took my hand, then moved out of the way as I led my bride through the streets we had just traveled. Behind us, Bettina's friends followed, trailed by her parents and a train of relatives.

At my parents' home, the courtyard gate had been flung open and garlanded with flowers. I led my bride into the open area, where servants came running with wine for our guests. Though the custom was for the bride and groom to mingle, eat, and drink, I led Bettina around the house to the garden, where the chuppah waited. The silk-draped shelter—my father's special contribution—symbolized the tents in which Abraham married Sarah, Isaac married Rebekah, and Jacob married Rachel and Leah.

I gripped Bettina's hand. As we waited for Abba to join us, a thought blew through my mind: when Abraham married Sarah, did he know what HaShem would do through him? Did Isaac suspect he would wrestle with the Angel of Adonai? Did Jacob know his sons would establish the twelve tribes of Israel?

My marriage, if HaShem was willing, might be as significant as those of the patriarchs.

With Bettina by my side, my father took his place and pronounced the traditional blessing. As the words poured from his lips, I turned to look at the face behind the diaphanous veil.

When Bettina and her family came to Ima's feast last week, I had almost been afraid to look at the woman I had not seen in months. What if she was not as pleasant as I remembered? What if she had burned her face or developed a noticeable scar? Yet Bettina looked exactly as I remembered her—clear-skinned, dark-eyed, and neither plain nor extraordinarily beautiful. She was as pleasing as a serviceable linen tunic, and her appearance suited me well.

Gabor, the Torah teacher, joined us beneath the chuppah. As he recited the seven blessings, I looked past my bride and remembered an afternoon I spent arguing with one of my fellow yeshiva students. "Did the Creator not create all things beautiful?" he had asked. "If so, He prizes beauty, and a man with a beautiful wife has been blessed by HaShem."

"But was Satan not the most beautiful of all angels?" I countered. "Great beauty leads to pride, and pride leads to sin. Therefore, beauty in either man or woman is not something to be desired, but something to be held lightly and easily surrendered. A man will be far happier with a simple wife than a great beauty."

"Rebekah was beautiful," my companion argued.

"And caused Isaac great concern when she was coveted by the king of the Philistines." I shook my head. "Give me a plain wife, and I will be a happy man."

Apparently HaShem had answered my prayer. I looked at my wife's plain face and smiled, sending a ripple of humor throughout the assembled guests.

"Look how eager he is," one of the old men said, his crusty voice cutting through the recitation of blessings. "What I would give to feel eager blood in my veins again."

Gabor finished the benediction, and Bettina and I turned to face the crowd of witnesses as man and wife. In that moment, I recognized my father's wisdom: we were celebrating the wedding outdoors, so the house would not be ritually contaminated by Gentiles. After the eating and dancing, the Gentiles would leave, and the Jews would continue the celebration inside the house.

Knowing we had an entire week to enjoy food, music, and dancing, I took my bride's hand and led her toward the bridal chamber. Bettina's fingers trembled, so I gripped her hand more tightly and led the way.

I might have been a reluctant husband, but to honor HaShem, I would do my best to be a good one.

After leading Bettina into the bridal chamber, I closed the

door and waited until the excited whispers from the other side faded away. Our guests would eat, drink, and dance while my bride and I consummated our marriage.

I turned to Bettina, who stood waiting beside the bed, her veil trailing over her back. Smiling shyly, she pulled on the sheer fabric and let it slide until it fell to the floor.

I stared, fascinated by the dark stream flowing over her shoulders. Bettina may have possessed an ordinary face, but her true beauty lay in that glorious river. Like any modest woman, she had covered her hair since our betrothal, and I had not realized how amazing it was . . .

I shook my head. I could not allow myself to be distracted from my duty. I was a husband, and she a wife. We had married in obedience to HaShem, and I needed to remind her of the laws and traditions that would henceforth govern our lives.

"Sit, please." I gestured to the bed and nodded when she sat on the edge. "I have spent time studying marriage, and I want to make certain we are beginning our life on a solid foundation. When remarking on HaShem's use of Adam's rib to create woman, one of the sages said, 'It is as if Adam exchanged a pot of earth for a precious jewel.' So I will always honor you, for you are my jewel, fresh from HaShem's hand."

I smiled, hoping she understood, and in her eyes I saw eagerness and confusion. She had never studied the oral traditions, so perhaps she would require more explanation.

"You will be as a precious and rare jewel to me," I repeated. "Do you understand?"

"Yes, husband."

"Excellent. Another sage said men marry for one of four reasons: passion, wealth, ambition, or the glory of HaShem. Time has proven that men who marry for passion raise rebellious sons. Men who marry for wealth have children who will eventually be poor enough to beg for food. Men who marry for ambition—well, consider Athaliah, who murdered all the royal sons once her husband died, proving that unbridled ambition leads to death. But men who marry for the glory of HaShem—their children will preserve Israel." I studied her face, which now held a touch of sadness. "Do you understand?"

She blinked. "So why did you marry me?"

I looked away, resisting the urge to slap my forehead. Had this girl no powers of deduction?

I forced a smile. "I married you for the glory of HaShem, because a man who wishes to obey God must do his part to replenish the earth. Together we will raise righteous children. One of them might even become our Messiah."

Her lashes fluttered. "Thank you for explaining."

I wiped my damp palms on my tunic and sat beside her. "I am glad we are married," I said, "and I will do my best to be a righteous husband. My life's purpose is to obey the Law in all things, including marriage. I pray HaShem will bless us with children and make their names great in Israel."

I lay back, folding my hands on my chest as I smiled at the gauzy linen over our bridal bed. "I would love to have a son. A boy who will go with me to the Temple, a child I can teach to honor HaShem and the Law. He will be a righteous man, a scholar, and his name will become as renowned as Gamaliel's and Hillel's. I will be a link in a chain of esteemed Torah teachers and members of the Great Sanhedrin."

Bettina looked down at me. "So you married me . . . out of duty."

I winced but could not deny the truth. "Yes."

"And you will lie with me out of duty."

"Yes."

She glanced away, then lay beside me, her eyes wide and expressionless. "Do you hate me, Sha'ul?"

The question caught me off guard. "Of course not."

"But you do not love me."

"I . . ." I halted. "If you mean passion, I have already—"

"I am not speaking of passion, but of love. I understand if you do not love me; I do not love you, either. But I am willing to serve you, obey you, and be faithful to you. In doing so, I hope to learn what love is."

When she looked up at the bed canopy and smiled, I felt as foolish as a toddling child. In some ways, my bride was wiser than I was.

"Thank you," I whispered. "For being honest and wise."

"I hope," she said, "we have a son. Then perhaps your duty will become love."

I propped my head on my hand and studied the curved form of my bride. She was wise *and* comely, my wife; well-formed and compact, with rounded breasts and sturdy legs that would serve her well on the hilly streets of Jerusalem. My children would enter the world between shapely thighs, and when we lay together, that long thick hair would lie against my chest, warming me on chilly nights . . .

No longer thinking of Jerusalem, I reached for her and smiled when she sank into my embrace.

Later that afternoon, as Bettina napped beside me, I lay on my back and stared at the ceiling. Music filtered through the walls of the chamber, mingling with the rumble of conversation and the laughter of celebration. Someone was singing from the Song of Songs, but it was a man's voice, not Aya's.

Had Aya asked Abba if she could sing at my wedding? I didn't think so—her wedding feast had just ended, so she had probably been thinking about other things.

The same things that filled my head now.

The Law had taught me many things, but being a scholar—celibate, disciplined, and devoted—had done little to prepare me for being a husband. I had studied the Song of Songs, which our Torah teachers insisted was a declaration of God's love for Israel, demonstrated at the Passover in Egypt. After one discussion of Solomon's book, Gamaliel led us in a debate about which should be greater—a husband's love for his wife or his love for HaShem. When I argued that a man's love for HaShem should be greater than his devotion to anything else, Gamaliel smiled. "You are correct, Sha'ul," he said. "But you did not hesitate to answer, which tells me you have not yet experienced this sort of love"—he tapped the Song of Songs scroll—"for a wife."

Now I understood the emotion behind my master's smile. When I held Bettina and found myself lost in her eyes, the rest of the world ceased to exist. Afterward, when we lay together in silence, tears ran from my eyes and my spirit soared like a bird wheeling through shafts of sunlight.

My respect for Solomon's writing diminished in that moment. He had written many beautiful things, but his words did not adequately describe what I had experienced.

I did not expect to be smitten by a womanly look of surrender. I did not expect to feel my heart slam against my ribs when her arms wrapped around my neck. I did not expect reason to leave my head as my lips devoured a woman's.

Except for Ima and Aya, no woman had touched me in years. Yet here I was, lying beside a woman I barely knew, a virgin who had given herself to me without hesitation or fear.

Unlike my sister, Bettina had embraced the idea of marriage as eagerly as she embraced me. She would be a willing partner in anything HaShem led me to do.

I heard the soft sound of her breathing and realized she was shivering. I wrapped my arms around her and thought of how often I had trembled in contemplation of HaShem's love. Were they so different, the love of a woman for a man, and the love of a man for HaShem? Woman was created to serve man; man was created to serve his Maker. Perhaps marriage was more about service than procreation.

When Bettina stopped shivering, I slid my arm from beneath her neck and pulled the linen covering over us. I felt her hand touch my shoulder. "Is all well?" she asked, her voice a faint whisper. "Do I please you, Sha'ul?"

"Yes," I said, my voice gruffer than I intended. "You please me well, Bettina. You should sleep, for we must endure a week of celebration before we prepare for our journey home."

Her hand slipped from my shoulder, and before long I heard her deep, even breathing again.

TEN

Aya

To my great dismay, Sha'ul and Bettina left for Jerusalem a few days after the conclusion of their wedding feast. Avidan and I went to my father's house to bless their journey, and afterward I fervently embraced my new sister-in-law. "I am delighted to finally have a sister," I told Bettina. "I pray that HaShem will bring us together again, because I want to get to know you better."

When Bettina blushed in response, I realized my outgoing brother had married a woman who was as quiet as he was loud. Perhaps that is why Abba chose her for Sha'ul—she would never outshine him in public.

For the first month of our marriage, Avidan and I lived in a small chamber built onto the back of his parents' house. I had been hoping he would find us a permanent home with room for children, but his mother said our future would lie in Jerusalem, not Tarsus.

"My son has been preparing for you through Torah study," Zara said, pressing her hands to her chest as though her great love for him might cause her heart to burst. "He wanted to honor us by being the best yeshiva student in Tarsus. Now he wants to honor you by being the best student in Jerusalem."

I did my best to hide my distress, though I could not imagine how Avidan's Torah study would benefit me in any way. Leave Tarsus and move to Jerusalem? That is not what I expected.

The bliss I enjoyed at our wedding feast vanished as the last guest departed. I reluctantly accepted that we might live in Jerusalem *someday*, but until then I would have preferred to live in a home that did not permit Avidan's mother to constantly thrust her head through the doorway to see if my husband wanted food or drink.

After a few weeks, I told Moselle I had changed my mind. I would happily go to Jerusalem—or even Sheol—rather than remain in Matan and Zara's guest chamber.

When I pressed Avidan about how long we would remain in Tarsus, he told me he had to complete a course and pass an examination before his Torah teacher would recommend him to the authorities in Jerusalem. This was troubling news, because by that time I had realized Avidan was not like Sha'ul. He was not stupid, but neither was he bright, and he seemed to labor over the scrolls he read by lamplight. Each morning when Avidan left for the synagogue, I watched him go with mixed feelings. Part of me wanted him to make slow progress, delaying our move to Jerusalem. Another part of me wanted him to take his exam as soon as possible. Until he did, I would have to live in his home and obey Zara and Matan.

Avidan's parents were not bad people. Matan had always wanted to study Torah full time, but his family could not afford to support a scholar. So he made a living importing wine from Judean vineyards. He had met my father in the marketplace, and they often talked about business together.

Avidan's mother, Zara, loved HaShem, her husband, and her son with single-minded devotion, yet she did not love me. Each morning when I left our small chamber, I had to walk through my mother-in-law's house to reach the street. Though I tried to slip away without attracting attention, I could feel her scrutiny and silent appraisal. And though she never criticized me directly, her casual comments made it clear that I had been weighed in the balance and found wanting.

"My hair used to curl like that," she remarked one morning. "But when it did, I had enough sense to hide away in my bedchamber."

Another time she studied my tunic and remarked that a married woman ought to look "more married." I had no idea what she meant—I was already covering my hair in public and wearing long tunics, so what else was I to do?

Every night, after the evening meal with Avidan and his parents, Zara gave me a light embrace and sent me off to bed proclaiming that I had "delighted them long enough." If I lingered in the hallway, I would see her kiss her son, bless him, and ask if he wanted to stay for another cup of wine and some honeyed fruit. Most nights, Avidan refused and followed me. Many nights, he did not.

With no house to care for and no need to prepare my husband's meals, I didn't know where I fit in Avidan's family. I offered to help with the meals, but Zara said too many cooks crowded a kitchen. I offered to help with the shopping, but Avidan's father gave me no money, and Avidan had none of his own. While I thought about offering to wash or mend clothing, the servants tended to those chores.

During the first month of our marriage, I escaped to my parents' house on several occasions. I did not complain while I visited but sat quietly in the atrium and enjoyed the familiar surroundings. Even though Ima was busy with her social obligations and Abba was occupied with customers, I felt at home.

When I went home, Ima did not seem surprised to see me, but simply lifted a brow and asked if I wanted something to eat. I chatted with Lyris, half wishing she had been given to me as a wedding gift, and napped in my former bedchamber, which seemed to have grown larger and colder.

My harp called to me, so I carried it with me when I returned to Avidan's house. After that, whenever Avidan went to study at the synagogue and Zara chased me out of the kitchen, I went into the garden and took refuge in my music. I sang songs I had learned at synagogue and invented a few songs of my own. I sang about HaShem, but I also sang about love. If Solomon's bride could sing about what she felt with him, why couldn't I sing about what I felt with Avidan?

So I played and sang and experimented with music. Occasionally the shutters would slam as I sang, but I kept singing.

One afternoon I finished a song and heard an unfamiliar voice float over the garden wall. "Hello! Musician?"

I looked up, startled that a stranger would address me. "Yes?"

"I must speak with you. Can you meet me at the front of the house?"

I had no idea who stood on the other side of the wall, but the woman's voice rang with approval, and I hungered for it. I hurried through the house and walked to the courtyard gate.

A moment later, a woman came around the corner, flanked on both sides by servants in short tunics. She was not Jewish, for she did not cover her hair but wore it in the Greek style, braided, curled, and studded with pearls. The woman was neither young nor old but had taken pains to enhance her appearance. A soft blue himation covered her throat and shoulders, while a white tunic draped her slender form.

She had been wise to meet me outside the house—Avidan's parents would have fainted at the thought of a Gentile crossing their threshold. I could not imagine what business this woman had in the Jewish district, but who was I to question her?

I gave the woman a cautious smile.

"You are the singer?" She regarded me with an appraising look. "The one I heard a moment ago?"

I nodded, afraid to say more. Avidan might not approve of my speaking to a Gentile, but if this conversation proved to be trivial, he might not need to know about it.

I pulled the edge of my headscarf closer to my throat. "May I be of service?"

She smiled. "I heard your beautiful song . . . I never thought to hear such music in this part of the city." She lifted a sculpted brow. "The music was your own? You are the singer and the harpist?"

I nodded again, but barely. What was I getting into?

She smiled, apparently satisfied with my answer. "Consider this a formal inquiry as to your availability for hire. I will be entertaining guests from Rome. I am holding a banquet and sorely need a musician to entertain them."

I hung my head, at once pleased and embarrassed. "I am sorry, but I am—I do not sing for hire."

"Why not? You have such a gift, why not share it with those who appreciate it?" She took a step back and sharpened her gaze. "You are young, but by your dress I assume you are married. Would your husband not appreciate your willingness to help support your family? All young couples need help when they are starting out."

I looked away. For years I had longed to do something with my music, and HaShem had just sent me an incredible opportunity. But I was a different woman now. Did Avidan's wife sing?

"I am sorry to disappoint you," I finally told her. "I love music, but now that I am married, I must care for my husband and my home."

I said the words my parents would want me to say, but were they the truth? I did not yet have a home. And how could I care for my husband when his mother did everything but warm his bed?

The woman made a *tsk*ing sound. "I do not care that you are Jewish. I want to honor my guests with the best musician I can find, and I have found nothing as lovely as what I heard a moment ago. At least tell me what you were singing."

"I . . . I was singing a love song . . . for my husband."

"Charming. And quite unique." She clasped her jeweled hands. "I will leave you now, but if you change your mind, please send word to me as soon as possible. I will pay you handsomely, and I believe your husband will be happy to know how you have honored him."

I was about to repeat that I could not possibly sing for Gentiles, but the words did not come.

"I cannot give you an answer now," I finally said. "But if you will send a servant to this house tomorrow, I will give him a reply. When is your banquet?"

"In ten days," she said. "At sunset." She narrowed her eyes, probably wondering if I was worth so much trouble, then dipped her chin in a firm nod. "Very well. My servant will come here tomorrow at about this hour. I look forward to hearing your answer."

Before Avidan returned from the synagogue, I donned my most attractive tunic and applied a stroke of perfumed oil behind my ears and between my breasts. I planned to ensure he had a pleasant night. Tomorrow, when he woke, I would ask if he would allow me to sing for a woman who wanted entertainment for her banquet. I would not specify who she was or where she lived, but if Avidan asked, I would not lie.

I had debated the question all afternoon. My father frequently did business with Gentiles, stating that the Tanakh required Jews to treat Gentiles well. So what would be the harm in singing for this woman's dinner? None of her guests would know me. As hostess, she would be too busy to call attention to me. To her guests, I would appear to be a servant who quietly sat in the corner and played a harp. My father would not protest because he would never learn about it, nor would Avidan's parents. As to Avidan, he had not been taken aback when he saw Gentiles at my brother's wedding. Perhaps he would not mind if I took this opportunity.

I closed my eyes. If I was not supposed to sing for this woman, why did HaShem send her to me? Adonai could have directed her steps to a street where she would not have heard my music. I could have chosen another time to sing in the garden. So perhaps HaShem *meant* for me to sing when and where this woman would hear me, and she was meant to invite me to sing for her banquet.

Or perhaps this was HaShem's way of allowing me to fulfill one of my dreams. If only for a few moments, I could freely exercise my gift before people who would be impartial. They would see and hear me as I was, and if my music pleased them, I would *know* I had a gift . . .

I was sitting on a dining couch, my hair down and my garment arranged artfully around me, when Avidan came into the triclinium. Grateful that his parents had not yet entered the room, I held out my arms and he hurried forward.

But he was not thinking about love.

"It has happened," he said, his eyes shining. "Praise HaShem, my prayers have finally been answered."

"Which prayers?"

"Jerusalem." He dropped to his knees. "We are going to Jerusalem sooner than I hoped. Sha'ul, may he be blessed forever, has spoken to Gamaliel and I have been accepted into his yeshiva. I will be studying in the same yeshiva as your brother, under the most esteemed Torah teacher in Jerusalem. Perhaps"—he gripped my hands—"we can even live near Sha'ul and Bettina."

The hope that had blossomed in my heart abruptly withered. I would never sing at a banquet. That possibility could exist only in Tarsus. In Jerusalem the Law was more than the texture of a Jew's life—it was tough, unyielding fabric, keeping the inhabitants of Jerusalem imprisoned in a cocoon of uniformity.

Tarsus had a Gentile governor, but Jerusalem was governed by the high priest. Tarsus offered schools of Greek philosophy, gymnasiums, and classical literature; Jerusalem had dozens of yeshivot, where Jewish men, young and old, studied Torah and the oral traditions. The governor of Cilicia ruled diverse groups, respecting the beliefs of each, but in Jerusalem the religious authorities dictated everything from how long a corpse could remain unburied to whether or not a housewife could plant a garden in her courtyard. Sha'ul had explained many of Jerusalem's laws, but he delighted in the restrictions that kept impurity from the Holy City's streets, homes, and especially the Temple.

"So when . . . when should I pack our things?" My voice sounded strangled to my own ears.

"That is for my father to decide." Avidan squeezed my hands. "I did not tell you that I asked Sha'ul to inquire on my behalf because I did not want you to be disappointed if I was not accepted."

"I would not be disappointed."

"But a letter arrived today! I cannot believe HaShem has so honored me! I will be studying with the grandson of the great Hillel. At the conclusion of my studies, I should be a wise man; perhaps I will become a Torah teacher. In time, other scholars may read my writings and extol my name in Israel . . ."

He was rambling now, fashioning dreams out of empty air. By that time I knew him well enough to see his sincerity and utter lack of pride. Avidan lived to please HaShem, his father, and me. If only he had thought to ask what I thought about living in Jerusalem.

But men followed HaShem, and women followed their husbands.

"How long," I managed to croak, "must we stay in Jerusalem?"

Avidan stared into space. "My father will support us, of

course—he is happy to do it because he has always wanted me to answer the highest calling a man can have. We will find a house, or my father's agent will, and we will furnish it. Most of the work will be done by my father's servants, so we can leave by the end of the month, I am certain. Of course, you will want to say farewell to your parents, but I know they will be overjoyed to know you will be near your brother." An impulsive laugh bubbled from his lips. "Perhaps your parents will move to Jerusalem, since both their children will be living in the Holy City."

"No." I shook my head. "Abba will never leave Tarsus. His business is here, and the city has been our home for generations."

Avidan was guileless, righteous, and incapable of understanding what I grasped intuitively: better to be a well-fed fish in a lake than a starving fish in the sea. My father was a leading citizen of Tarsus, wielding considerable power in the Jewish and Roman communities. Though he was devout, he would never exchange his influence for a place in the Holy City.

"I am so happy, Aya." Avidan placed his head in my lap and smiled like a contented child. "You will love living in Jerusalem, and your brother will be thrilled to be near us."

My husband did not know my brother, and neither did he know me. All my life I had lived in my brother's distant shadow . . . why did he think I would enjoy living with that shadow close by?

Avidan kissed my forehead.

"What smells so delicious?" He parsed the air. "You have outdone yourself. How fitting that we should have lamb stew on this significant occasion!"

"I did not prepare it," I said. "Your mother did."

"Praise be to HaShem!" Avidan rose and hurried away, probably in search of his father.

I washed my hands and tried to be content for my husband's sake.

But as we dined with his parents, with every mouthful I thought of the banquet at which I would never sing and the opportunities I would never have. I still wanted to do something to prove my gift, and Tarsus was the ideal city in which to achieve my goal. I would never achieve anything in Jerusalem. I would never be *seen* in Jerusalem.

In my parents' house, I had been overshadowed by Sha'ul, even though he was far away. In Avidan's house, I was nearly invisible. In Jerusalem, I would be one of thousands of dutiful Jewish wives. When I stood in the vast crowd of women at the Temple, not even HaShem would see me, because He would be focused on the priests in the heart of the sanctuary.

Later, right before we went to sleep, Avidan said he had spoken to his father, who wanted to depart for Jerusalem on the morrow. They would leave just after sunrise, to get an early start.

I would stay behind to pack.

⸻

"I am sorry to leave you," Avidan said as he dressed the next morning, "but we will soon be together in Jerusalem."

A fresh wave of despair swept over me. "Are you *sure* you want to leave Tarsus? You could continue with your studies here—"

"I am sorry, Aya, but I must find a house, I must meet my teacher and my fellow yeshiva students, and I must be examined by the council. Once everything is settled, I will send for you."

He had not even heard my question; his head was too filled with anticipation. Avidan beamed, certain I was as happy as he was. Was this to be a pattern in our lives?

"I am pleased you will be able to study under a great teacher," I told him. "But hear me, Avidan—I need time to adjust to the idea. I will follow you to the Holy City, but I will miss my family and I will miss Tarsus. Jerusalem is so . . . different."

"The Holy City is the center of the world," Avidan assured me. "The air itself is sweetly scented there. The limestone buildings shine in the sunlight." He drew me into his arms and planted a kiss on the side of my neck. "I am only sad to be leaving you. But my mother will take care of you, and I will count the days until I see you again."

I inhaled his scent, still sharp and new to me. In time I would grow familiar with it, but not if he kept leaving me behind.

"How long do you think I will have to wait?"

He smiled. "No longer than one month, I am certain. I could not be without you longer than that."

I sighed as he released me and left our bedchamber.

One month. I had one month to prepare for Jerusalem and say good-bye to my parents. One month to pack, to buy the things we would need, to visit Moselle and say farewell forever.

Then I would join my husband and adjust to the city he loved. I would again be a scholar's wife, only this time the pressure would be stronger, more intense. My husband and brother were students of Gamaliel, the greatest Pharisee in Jerusalem.

I would be so insignificant I might disappear.

All my life, I had dreamed and kept my dreams hidden. My father had encouraged my talent, but only to a point—I could sing before Gentiles, but only if he approved of the venue.

I had not been married long enough to know how permissive Avidan might be, yet when we lived in Jerusalem, he would undoubtedly do as all the Pharisees did, which meant I would never sing anywhere.

But at least I would have a month to revel in Tarsus. Perhaps this month was a gift from HaShem.

I no longer lived in my parents' house, so I was no longer under their authority. I was under my husband's, but Avidan would not be here. He would entrust me to the care of his parents, but Matan would be busy with his wine business, and Zara would avoid me as much as possible.

I would have one month to do . . . whatever I dared.

I opened the window and drank in the sights of the city that had allowed me to celebrate the best of Jews and Gentiles. I would inhale the pleasures of Tarsus while I could, exploring my freedom while I remained unfettered.

And I would sing for that woman's banquet.

I would send word with her servant and begin to practice my songs. The night of the banquet, I would slip away from Avidan's house. His parents would assume I had gone to visit my parents, so no one would care that I had gone out.

And afterward, when I traveled to Jerusalem, I would know that I had accomplished one of *my* dreams. With renewed confidence, I would settle down and determine to be a good wife. I would support my husband and bear his children. When Avidan was ordained and obtained a seat on the Sanhedrin, he would be as great as my brother, perhaps even greater.

As my husband's star rose, so would mine. I would be the mother of beautiful, talented children, and I would be known, not as Sha'ul's younger sister, but as Avidan's wife.

My parents would be pleased. My husband would take pleasure in me.

And Sha'ul would be surprised.

ELEVEN

Aya

For the Gentile woman's banquet, I chose a simple linen tunic and modestly covered my hair with a matching headscarf. Knowing Avidan's mother would bar the door if she knew my plans, I slipped away while she was preparing dinner.

Within minutes I had left the Jewish district and entered a wealthy residential area. The servant who had come to get my answer told me his mistress was Isadora, a Greek widow who enjoyed entertaining.

A doorman greeted me when I arrived at the house. He seemed surprised to see a stranger at his mistress's door, but when I explained that I had come to sing for the banquet, he escorted me to a long atrium with a pool at its center. The shallow pond held water lilies, lotus plants, and fish that floated on the surface and gaped at the world above. To the right of the pool, three slaves in white tunics were arranging dining couches in a semicircle. None of the guests had arrived, though the doorman said his mistress expected them within the hour.

"When they get here," he said, regarding me with a superior

look, "they will go to the garden, where they will drink and talk for a while. Then they will enter the triclinium. That is when you should begin to play." He pointed to a small stool behind a potted palm. "That is where you will sit."

I nodded, relieved to see I would not be the center of attention. I had suffered twinges of guilt as I stepped over the Gentile woman's threshold, and the thought of being ogled by strangers made my stomach churn. But if I could sit behind the guests, playing softly, I might be able to pretend I was in my garden, singing for myself and HaShem.

I took my seat and slipped out of my sandals. I would have left my shoes at the entrance, but the doorman had not offered a basin or a towel. Either the Gentiles did not care about bringing dirt indoors, or my status did not merit that level of hospitality.

Grateful for a private moment to indulge my curiosity, I looked around. I expected to see idols, indecent images, and vulgar displays. I had heard that Gentiles—particularly the Romans—had no fear of HaShem because their gods were like spoiled children who had to be fed, cajoled, and pampered on a daily basis. I expected the walls to be painted in garish colors, and on that point I was not disappointed—Isadora's walls were blood-red and shimmered in the flickering torchlight.

I expected to see statues of Isadora's gods, yet I saw nothing that resembled the images in my imagination. Several life-size masks hung on one wall, and I assumed they were death masks of respected ancestors. I saw nothing else but a small bowl of incense burning in a niche.

I ran my fingers over the strings of my harp and tightened two of them. From someplace beyond the triclinium, I heard the sound of voices and assumed Isadora's guests had begun to arrive.

I had not used my voice much during the day, so I lowered my gaze and began to sing, hoping to warm up my throat as well as my fingers:

By the rivers of Babylon,
we sat down and wept,
when we remembered Zion . . .

Despite my best intentions, anxiety made my voice quaver. I
drew a deep breath, remembering my young students' efforts to
hold their belts against their ribs. I should have worn a belt to
remind myself that I would have to support my voice, especially
in a room as large as this one.

On the willows there
we hung up our harps.
For there our captors demanded songs
and our tormentors asked for joy:
"Sing us one of the songs of Zion."
How can we sing a song of Adonai in a foreign land?

I stopped, a wave of embarrassment heating my chest, when
I realized the distant sounds had ceased. I lifted my head and
saw people behind the couches, several of them staring at me. A
man in a red toga with a leather breastplate had already seated
himself on a nearby couch. When my gaze crossed his, he smiled
and lifted his silver cup. "Do not let us interrupt you," he said,
speaking Greek. "Please continue."

Isadora, wearing a one-shouldered tunic that dripped with
silver bangles, placed her hand on the Roman's shoulder. "You
have taken the wrong couch," she said, urging him to rise.
"Please, your place is in the center of the room, for you are
our guest of honor." She smiled at the others, most of whom
had begun to choose seats of their own. "All of you, enter and
make yourselves comfortable. Take any seat you like, but leave
the central couch for Claudius Lysias, who has deigned to grace
my humble house with his presence."

Claudius Lysias had to be an important man, judging from
the way Isadora catered to him. I was not pleased that he no-

ticed me, and my anxiety sharpened when he sat on the center couch and shifted so he could look in my direction.

"Please," he said. "Continue with your song. I have never heard such a melancholy melody."

"If you would prefer something else—"

"I like that song. It reminds me of home."

Not knowing what else to do, and determined not to speak again, I lowered my head, strummed my harp, and continued to play.

For Isadora's guests, I realized, a banquet was less an exercise in eating than in socializing. As servants brought in trays of meats, fruits and vegetables, and pastries, the guests nibbled at the delicacies and brazenly flirted with everyone else. Isadora had invited seven men and four women, none of whom sparkled as much as their hostess. Because the ratio of men to women was unequal, all five women received lavish attention and frequent compliments on their beauty, wit, and charm.

I kept my head down and my fingers busy. When I was not singing, I played softly and tuned my ear to nearby conversations. My initial feelings of shock and surprise had faded, and my curiosity had been thoroughly awakened. When would I have another opportunity to visit a Gentile home? Surely not in Jerusalem, where I would be under the watchful eyes of my husband and brother. Even if I did happen to be invited to a Gentile home in the Holy City, I was certain I would see nothing like this.

My guilt vanished as I watched and listened. If I could give Avidan an honest report of what went on at these banquets, perhaps I could convince him that no harm would come if I entertained at similar occasions in the future.

Thus far I had not observed anything that would cause me to sin against HaShem. The servants had brought in a large hog with a lemon in its mouth, but no one forced me to eat it. A man in a dark corner kept nibbling the ear of a woman, but I did not feel inclined to imitate their example. At one point, the guest of honor leaned toward another man and said something in Latin. The second man flushed and barked a laugh, but since I did not understand the language, the coarse jest did not even enter my thoughts.

So why were my people forbidden to mingle with Greeks and Romans?

I understood that the Pharisees—my father and brother among them—did not mingle with Gentiles because of the purity laws. The "set apart" could not touch anything unclean—a dead animal or person, a bodily discharge, or even the dust from a graveyard. The law was absolute, so if a Gentile sat on a stool a menstruating woman had used, he would not only be unclean but would transfer his uncleanness to anything he sat upon. The unwary Jew who sat on a seat used by that Gentile would therefore be unclean and unable to attend synagogue or Temple until he had been cleansed. Most Jews did not know or care who sat on a public bench, but the Pharisees did, and that was why they avoided anything a Gentile or woman could render impure.

I sighed, realizing I had defiled myself by visiting this house, so I would have to visit the mikveh before returning to Avidan's home.

Isadora's voice cut into my thoughts as she bade her guests farewell. Most of them followed her to the tiled entry while the Roman remained on his couch and watched her go. I wondered why he remained, then realized he might have been invited to stay overnight. The Romans, I had heard, had no moral law governing the sacred act of marriage but slept with whomever they wanted, whenever they wanted.

I was sliding my harp into its protective cover when the Roman turned in my direction. "I should tell you how much I enjoyed your music."

I gave him a polite smile. "Thank you."

ANGELA HUNT

"I have never heard such melodies. So gentle and yet so sad."

"My people have suffered greatly over the years. We were slaves in Egypt and exiles in Babylon."

"Yet most of your people have returned to their promised land."

I should have kept silent; I should have remembered my place, but I could not restrain a sudden flash of defensive spirit. I wanted him to see that one Jewish woman, at least, had not accepted Roman rule.

"Most of us *are* in our Promised Land, yet we are not free. Some would say we are as enslaved now as when we lived in Babylon."

The corner of his mouth twisted. "Is that so? I, on the other hand, believe your leaders are uncommonly wise, for they have learned to cooperate with Rome. This wisdom has helped you survive when other nations did not."

This conversation could not be beneficial for either of us, so I stood, determined to leave before I said something I would regret. "We did not save ourselves; we were saved by HaShem."

"You call him *the name*? Has he no name?"

"Of course He has a name, but it is too holy to utter in casual conversation. So—"

"Is that what this is? Only a casual conversation?" A smile played at the corners of his mouth. "I am enjoying a spirited discussion. I know so few Jews, and no Jewish women."

My stomach tightened. The conversation had taken a turn and I needed to leave, but the Roman blocked my path. Fortunately, Isadora breezed back into the triclinium, her eyes alight. "Claudius! Forgive me for neglecting you. I should have had the servants escort the others out, but Drusilla had a special message for—"

She halted, her eyes slanting from the Roman to me. "Am I interrupting something?"

I stepped forward. "I was leaving."

"Wait."

Reluctantly, I turned. Isadora offered a chilly smile. "The doorman has your wages. And thank you—several of my guests remarked on your beautiful music."

"Beautiful and unusual," the Roman agreed, grinning with more familiarity than was proper for a guest of honor. "If I were not leaving Tarsus soon, I would hire you for one of my own banquets."

"Leaving Tarsus?" Isadora's hand rose to her throat. "Where on earth is he sending you?"

"The governor has been in touch with Rome and has recommended me to a post in Jerusalem—hence my interest in the Jews." His dark eyes shifted to my face. "I am to be commander of the Fortress Antonia. If you ever find yourself in Jerusalem, little singer, perhaps you will sing for me again."

"That would not be possible." I gave Isadora a quick smile. "Thank you."

"Can I engage you next week?"

I shook my head. "I cannot."

"Whyever not?"

What could I say? I did not want to tell her I was going to Jerusalem, not when her honored guest had said he would be transferred to the same place.

"I have other plans. Thank you. It was an honor to sing for you."

I tucked my harp under my arm, collected my wages from the doorman, and left the villa. I could not wait to tell Moselle that I had finally—and probably for the last time—fulfilled my greatest longing.

Three weeks later, I climbed onto a wagon loaded with all the provisions our parents could procure for our new home. Avidan's father also provided the wagon, a mule, and a family

108

who also wanted to go to Jerusalem. The man would drive the wagon, and his wife and children would keep me company on the journey.

Matan gave the driver a few parting instructions, then walked over to me. "Sell the wagon and the mule when you arrive in the Holy City," he said. "Those who live in the city have little use for such animals, but he will fetch a good price from a farmer. Do not be afraid to sell anything you cannot use."

In addition to providing the wagon and mule, Matan and Zara also donated our mattress and bed and a small mill for our table. I thanked them, especially for the millstone, since having it would enable me to purchase less expensive whole grains at the marketplace.

My parents arrived as we packed the wagon, bringing with them a beautiful carved bench, with storage beneath the hinged seat. "Thank you, Abba." I struggled to hold back tears as I embraced my father. "I will never see this without thinking of you."

"I chose it so you will never forget Tarsus," he said. "If you look closely at the carving, you can see the columns that stand before the School of Philosophy, and in the foreground you can see the black goats that provide the leather for our tents. The edge has been carved to remind you of the river that runs through the city."

"It is beautiful, Abba."

"And here is one more thing." Ima stepped forward and unwrapped a large platter. The sculptor had worked a message into the wet clay before firing it:

> May this home have light and gladness,
> Shalom and companionship.
> Bestow abundant blessings and holiness in every room
> And love in every corner.
> May the windows be illuminated by Your
> Holy Torah and Your commandments.

"I love it. It is the perfect gift. Thank you, Ima." I kissed her and turned to my father, who stood ready to help me into the wagon.

The lines in his face softened as he smiled. "I never thought we would send you away," he said, holding out his arms. "Goodbye, sweet Aya. May the Lord God bless you until we meet again."

I stepped into Abba's arms, tears blurring my vision as I breathed in the scents of wool, beard oil, and home. I did not know when, if ever, I would see my parents again, but my heart warmed to think they might miss me as much as they had missed my brother.

TWELVE

Aya

After drawing a deep breath, I stepped into the one-room house Avidan had rented in the lower city. The table, Avidan quickly pointed out, came with the house, but I found myself wishing it had not. Two of the four legs were barely attached, and a splinter pierced my palm when I wiped my hand over the rough surface.

Avidan placed the bench my parents had given us beneath the front window, where it looked beautiful and out of place. When my husband looked to me for approval, somehow I managed to smile.

In Tarsus, a similar mud-brick structure would be suitable only for slaves. When I looked upward, instead of elaborate designs on plaster I saw wooden beams beneath mud-stiffened rushes. When I looked down, I was not standing on artfully designed tiles, but on packed earth. The home's single window must have been cut into the wall as an afterthought because the top edge was definitely wider than the bottom.

The house had one saving grace—a flat roof, with a low parapet built around its edges. I would have to reach it by climbing a ladder, but it would provide useful space for eating and sleeping in the hot summer months. If Avidan would secure a rope to one of the roof beams, I could pull up a basket and dry our wet clothing in the sun.

We would have no garden. Our home shared two walls with neighbors on each side, though the flat roofs varied in height—an effort, I supposed, to give the illusion of private space where none existed.

I knew I should be grateful we had a home—many came to Jerusalem and lived with other families because they could not afford housing. And though many people slept on the floor, Avidan and I had been blessed with a proper bed frame and straw mattress.

I thanked HaShem that my parents had not come to Jerusalem. My mother would have refused to leave me in such a house, and my father would have insisted on buying more furnishings than the house could hold.

A former resident had mounted a shelf onto the far wall, a solid beam worn by use. A few clay shards lay on the floor, along with a cracked pitcher. I had brought a few dishes and the mill from Tarsus, but we still needed several items to set up a functional home. Until we could afford them, perhaps I could borrow a pot from Bettina . . .

I turned to Avidan. "Where is Sha'ul's house? Can we visit him?"

Avidan knotted the last rope in the bed frame. "You want to see them *now*? We have not finished unpacking."

"I only want to see where they live," I said, walking over to him. "Is that so much to ask?"

In truth, I wanted to see if Sha'ul and Bettina lived also in a one-room house with a crooked window and a dirt floor. Or had he managed to find something better?

When Avidan hesitated, I knew he would never understand. As his parents' only child, he had never felt second best or worried that he could never compete with a sibling. He had been celebrated from the moment of his birth.

"I never had a sister," I said, slippery words coming easily to my lips. "In the coming days, when you and Sha'ul are at the yeshiva, I will want to spend time with Bettina. So I would like to know where they live."

Avidan's mouth curved in an easy smile. "Of course. Yes, once I have assembled the bed, we can visit them. Their home is not far, and Bettina will be happy to see you."

"Shall we eat with them? I could pick up some food at the market—"

Avidan shook his head. "We cannot spare the time. I must study this afternoon."

I swallowed my disappointment, then went back to the window. At least we were not far from the Pool of Siloam, so I would not have to venture far to draw water.

Movement from next door caught my attention. I turned to see a woman, possibly a year or two older than me, stepping out of the house. She stood tall and erect, and walked through her courtyard tapping a stick on the ground. When her stick hit the wooden gate, she stopped and opened the gate.

She was blind. I stared, awed by her skill, and watched as she stepped out of her courtyard, hesitated, and turned toward my window.

"Shalom," she called, her voice bright. "Welcome. I have been listening for you."

"For me?" Amazing, how much pleasure this news brought me.

"I am Eden," she said, tapping as she moved closer. "My husband met your husband, who told us you would be coming. So I have been waiting for you."

I smiled in pleased surprise. "I am Aya. I cannot tell you how nice it is to see a friendly face."

She rested both hands on the top of her walking stick. "My husband is also a yeshiva student. We will undoubtedly spend many hours together, but now I am sure you have important things to do. If you need anything, you have only to knock on my door."

"I will," I promised. "And thank you."

She turned and walked back into her house, but her appearance erased the gloom I felt at the prospect of living in such a humble home. What a wonder she was! Her place appeared to be no larger than ours, and if her husband was also a student, they would be living on charity just as we were.

After meeting Eden, Jerusalem seemed a much brighter place.

⸻

To my great surprise and pleasure, Sha'ul and Bettina lived in a house much like ours. It looked better, of course, since they had been in Jerusalem for several weeks and Bettina had added many decorative touches. Like us, they had a bed and an old table that must have come with the house. But Bettina had breathed life into the place, hanging colorful fabrics on the walls and setting bowls of fruit and flowers on trunks and stools. Dried flowers and herbs hung from hooks in the wall, and a bowl of figs occupied the center of the table.

"This looks like a home," I told her after we embraced. "You have brought this place to life."

"Thank you." Bettina blushed. "Do you like your house?"

I laughed. "I have only just arrived, but I wanted to see where you lived. I hope we can share many happy hours in the days ahead."

Sha'ul and Avidan had already withdrawn into a corner, where they were conversing in low voices. I frowned at them— why did men automatically pull away from women? I understood why they did so in public, but we were alone and we were family. Now that my brother and I lived in the same city, I wanted to be part of his life.

I pulled up a three-legged stool and sat next to Avidan. "Tell me, brother," I said, smiling at Sha'ul. "Since I am unacquainted with the education offered in Jerusalem, please explain how you both can be under the same teacher when you have been studying for years and Avidan has just arrived."

I did not intend to belittle my husband, but Sha'ul glared as if I had said something inappropriate. "All men who study Torah are blessed," he said, lifting his chin, but Avidan gave me an indulgent smile.

"It is not complicated," he said. "The yeshiva of Gamaliel has several levels. Sha'ul is at the highest level, studying advanced interpretation and judicial learning, along with astronomy, mathematics, and speculation. I will be in the *bet midra*s, studying the traditions of the fathers. When the time is right, I will sit for examination. If I pass, I will advance. Because I received a solid education in Tarsus, it should not take me long to sit for my exam."

I thanked him and met Sha'ul's gaze. "You could have explained that. I am not so simple that I cannot understand."

Sha'ul smiled at his wife. "Bettina, can you prepare a platter of figs and honey? Perhaps our guests would like something to eat."

How like a man to put a woman to work.

I went to help Bettina because that is what a well-bred woman should do. But though I spoke gently to my sister-in-law, I felt nothing but irritation toward my brother. Now that we were both married, I had hoped we could treat each other as equals. But with Sha'ul's curt dismissal, I realized that because HaShem made me female, my brother would never see me as anything but weak.

THIRTEEN

Sha'ul

I adjusted the folds of my new robes, then stood perfectly still, my hands folded as Gamaliel gave the order to proceed to the *semikhah* ceremony.

With two others of my chaburah, I left the Temple Mount and crossed the Xystus, a large colonnaded enclosure where public assemblies were often held. As our sandals moved over the ancient stones, I felt an odd connection to the Maccabean-era architects who had turned the atrocity of a Greek gymnasium into a dignified structure. They, too, were Pharisees who understood the importance of the Law.

We left the Xystus and came to the entrance of the Chamber of Hewn Stone, home to the Great Sanhedrin. Our escort, a clerk to that august body, peered through a crack in the door to see if all was ready, then swung the door open and stepped aside.

I swallowed, momentarily speechless at the thought that I had finally reached this point. My father always wanted me to be a great scholar, but I took his dream a step further: I was about to earn a seat on the highest religious court in the land

and would go down in history as the youngest man to have done so.

My two companions nodded to me before proceeding—out of deference to my accomplishment, they wanted me to enter the building first. So I led the way to the first row of stone seats in the judicial chamber.

Once seated, I looked up at the assembled members of the Sanhedrin. They sat in three rows that formed a great semicircle, thirty-five members on one side, thirty-five on the other. The high priest sat at the center of the third row on an elevated dais, and two scribes occupied tables in the empty space at the middle of the room. More than one hundred scholars were eligible to be seated as part of the Great Sanhedrin, but seventy were required to hear and judge a dispute.

My teacher, my spiritual father, had taken his seat among the Pharisees. Though Gamaliel would say pride was a sin, he would also admit he took especially great pleasure in seeing me before the council.

The high priest spoke, his voice reverberating throughout the chamber. "Who comes to be examined and tested in the ways of the Law?"

I stood. "I do, honored Caiaphas. I am Sha'ul Paulos of Tarsus, a student of Gamaliel."

From the corner of my eye, I saw movement among the men sitting near my esteemed teacher—his friends and rivals, any one of whom might decide to pose a question to trick me. Not everyone in the Sanhedrin agreed on interpretation, and Gamaliel had warned me not to get into an argument. "They have heard of you," he said, "and because they distrust your youth, they may try to confuse you. So think before you speak, Sha'ul. Be confident of your answers."

My teacher did not need to warn me. I had never lacked confidence.

"The highest honor of a scholar," Caiaphas said, "is that he be like a reinforced cistern that does not lose a single drop of what has been poured into it. In cases of discussion or argument, you must always appeal to a greater authority, whether to your teacher or a decree by the Sanhedrin. To decide differently from such an authority is the mark of ignorant assumption or the outcome of rebellion."

I bowed my head. "I hear and understand."

"Have you come here to be ordained to the office of teacher-elder-judge?"

"I have."

"Have you been examined and approved by your teacher?"

Gamaliel stood. "He has, honored Caiaphas."

"Then come forward."

I waited while Caiaphas asked the same questions of my two companions. My thoughts wandered, and who could blame me? For years I had striven for this moment. Since the age of ten I had sat at my teacher's feet, and the knowledge that he approved my efforts brought a flush to my face.

Just before walking to this chamber, I had stood before my master and felt his hands on my shoulders. "Sha'ul Paulos," he said, the hint of a smile gleaming through his beard, "you are a Pharisee of the highest order, a son of Moses, of the tribe of Benjamin, a citizen of Tarsus and Cilicia, and now a married son of Israel. I will be honored to support you for the Great Sanhedrin." I had kissed his hand, overcome by gratitude, knowing my teacher was more of a father than the man who had sired me.

Gamaliel had encouraged me to study, sharpened my focus on the Law, and taught me the nuances between Torah and the Oral Torah. He taught me how to put on the tallit, sponsored me as I entered the fraternity of Pharisees, and was the first to encourage me to marry. *"Marriage is a man's duty,"* he had advised me, *"but even more important to you is the requirement that a man be married before he is eligible for the Great*

Sanhedrin. So go home, young Sha'ul, and betroth yourself to a virtuous daughter of Abraham. Only then can you achieve greatness in Jerusalem."

My wife now stood in the Court of the Women at the Temple, waiting to rejoice with me after the ceremony. But first my companions and I had to be tested so we would be worthy to teach others.

When all three of us stood before the assembled elders, the high priest rose. "Honored Gamaliel, are these your students?"

Our teacher folded his hands. "They are."

"Then let us test them. If they answer correctly, they will be known as Torah teachers and able to settle disputes among the people. If they do not answer correctly, they will be banned from among us."

Even though the three of us were not touching, I could feel my companions' anxious trembling. They had been good students, though not great, and had to be nervous, but I felt as cool as a winter breeze. Life had taught me that my value lay not in who I was, but in what I could contribute. So I had learned to contribute much by learning much.

"Sha'ul, I shall begin with you." Gamaliel turned. "Tell me, of all 613 mitzvoth in the Torah, which is the greatest?"

I drew a quick breath. "The greatest mitzvot is found in the Ten Commands—'You shall have no other gods before Me.' For if we observe this, never bowing to idols or false gods, we will keep our minds set on obedience to the entire Law, every jot and tittle."

"In the Oral Torah"—the scholar next to Gamaliel stood and moved to another topic—"it is said that Abraham took wood for the burnt offering and laid it on Isaac, similar to how a cross is laid on the shoulders of a person about to be crucified. What can we deduce from these words?"

"Isaac was intended to be the sacrifice and may have realized his father's intention," I said. "And even though such a death would involve great shame and human sacrifice is against HaShem's Law, so great was the faith of both men that God supplied a ram for the altar."

An hour later, after all three of us had been thoroughly tested on several subjects, Gamaliel turned to the high priest. "You have seen and heard their answers," he said. "I present these three men for ordination to the office of teacher-elder-judge."

Caiaphas dipped his chin in a solemn nod, and the members of the Sanhedrin stood in unanimous agreement. As my companions and I knelt on the stone floor, the members passed by us, each man stopping to place his hands on our heads, symbolically transferring the authority of teacher-elder-judge.

When they had returned to their seats, the high priest lifted his hand. "And so I say: let them teach, let them judge, let them decide on questions of firstborn; let them decide; let them judge!"

The three of us rose and walked past the scribe's desk, where we were given a scroll bearing our orders. The scroll validated our authority throughout the Roman Empire, so no matter where we went, we would have the authority to teach, judge, and settle matters between Jews.

As I accepted my scroll, I felt a mantle of responsibility settle on my shoulders. Never again would I be Sha'ul, yeshiva student. From this moment forward, I would be Sha'ul Paulos of Tarsus, Torah teacher, judge, and member of the Great Sanhedrin, a man who wielded authority in the high priest's name.

I lifted my chin, swallowed hard, and blinked back unexpected tears.

FOURTEEN

Aya

Avidan and I were invited to Sha'ul's home after his semikhah. We had not been allowed to witness the ordination ceremony, for access to the Chamber of Hewn Stone was forbidden to anyone but members of the Sanhedrin and the high priest's family. Sha'ul and Bettina had not returned from the Temple when we arrived at their house, so we sat in the courtyard to wait. When my brother finally arrived, one look at his face told me he had done well. I was not surprised.

"Congratulations." Avidan embraced my brother, a look of unadulterated admiration shining in his eyes. "In a few years, perhaps I will join you in that chamber."

Sha'ul smiled. "Anything is possible if HaShem wills it."

I hugged my brother, as well. "Congratulations. Abba would be so proud."

"I wish you could have been present," he said, releasing me. "It was an amazing experience. During the examination, words came to my lips as if they had flown from the heavens, and my voice did not tremble as I answered. I wish I could say the same for my companions, but at least they did not fail. All three of us received our orders."

"I am happy for you." I turned to look for Bettina. "And where is your wife?"

Sha'ul glanced down the street. "She is coming. I have also invited Gamaliel, who has promised to honor us with his presence. Bettina probably stopped by the market to get food for the feast—nothing less than the best will do for my teacher."

I left the men and went in search of my sister-in-law, who was certain to need help with the meal preparation. I found her walking up a hill with a large basket, her forehead dotted with perspiration. "Can I help?" I asked, alarmed at her flushed face. "You do not look well."

Bettina handed me the basket of fruit and bread, then rested her arm on a wall and drew several deep breaths. "I am fine," she said, panting. "If I look unwell, it is because I am with child."

A dozen different emotions smote me: happiness, for what woman did not want to bear children? And alarm because Bettina should not be hauling heavy baskets in the heat. I also felt a measure of jealousy because I had married before Bettina. Why had I not conceived?

I told myself I was being petty. Ima had warned me that sometimes HaShem was slow to send children, so I should not fret if I did not conceive right away. But still, I did not think HaShem should allow Bettina to have a child before me.

I lifted the basket and urged Bettina to follow me. "Sha'ul is excited about entertaining his teacher," I said, keeping my voice light. "If you are not feeling well, I will prepare the meal."

"Everything is already prepared." Bettina used her headscarf to wipe her forehead. "I have only to set it on the table." She glanced over at me. "Does he seem pleased?"

I blinked, surprised by the question. "Did he not seem pleased when he came out of the ceremony?"

"I know he is happy to be part of the Sanhedrin," she said,

panting again as we climbed the hilly street. "I was asking if he seemed pleased with *me*."

I stared, shocked again. "Of course he is."

"Does he say so? Does he ever speak of me?"

I scoffed. "What man talks about his wife? I can tell you this—I have not heard him complain about you." I peered at her. "What does he think about the coming child?"

Bettina pressed her hand to her lower back. "I have decided to wait before telling him. I want to be sure everything is as it should be."

"How long will you wait?"

She shrugged. "Three months . . . perhaps. Unless he realizes I have stopped my monthly bleeding."

We had reached her gate. She pressed her finger to her lips in the sign for silence, then walked through the courtyard and into the house, offering a shy smile to Avidan and Sha'ul.

I followed with the basket. Now that Bettina was no longer watching, I allowed myself a moment of self-pity. For the last several weeks I had been telling myself that if I could not be a singer, perhaps I was meant to be a mother. I had always enjoyed children, and I could indulge my love for music by teaching my sons and daughters how to sing and play the harp and flute and trumpet . . .

When my babies arrived, perhaps I would finally find my life's calling. I could only hope HaShem sent children soon, because the Holy City offered nothing else for me.

FIFTEEN

Sha'ul

I had just offered the blessing for our evening meal when someone knocked on the door. Bettina's eyes widened. "Have you invited a guest?"

I lowered my head, skimming memories of the day's events, and could not recall asking anyone to visit. "I have not. But when one is a member of the Sanhedrin, one never knows when he will be needed. Something might have come up."

I opened the door, but the man outside was no messenger. Avidan stood in our courtyard with a troubled look on his face.

"Shalom, brother. Is something wrong?"

Avidan dipped his head in an abrupt nod. "I am sorry to interrupt. If I might—may we talk? Somewhere private?"

I glanced at Bettina, who was watching from the table. "Go ahead and eat, woman. We will speak in the courtyard."

Bettina rose from her seat. "Is Aya well?"

"I am sure she is."

I closed the door behind me and gestured to the bench against the wall. "I am sorry this is not more comfortable."

"I would sit on a rock."

We sat. Avidan leaned forward and tugged on his beard. "I do not know where to begin. What I have to share is . . . personal."

"You are now my brother. You can speak freely." I lifted a brow. "Are you and Aya having difficulties?"

Avidan shook his head. "She is a fine wife, but sometimes she can be . . . distracting. She might be sitting at the table, doing nothing of importance, but she looks so beautiful in the lamplight that I can no longer concentrate—"

I chuckled. "All women can be distracting, which is why a man needs to withdraw in order to focus." I studied him, noting the shadows beneath his eyes. "You are not sleeping, so what troubles you?"

He cleared his throat. "I am not a young man, Sha'ul."

I coughed rather than release the laugh that threatened to escape my throat. "You are only, what, twenty and six? That is far from threescore and ten."

"I know I am far from being an elder, but the other men in my study group are younger. Their minds are like sponges; they repeat whatever Gamaliel says without hesitation. They devour scroll after scroll while I struggle to read one. I know they are laughing at me, though none of them would do so to my face."

I frowned. "Which is more difficult—reading the scroll or understanding it?"

Avidan hesitated. "Reading is difficult. Sometimes the letters blur before my eyes, and at other times reading makes my head ache. I try to persevere because I know I will be blessed if I study Torah, but sometimes I wonder if HaShem meant me to be a scholar."

"Aya says your greatest wish is to become a Torah teacher."

"It is what my father has always wanted for me, and is that not the highest work a man can do? Abba has worked a lifetime selling wines to men and women who have far more than they need, all so I could have the opportunity to study Torah. Now he has made it possible for me to live in Jerusalem and study

under the finest teacher in Judea, but I am not the student I want
to be. I should be the leader of my group. I should be guiding the younger men. Instead, I find myself listening to them,
hoping I can pick up what they have read because I struggle to
read on my own."

"Did you have this problem in Tarsus?"

Avidan shook his head. "My teacher at the synagogue read
the scrolls, and I memorized them."

A sudden thought occurred to me. "Look at me, Avidan."

Slowly, my brother-in-law turned to meet my gaze. I peered
at his eyes—they did not seem unusual. The pupils were round
and dark, lit by glimmers of light reflected from the bleached
stones around us.

"I see nothing wrong with your eyes." I held up my hand.
"Can you see my fingers?"

Avidan snorted. "Of course."

I walked to the courtyard gate, then held up two fingers.
"How many fingers have I raised?"

He gave me the look a man would give a stubborn child.
"Two."

I went back to the bench, leaned toward Avidan, and held my
hand close to his eyes. "How many fingers this time?"

Avidan pulled away, but I caught his shoulder and held it.
"How many?"

"Three."

"Can you see them clearly?"

"What does it matter? I can see them."

"But are they clear?"

He shook his head.

I told him to wait while I went into the house. A quick search
yielded the items I sought—Bettina's wooden needle and a ball
of spun wool.

Carrying the items to Avidan, I placed the wool in one hand
and the needle in the other. "I believe the problem is your eyes."

"But you saw nothing wrong with them."

"Then thrust the thread through the needle."

Avidan held the needle at arm's length. "This is not fair. There is no opening in this needle."

"There is." I spoke softly, not wanting to shame him for something that could not be helped. "The needle has a narrow opening, but one I can easily see."

"You are mistaken."

"Run your fingernail along the wood. You will feel the opening even if your eyes cannot see it."

Avidan obeyed. When his countenance fell, I knew he had realized the truth.

"You are not stupid," I told him, lowering my voice. "You cannot read because you cannot clearly see things close to your face."

A red tide washed up from Avidan's throat. "What am I to do? My father has spent so much to send us to Jerusalem. I cannot disappoint him, and we cannot go home. I would die of shame before I could tell Abba I will never be a Torah teacher."

"You do not need to stop studying," I told him. "You need someone to read the scrolls like your teacher in Tarsus did. You will listen as they read, and you will remember what you hear. If something fails to take root in your memory, ask the reader to repeat the passage. Learning can be a matter of hearing what has been written and committing it to memory."

Avidan snorted. "You make it sound easy."

"It *is* easy once you understand how the mind works. The Greeks have long used methods of recitation and questioning to learn. We can do the same. After you have learned, once a week you must come here, and I will ask questions about your study material. You will answer and, doing so, you will reinforce the lesson in your mind."

A wave of relief swept over Avidan's face. "Truly you are a generous man," he said, catching my hands. "I will appreciate every moment taken from your studies and your wife. I know how precious those moments are—"

"We need to find someone to read to you," I said, embarrassed by his effusive thanks. "You could hire someone."

Avidan flushed. "I would rather not let anyone else know of this problem."

I hesitated as a phrase from the sages ran through my mind: *Women need to cook, not study Torah.* But Aya wouldn't be *studying*; she'd only be *reading*.

"Have Aya read to you. She reads well."

Avidan frowned. "A woman reading the Scriptures and holy writings? I know she knows the Torah, but to handle the sacred scrolls?" He lowered his voice. "What about her time of *niddah*? She will be unclean."

I shook my head. "You need not worry. Though the Law states that a woman may not *write* a Torah scroll for public use, she may read it. And the time of her uncleanness will not stop you from learning. The words of the Torah are not susceptible to ritual impurity. During the time of niddah a woman is permitted to both hold and kiss a Torah, so she may certainly read it."

Avidan gave me a smile of pure relief. "For the first time in days, I feel hope—and gratitude, because HaShem has given me a wise brother-in-law."

I held up a warning finger. "I have told you the truth in these matters, but I would not tell your fellow students about your arrangement with Aya. No one else needs to know."

"Again, you have proven yourself wise." Avidan clamped his arm around my shoulder. "May you be blessed above all men!"

I waved his words away but could not help feeling pleased that we had found a solution.

SIXTEEN

Aya

I listened quietly as Avidan told me what he and Sha'ul had learned: my husband was not a poor student, but a poor reader due to weak eyes. "But when your brother suggested that you read to me"—Avidan looked up, a smile blossoming in his beard—"I thanked HaShem for sending me such a wise brother-in-law. I know you will give the sacred words meaning for me. My learning will progress, and my father will have no reason to be ashamed."

I listened with mixed feelings. My heart warmed to the compliment in my husband's words, yet he did not seem to realize that my days were already quite full. Every morning I rose with the sun, said the morning prayers, and prepared food to break our fast. When Avidan left the house, I cleaned the cooking area, damped the fire, and went to the market to buy food for the day. I came home, put the food away, and said the midday prayers. Then I hung my water jars on the pole I carried across my shoulders and walked to the Pool of Siloam, where with dozens of other wives I waited for my turn to step into the pool, fill my jars, and walk home.

Occasionally Eden joined me on the short walk to the pool. Her husband had crafted a pushcart for her. The wheeled base was as wide as her body, the wheels small and smooth, and the handle long enough for her to hold without bending over. Not only did the pushcart transport her water jar, but it also served the same purpose as her walking stick, warning her of obstacles in the road.

I thought it a terribly clever idea, and she laughed when I told her so. "My husband," she said, blushing, "cares far too much for my comfort. He is always behind in his lessons because instead of reading, he has spent half the night trying to make life easier for me."

"Then he is a prince in Israel," I said. "More men should be like your husband."

While Eden and I waited at the pool, we listened to the conversations of women who seemed to know everything that transpired in Jerusalem, Judea, Samaria, and Galilee. Eden had exceptional hearing; often she could hear whispers from the far side of the pool. The neighborhood women spoke of people both highborn and low, of events in places from the Holy City to Rome, and of ideas spreading throughout the region.

We heard about an itinerant teacher from the region of Galilee, an uneducated man who healed the sick and spoke with great authority. "They say," one woman reported, "he has made the lame walk and the blind see."

The woman next to her scoffed. "When he can make the fat skinny, then I will listen. We have Torah teachers in abundance—why would we need an uneducated fisherman from Galilee?"

I was not interested in local gossip, though I heard plenty of it, but felt a keen interest in news of banquets and significant events—occasions for which a hostess might wish to employ a singer. I had no intention of inquiring after a job because I could not do such work without damaging Avidan's reputation at the yeshiva. Yet the thought of making music, of lightening hearts and soothing troubled minds, dangled over my head like forbidden fruit.

Once I tried to tell Bettina that I yearned to become a paid singer. She only shook her head. "Once you have a child," she had said, rubbing her expanding belly, "your world will center around the baby. These other thoughts will leave your head, dear sister, because your heart will settle on the task HaShem has given you."

I did not argue with her, but I could not reconcile her belief with my desires. I had resigned myself to being a wife and mother, and yet HaShem had not placed a child in my womb. What if He never did? The sages had a saying: "He who had no child was like one dead." When a man died, all his seed died with him, so his line came to an end. Surely the saying was true for a woman, too.

If HaShem had ordained that I die childless, perhaps it was because He had other plans for me . . .

I looked at my husband, saw the burning desire in his eyes, and felt my heart soften. Perhaps I was meant to serve him as he attended the yeshiva. A wife's duty was to help her husband, so if Avidan needed someone to read the sacred writings, that is what I would do . . . though, with little time to cook, we might eat nothing but boiled eggs and vegetables for months.

"I would be happy to read for you," I told him. "Shall we begin tonight?"

"I would not interrupt your cooking," Avidan replied. "So we will read after dinner, if it suits you."

Ah, after dinner, when I usually found a few minutes to rest. But what choice did I have?

I served a stew that had simmered for hours on the cook fire. When we finished eating, I cleared away our bowls, lit an additional lamp to counteract the growing gloom, and took the scroll Avidan handed me. It was not part of the Tanakh, but the oral tradition.

"'The *Akedah*, the story of Isaac's binding,'" I read, glancing up to make certain Avidan was absorbing my words. "'The son of Abraham was thirty-seven at that time. The binding was the cause of Sarah's death, who was not informed of Abraham's intention until he and Isaac were on the way to Mount Moriah. Not only did Isaac consent to the sacrifice, but on the way to the mountain, Isaac was addressed by Satan, who said to him, "Unfortunate son of an unfortunate mother! How many days did thy mother pass in fasting and praying for thy birth! And now thy father, who has lost his mind, is going to kill thee."'"

"Indeed," Avidan murmured. "Isaac must have wondered if Abraham had gone mad."

I continued reading: "'But Isaac rebuked Satan and said he was not willing to oppose the wish of his Creator and the command of his father. While Abraham was building the altar, Isaac hid himself, afraid Satan would throw stones, wound him, and render him unfit for sacrifice. The same fear caused Isaac to ask to be bound on the altar. "Because," he said, "I may tremble at the sight of the knife."'"

I lowered the scroll. "I have never heard these words. What is this?"

Avidan lifted his head. "The Akedah. Gamaliel says Isaac knew he was the promised son, the one who would fulfill HaShem's promise and bless all nations of the earth. Yet as they climbed the mountain of sacrifice, so great was Isaac's trust in his father and HaShem that he went willingly, allowing himself to be bound and placed upon the altar, confident that even if the blade cut his throat, HaShem had the power to restore his life and fulfill his promise."

I shivered, imagining the terror Isaac must have felt. I might have trusted HaShem in the beginning, but if I were bound and placed on an altar, I would have a terrible time trusting the man holding the blade. What if he had misunderstood HaShem?

But then . . . HaShem had provided a substitute.

I lifted the scroll again. "'Then Abraham lifted up his eyes and behold, there was a ram, caught in thick bushes by its horns. So Abraham took the ram, and offered it up as a burnt offering instead of his son.'"

"HaShem always intended to provide a substitute," Avidan said.

"Might have been easier if HaShem had provided the ram earlier," I said. "Abraham and Isaac would not have suffered. And Sarah—they say the shock of what Abraham was about to do killed her."

"If a ram had appeared earlier, Abraham and Isaac would not have been tested."

"So HaShem would not know if their faith was strong?"

Avidan shook his head. "HaShem knows all things. Abraham and Isaac suffered through testing so *they* would know the extent of their faith."

"That is not what the Scripture says," I argued. "HaShem said, 'For now I know that you are one who fears God because you did not withhold your only son from me.'"

Avidan's face twisted. "Why would HaShem test Abraham if He already knew the outcome?"

"Why would He make Abraham and Isaac suffer?" I countered.

The words echoed in our small house, and neither of us could answer the other's question.

I turned back to the scroll. "'At first Abraham did not have the courage to tell Isaac his true intention,'" I said, running my finger along the lines of Hebrew. "'The Lord will provide the sacrifice.' That is probably not the answer Isaac wanted to hear."

"Would he have wanted to hear the truth?" Avidan argued. "Could he have borne it at the beginning of their journey?"

"I don't know. Can a child understand the fullness of HaShem at the beginning of his life?" I gave my husband a small smile.

"And in the Scripture, Isaac asked who would supply the *lamb*, so why did HaShem supply a *ram*?"

Avidan leaned forward. "Will you read the passage?"

I went to the carved chest beneath the window and pulled out the scroll of *Bereshit*, the first book of Moses. I laid it on the table and searched for the story of the Akedah. "Here it is: 'Then Abraham took the wood for the burnt offering and put it on Isaac his son. In his hand he took the fire and the knife. So the two of them walked on together.'

"'Then Isaac said to Abraham his father, 'My father?'

"'Then he said, 'Here I am, my son.'

"'He said, "Look. Here's the fire and the wood. But where's the lamb for a burnt offering?"'

"'Abraham said, "God will provide for Himself a lamb for a burnt offering, my son."'

I ran my finger down the parchment until I came to the conclusion of the passage.

"'Then Abraham lifted up his eyes and behold, there was a ram, just caught in the thick bushes by its horns. So Abraham went and took the ram, and offered it up as a burnt offering instead of his son. Abraham named that place *Adonai Yireh*—as it is said today, "On the mountain, Adonai will provide."'"

Avidan closed his eyes, absorbing the sacred words of Moses. "Please read Abraham's answer again."

I read it, translating the Aramaic into Hebrew: "'God will provide for Himself the lamb, for the burnt offering is my son.'"

Avidan fingered his beard. "Some Torah teachers say Abraham killed Isaac, and HaShem raised him from the dead. Therefore, HaShem is beholden to us, because Abraham was righteous enough to sacrifice the promised son."

I shook my head. "That is not what Moses wrote. Listen."

I read the Hebrew slowly, word by word: "'God will provide Himself a lamb for the burnt offering. God will provide Himself a lamb in His son.'"

"But God has no son," Avidan said.

I shrugged. "Then this is a mystery."

"I will have to ask Gamaliel," Avidan said. "Or Sha'ul."

"Please do." I yawned. "But now, husband, I am tired and I do not know the answers to your questions. My eyelids are heavy."

"I am sorry—and I know you have worked hard." Avidan stood, took my hand, and led me to the bed, where he unbraided my hair and stroked it until I fell asleep.

Two months passed. Avidan came home in increasingly better moods, as our evening sessions did much to improve his understanding and retention. He did not complain about our simple meals and the occasionally unswept floor, and I came to enjoy our study time. Like most young girls, I had learned to read and write at my mother's knee, but apart from lessons at our synagogue, I had never been given an opportunity to study Torah and the oral traditions.

During those months, as I watched Bettina's belly swell to the size of a melon, I noticed that my monthly show of blood did not appear. I held my breath, afraid to mention anything to Avidan, until two months had passed with no sign of blood.

Once I was certain, I went through my daily routine as if I were sleepwalking. When not involved in a task, my hands would hover near my belly, compelled to caress the unborn child within. Every night I crawled into bed beside my husband and held my breath as he loved me, afraid he might injure the developing infant. But day after day passed, and still I did not bleed.

My appetite departed during those early weeks, and not even my favorite dishes could tempt me. Every morning I set out bread, honey, and cheese for Avidan, then quietly covered my mouth and hurried into the courtyard lest I vomit in his presence. I do not think Avidan noticed my nausea because his attention was so focused on his studies. Sha'ul's ascent to the Sanhedrin had wakened my husband's slumbering ambition, and he spent every available minute studying his lessons, reciting the prayers, or jotting down questions to ask his teacher. He had never been a witty conversationalist, and he became even less inclined to converse . . . unless, of course, I wanted to debate some point from the Scriptures.

Eden was the first to notice my condition. One afternoon I found her sitting on her courtyard wall, her arms crossed and her brows raised.

"What is wrong?" I asked, alarmed at her indignant expression.

"Were you not going to tell me?"

My mouth dropped open. "How did you know?"

She smiled. "I heard you vomiting. Congratulations and shalom, my friend. May this be the first of many."

Finally, after three months without bleeding, I sat across from my husband and told him we would have a child in the fall. He blinked, put down the scroll in his hand, and lowered his gaze to my belly. "I am to be a father?"

"You are, HaShem willing. It has been three months since I last bled."

His eyes brightened, and for a moment I thought he might shout and alarm the neighbors. Then he remembered he was a serious Torah student and gave me a dignified smile.

"Praise Adonai," he said, his eyes crinkling at the corners. "I must send a letter to our parents."

"Let us hope your letter reaches them before the baby is born," I answered, patting my belly. The child had not yet quickened, but that moment could not be far away.

Avidan stood and kissed the top of my head. "You have made me very happy," he said, reaching for his bag. "I will be home late tonight."

"Don't you want me to read?"

"I must study with men from the yeshiva. Do not wait up—you need your rest."

I watched him go, a kernel of joy warming the center of my being. Surely, I was born for this—bearing children and helping my husband.

Who could have guessed? Ima had been right all along.

———————•———————

After sharing my news with Avidan, I packed a basket with food and walked to Sha'ul's house. My sister-in-law had not been feeling well, but I hoped my news would cheer her.

I found Bettina sitting on a bench in the front room. She rose to greet me and blushed when I exclaimed over her round belly. "Look how you have grown!"

She bit her lip. "Sha'ul says I should not go out looking like this, but it is easier to go out than to send Huldah. She struggles with the water jugs even more than I do."

"Who is Huldah?"

"Oh—we have a servant now. She has gone to get water."

I frowned. "Why does she struggle with the jugs?"

"Because she is old." Bettina pressed her hand to her lower back. "She owed a debt to one of the leading Pharisees. When he saw how slow she was, he sent her to us."

Though I was itching to share my news, politeness demanded that I ask about my brother. "And how is Sha'ul? I have not seen much of him since his ordination."

"Oh." Bettina blew a wisp of hair from her damp forehead. "He is restless. The religious authorities have not yet given him a job. He wants to teach, but at the highest level, of course. The ruling council has not yet decided where he should serve."

I clicked my tongue against my teeth and sat on the bench. "Sit down, for I have news to share. I, too, am expecting a child."

Bettina gasped, then a smile spread over her youthful features.

She sat and clasped my hands. "I am so glad to hear it! I am relieved to know I will not have to go through this alone. If you are with me, I will not be afraid."

"*Are* you afraid?"

A blush ran over her pale cheeks. "Sha'ul says it is a sin to doubt HaShem, but my mother died giving birth to me. Sha'ul says not to worry, all will be well, but he is a man. I am not fond of pain, and I wonder if I am like my mother. What if I am not able to survive childbirth?"

"Sha'ul is correct; you should not worry so much." I squeezed her hands. "We must rejoice in the blessings HaShem has bestowed. We must look forward to presenting these babies at the Temple. Think how happy our husbands will be that day! We will redeem our children and dedicate them to Adonai, and we will raise them to honor their fathers, love their mothers, and obey HaShem. Is that not what He created us to do?"

"Yes." She nodded. "Of course you are right."

"All will be well." I squeezed her hands again, then reached for my basket. "I have brought delicacies for us to enjoy. I have toasted grain, barley cakes, and globi. We will spend the day together and talk about the joyful days to come. "And"—I leaned toward her—"if at any time you want to speak to a woman who will understand, you should come to me. I will listen, I promise."

A tear rolled down her cheek, but she swiped it away. "You don't know how I have longed to hear those words. I know so few people in Jerusalem, and I cannot help being shy. I wanted to talk to you about the baby but thought your heart might ache for a child of your own."

"It did," I admitted. "I had even begun to beg HaShem for a sign that I was not meant to be childless. Fortunately, He answered that prayer."

"I am happy He did."

She pulled a handful of toasted grain from my bowl, then

tossed it in her mouth. "Perfect," she said, crunching the kernels.

"Not too salty?"

"You have it exactly right."

And for the first time since Sha'ul's marriage, I felt a true kinship with my sister-in-law.

SEVENTEEN

Aya

As the celebration of Pesach approached, I noticed an unusual flurry of activity among the women in my neighborhood. Not only did they sweep their houses from floor to ceiling in search of tiny specks of leaven, but they also aired linens, tightened bed frames, and dusted every basket hanging from their ceiling beams. They planted flowers in window boxes and ordered new leather hinges for their doors and shutters.

I had never anticipated Passover as a resident of the city. As a visitor, I assumed the Holy City was always blooming and in good repair. But for the first time I saw how much work went into preparing the city for thousands of international visitors.

Somehow I supposed that the pilgrims who flooded Jerusalem would avoid our humble home, but when a woman at the Pool of Siloam asked how many guests my husband and I would host, the question caught me off guard. "How many?" I gaped in astonishment. "Our house barely holds us."

The woman's raucous laughter drew attention from others in line. "She thinks her house is too small to host guests," she announced as my cheeks burned. "As if she has never before experienced Pesach!"

"I haven't," I stammered. "Not while living in Jerusalem, that is."

An older woman walked over and patted my shoulder. "Little wife, you must open your door to anyone who wants to enter," she said. "Showing hospitality is a commandment. But do not worry—once your home is filled, the others will go in search of a more comfortable space. All Jerusalem becomes an inn during the pilgrimage festivals."

My heart sank at this news. I had finally begun to think of our house as a cozy home, but soon it would be overrun with strangers who would soil my linens, crowd my table, and drool on my pillows. Despite my pregnancy, I would have to surrender my bed to an elder, so Avidan and I might end up sleeping on a rug.

I would find it difficult to feel hospitable while lying on our dirt floor.

"Having guests is a blessing," another woman said. "You will need extra mouths to eat your entire lamb, for nothing can be eaten the next day."

"Is this the first year you will be roasting a lamb?" another woman asked.

I nodded.

She smiled. "Just be sure not to break a single bone. You will do well, as long as not a single bone is broken."

Eden rolled her pushcart toward me. "Aya, did you not visit Jerusalem with your family?"

"Not every year," I replied, my tone more defensive than I would have liked. "The distance was too great. But Abba tried to bring us every two or three years, especially after my brother began to study at the Temple yeshiva."

"And while you were in the Holy City, where did you stay?"

"Sha'ul found us a place with a family he knew." A wealthy family, I might have added, but did not.

Eden's smile deepened. "Did you not notice your host's efforts to ensure your comfort? Surely we can do no less for those who will be visiting from great distances."

In truth, I had not noticed, because what young person notices such things? But now I would be a hostess by holy command, so I resigned myself to my responsibility. Within a few days, thousands upon thousands of Abraham's descendants would enter Jerusalem, and some of them would sleep in my home.

Perhaps, if I closed my eyes and pretended I had traveled all the way from Tarsus, I would not mind.

———— • ————

We women were not the only people who had to prepare for Passover. A month before the festival, officials from Judea, Samaria, and Galilee had sent out laborers to repair the roads and bridges for the onslaught of pilgrims. Outside Jerusalem, a crew of workers visited graveyards to whiten the sepulchers lest a speck of dead man's dust attach to a pious traveler. Those who served in the Temple were busy erecting fences to contain the animals rural families would bring as their tithes.

Exactly one month before the feast, money changers, known as *schulchanim*, had opened stalls in every Judean town. These men, authorized by the Temple authorities, took whatever goods or coinage the pilgrims offered and exchanged it for Tyrian coins so families could pay the annual Temple tribute of half a shekel. The schulchanim did not offer their services out of charity but charged a fee, and those operating in Jerusalem charged the highest fees of all.

A few days before the beginning of Pesach, Avidan took me to the Temple Mount. The area was already crowded with worshipers, foreign visitors, and Levites who had left their villages to serve during the festival. Avidan and I entered through the Royal Portico and stepped into the teeming Court of the

Gentiles. We threaded our way through carpenters, scribes, and money changers. The odors of animals and manure wafted past my nose as foreign languages, most of them unknown to me, tickled my ears.

At one point, Avidan turned and put his arm over my shoulders. "Wait here," he said, guiding me to a shady spot near a pillar. "I must find my Torah teacher, but I do not want to drag you through this crowd. I will return soon."

"Please don't leave me," I begged, alarmed by the confusion and noise. "I may never find you again."

"Of course you will. Stay exactly where you are, and I will return soon."

I watched as he disappeared into the boisterous crowd, then shifted my gaze to a pair of bickering money changers. How could anyone who lived in Jerusalem consider Pesach a time of joy?

I was watching a shepherd apply whitewash to a blemish on one of his lambs when the sound of a familiar accent caught my attention. My father once sold a set of tents to a Galilean merchant, and the man's accent had fascinated me. Abba said people from Galilee had a reputation for being brutish and poorly educated, yet fish and textiles from that region were highly prized.

I watched as a group of Galileans, men and women, entered the court, and noticed that they seemed to defer to the man who led them. He looked like the others—tanned, with simple clothing, a leather girdle, and an untrimmed beard. Though the others seemed wary and alert, he moved with perfect calm, like a priest who felt at home in this sacred place.

Could this be the teacher mentioned by the women at the Pool of Siloam?

I leaned against the pillar, fascinated by the man who surveyed the milling crowd of animals, pilgrims, and Levites; then his eyes narrowed. Without warning, he approached a table of money changers, grabbed the edge, and tipped the table over, scattering coins onto the pavement. Then he removed his corded girdle, lifted a rail from a holding pen, and waded into a herd of sheep, brandishing the girdle. "How dare you," he shouted to the astonished onlookers as he drove the sheep out of the pen, "turn my Father's house into a market?"

While sheep bleated and shepherds shouted, the Galilean opened a cattle pen, scattered the beasts, and then strode to a table of pigeon cages. There he lifted the lids, setting the birds free, and tossed the wooden cages onto the pavement.

Horrified, I looked for the Temple guards, who had removed their swords and stepped forward, but they seemed confused about what to do. The money changers were too busy scrambling for coins to chastise the man, and the shepherds were chasing their bellowing beasts.

Finally, a group of priests appeared, and their presence spurred the Temple guards to action. With swords drawn, they cornered the Galilean and a few of the men with him.

One of the white-robed priests strode forward to confront the man. "By what authority have you done all this?"

"You have turned my Father's house into a market," the man replied, not retreating from the priest's hot gaze. "This should be a house of prayer."

"Your Father?" The priest stiffened. "HaShem is Father to *all* children of Abraham, so why do you have the right to sow such confusion? Give us a sign to show us you have the authority to do this."

"I have the authority." The stranger lifted his head, then stared pointedly at a guard who was brandishing his sword. "You want proof? I tell you this—destroy this Temple, and in three days I will raise it up again."

A group of Judeans—I was astounded to see Sha'ul and Avidan among them—turned to each other and laughed. "Forty-six years this Temple has been under construction," one of the

Judeans said, his voice rising above the crowd, "and you are going to rebuild it in three days?"

My heart pounded as I looked toward the Antonia tower, looming above the north wall of the Temple. Were my brother and husband about to become involved in a riot? The Romans frowned on public disturbances and would not hesitate to intervene if the situation escalated.

In the hollow of my back, a single drop of sweat traced the course of my spine. I held my breath, afraid the Galilean would urge his followers to charge the priest, but he only gave the Judean a sharp look and walked away, his followers trailing behind him.

With my hand on my chest, I felt my heartbeat slow as the crowd dispersed. I searched the crowd and finally spotted Avidan coming toward me. "I am sorry to be gone so long," he said, taking my hand. "But you probably saw why I was detained."

"Who was that man? I have never seen a Galilean act with such boldness."

"You have never seen anyone act with such *foolishness*," he said. "That was Yeshua of Nazareth. Apparently, he has developed a reputation as a healer. Some say he is a prophet."

"But we have not seen a true prophet since Zachariah. Some claim John the Baptizer was a legitimate prophet, but Herod—"

"You have been listening to women's gossip." Avidan gave me an indulgent smile. "And the stories about John the Baptizer are nonsense. You should ignore them as well as anything you hear about this Yeshua."

I rose on tiptoe, but the Galilean had disappeared. "Whoever he is," I remarked, "he is certainly zealous for the house of God."

Avidan's eyes narrowed. "Zealous or foolish? It can be difficult to discern the difference."

I did not see Yeshua of Nazareth again that year, though we continued to hear about him. We heard reports of healings—a blind man who received his sight, a child healed of leprosy, a man who had been lame for years walking again. The people who told these stories were convinced they had witnessed genuine miracles. They said Yeshua was a healer sent from HaShem. Some speculated that he might be our promised Messiah.

Avidan and Sha'ul also heard these stories, and their reactions could not have been more different. One night, as Sha'ul and Bettina dined with us, Avidan quoted from a psalm of David: "'I have become a stranger to my brothers, a foreigner to my mother's children. For zeal for Your House consumed me—the insults of those who insulted You have fallen on me.'" He turned to Sha'ul. "Could those words not apply to the man who overturned the money changers' tables? He certainly received many insults that day."

Sha'ul's mouth curled and rolled like he wanted to spit. "You have not been studying long enough to interpret the Scriptures correctly, Avidan. Do not overreach."

"But the prophet Malachi speaks of a messenger who will come to the Temple and refine it," Avidan insisted. "The prophet wrote, 'Suddenly, He will come to His Temple—'"

Sha'ul looked at my husband as if Avidan were a young child. "Surely you realize dozens of false messiahs have appeared through the years. This Galilean is one of them. He will fade away, as did the others before him, and he will amount to nothing . . . unless he falls afoul of Rome. Then he will most certainly perish in ignominy."

When Avidan glanced at me, I knew what he was thinking. We had been reading the story of Joseph and his brothers, and both of us were struck by the brothers' blindness when they finally met Joseph in Egypt. Though Joseph was wearing Egyptian garb and had probably shaved his head and beard, how could they not recognize his voice?

Avidan insisted that the passing years had obliterated their knowledge of Joseph, but I pointed out that the brothers realized almost immediately that their trouble with the Egyptian had something to do with the treachery they had committed. Their sin against Joseph was uppermost in their minds . . . so how had they not recognized him?

Avidan gave me a small smile and turned to Sha'ul. "Is it not possible," he said, folding his hands, "that this Yeshua could be a prophet and we have been blind? After all, Joseph's brothers did not recognize him when they met him in Egypt."

A warning cloud settled on Sha'ul's features. "Has someone in your yeshiva suggested that Yeshua is from HaShem?"

Avidan shook his head. "But—"

"Such blasphemous speculation is a waste of time." Sha'ul turned to Bettina, who had grown pale at the vehemence in her husband's words. "Are you ready to go? You must be tired after such a long day."

Like a dutiful wife, Bettina nodded, and Sha'ul stood to say the blessing for the end of the meal. "Blessed are You, Lord our God, King of the universe, benevolent God, our Father, our King, our Strength, our Creator, our Redeemer, our Maker, our Holy One, the Holy One of Jacob, our Shepherd, the Shepherd of Israel, the King who is good and does good to all, each and every day. May the Merciful One send abundant blessing into this house and upon this table at which we have eaten. May the Merciful One send us Elijah the prophet— may He be remembered for good—and let Him bring us good tidings, deliverance, and consolation. May the Merciful One bless my father, my teacher, the master of this house, and my mother, my teacher, the mistress of this house, and all that is theirs. Just as He blessed our forefathers, Abraham, Isaac, and Jacob, in all things, by all things, with all things, so may He bless all of us together with a perfect blessing; and let us say, Amen."

My brother had never been one to use five words when fifty were available.

When Sha'ul finished, he prodded Bettina toward the door, and they left without another word.

Avidan cleared his throat. "Your brother does not take kindly to differing opinions."

I sighed. "He is adamant in his beliefs. He has always been that way."

"I suppose that is why he is such a strong leader."

"Perhaps." I stacked the dishes near the water jar, then pressed my hand to Avidan's cheek. "But strength is not always necessary, husband. Sometimes a gentle approach is best."

He took my hand, kissed my palm, and led me to our bed.

———————◆———————

In the fourth month of my pregnancy, I began to bleed. Not knowing what this meant, I sent Avidan for the midwife, who at first refused to come. Only after much pleading and the promise of payment did the woman agree to assist me. She bade me lie down and placed a thick cotton cloth beneath my thighs. Then she lifted my tunic and pressed hard on my belly, her face as expressionless as stone.

My body responded with cramps and more bleeding. Every so often the midwife would remove the cloth, examine it, and replace it with another. When the severe cramps finally ceased, the midwife took the folded cotton from beneath me and held it to the light from the window. "The child you carried has died," she said, each word hammering my heart. "Your child was the size of a locust. The eyes are like two specks at some distance from each other; so are the nostrils. The feet are like two silken cords; the mouth like a hair . . . and I cannot determine whether it was male or female."

She folded the cloth over the remains of my baby, then pressed her palm to my forehead. "You have no fever, so you will recover soon. Wait fourteen days, then visit the mikveh for your purification. Afterward you will be able to lie with your husband and conceive another child."

I stared, astounded both by her blunt advice and her air of detachment, and watched as she went to Avidan for payment. Pale and stricken, he walked to the cupboard, removed three loaves I had hoped to sell at the market, and gave them to the midwife.

She left our house without a backward glance, her indifference cutting me like a knife.

My husband and I sat in silence for a long while, neither of us looking at the other. Finally, I found my voice: "Why has HaShem taken our baby? We are serving Him. We left Tarsus to come to His Holy City, and you are studying His Law—"

"Adonai gave and Adonai has taken away; blessed be the Name of Adonai," Avidan replied, his voice flat. "Job lost his children, his possessions, and his health—are we more righteous than he was?"

I had no answer, but my husband's logic did little to assuage my grief. In my mind, once again HaShem had blessed Sha'ul and shown me the back of His hand. Sha'ul was firstborn, brilliant, and worthy of my parents' praise. He had been blessed with the best Torah teacher, the most fertile bride, and soon HaShem would bless him with a child.

Once again, HaShem had smiled on my brother and ignored me. Avidan would not agree, nor would Sha'ul, but they could not argue with the bloodstained cloth at the end of my bed.

I did not go to the Pool of Siloam during the time of my uncleanness, and I wore sackcloth when I finally returned. The neighborhood women took one look at my flat belly and understood.

"In due time," one woman told me, "you will not think of

this pain. When your arms hold another baby, your heart will be full."

"You will be too busy to think about what you have suffered," another woman added. "Your heart aches now, but when another baby fills your womb, you will think only of the future."

"But why did this happen?" I asked, suddenly longing for my mother. "I did not fall, nor was I sick—"

"Why do the Romans control Jerusalem?" a woman countered. "To teach us how to suffer? Who can say?"

"I do not think we need to be taught how to suffer," I said, thinking of that bloodstained cloth. "Have we not suffered enough? The Egyptians made us slaves; the Babylonians took us from our Promised Land. Haman would have eradicated us from all the domains of Persia, and the Seleucids tried to destroy our worship and our way of life—"

"You have been reading again." Eden smiled as she carried her water jar out of the pool. "Perhaps you should bake more and read less."

"In any case," another woman said, "the Lord is faithful to Israel. Now, fill your jars and lift your head. HaShem will not allow you to remain childless forever."

But what if He did? If I could not bear a living child, Avidan's seed would die with him. He would grow old knowing he had not been able to fulfill HaShem's command to fill the earth . . .

"The midwife was no comfort," I said, slowly stepping into the pool. "She did not even shed a tear over my child."

An older woman who sat on the edge of the pool lifted her head. "You must not blame her," she said. "If she dissolved into tears at every lost baby, nothing of her would remain. Instead, she allows you to weep for your child, and carries none of your grief away with her."

I pressed my lips together and filled my water jars, resolved not to speak another word. Job suffered mostly in silence when his so-called friends visited, each of them determined to find some secret sin in Job's life. I was far from perfectly righteous, but I had committed no sin that should result in the death of my child.

Thoughts of Job's judgmental companions remained with me as I trudged home. They offered about as much comfort to the suffering Job as those women offered me, and I could not help but feel resentful. Their glib advice did little to ease my grief, and not even the promise of another child could erase the dreams I held for the baby who never drew breath.

If HaShem was faithful to Israel—and to me—why did He allow us to suffer so?

I turned a corner and halted, a thrill of fear shooting through me. In the road ahead stood a familiar figure, one I had not seen since Tarsus. For an instant I thought I was imagining things, and then the man turned and I saw his face. The Roman Claudius Lysias, commander of the Fortress Antonia, was standing a few steps away.

Instinctively, I ducked behind the corner, then lowered my water jars and peered at him again. The man was as tall and broad as I remembered, but his uniform and helmet were embellished with more gold. What was he doing in this humble part of the city?

The reason for his presence became clear when a merchant led a handsome horse out of an alley. Claudius patted the horse's flank, said something to the merchant, and handed the reins to another Roman who stood nearby. I relaxed against the wall, relieved to see that their transaction had been concluded. In a moment he would leave, and I could continue without being noticed . . .

As the second Roman led the horse away, a rat skittered out from beneath a bale of straw and ran toward me while the Roman watched. When he lifted his gaze, our eyes met.

I lowered my head, my face heating, and hoped he would not recognize me. After all, two years had passed since we met at the banquet in Tarsus, and I was no longer a young bride.

151

"By all the gods." His voice, deep and vibrant, made my stomach sway. "Imagine seeing you in Jerusalem."

I looked up, not wanting to offend. "Shalom, Commander."

"Tribune," he said, smiling.

"I apologize."

"I do not expect you to be familiar with the ranks of Roman legionaries."

I looked away, hoping none of my neighbors would pass this way. How would I explain knowing a Roman?

"It is good to see you, Aya. Are you still singing?"

"Only around the house." I blushed. "I am married, and Jerusalem is not Tarsus."

"Indeed not." A line appeared between his brows. "You are wearing sackcloth. Are you in mourning?"

"Yes."

He waited, and when I did not explain, he bowed his head. "I must be off. I hope your God brings you comfort."

"Thank you. Shalom."

I watched him go, my heart beating like a frightened rabbit's, and wondered why the man had remembered me. I had been little more than a servant when we met. So why had he recalled my name?

I picked up my water jars and walked away, realizing I might never know.

EIGHTEEN

Aya

I was preparing to light the Shabbat candles on a warm summer evening when one of my neighbors called through the window. "Aya! Your sister-in-law has sent for the midwife!"

I glanced at Avidan, who had just seated himself at the table. "May we go to her on Shabbat?"

"Walking from one house to another is permissible," he said, standing. "And I know Bettina would want you by her side."

I grabbed my head covering and heard the pounding of my pulse, even though my heart still felt hollow. How could I rejoice at the birth of Bettina's baby when my own loss was still fresh? Eight weeks had passed since I lost our child, and though I no longer felt engulfed in despair, I did not think I could look at a baby without weeping.

But perhaps I was wrong. Perhaps I could focus on helping the midwife and comforting my sister-in-law. Helping hands were always appreciated, and I was Bettina's nearest relative in Jerusalem.

Avidan and I hurried to Sha'ul's house. Avidan did not knock but walked straight through the courtyard and into the house, where he found Sha'ul reading a scroll. I went to the bedside, where the midwife had rolled up the sleeves of her tunic. Her hands were pressed against the thin undergarment over Bettina's round belly.

"How long?" I asked, moving to the opposite side of the bed.

The woman looked up. "What?"

"How long has she been in labor?"

The midwife shook her head. "Half a day, I would think. She did not send for me until the sixth hour." She squinted at me and nodded. "Have you recovered from your loss? Are you strong enough to do this?"

I nodded. "I am."

"Have you ever attended a birth?"

"No, but I want to help. Bettina is my sister-in-law."

"Good. But you must mind me and be quick to move if I tell you to do something."

I looked down at Bettina, who did not seem to realize I had arrived. Her eyes were tightly shut, her right hand curled into a fist against her mouth. I gasped when I saw that she had bitten her hand, staining the top of her tunic with blood.

"Bettina." I sat on the side of the bed. "Sister, I am here. Do you need anything?"

Her eyelids fluttered, then opened. "Aya." A brief smile curved her lips and then vanished. "Ohhhh. No one said travail would be so painful."

"It will pass. Did HaShem not say He would increase our pain from conception to labor?"

"Then it is a wonder"—Bettina gasped—"any of us are born at all." She drew a deep breath and grimaced, then let out a scream that lifted the hair on my arms. "Something is wrong. I can feel it."

I looked at the midwife, who was prodding Bettina's belly. "Is this . . . normal?"

"The baby has turned," she said, her voice so low I could barely hear her. "It can't be birthed in this position. If I can't turn it again . . ."

She shook her head, allowing me to interpret her silence. I swallowed hard and glanced at the table, knowing that Avidan and Sha'ul were pretending not to hear Bettina's cries. I was certain—at least I hoped—they were praying.

I caught Bettina's free hand and held it, though her grip threatened to break my fingers whenever the pain seized her. I watched, horrified, as the muscles in her belly shifted and contracted, but still the baby did not move.

For hours I whispered words of comfort to Bettina. I wiped her wet forehead, bathed her neck, and brought water to her lips. Once I looked toward the table and saw that Sha'ul and Avidan had disappeared. I felt certain they had gone to our house where they could pray without distraction.

The moon had risen high above the darkened window when Bettina screamed so loudly even the midwife startled. A red stain blossomed on the bed, and the midwife's lips flattened at the sight of it.

I stared in disbelief as the woman jerked her head toward the door. "You should get her husband. If he wishes to give her the respect she deserves, he should come at once."

I flew out the door and ran home, my sandals slapping against the street. Sha'ul must have heard me coming, because he was in the doorway when I reached the house. "Go!" I told him.

He took off, leaving me with Avidan, who drew me into his arms and held me. I leaned against him, weeping silently, then we sat together on the courtyard bench. As we sat in silence, my mind flitted back to the story of Rachel giving birth to Benjamin, which Avidan and I had read a few nights before. Benjamin survived a difficult birth, but his mother did not. Isaac buried her at Bethlehem and erected a stone marker in her memory.

And so it was said, even now, that Rachel looked after every child who passed by the marker. With that gravestone in mind, the prophet Jeremiah had written, "Thus says Adonai: 'A voice is heard in Ramah—lamentation and bitter weeping—Rachel weeping for her children, refusing to be comforted, because they are no more.'"

I had not been able to shake the story from my thoughts. I had asked Avidan whose children Rachel wept for, but he could not give me an answer.

Yet the melancholy question remained with me—did Rachel weep for Bettina's child, mine, or all the children of Israel who would die too soon?

NINETEEN

Sha'ul

I sat on a bench in the front room, deaf to the midwife's instructions. "Your place is outside," she said, gesturing toward the door. "Let the women tend to your wife. It is the custom, after all."

I did not move. My mind kept replaying the events of the last hour and would not stop.

Bettina had closed her eyes by the time I arrived, but she was still breathing. I knelt beside the bed, knowing I should urge her to confess her sins before God. The traditional words were supposed to be spoken in the last moment of life, and the dying one's last breath was to be spent repeating the Shema . . . but Bettina did not open her eyes.

In times of great illness, a dying person could confess sins with only her mind and heart, so I said the words for my wife, hoping she was silently repeating them: "I acknowledge before You, my God and God of my ancestors, that my recovery and my death are in Your hand. May it be Your will to heal me completely, but if I should die, may my death be an atonement for all sins I have committed. May You grant my share in the Garden of Eden, and privilege me for the world to come that is concealed for the righteous . . ."

I was about to say the Shema when the midwife placed a feather on my wife's lips. "She is gone," the woman said, focusing on the feather. "If it does not move, she has left us."

We watched and waited for several moments, then the midwife lifted the feather and shook her head. "*Baruch dayan ha'emet*," she said. Blessed be the true Judge, who gives life and takes it as He wills.

Then she extended Bettina's arms alongside her body and covered her face with a linen cloth. While I watched, unable to move, the midwife tied a strip of linen around my wife's head to close the lower jaw and prevent the mouth from opening.

"Now you must help me," she said. "We must place the body on the floor, feet toward the door."

I did not question her but helped her complete her task. When my wife lay on the floor, the midwife spilled the basin of water by the bed—to prevent the spread of death, she said—and placed a long linen sheet over Bettina's body.

"When Shabbat ends," she said, looking toward the dark window, "women from the *hevra kadisha* will come and prepare the body. They will bathe her, make a proper shroud for her, and arrange her for burial. You, of course, will begin your time of mourning."

I knew the customs and the Law. The numbness I felt in that moment was part of the *aninut*, the mourning period between death and burial. Then I would go through *shiva*, the seven days after burial; then *sheloshim*, the time until the thirtieth day after burial. I would not mourn longer than thirty days, because I could not feel more compassionate toward Bettina than HaShem himself.

Since I had touched the dead, I would also be unclean for the next seven days. My house would be unclean, along with any open vessels inside it. Anyone who touched me would be unclean, so I would sit alone in my courtyard, receiving consolation from outside the gate.

Remaining apart from the community seemed a small price to pay for my guilt. My wife was dead, with my unborn child entombed in her body. They would be buried together before sunset on the first day of the week.

When the sun rose, continuing Shabbat, neighbors gathered outside my gate and observed me sitting silently, my tunic torn and my head covered with dirt. Through the open door they could see my wife's covered body, and that told them all they needed to know.

"Baruch dayan ha'emet," they murmured. *Blessed be the true Judge . . .*

When the first three stars appeared in the evening sky, the women from the hevra kadisha arrived with baskets of cloth, herbs, and dried flowers. I watched through the open door as they placed Bettina on a special board, removed her soiled clothing, and bathed her while reciting a series of Scriptures. "'May He establish His kingdom in your lifetime and during your days, and within the life of the entire House of Israel, speedily and soon; and say, Amen.'"

They performed the *tahara* ceremony, the pouring of warm water over the body while it was held in an upright position. I had never seen the ceremony performed and watched with detached interest as the women gave Bettina her last bath.

"'Blessed and praised, glorified and exalted, extolled and honored, adored and lauded be the name of the Holy One, blessed be He, beyond all the blessings and hymns, praises and consolations that are ever spoken in the world; and say, Amen.'"

They laid her down, combed her hair, cut her fingernails and toenails. When the cleansing was complete, one of the women began to sing quietly while the others sewed my wife into a linen shroud. Unlike the people of other nations, we buried our dead without food, coins, or precious stones, because only Torah study and our good deeds could go with us into the next world.

Avidan and Aya came to mourn with me, but I sent them away. Though they were family, I could not bear the sight of Aya's tears, and I did not want Avidan to miss a full week of Torah study. When I told them to spare themselves this exercise in sorrow, something inside Aya broke. Her somber facade shattered, and Avidan led my weeping sister from the house, leaving me alone with the women of the hevra kadisha.

The women completed their work in darkness and slipped away to their homes. One of them paused to tell me that Bettina should be buried at first light. She offered to procure the required flautists and a mourner, and I nodded my assent.

Then I sat beneath a canopy of stars, oblivious to everything but the necessity of properly mourning the wife I had not appreciated or loved as she deserved. After returning from the burial, I would sit for seven more days, then I would go to the Temple to be sprinkled with the water of purification, a mixture of spring water and the ashes of a red heifer. Only after bathing, washing my clothes, and sprinkling my house and its furnishings could I be considered clean.

I struggled to think—the Law had exact requirements for purifying the outside of a man. What would I have to do to cleanse my soul of guilt?

After sunrise, neighbors gathered at my courtyard gate. Several men moved into the house, where they lifted my wife's body and carried her toward the burial ground outside the city.

Walking behind the flautists and the professional mourner, I followed the funeral bier, taking slow steps to keep time with the heavy beating of my heart. *HaShem, what have I done?*

I sought solace in the traditional mourner's prayer, reciting it in a loud voice: "'Glorified and sanctified be God's great name throughout the world, which He has created according to His will.'"

I had married a child, barely sixteen, whose frail body could not handle the stress of childbirth. I loved her as I might have loved a favorite book or garment—she was a ritual, a rite of passage, a passport to ordination and the Sanhedrin. Even the baby had been an accomplishment, another commandment satisfied, my acknowledgment of HaShem's command to replenish the earth. A son would have been a credit to my name, a child of Abraham into whom I could pour my knowledge and lead in the path of righteousness.

"'May His great name be blessed forever and to all eternity.'"

My young wife, whom I might have learned to love earnestly, had kept my house, prepared my meals, and warmed my bed . . . and I had given her very little in return.

I had never even made an effort to know her.

"'May there be abundant peace from heaven, and life, for us and for all Israel; and say, Amen.'"

I should never have married. My heart held no room for a wife because long ago I devoted it to study. I knew members of the Sanhedrin who had developed loving partnerships with their wives, but they were not as driven as I, not as ambitious . . . or perhaps their ardor for HaShem had cooled over the years. Their passion for the Law evolved into adoration for their children, a fondness they demonstrated by paving the way for their sons to enter a religious fraternity and for their daughters to make good marriages.

"'He who creates peace in His celestial heights, may He create peace for us and for all Israel; and say, Amen.'"

I gripped my dirt-encrusted hair and refused to look at Bettina's shrouded body, still round with the unborn child. My father, if he were here, would tell me to find another wife, perhaps a young widow who had successfully birthed children. He wanted me to raise many sons, all of whom would bring honor to the family.

He had always based my value on what I could bring to the family.

But my mother, if she were here, would hold my arm and

tell me to move on. "You are too single-minded and stubborn," she would say, her honesty both repellant and attractive. "If you want to be a man of the Law, apply yourself to the Law and let nothing distract your pursuit of righteousness. But if you want to be a husband, marry a woman you can love, and love her with all your heart. Because a good wife is a treasure from the Lord, but marriage demands a price you may not be able to afford."

Ima knew me better than anyone; she always had. My father praised my success, but Ima understood my nature.

So why didn't I?

Yesterday I had been satisfied with my life, content to know I had followed the Law in every aspect of life. And then HaShem, blessed be His name, had chosen to send a whirlwind that took my wife and exposed my stony heart.

Today I saw myself as I was—stubborn. Resolute. Determined. And indifferent, perhaps, to the emotional needs of others. I had wronged my wife and would pay for it in this life or the next.

But I did not need a wife. I would be a stronger and more effective Torah teacher on my own, and I'd have far more freedom to follow HaShem's commands.

So I would not marry again. Not because I did not have a man's desires but because I would surrender them to HaShem.

As we walked through the Water Gate, on the way to the tombs, I made a resolution.

Baruch dayan ha'emet. *Blessed be the true Judge . . .*

I had done what was required of a righteous man. I had taken a wife and gained a seat on the Great Sanhedrin. That seat would enable me to serve HaShem on a greater scale than an ordinary man. A far greater scale than my father. If I had to forgo the ordinary pleasantries of life and sever emotional ties, then so be it.

HaShem ruled in all things, even in this. So I would willingly bear this grief and never marry again.

TWENTY

Aya

Grief colored the months following Bettina's death, yet Sha'ul's loss changed my perspective. Apparently, HaShem had not granted my brother an exemption from suffering, and in many ways his suffering seemed worse than mine. Though he continued to work with Avidan, he seemed more distant than ever, and more determined to mold Avidan in his image.

The season of Pesach returned, though this year promised to be more somber than the festivals of years past. I set about the work of preparing for the pilgrims, and Avidan hired a woman to help me. He did not want me to overtire myself, because I was again carrying a child.

I conceived in the month of Elul and felt the quickening of my womb at the time of Yom Kippur. I realized I should give birth, Adonai willing, in late spring, which meant I would be heavily pregnant during Pesach. With thoughts of Bettina ever present in our minds, Avidan promised to hire whatever help I needed to ensure my well-being.

Avidan, Sha'ul, and I were still quietly grieving, but most

people in Judea were focused on Yeshua of Nazareth. For the fourth time, he and his followers came to Jerusalem, and his entourage was larger than ever before. Sha'ul and Avidan were greatly concerned about the man's intentions, though they took pains to hide their anxiety from me. But one night I went to bed early, pleading exhaustion, and pretended to sleep as Avidan and Sha'ul discussed recent events.

"You have heard about Lazarus of Bethany," Avidan said, his voice low. "The man who was dead four days before Yeshua brought him back to life."

"It is impossible," Sha'ul snapped. "But the alleged witnesses have been persuasive. Their influence only increases the potential for trouble."

"I heard that Caiaphas sent scouts throughout the city. He even convened a special meeting of the elders—"

"Yes, a plan has already been set in motion. They have paid one of the Nazarene's *talmid* . . . thirty pieces of silver proved sufficient to purchase the man's cooperation."

"To do what?"

"To signal them. After the informant reports a time and place, the Temple guards will seize this false messiah and deliver him to the high priest."

My thoughts raced as I lay motionless beneath my blanket. I had heard that Yeshua's *talmidim* had sworn allegiance to him—how, then, could one of them be bought for the price of a slave? Had the man seen or heard something that made him doubt his master? Or had he been falsely loyal from the beginning?

I wanted to ask the question aloud, but I knew Sha'ul and Avidan would only change the subject. They did not want me to worry about secret meetings and covert plots.

The night before Passover, Sha'ul dined with us and the six guests who were staying at our house for the festival. When the pilgrims retired to their cots and blankets, Sha'ul motioned for

Avidan to meet him in the courtyard. Curious, I followed my husband.

Sha'ul did not even glance at me. "The high priest has called a meeting of the ruling council," he told Avidan. "Witnesses have been summoned, and the council will begin its deliberation tonight. If they find the accused guilty, the full Sanhedrin will begin his trial at daybreak."

I stared at my brother. "What are you talking about?"

"This does not concern you, Aya."

"If it concerns you and Avidan, it also concerns me. What trial do you mean? It is illegal for the Sanhedrin to convene during a festival—"

He cut me off with an uplifted hand. "If you want to know the business of the religious authorities, ask your husband. Better yet, wait for him to tell you."

I choked back a terse reply. If not for my help, Avidan would not be the scholar he was. But I would hold my tongue for his sake.

Sha'ul bade Avidan farewell, then stepped into the gloom and hurried toward the Temple Mount.

"This is about the Nazarene, isn't it?" I whispered, clinging to Avidan's arm. "I heard he cleared the Temple courtyard a second time."

"He did." Avidan led me into the house. Together we crept through the semidarkness, careful not to step on any of our slumbering guests.

When we were finally in bed, Avidan drew me into his arms. "I do not want you to become anxious about this. The Sanhedrin will seek the will of HaShem concerning this man. Everything will be as HaShem wills."

"Even though the Sanhedrin is disregarding its own laws? And what did I hear about Yeshua restoring a man who had been dead four days? Such a thing should be impossible."

"It is," Avidan answered, "because once a soul has entered

Sheol, it cannot return unless HaShem allows it. You will doubtless remember how the witch at Endor summoned Samuel the prophet for King Sha'ul."

"I remember."

"Yes. Well, HaShem allowed that." Avidan swallowed. "Since this Nazarene is not HaShem, the story cannot be true. If he claims it is, he is committing blasphemy."

He tucked our blanket over my round belly. "You look tired, wife. For the sake of our child, perhaps you should sleep."

Reluctantly, I agreed.

TWENTY-ONE

Sha'ul

I woke in darkness, then rolled out of bed. "'I gratefully thank you, O living and eternal King, for You have returned my soul within me with compassion—abundant is Your faithfulness!'"

As tradition demanded, I picked up the cup of water with my right hand, passed it to the left, and poured water over the right. With the right hand I poured water over the left, then repeated the process three times.

"'The beginning of wisdom is the fear of HaShem—good understanding to all who practice them; His praise endures forever. Blessed is the Name of His glorious kingdom for all eternity.'"

I reached for my tunic and slipped it over my head, then held up my prayer shawl. "'Bless, O my soul, HaShem; HaShem, my God, You are very great; You have clothed Yourself in majesty and splendor; wrapped in light as with a garment, stretching out the heavens like a curtain.'"

When I had finished saying the prayers for the wearing of the fringe, the prayer shawl, and the tefillin, I left the house and looked toward the eastern horizon. The rising sun appeared swollen and blood-red as I walked to the high priest's palace, burnishing the city with a coppery glow. I knew the council had passed a sleepless night. Undoubtedly the Nazarene had, as well.

The doors to the stately building were open, and several of my fellow Pharisees stood in the forecourt, conversing in low voices. I stopped by a group of men I knew. "Well?"

Nissim of Caesarea gave me a humorless smile. "Caiaphas and the council examined the Nazarene last night."

"And?"

Nissim shrugged. "Several witnesses were called, but none of them agreed with each other. But as all hope seemed lost, two men agreed that they had heard the Nazarene say he would destroy the Temple and raise it again in three days. That was enough to validate a charge of blasphemy."

"Thanks be to HaShem, who will allow us to finally remove this troublemaker from the populace." I crossed my arms. "So the Sanhedrin will settle the matter today?"

"This hearing is only a formality," Nissim said. "The high priest has already heard the evidence of blasphemy."

When one of the clerks sounded a gong, we moved into the building and sought our seats. The chamber smelled of burning oil, and light from the flickering torches cast a golden glow over the chamber. I sat and looked around. Even on short notice, the high priest had managed to fill every seat, so no one could complain that the Sanhedrin had met with less than a full complement of members. Others might protest the council meeting and the transaction of business on the Feast of Unleavened Bread, but surely this matter transcended such details.

I looked across the room and nodded to several familiar faces. Though I had been a member of this court for more than a year, I still did not know many of the members. I counted most of the Pharisees as friends, having met them at meetings of my chaburah, but the Sadducees did not mix with us unless compelled to do so. They operated in the realm of wealth and politics, a world I had not entered . . . yet.

We rose when Caiaphas entered and took his seat. A pair of scribes sat at the tables on the lower floor, their writing implements spread before them, and two Temple guards opened the double doors at the back of the hall. I leaned forward as additional guards led a shackled man into the room.

I had glimpsed Yeshua of Nazareth from a distance and thought him an ordinary-looking fellow, but the beaten and bruised creature before me bore little resemblance to the man in my memory. While I did not know where he had been before entering this chamber, his face bore the marks of a determined fist, and one eye had swollen shut. He wore a blood-spattered tunic and mantle, the clothing of a poor man, and nothing about him indicated messianic ambition.

Still, clothing did not always reveal the true measure of a man.

"Brothers," Caiaphas began, his voice brimming with depth and authority, "you see before you Yeshua of Nazareth, who has been accused of blasphemy. Last night he stood before a council of scribes and Torah teachers, who heard witnesses testify to his blasphemous words. Today you will hear from those same witnesses, that we may judge him."

I frowned. Though I would never support this man's claim to messiahship, the Sanhedrin should not allow Caiaphas, who last night acted as accuser, to act as judge today. The Scriptures clearly stated that the accuser and the accused should stand before the priests and judges.

Joseph of Arimathea, a highly esteemed Pharisee, must have been thinking the same thoughts. "Honored Caiaphas," he said, standing, "who accuses this man of blasphemy?"

Caiaphas lifted his chin. "We have two witnesses, and you shall hear them presently."

"Yet it is my understanding that these witnesses were not found until you had already formulated the charge of blasphemy. So are you not the accuser?"

I smiled, admiring the older man's logic.

Caiaphas did not share my admiration. "I may have been the accuser last night," he said, his mouth taking on an unpleasant twist, "but today the witnesses shall fulfill that role."

I lifted a brow, wondering if anyone would question the high priest's answer. The Nazarene seemed indifferent to the discussion.

The double doors opened again, and several men entered. They stood in a silent knot at the back of the room until Caiaphas summoned the first man. "Jared ben Natan." He lifted his head. "Come and give us your testimony."

I leaned forward, keenly aware of an important oversight. Tradition and the rules of the Sanhedrin demanded that witnesses be reminded of the heavy responsibility the court had placed upon them before uttering a word, yet Caiaphas had neglected to administer the proper oath and charge the witnesses with telling the truth. Was this a mistake, or had he a reasonable explanation?

Without looking at the accused, Jared moved to the center of the chamber. "Three years ago, I was in Jerusalem at the Passover feast," he said, his gaze shifting from left to right. "I heard this man say, 'I am able to destroy the Temple of God and rebuild it in three days.'"

I looked at Yeshua, who did not respond.

Caiaphas pointed at the prisoner. "Have you no answer? What's this they're testifying against you?"

Yeshua remained silent, his bruised face as expressionless as a mask.

Caiaphas gestured to the second witness. "Come forward and tell us what you heard."

The man obeyed. "I am Yair of Capernaum," he said. "And

I heard this man say, 'I will destroy this Temple made with hands; and in three days I will build another one, not made with hands.'"

The witnesses' testimonies did not agree. I looked around to see if anyone would object to the irregular proceedings, but Caiaphas broke the silence with a roar: "I charge you under oath by the living God, tell us if you are Mashiach Ben-Elohim!"

The Nazarene's left eyebrow rose slightly. "I am," he replied. "Besides that, I tell you, soon after you will see the Son of Man sitting at the right hand of power and coming on the clouds of heaven."

Caiaphas clutched the neckline of his tunic and tore it. "Blasphemy! Why do we need any more witnesses? Are you not going to answer?"

I stared, astounded by the actions and fury of our high priest, who was considered to be infallible among us. The man sitting to my right, a wealthy scholar named Nicodemus, must have been similarly shocked, because he made a noise that sounded as if he were strangling on suppressed words.

A murmur spread through the group, cries of support for Caiaphas, cries of indignation from a smaller contingent. Nicodemus turned to me, his eyes wide. "I heard he said the same last night, and he tore that garment too, though the high priest is never to rend his garments, not even in grief. Furthermore—"

Nicodemus stood, a bulwark in a sea of dissent, and did not speak until the noise died down. "Honored Caiaphas," he said, his face flushed, "though we value your opinion, you cannot deprive us of our right to vote on this man's fate. Each of us must be given the opportunity to say 'I absolve' or 'I condemn.' Furthermore, the Law demands that we dismiss and assemble by twos to discuss the matter, then reconvene on the morrow."

"Thank you, Nicodemus," Caiaphas said, barely turning to acknowledge the man. "But what need have we of further witnesses or debate when this man's blasphemy is obvious? Tonight begins the Passover, when no business should be conducted. So let him be judged guilty, and let him be taken to Pilate."

Several members shouted their agreement while Caiaphas gestured to the guards, who stepped forward and dragged Yeshua of Nazareth from the chamber.

Mixed feelings assailed me as I watched. I agreed with the verdict and believed Yeshua a dangerous man, but Caiaphas's disregard for the Law troubled me. As the other judges left their seats, I glanced at Nicodemus, who remained seated, as did I.

"Were you at the council meeting last night?" I asked.

The older man shook his head. "I refused to go. The Law says, 'Let a capital offense be tried during the day, but suspend it at night.' I could not attend an illegal meeting, but I received a trustworthy report early this morning. Not only did they call a stream of false witnesses, but they neglected to administer an oath to those about to testify. And they were harsh with Yeshua, completely ignoring the Law's admonishment to speak gently with an accused man, urging him to confess his sin, if guilt can be proven."

He turned, his nostrils flaring. "But the worst was what happened afterward. After Caiaphas pronounced him guilty, those present spit on the accused and beat him. They blindfolded and mocked him, saying 'Prophesy! Who hit you that time?'"

I stared, speechless. I could not imagine the esteemed council members resorting to such immature behavior, but how could I judge? I had not been present and had no idea what the accused might have said or done to reduce them to such churlish conduct.

A sudden thought struck: "Was Gamaliel present at the meeting? Was he among those who—?"

"Yes," Nicodemus said, his voice flat. "He was at the meeting, but no, he did not participate in the cruelty. He departed, as did others, once Yeshua was handed over to the Temple guards, who continued to berate and mistreat him." He shook his head. "Not since the Philistines beat and abused Samson has a prisoner been treated in such a manner."

Nicodemus's words haunted me as I left the chamber, yet I took comfort in knowing that my teacher had shown admirable restraint and wisely removed himself from the situation when he could.

One thing was clear: Gamaliel had been part of an action to remove a dangerous false prophet from Israel. That act might well prove to be his legacy.

TWENTY-TWO

Aya

Despite the advent of Passover, the news filled Jerusalem: Yeshua of Nazareth, found guilty of blasphemy, had been taken to Pilate, who put him to death . . . not because he claimed to be God, but because he claimed to be a king.

I was busy with Passover preparations that day, yet I felt a chill streaming from the rocky knoll outside the city. The Romans crucified most of their prisoners at the hill known as Golgotha, the place where Adam's skull had reportedly been buried. The infamous spot was easily visible from the road leading into Jerusalem, and I had seen enough crucifixions to know I did not want to see another one.

Avidan and one of our guests had gone to the Temple to choose a lamb for our feast. The Passover lamb was always purchased for a group so it could be entirely consumed without waste.

Once a man had selected his lamb, the priests would divide the people into three large groups. At midday, the shofar would

174

blow, the first group would be admitted into the Temple court, and the gates would close. The men would slaughter the lambs while the priests, who stood in long rows, would catch the blood in silver bowls and pass the bowls down the line until they reached the altar of sacrifice. The priest stationed there would sprinkle the blood on the base of the altar. During the ritual, the Levites would chant the Hallel . . .

The freshly slaughtered lambs were hung on hooks, skinned, and the entrails removed. The portion intended for the altar was then cut out, put in a vessel, and burned on the altar. When the process had been completed, each man would take his lamb home to be roasted.

At midday, as the shofar blew, the sun weakened and daylight disappeared, leaving Jerusalem as dark as pitch. Startled by the abrupt darkness, I knocked a clay cup from my table and sent it crashing to the floor. I lit a lamp and knelt to pick up the pieces, but Hannah, one of our Passover guests, caught my hand. "What is happening?" she asked, a quaver in her voice. "I cannot recall a Passover like this one."

"The darkness will not last," I said, trying to remain calm despite the creeping uneasiness that pebbled my skin. "These things happen when a storm is approaching."

"Perhaps it is an omen." She wrapped her arms around her young son. "I wish my husband were here. It is not right that he should leave his wife and child alone at a time like this."

"You are not alone." I squeezed her hand. "I am with you, and I am not afraid. My husband is a scholar, and he will explain all that happened today. I am sure we will find that we had nothing to fear."

With difficulty, for my belly had grown to the point where I could no longer see my feet, I pulled myself up from the floor.

"Perhaps this darkness has something to do with Yeshua of Nazareth," Hannah said, standing with me. "Some say he is our Messiah."

I scoffed. "How could HaShem allow the Anointed One to hang on a cross? He who hangs on a tree is cursed, everyone knows that. No, Yeshua was misguided and dangerous. And now he will no longer divide our people."

Avidan, and Hannah's husband, returned with our lamb, since they had been in the first group. While I hung the meat over the cook fire, careful not to break a bone, Hannah set the table with clay plates, goblets, and bowls for the bitter herbs and dipping sauce.

During the long afternoon, the shofar sounded twice more, signaling the sacrifices of two additional groups. The darkness remained.

I looked at Avidan. "Why is the sky still dark?"

He shook his head. "I do not know. I saw Gamaliel in the Temple court and asked what he made of it, but he simply walked away."

At the ninth hour, the shofar blew a final time, signaling an end to the sacrifices. I gave Avidan a fleeting smile, but my expression froze as the earth trembled beneath my feet. Hannah's little boy screamed, and she went pale as she held her son close.

When the earth stopped shuddering, we drew deep breaths of relief. Avidan stepped outside to check for damage, and through the open door I caught a glimpse of bright sunlight.

"It is over," I whispered. "It is done."

Hannah stood with her son, and together we surveyed the table. No dishes had broken, nor had the lamb fallen off the spit.

Avidan came back inside, his expression calm and reassuring. "All is well," he announced. "None of the houses on this street were damaged. I hope the rest of the city fared as well."

"And the Temple," Hannah added.

"The Temple was built to last a thousand years," her husband said. "Do not worry about it."

"Come." I extended my arms to my guests. "Let us forget

about these odd occurrences and celebrate our liberation from slavery. We have yet to bake the unleavened bread."

I pasted on a smile and reached for my millstone, determined to dispel the lingering melancholy with festivity. "Tonight," I told my guests, "we will commemorate the blood that was shed for our freedom." I smiled at Hannah's son, hoping I would soon hold a son of my own. "That is why this night is different from all others."

On the first day of the week, all Jerusalem celebrated the Feast of Firstfruits. We rose early on the special Sabbath and went to the Temple, where the priests offered the first of Israel's new grain to the Lord. The special burnt offering consisted of two young bulls, one ram, and seven yearling male lambs, all without blemish. Those offerings were accompanied by grain offerings of choice flour moistened with olive oil.

Extraordinary news reached us as we broke our fast with a challah loaf. Hannah's husband strode into the house, his face flushed. "Yeshua of Nazareth lives! He has been seen by several women and some of his disciples."

Sha'ul scoffed. "Of course his followers would make such a claim," he said, dipping his challah into a bowl of honey. "And of course his tomb is empty. His disciples have stolen the body and hidden it. Or they have chopped it into pieces and buried it in diverse places."

I shuddered at the revolting thought, but the men at our table did not flinch.

"The tomb was sealed by the Romans and watched by Temple guards," another guest remarked, his face troubled. "I cannot believe they would shirk their duty."

"Have you ever tried to stand guard all night?" Avidan grinned. "I used to guard my father's wine exports, and let me assure you, the task is not easy. First your legs tire, then your back begins to ache. So you sit, but after a while your eyelids grow heavy. So you sing, or tell yourself a story, anything to remain awake. Then you get up and walk again—"

"Eat," Sha'ul interrupted, passing a bowl of roasted chicken down the table. "By tomorrow Yeshua of Nazareth will be only a memory. Eat, my friends. Next year we will celebrate Pesach without a moment's thought for the Nazarene."

TWENTY-THREE

Aya

The women at the Pool of Siloam kept eyeing my belly and telling me not to be anxious, but as my time drew closer, my fear overshadowed my courage. Every day I studied the growing mound beneath my tunic and remembered how a similar mound had killed Bettina. Sometimes I woke in the dead of night and shivered with terror, unable to warm myself even when Avidan held me close.

And, truth be told, my husband was often too distracted to comfort me. He was as focused on his studies as my brother had been, and sometimes I wondered if Avidan longed to *become* Sha'ul. He was not as naturally gifted, but he was nothing if not determined. Avidan's stubborn streak was wide and deep, and he would not give up his dream. So every night I continued to read long portions of his assigned texts, and every week Sha'ul tested Avidan's knowledge of the Law.

After more than a year of study, Gamaliel told Avidan he was nearly ready for the test that would allow him to move from the intellectual mastery and interpretation of the sacred revelations of the past to study of the discourses and illustrations that helped a scholar interpret the Law and its application to daily life.

Many nights I lay awake, burdened by my concern for Avidan. What would become of us if he failed his exam? If he could not pass, he would have to return to Tarsus and surrender his dream. An ordinary man who failed the examination would be disappointed but would recover and find another way to make a living.

But Avidan was not an ordinary man. He was brother-in-law to Sha'ul, a leading Pharisee and a member of the Great Sanhedrin. If Avidan failed the examination, both he and Sha'ul would be shamed, and I would not know how to encourage them. In addition, I would not know what role HaShem intended *me* in the future—was I to be the wife of a scholar or the wife of a wine merchant's son?

One morning I bade Avidan farewell and went about my usual work. When Sha'ul stopped by, I asked if he had heard anything about Gamaliel's plans. Sha'ul only shrugged. "Avidan knows what he knows," he said, searching for something to eat. "And you can rest for now. Gamaliel is in no hurry to test him."

I gave Sha'ul a chunk of cheese and pointed to the bread under a linen cloth. I was about to break the loaf when at that moment a searing pain shot through my back. Terrified, I braced myself against the table and felt a stream of water run down my leg.

"Sha'ul—" my voice came out as a squeak—"please fetch Eden. The baby is coming."

I did not have to ask again. Panicked by his memories, Sha'ul ran to fetch my neighbor. Within a few hours, if Adonai willed, I would either be a mother or a corpse.

Eden, who was also with child, came over and helped me spread a clean blanket on the bed. "You can walk or lie down while you wait," she said, smiling as though childbirth were of no consequence. "Walking will cut the pain, but you will

tire more easily. Are you comfortable now? If so, I will find the
midwife and tell her to come. I will come back to stay with you
until she arrives."

I do not need to record a lengthy description of my daylong
labor, but I would have had an easier time if I had not been
traumatized by Bettina's experience. Every time I felt a sharp
pain, I imagined the agony to be a fatal wound. Every time the
pain eased, I thanked HaShem for His mercy and begged the
child to come forth. Though my cowardice seemed silly in retro-
spect, the pain of childbirth turned me into a spineless creature.

Avidan was not much better. He and Sha'ul waited in the
courtyard, continually calling to the midwife for reports. Eden
finally sent them away, urging them to find some useful activity
that would fill the hours. Avidan told me they went to Sha'ul's
house, where they debated the meaning of *messiah* until they
fell asleep.

When morning dawned and the midwife placed a healthy
son in my arms, my chief emotion was astonishment that we
had survived.

I never knew if Avidan or Sha'ul harbored similar fears.
When they appeared again, searching for food, they congratulated me on a healthy baby and proceeded to break their fast.

Avidan asked what we should name our boy, and I suggested
Seraiah, which meant *the Lord's prince.*

"Why that name?"

"Because the Lord's prince is what I want him to be."

I looked into Avidan's eyes and saw that he understood. The
baby's father was a scholar. His uncle was a scholar. And one
day, if HaShem willed, this little one would be, too.

"Seraiah," Avidan whispered. "That is what he will be called."

———— • ————

During the next month, I experienced a joy deeper than any I
had ever known. My baby brought more fulfillment than being a

wife, even more than being a musician. I would have fought anyone or anything in order to protect the child HaShem sent me.

My mother's voice came to me on a wave of memory: *"One day you will have children, and you will do anything in your power to keep them from harm or shame. You will forbid them to travel alone. You will shield them from people who could sully their reputations. You will choose their teachers and companions, forbidding them to associate with anyone who might poison their minds or lead them from the worship of HaShem."*

Again I marveled at my mother's wisdom. She knew this sort of love. How silly I had been to question her.

I adored caring for Seraiah—bathing his tiny hands and feet, nursing him, washing his dark hair. His first smile brought tears to my eyes, and the sound of his crying immediately woke me from sleep. The fear and pain of childbirth faded because Seraiah brought us so much.

Avidan loved the baby but could not allow himself to appear as besotted as I was. His love was quiet but strong. He frequently took breaks from studying to help me with the baby, and yet he could not ignore the examination that loomed ahead of him.

Sha'ul visited more frequently than before. He would say he had come to help Avidan prepare for his exam, but I think he was secretly fascinated by Seraiah. I often caught him watching our baby with a forlorn expression. Did he wonder what life would be like if HaShem had not taken his wife and child? Did he resent our happiness?

On the eighth day after Seraiah's birth, we circumcised our son according to the Law. Sha'ul was present, along with Gamaliel and many of our neighbors. They rejoiced with us and shared our wine, then I carried my little boy into a corner and nursed him, hoping he would forget the pain of the knife. "Sometimes," I whispered as he suckled, "HaShem asks us to endure a bit of pain in order to be obedient. But His ways are always best."

I must admit—during the months of pregnancy and early motherhood, I scarcely thought about my music. The desires of my heart shifted, and though my mother was far away, I knew she would approve. She had never understood my love for music, and I had never understood the happiness I could experience as a wife and mother.

Everything was different now.

"If only your *safta* were here," I told Seraiah. "She would cover your little face with kisses."

I wrote my parents and Avidan's, telling them they had a fine grandson. My parents were not the best correspondents, and Avidan's even less so, but I knew this news would delight them. I was not surprised when Ima wrote back, telling me that they were happy to bless the child in their nightly prayers.

Abba would appear at our threshold, but the journey would be too arduous for them. They had not come for Passover that year, and Ima wrote that Abba was not feeling well. My father had always been so strong, I could not imagine him sick, so I put the distressing image out of my mind and prayed for his good health.

One day, after Sha'ul dropped by and hinted that his belly was empty, I prepared a meal. Because Avidan and the baby were out, I sat next to my brother as he ate. When he looked over, a question in his eyes, I rested my hand on his arm. "I wish you had a son, too. I am sorry HaShem's will is hard for you to bear."

He lowered his gaze. "Should we accept the good from HaShem and not accept the bad? If I look at your son with longing, it is only because I wish I could spend more time with him. My son is with HaShem. One day I will teach him the many things I have learned. I would love to teach your son as well, but Seraiah has a father . . . and I have other responsibilities."

I withdrew my hand. "I am sorry if I misread your expression, but know this—you are always welcome in our home. Seraiah will be doubly blessed, because he will have a father and an uncle to teach him through words and example."

Sha'ul nodded, but the shadow of grief did not leave his eyes.

Though I missed Bettina and ached for my brother's loss, I had to admit her passing had caused Sha'ul to grow closer to me and Avidan. Now that he had completed his studies, he seemed to have more time on his hands, time he spent with us. He would stop by the house on impulse, sometimes to talk with Avidan, sometimes to eat, sometimes to read. I suspected that his empty house haunted him, so I was happy to welcome him to ours.

My feelings for Sha'ul shifted from resentment to affection. He was still a brilliant scholar, but I had become a *mother*, a role he would never be able to fill. When he came to the house, hungry or in need of someone to mend his tunic, I would *tsk* over his helplessness and do whatever needed to be done. In turn, he was kind and helpful to my husband, and seemed honestly impressed that I had done more than read to Avidan. I had absorbed what I read and could participate in their debates as energetically as a yeshiva student.

But I didn't live for the joy of debating. I lived for my husband, my son, and HaShem. God had given me a role to fulfill, and though I was slow to find joy in it, I would not have surrendered it for all the wealth in the world.

"So"—I brightened my voice, determined to brighten Sha'ul's mood—"tell me of life beyond these walls. I have not stepped outside since Seraiah's birth, and the time of my purification cannot come soon enough."

One of Sha'ul's brows rose. "Consider yourself fortunate, because the city has gone mad."

"Has Rome issued some sort of—?"

"The trouble lies not with Rome but with the followers of

Yeshua of Nazareth. Surely you heard the rumor that he escaped his tomb."

I nodded. "It is all Eden talks about. But surely by now they have found his body and exposed the truth."

"They have not. In fact, many have testified of seeing him alive in Jerusalem and Galilee, even to a crowd of more than five hundred. I have seen his followers in the Temple—they are easy to spot because they walk around with wide eyes, as if expecting Yeshua to appear at any moment." He shook his head. "The high priest does not know what to do. He and the elders had hoped to squash the Nazarene's claims to messiahship, but the fever that infects his followers is spreading."

I frowned. "Surely this fever will dim. How long has it been since his execution—a month?"

"His followers claim he rose at Firstfruits—they say HaShem viewed him as *the* first fruit, the first of many who will rise to eternal life. Such an idea is ludicrous, but his followers overflow with ridiculous notions. Some say he ascended into heaven a few days ago."

"From the Temple?" I guessed.

"From the Mount of Olives."

I laughed. "Why that place?"

Just then Avidan came into the house, his face shining above our son's dark head. "Seraiah is asleep," he said, glancing at the baby against his chest. "Let us hope he sleeps for more than an hour before demanding to be fed again."

Avidan's gaze shifted to Sha'ul. "Have I interrupted something?"

Sha'ul shook his head. "I was telling Aya about the latest rumor—Yeshua ascending to heaven."

"I don't understand what's so special about the Mount of Olives," I said. "There's nothing significant about an olive grove."

"Zechariah wrote about it," Avidan said. "'On that day his feet will stand on the Mount of Olives, east of Jerusalem. And the Mount of Olives will split apart, making a wide valley running from east to west. Half the mountain will move toward the north and half toward the south.'" He grinned. "I believe I may be ready for my examination."

"I would not quote that verse in reference to Yeshua." Sha'ul glanced at me. "I don't know why Yeshua was fascinated with the place."

Still holding the baby, Avidan sat at the table. "I heard Yeshua's followers are expecting him to reappear at the Festival of Weeks. Many who left Jerusalem after Pesach are returning for the festival. Never have I heard so much talk about what is usually a quiet feast."

"Shavuot?" I straightened. "Shavuot is forty days after Seraiah's birth, the day of my purification. I cannot postpone—please, Avidan, tell me we can still go to the Temple that day."

Avidan stood as the baby began to squirm. "We will go early, if we must, though I do not see why it would hurt to wait—"

"Forty days of confinement is long enough," I said, trying to explain my frustration to someone who was not rendered impure after childbirth. "I am glad I did not give birth to a girl. I do not think I could stand eighty days of confinement."

"I would not fret overmuch," Sha'ul said, watching Avidan place Seraiah in his cradle. "On Shavuot, let the Nazarene's followers wait for a miracle—they will not be a problem because they are not likely to get one."

Forty days after the birth of our son, Avidan woke me early, led the morning prayers, and together we prepared Seraiah for his first visit to the Temple. We wrapped him in swaddling cloth and dressed in our best, then we hurried out, knowing we needed to arrive by the time the priests lit the incense on the golden altar.

We heard the first three blasts of the Levites' trumpets as we left the house. That meant the gates of the Temple had been thrown open, so we walked quickly, eager to find our place before the throngs of Shavuot pilgrims arrived. As we entered the Court of the Gentiles, we could hear the Levites singing the psalm of the day, which meant the drink offering was being poured out. At the end of the psalm, the trumpets blew another three blasts, and we joined the worshipers.

With the baby in my arms, I left Avidan and went to stand at the Gate of Nicanor with several other new mothers. Behind me, in the Court of the Women, Avidan waited with—I hoped—Sha'ul. I climbed to the top of the Levites' steps, where I could see everything taking place in the sanctuary.

Shavuot marked the fiftieth day after Passover and was known as *Pentecost* to those who spoke Greek. The festival, which celebrated the end of the barley and the beginning of the wheat harvest, was generally a happy time, and I had been delighted to realize that my purification sacrifice would coincide with it.

I watched as a priest took two loaves, each baked with flour and leaven, and waved them before the Lord. Since freewill offerings were encouraged, worshipers also brought loaves, and joyfully offered them to the Lord.

While the worshipers piled their loaves around the base of the altar, one of the officiating priests came to the Gate of Nicanor and asked for my purification offering—a pair of turtledoves, all Avidan and I could afford. After taking my doves, the priest turned and killed them, then returned to me with a small bowl of blood in his hand. He dipped his fingertips into the bowl and sprinkled me, an act designed to remind me of how HaShem spared the firstborn of Israel when the angel of death swept over Egypt and took the firstborns of those who had enslaved us.

I joined in the prayers of thanksgiving and gave the priest the price of my son's redemption: five shekels of silver. The priest pronounced two benedictions: one for the happy event that had enriched our family, the other for the law of redemption HaShem had given to Israel. With the ceremony completed, I made my way down the steps, eager to join Sha'ul and Avidan.

Avidan planted a kiss on my forehead and then kissed Seraiah, but Sha'ul seemed distracted. He kept looking past me, and I couldn't believe he would allow himself to be distracted on this significant day.

"Are you not happy your nephew has been redeemed?" I asked, turning the baby toward him. "You should bless him, Sha'ul."

Sha'ul shaded his eyes and looked toward the city beyond the walls. "Do you not hear it? Something is happening outside." His brows lowered. "We cannot afford unrest, not now. The Romans have been warned to watch for trouble and will not tolerate a disturbance."

To my dismay, Avidan turned toward the street as well. "What do you hear?"

"Listen."

All three of us stared past the outer courtyard, our ears tuned for commotion, but I did not hear shouting. Instead, I heard the ordinary sound of men in the street, but louder than usual, as if every living soul in Jerusalem had decided to speak at once.

Sha'ul strode forward, and Avidan followed without hesitation.

I lingered only a moment, then hurried after them. We crossed the Court of the Gentiles and stood on the steps of the portico, watching as the crowd shifted as if a giant paddle was stirring an unruly broth.

Sha'ul grabbed the fringed robe of a Pharisee. "Shalom, brother," he said, a frown crinkling his brows. "What is this commotion? Today is a special Sabbath, yet there is such noise in the street . . ."

"Have you not heard?" The man laughed. "The followers

of the Nazarene are drunk. Though the hour is yet early, they
have spread throughout the city, boldly speaking gibberish."

"Drunk?" Avidan gaped at the man. "Impossible. I have
heard many things about Yeshua's followers, but they are not
drunkards."

"They are today," the Pharisee replied. "I know one of them,
a man from Capernaum. He usually speaks with a thick Galilean accent, but this morning he was babbling as though he
had taken leave of his senses. The men with him were doing
the same thing."

Sha'ul strode deeper into the crowd, and Avidan followed. I
barely managed to catch the edge of my husband's sleeve, but
I clung to it, afraid the baby and I would be lost in the tumult.

The crowd was flowing now, moving northeast. I struggled
to hold the baby and stay on my feet as we walked past the
repository of the archives and the Chamber of Hewn Stone. At
one point we climbed a hill, and I was able to see the Xystus,
the open structure used as a public meeting place. A man stood
at the center, his hand uplifted.

The crowd surged toward him.

I lost sight of him when the road dipped again, and we continued to move, bobbing like corks in a current. Another man
stood on an elevated block, speaking to anyone who would
listen. "We are utterly and completely amazed," he said, his
eyes wide. "Were not all of Yeshua's followers Galileans? So
how is it that each of us hears them in his native language? I
stayed in a house with Medes, Elamites, and Egyptians. When
the followers of Yeshua walked by the place, we all heard their
message in our own tongue!"

"Impossible," Sha'ul muttered under his breath, shouldering
his way forward. "That man has been drinking, as well. Either
that or someone has knocked him on the head."

We walked on, then stopped, unable to move because the
crowd had consolidated around the covered colonnade of the

Xystus. Though several men stood in the open space, a tall fellow with curly hair occupied the dais. "My fellow Judeans and all who are staying in Jerusalem," he called, his face alight, "let this be known to you, and pay attention to my words. These men are not drunk, as you suppose, for it's only the third hour of the day! But this is what was spoken about through the prophet Joel:

> 'And it shall be in the last days,' says God,
> 'that I will pour out My Ruach on all flesh.
> Your sons and your daughters shall prophesy,
> your young men shall see visions,
> and your old men shall dream dreams.'"

I glanced at the people behind the bold speaker. Many had the rugged look of Galileans, but a few were well-dressed, and several women stood with them. They represented all walks of life, but without exception, their faces radiated joy. They reminded me of Moses, whose face shone after his encounter with HaShem on Mount Sinai.

"Men of Israel," the tall man continued, "hear these words! Yeshua ha-Natzrati—a Man authenticated to you by God with mighty deeds and wonders and signs HaShem performed through Him in your midst, as you yourselves know—this Yeshua, given over by HaShem's predetermined plan and foreknowledge, nailed to the cross by the hand of lawless men, you killed. But HaShem raised Him up, releasing Him from the pains of death, since it was impossible for Him to be held by it."

I did not understand the man's message, but I believed his joy. Without a trace of self-doubt or fear, he stood before the crowd—which must have numbered in the thousands, considering all the festival pilgrims—and proclaimed that Yeshua was not only a prophet but HaShem himself. With breathtaking audacity, he spoke clearly, simply, and convincingly, quoting

Scriptures and tying them together with knowledge and assurance.

I turned to Sha'ul. "Do you know this man?"

His nostrils flared. "I know *of* him. He is Simon Peter, an uneducated fisherman from Galilee."

"He speaks well," I whispered. "He speaks with authority."

A rumbling sound came from Sha'ul's throat.

"Brothers," Simon Peter continued, "I can confidently tell you that the patriarch David died and was buried—his tomb is with us to this day. So because he was a prophet and knew HaShem had sworn with an oath to seat one of his descendants on his throne, David saw beforehand and spoke of Messiah's resurrection—that He was not abandoned to Sheol, and His body did not see decay.

"This Yeshua HaShem raised up—we all are witnesses! Therefore, being exalted to the right hand of God and receiving from the Father the promise of the Ruach HaKodesh, He poured out what you now see and hear. For David did not ascend into the heavens; yet he himself says,

> 'Adonai said to my Lord,
>   "Sit at my right hand,
> until I make Your enemies a footstool
>   for Your feet."'

"Therefore, let the whole house of Israel know for certain that HaShem has made Him—this Yeshua whom you had crucified—both Lord and Messiah!"

Sha'ul clenched his fist. "How can we stand here when this man speaks blasphemy?"

Avidan glanced around, and for an instant I was afraid he would repeat Sha'ul's charge. If he had spoken, or if Sha'ul had lifted his voice, we would have been in trouble, because even I could read the attitude of the crowd. They were not of my brother's mindset; they had understood and accepted the Galilean's words. They *believed*.

"Brothers!" a man called from the colonnade, "what shall we do, then?"

Simon Peter looked at those who stood with him. "Repent and let each of you be immersed in the name of Messiah Yeshua for the removal of your sins, and you will receive the gift of the Ruach HaKodesh. The promise is for you and your children, and for all who are far away—as many as Adonai our God calls to himself."

"Blasphemy!" Sha'ul cried, but I hissed in his ear.

"Have you forgotten that I am carrying a baby?" I caught Avidan's eye. "Husband, help me get him home. We do not want to cause a riot today."

My words activated Avidan, and for once he sided with me instead of Sha'ul. Together we dragged my brother away from the gathering.

"Yes, he speaks blasphemy," Avidan whispered in Sha'ul's ear. "But this is not the place or the time to confront him. Later, brother, we will act, when we are better prepared."

TWENTY-FOUR

Aya

I was never so happy to return home. I nursed the baby and put him to bed, then set out the simple meal I had prepared for our festival dinner. Avidan was content to sit and eat, for he had not been as upset by the Galilean as Sha'ul.

My brother sat at the table with his hands folded, his head lowered, and his eyes closed. Not even the barley cakes, stuffed grapevine leaves, and lamb stew could snap him out of his dark mood.

Sighing, I wondered if HaShem had been merciful to take Bettina and her son from my brother's home. I knew Sha'ul. Once he determined to achieve a goal, he cared for little else, and apparently he had set his mind against Simon Peter.

When Sha'ul left a short while later, he stalked away like a man on a mission. I watched him go, fearing he would set himself on an irreversible course. I had waited years for an opportunity to establish a relationship with my brother. We were closer than we had ever been, but if he went to Galilee in order to pursue this fisherman, would I lose him?

Avidan helped me understand Sha'ul's obsession. "He is

looking for something new," he told me when I went back into the house. "He wanted to become a scholar; he became one of the best. He wanted to sit on the Sanhedrin; he is the youngest to attain that honor. Now he needs to apply his authority and knowledge to a new cause."

"I hate to see him so upset." I reached for the platter of uneaten barley cakes. "He has no appetite when he is unhappy."

Avidan grunted. "He would be happy to rid Jerusalem of Yeshua's followers."

"He will have a time of it. The people we saw today were bold and unafraid."

"Yet people can sincerely believe a lie," Avidan said. "Look at the Romans, who worship gods of iron and stone with complete devotion. Their belief cannot empower false gods, but can a false god give men the power to speak languages they have never heard?"

I lifted a brow, surprised by his comment. "Would you defend these people?"

He shrugged. "I have no wish to defend them, but as you said, they did not appear drunk, foolish, or deluded. I cannot believe the Nazarene was the son of HaShem, but neither can I say he had no power. He healed people. And apparently his spirit has given them the ability to speak in languages they never learned."

I did not know how to respond, so I shook my head and nibbled at the meal Sha'ul would not touch.

Over the next few months I focused on my child, my husband, and our home. Seraiah was a delight, and I marveled at each new smile, his ability to turn over, and the way he clung to my finger. Avidan often came home early to play with the baby. We would lie on the bed with Seraiah between us, amazed that HaShem had blessed us with such an amazing child.

Avidan passed his long-awaited exams and continued his studies under Gamaliel but with a cohort of older students.

At this level his studies focused on the application of the Law to daily life—the *halakhah*. I found some of the material fascinating. Some I found infuriating. For instance, at the death of his wife, every Jewish husband was required to provide two flautists and one professional mourning woman for her funeral. Who had chosen those numbers? And why would it matter if a man could only afford one mourner and one flautist?

After dinner and evening prayers, we would study—I would read and Avidan would memorize the key points. When we had absorbed all the information we could hold, we would lie together in the dark while Avidan shared the latest news from the yeshiva.

One night he told me that believers of Yeshua were calling themselves "followers of the Way." "Yeshua said he was the way, the truth, and the life, and no one could approach HaShem unless through him."

"So none of the elders and scholars can approach HaShem? Is the high priest not approaching HaShem when he approaches the altar? That is a presumptuous notion."

Avidan pushed a wayward strand of hair from my face. "So you can see why the authorities are eager to eradicate this movement."

"Are there so many of them?"

"Their numbers are increasing. Remember when we heard Simon Peter on Pentecost? More than three thousand believed that day. Later, Simon Peter and another talmid called John healed a man who had been lame from birth. When people recognized him as the cripple who used to sit at the Beautiful Gate—"

"Wait." I lifted my head. "The bald man with the bony legs?"

"Exactly."

"I know him. He sits by the gate every day, begging for shekels."

"He sits there no longer, because now he walks as well as I do.

I cannot explain how two fishermen healed him, but when the astonished onlookers gathered around, Peter and John spoke to them."

"And?"

"He repeated many of the things we heard on Pentecost—that we killed HaShem's messiah, but HaShem raised him from the dead. And if we turn from our wicked ways, we will be blessed."

"Our wicked ways?" I sat up, energized by indignation. "*What* wicked ways? You and I live in the Holy City, we keep the Law, you study Torah every day. I am helping you raise a son of Abraham—"

Avidan patted my shoulder. "Do not wake the baby. And do not worry about Peter and John—the priests and the captain of the Temple guard put them in jail."

"Oh." Mollified, I sank back to my pillow. "I'm glad they put an end to it."

"Not soon enough, though." Avidan rolled onto his back and blew out the lamp. "Some of the listeners believed, and now more than five thousand people of Jerusalem call themselves followers of the Way."

I absorbed the news in silence. Five thousand seemed a large number, yet I had heard Sha'ul say the people of Jerusalem numbered six hundred thousand, and that number doubled during the pilgrimage festivals.

"This Peter and John, how long will they remain in jail?"

I could no longer see Avidan, but the soft sound of rustling fabric told me he was ready to sleep. "Who can say? The people love miracle workers."

I closed my eyes. "Let us hope they remain in jail long enough for the movement to die. Because until it does, I do not think we will see much of my brother."

TWENTY-FIVE

Sha'ul

The sages tell us that though the fallen angels are held in chains until Judgment Day, the souls of their offspring—the giants born to women and the disobedient angels of God—still roam the earth, inhabiting human bodies and seeking vengeance against the Most Holy One.

I cannot deny that followers of the Way have power—I have witnessed the results of their troubling mischief—but the source of that power cannot be HaShem. Since both light and darkness exist, and HaShem is light, the people who work miracles in Yeshua's name must do so through the powers of darkness.

I was happy to hear that Simon Peter and John had been arrested and imprisoned by the Temple guard. The next morning, I joined other religious authorities, elders, and teachers of the Law in the Chamber of Hewn Stone. Caiaphas, our high priest, and Annas, our former high priest, were present. Also in attendance, in the observers' seats, were the formerly crippled man and his parents.

While we waited for the accused prisoners to arrive, I stood to address the council. "We know these men are not from God,"

I said, looking at the semicircle of somber faces, "so we must convince them to admit they performed these healings through the power of evil."

"Others attempted to trap Yeshua with the same argument," Caiaphas said. "The Nazarene confounded his questioner by asking how he could cast out devils if he worked through the power of Beelzebub. He said a kingdom divided against itself could not stand."

I scoffed. "Honorable Caiaphas, let us say you have two students. Is it impossible for you to ask one to strike the other? Of course not. Yeshua's answer was not sound."

Caiaphas gestured toward the stately double doors. "Let us hear what these two have to say."

The doors opened, and a pair of Temple guards led the prisoners in. I recognized the tall man who had addressed the crowd on Shavuot. Simon Peter looked up at the assembly and smiled, an expression I found completely inappropriate and highly disrespectful. He was uneducated, a mere rustic, while the men before him had studied for years under the greatest teachers of Israel. And had he forgotten how these same men ruled against his master?

"Simon, called Peter, and John, son of Zebedee," Caiaphas began, "we have but one question for you. By what power or name did you heal the lame man who begs by the Beautiful Gate?"

One of the clerks motioned to the cripple, who stood and walked forward, exhibiting proof that he had been healed. In his legs I saw no weakness or deformity, nor did he limp. He did, however, embrace both Simon Peter and John before being reprimanded by a scribe.

Peter glanced at John, then stepped forward. "Rulers and elders of the people," he said, his voice reaching every corner of the room. "If we are on trial today for a *mitzvah* done for a sick man, as to how this fellow was healed, let it be known to all of you and to all the people of Israel that by the name of Yeshua *ha-Mashiach ha-Natzrati*—whom you had crucified, whom God raised from the dead—this one stands before you whole. This Yeshua is 'the stone—rejected by you, the builders—that has become the chief cornerstone.' There is salvation in no one else, for there is no other name under heaven given to mankind by which we must be saved."

I glanced around, expecting to hear shouts of derision from my fellow scholars. Though many wore disapproving expressions, others watched with interest.

"Look at them," the man in front of me whispered to the fellow at his right. "These are rough, ordinary Galileans, yet this Peter speaks as one with wisdom and great learning."

"They say Yeshua also spoke with authority," his companion answered. "Yet he never studied in Jerusalem; neither was his father a yeshiva student."

"Few scholars reside in Galilee," the first man answered. "None come from Nazareth."

While murmured conversations rippled through the chamber, Caiaphas commanded that the formerly lame man, his parents, and Yeshua's disciples be removed. The guards led them away, then the high priest stood and surveyed the judicial body.

"What shall we do with these men?" he asked. "For it is obvious to everyone that a remarkable miracle has occurred. We cannot deny it."

Objections rose from both sides of the room:

"But can we ascertain the source of this miracle?"

"Can we forget that Yeshua was convicted of blasphemy by this court?"

"Are you aware of the rumors of his resurrection? Dare we give these men liberty to spread these rumors further?"

"But the people support these men. How would we look if we punished those who have done good? Can we punish them for being a blessing?"

Caiaphas lifted his hand, calling for silence.

"I have heard you," he answered, closing his eyes. In that moment, I could see the stress of the past few months on his lined face. "We are trapped in a difficult situation. If we punish these men, the people will revolt. If we do nothing, their blasphemy will continue. So to prevent this movement from spreading further, let us warn this Peter and John not to speak again—to anyone—in the name of Yeshua."

A murmur of assent rumbled through the room as Caiaphas ordered the guards to bring the prisoners in.

While we waited, the Pharisee seated next to me turned. "Do you think this will stop them from speaking of Yeshua?"

I blew out a breath. "The fever that grips these men is far too hot. No, I believe there is only one way to stop this disease from spreading."

"And that is?"

"When a tumor invades the body, the surgeon cuts it out, no?"

The two disciples entered and stood before the high priest, who formally commanded them not to speak or teach in the name of Yeshua of Nazareth.

If Caiaphas thought they would nod and walk away, he was mistaken. When he had finished, Peter stepped forward and looked around the assembly. "Whether it is right in the sight of God to listen to you rather than to God, you decide. For we cannot stop speaking about what we have seen and heard."

The Pharisee turned, surprise in his eyes. "How did you know that would be their response?"

"Because," I answered, "their malignant desire to spread news of the imposter Yeshua is almost as strong as my godly desire to silence them."

After the arrest of Peter and John, those who called themselves "followers of the Way" did not stop preaching, teaching, and gathering. They were brazen enough to meet openly in Solomon's Colonnade, the eastern porch off the Court of the Gentiles. In this elegant structure, flanked by tall columns of the purest white marble, Yeshua's followers were sheltered from sun and rain while they listened to the teachings of the Nazarene. Others visiting the Temple could not help noticing their enthusiastic prayers, praises, and miraculous healings.

When those of us who remained faithful to Torah saw and heard these meetings, we gritted our teeth and prayed that HaShem would remove the blasphemers from our midst. My stomach tightened whenever I saw them gathering. I often walked by with clenched fists, ready to strike the first man who spoke Yeshua's name in my presence.

Then I realized that an impulsive response would never be effective—we needed a careful, well-crafted plan to remove the blasphemers.

One afternoon I loitered near Solomon's Colonnade—within hearing distance, but not so close I would be recognized. I watched as men and women brought their sick into the shelter, carrying them on stretchers and mats, in carts and wagons, desperately hoping Peter would notice or even that the disciple's shadow might fall on the sick one as he passed by.

How could any son of Abraham fall so low? How could a Jew believe that the shadow of an ignorant fisherman could wield the power of *Yahweh Sabaoth*?

Those who sought Yeshua's disciples also brought friends and family members who were tormented by evil spirits. I watched in amazement as Yeshua's disciples commanded the demons to come out of those they inhabited.

The disciples' power to command demons unsettled me at first, but later reinforced my conviction that Peter and John were exercising dark powers. I could not cast out a demon, nor could any of my fellow scholars, so surely our inability proved our lack of affiliation with the forces of evil.

After many attempts, I finally managed to convince the high priest and several influential Sadducees that Yeshua's followers were stealing the hearts of the people. Goaded to the point of action, Caiaphas had the Temple guard arrest the apostles—all twelve of them—and imprison them in the public jail.

The next morning, I was among the first to visit the Temple Mount. I had planned to take a front row seat in the Chamber of Hewn Stone, but to my astonishment, Yeshua's apostles—all twelve—were freely mingling in the outer courtyard, preaching and teaching about Yeshua's death and resurrection.

I left the Temple Mount and hurried to the high priest's palace. After persuading several stubborn servants to admit me, I was finally ushered to the triclinium, where I found the high priest and his father-in-law breaking their fast.

"How," I asked, pushing my way past another servant who tried to block my entrance, "can we be expected to safeguard the nation if our Temple guards are utterly incompetent?"

Caiaphas lowered his cup and stared as if I were mud beneath his shoe. "How," he mocked, his voice dry, "can you be so ill-mannered? The day has scarcely begun, but here you are, complaining already."

"They are at it again." I stood my ground and glared at each of them. "As I speak, Yeshua's disciples are teaching in the Court of the Gentiles."

Caiaphas smiled. "Father," he said, dipping bread into a bowl of honey, "I believe Sha'ul did not get enough sleep last night. He has confused a dream with reality."

"At sunrise I was waiting at the Beautiful Gate," I interrupted. "I counted several of Yeshua's disciples waiting with me. When the gates were opened, the disciples separated, each going to a separate area where they began to preach about Yeshua—"

"Who *are* you?" Annas, who did not know me well, narrowed his aging eyes and peered in my direction.

"I am Sha'ul, formerly of Tarsus," I said, exasperated. "A student of Gamaliel, a Pharisee and member of the Great Sanhedrin."

Annas shook his head. "Sha'ul of Tarsus"—he lifted his cup with a trembling hand—"allow your high priest and his father-in-law to eat in peace. We will convene the Sanhedrin at midday, and we will hear you then."

Infuriated, I strode out of the room.

When the Sanhedrin met at the third hour, I sat among the members, my arms crossed and my patience worn thin. Annas and Caiaphas entered and took their seats of honor, then Caiaphas summoned the Temple guards and asked that the prisoners be escorted into the chamber.

Ten minutes later, the guards returned, shame-faced and with the answer I expected: the prisoners were no longer in the jail.

Caiaphas searched the crowd until he spotted me, then pressed his lips into a thin line. "Search the outer courts," he said, his voice clipped. "Find them and bring them to us. Immediately."

The captain of the guard hesitated. "What if they will not come?"

"Use force if you must."

"But the people approve of Yeshua's disciples. What is to prevent them from picking up stones to attack us?"

Caiaphas flushed as he glared at the guard. "Whom do you serve, the high priest or the people? Do whatever you must, but bring those men at once!"

Awash in guilty pleasure, I watched the high priest squirm. This morning neither he nor Annas had believed my report, but the guard had taught them a lesson: they should not doubt me again.

After half an hour, the guards returned, escorting Yeshua's twelve disciples. Peter and John had appeared rough and rural, but their aspect multiplied by twelve made the men seem as unkempt as a flock of unshorn sheep. They shuffled in, their sandals flapping against the polished tiles, and stood like beggars before the richly robed members of the Sanhedrin. Their short linen tunics exposed callused knees and scarred limbs; their tanned faces stood in stark contrast to the pale countenances of men who spent hours debating in lamplit chambers. None of the disciples was particularly handsome or physically impressive, and none had the silver hair that signified dignity and wisdom.

After giving the twelve a cursory glance, Caiaphas pounded the floor with his staff, then stared at Peter. "We gave you strict orders not to teach in this name," he said, "but look, you have filled Jerusalem with your teaching, and you intend to bring on us the blood of this man Yeshua!"

Peter had the temerity to smile. "We must obey God rather than men. The God of our fathers raised up Yeshua, whom you seized and had crucified. This One, God exalted at His right hand as Leader and Savior, to give repentance to Israel and removal of sins. And we are witnesses of these events—as is the Ruach HaKodesh, whom God has given to those who obey Him."

Wrong answer, fisherman. I smiled as Caiaphas's face flamed and many around him lifted clenched fists. "Kill him!" "Kill them all!"

I waited, gratified to finally see anger and resolve that matched my own. Mayhem ruled the chamber as members of the ruling council expressed their indignation and defiance.

Then Gamaliel stood and suggested that the twelve be sent outside. Caiaphas agreed, and the guards escorted Yeshua's disciples from the chamber.

When they had gone, Gamaliel turned to face the community.

"Men of Israel," he said, his stentorian voice echoing, "be careful what you are about to do with these men. For some time ago Theudas rose up, claiming to be somebody, and a number of men, maybe four hundred, joined up with him. He was killed, and all who followed him were scattered and came to nothing. After that fellow, Judah the Galilean rose up in the days of the census and got people to follow him. He also perished, and all who followed him were scattered. So now I tell you, stay away from these men and leave them alone. For if this plan or undertaking is of men, it will come to an end; but if it is of God, you will not be able to stop them. You might even be found fighting against God."

A heavy silence filled the chamber. With some dismay I realized that my teacher, who had spoken with his usual tact and wisdom, had given sound advice. We should not act while the crowds were enthused about these men. Those who met on Solomon's Porch were more enamored with Yeshua than they'd been at the time of his crucifixion.

We should allow the people to disperse, return to their chores and the realities of life. In time, hardship, poverty, and resentment toward the Romans would remove Yeshua from their hearts and minds. At that time, he would be added to the long list of would-be messiahs in Jerusalem.

All we had to do was exercise patience.

Caiaphas also realized the wisdom of Gamaliel's words. "We will have the twelve flogged," he said. "Perhaps the sting of the whip will remind them to stay away from the Temple. We will again command them not to speak in the name of Yeshua, and then we will send them home to lick their wounds."

"Hear, hear!"

The other members of the Sanhedrin voiced their assent, and I reluctantly joined in.

As we moved into the month of Kislev and observed the end of Hanukkah, Gamaliel said he had found a job for me. He wanted me to oversee a *bet soper*, a primary school for young boys. I accepted out of respect for my teacher but found it difficult to muster much enthusiasm for teaching children when I had no child of my own. The curriculum was basic and the children quite ordinary. I applied myself, however, and taught them the Hebrew alphabet, which they had to recite forward and backward so they would be able to read the biblical text.

We met in the Temple's north portico, and I often struggled to focus on my students when Yeshua's followers walked by. They were easy to spot, even when they walked alone. The man who prayed with his head uplifted and his eyes shining would believe in Yeshua, as would the woman who knelt at the disciples' feet and wiped tears from her eyes.

"They are emotional and dangerous," I told Avidan. "And they have infested the Temple like weevils."

Avidan shook his head. "What can we do?"

"We can stop them."

"The Sanhedrin has already warned the twelve—"

"Perhaps we need to take a more direct approach."

When I was not teaching, I began to recruit students from Avidan's yeshiva. "I need you," I told the first volunteers, "to go throughout Jerusalem and learn all you can about followers of the Way. Where do they meet when they are not at the Temple? Are they contributing money to their cause? Who supplies the most money, and what do they do with it? Do they gather weapons, food, or other goods? And do those who are healed *remain* healed?"

My spies were quick to respond. Though I lost a few who stopped to listen to Yeshua's followers, others brought back useful information. Avidan proved to be the best spy of all.

"They do collect offerings," he reported. "They use the money to care for the widows in their group."

Frankly, I was surprised to hear of such charity. I had expected them to be raising money for a revolt. Most would-be messiahs died in their attempts to rebel against Rome.

"The Temple has a fund to care for widows and orphans," I pointed out. "So why do they do it?"

Avidan shrugged. "Perhaps they prefer to personally help others. They often gather in homes where people explain their needs and others report on how the offerings were distributed. They sing hymns, they pray together, and they lay hands on the sick."

"There are no arguments? No rivalry?"

Avidan cleared his throat. "The group I visited raised one issue—apparently the widows of the Hellenes were being overlooked while the widows of observant Jews had their needs met."

I sat back and smiled. "Problems like that will fracture a community."

"But the widows are no longer a problem. The leaders elected men who were known to be full of the Ruach Ha-Kodesh and wisdom, and gave responsibility for the widows over to them."

I considered this information. "Do we know any of those men?"

Avidan blew out a breath. "You may know some of them, for many Levites were in the meeting. Some of the elected men were Hellenists—one was from Antioch, and another, a highly influential fellow, was called Stephen."

I leaned forward. "He is influential? Follow him. Find out all you can about this Stephen and let me know how he serves these people."

"He speaks in local synagogues," Avidan said. "He has worked wonders and miraculous signs, and many Levites believed in Yeshua through his work. He goes to the synagogue, heals the sick, and presents what he calls 'the Gospel of Yeshua the Messiah.' Many have tried to argue with him, but they cannot debate his wisdom."

I sat back. Arguing with a fool was so simple, even Balaam's donkey could do it. But arguing with a wise man, particularly if he claimed to be filled with the Spirit of God, was another matter.

I was not surprised to hear that many from the priestly tribe were following Yeshua. Levites who were not members of a chaburah often found it difficult to support their families. They tended to be resentful of wealthy religious leaders and might even yearn to overthrow the established Temple hierarchy. I understood why they would welcome a messiah who blessed the poor and criticized those who earned power and wealth through Temple service.

"This Stephen," I asked, "what does he teach?"

Avidan shifted uneasily. "He says the sacrifice of lambs and bulls is no longer effective for the remission of sin because Yeshua provided the ultimate sacrifice. He says this message has been proclaimed through the prophets for generations."

"How so?"

Avidan tugged at his beard. "Once I heard him say that HaShem sent Joseph to save Israel from death by famine, but the brothers did not recognize or receive him until their second visit to Egypt. Only then were they saved. In the same manner, God sent Moses to his people in Egypt. They rejected him on his first visit, but accepted him on his second, when he proceeded to deliver our people from slavery. In the same manner, HaShem sent Yeshua, who was intended to be our savior from death and the slavery of sin. He was rejected by most of Israel but will be accepted when He comes a second time."

"He believes Yeshua is coming again?"

"That's what he said."

"When should we expect him?"

Avidan shrugged. "No one knows but HaShem."

I digested this information. "What else did he say?"

"He said Yeshua told his disciples that we have turned the Temple into an idol, that we worship the Temple and its rituals instead of HaShem, who cannot be confined to one place or destroyed."

I drew in a quick breath. "He implied the destruction of the Temple?"

Avidan swallowed. "I believe so."

I made a fist. "Do you see why we must stop men like this? They are clever; they are smarter than those who have not studied the wisdom of the sages. We must stop those who would lead our people astray."

"But how do we stop such a clever man? He silences all his opponents."

I took a moment to consider the question. "When we needed to prevent Yeshua from bringing the wrath of the Romans upon us, the Temple authorities bribed men to say they had heard him commit blasphemy. The same approach should work with Stephen."

Avidan's face clouded. "Did they bear false witness against a brother?"

"How is this Stephen your brother? *I* am your brother, Avidan. We worship the same God in the same way. We follow the same Law. These people of the Way are Law breakers, they heal on the Sabbath, they preach about a man—may his name be blotted out—who claimed to be God, and they lead many astray. We must stop them, and we will begin by stopping one who is, as you say, *influential*."

"How?"

I smiled. "I cannot do it—Annas and Caiaphas do not fully trust me—but you can. All you need to do is follow Stephen and mark down what he says. In time, he will doubtless utter the same words Yeshua spoke in defiance of the Holy One. Be alert, Avidan, and be faithful. I am confident you will succeed."

TWENTY-SIX

Aya

Avidan, Seraiah, and I were leaving the Temple when we saw a Levite hurrying toward us. "Avidan of Tarsus?" he called.

We stopped, and Avidan gave the man an uncertain smile. "Yes?"

"I thought it was you." The man bobbed his head. "I wonder, sir, if I might have permission to address your wife."

Avidan's mouth nearly fell open, and I went speechless.

"I am Yosef," the man went on, "a Levite in charge of the Temple musicians. I have heard that your wife is a skilled singer."

Avidan shot me a look of surprise, but I could only shake my head. I had not spoken to anyone but Bettina about my love of music. I had sung around the house but never in public or with the window open.

"How would you know this?" Avidan folded his arms. "Because my wife does not sing in public."

"I am sorry; I did not mean to imply anything improper. I

210

was speaking to Sha'ul, your esteemed brother-in-law, and he told me that his sister sings quite well."

Avidan relaxed. "She does."

"Wonderful." Yosef nodded. "I don't know how familiar you are with the music of the first Temple—we know it was more elaborate than what we have today. For instance, the Scriptures describe an orchestra consisting of lutes, harps, and a cymbal. In other passages we read accounts of women who sing psalms, canticles, and other sacred poetry while they dance to a percussive accompaniment."

A frown settled between Avidan's brows. "But that is not the practice now."

"No—and the high priest does not want to alter the current practice. He believes it is enough to have trumpets and male singers. But he is not opposed to the idea of music outside our worship, and he has given me permission to train a female choir to sing in the outer courtyard on feast days. So I have been searching for skilled singers and was thrilled to hear about your wife."

I must admit, my heart began to pound after hearing this announcement. This man loved music as much as I did, and, like me, he had been forced to bury his dream. But, praise HaShem, his dream might soon be realized.

"Avidan." I clutched at my husband's sleeve. "I would love to participate in this choir."

Avidan's frown deepened. "But you have a baby."

"And I care for him all day. Surely, Seraiah would not suffer if he stayed with you for a few hours? Or I could take him with me—he could play on the floor while we learn our music."

I had placed Avidan in an awkward position by asking in front of the Levite, but my request was not outrageous. Furthermore, if Sha'ul had not approved of this choir, he would not have told this Levite about me.

I saw thought working behind Avidan's eyes, then he nodded,

211

albeit reluctantly. "I see no reason why my wife should not participate," he said, shifting his gaze to the Levite. "Send a message when you are ready."

"Thank you." The Levite bobbed his head again. "We have gone far too long without the sound of choirs in our Temple. When the people hear what they have been missing, perhaps the high priest will allow choir music to return to the sanctuary."

He thanked Avidan again, then hurried away.

As we continued to walk, I slipped my arm through Avidan's. "Thank you, husband. I did not realize how much I missed music until now."

"Are you not happy?" He threw me a sharp look. "Are Seraiah and I not enough for you?"

"More than enough," I assured him. "But my heart holds room for much more."

I don't know how he arranged it, but Yosef the Levite managed to reserve the Chamber of Hewn Stone for our choir rehearsal. The high-ceilinged chamber seemed well suited for our purpose, and the semicircle of rising seats made it easy for us to hear each other and see our director.

I had never been inside the hallowed chamber of the Sanhedrin, and I could not help but be awed at the sheer beauty of the room. More than a dozen decorative columns had been spaced around the chamber, and each was crowned by gilded leaves. A wide band of white marble connected the columns at the top, with gilded leaves at the upper and lower edges.

As I sank to one of the stone seats, I followed the lines of the columns as I looked upward. A wise man had designed this space because it forced an occupant to consider heaven.

Yosef began by asking each of us to sing a bit, then he moved us either to the right or left side of the semicircle. Within minutes I realized he was dividing us by the sound and range of our voices—women with deeper, lower voices sat on his left "in the Sadducee seats," he joked, while women with lighter, higher voices sat at his right, "with the Pharisees."

Once we were all seated, he divided the two sections into four, then sang a pitch for each group and told us to sing with him. "Keep singing," he urged each section before moving on to the next. Soon all four groups were singing a different tone, but oh, the harmony! I had never heard such a heavenly sound.

With one hand lifted, urging us to hold the pitch, Yosef closed his eyes and tipped his head back, caught up in a moment of ecstasy. "Ah," he said, allowing his hand to fall. "That is how the angels in heaven sing praises to HaShem!"

We women looked around, smiling at each other with joy and astonished wonder. Then Yosef opened a scroll. "Ezra the prophet," he said, looking around the chamber, "wrote of the exiles who returned from captivity in Babylon. Listen: 'The entire assembly totaled 42,360, not including their male and female servants, who numbered 7,337. *They also had 200 male and female singers.*'"

He lowered the scroll. "HaShem gives gifts to those who will use them. I bless you women for your willingness to sing in service to HaShem. I bless your husbands for allowing you to participate in this effort. I bless your children. And I praise HaShem for giving us the gift of music."

He set the scroll aside. "We are going to learn a simple psalm, but we will sing it to each other—two choirs singing and answering in harmony and rhythm. Listen as I sing it to you, then we will sing it together."

I straightened as every fiber of my being focused on the thin man in the white Levitical robe. He sang a lovely, flowing melody with Scripture for lyrics: "'My feet stand on level ground. In congregations I will bless Adonai.'"

Then, when he pointed to my group, I drew a deep breath and lifted my voice with the others.

My heart was still singing when I returned from choir practice and greeted Avidan with a kiss.

"I am glad you are home," he said, his expression serious. "Your brother has asked me to undertake important work for him."

"What sort of work?"

"He wants me to follow a man named Stephen."

When Avidan explained the situation, I opposed the idea. "He wants you to spy on this man and report him to the authorities?" I asked. "Why would they listen to you?"

"Perhaps because I am Sha'ul's brother-in-law," Avidan answered. "This is a way to advance in Temple service. If I do this thing and Stephen is silenced, the high priest and his brothers will be pleased. Sha'ul's warnings will be validated, and I will be lauded as someone who directed attention to a dire threat."

I nodded, grateful that Avidan had finally shown evidence of ambition. He would never be as driven as my brother, but lately I had begun to wonder if he would be content as an eternal student.

"How can you present a credible report?" I asked. "You must be careful—if your report is considered untrustworthy or exaggerated, you may be discredited."

"I know." Avidan gave me a rueful smile. "But Stephen is to speak at the Synagogue of the Freedmen on Shabbat. I will listen to him there."

"I have not heard of it."

"It is unique; the members are former slaves from all over the world—Cyrene, Alexandria, Cilicia, and Asia. They are proud, spirited men and do not suffer from the complacency that afflicts many Jews from Jerusalem. They will not accept Stephen's word easily."

"Some of them are from Cilicia?" The mention of our former

province sent a wave of nostalgia through my heart. "I wonder if any are from Tarsus."

"I will not be there to search for old friends. I am to listen to every word Stephen says. Given the freedmen's staunch support of the Law, the debate is bound to be heated. Anyone, even this Stephen, could slip and say something that is not strictly true."

"Would you like me to go with you? I could take the baby or ask Eden to watch him—"

"You should stay behind." Avidan lowered his gaze. "I will go alone."

He had presented his case, he had been guided by my brother, but when he could not look me in the eye, I wondered if Avidan truly believed he was following the right course.

I heard nothing more of Sha'ul and Avidan's plan until a few days later. I had just stepped into the water at the Pool of Siloam when Eden came over to ask about Seraiah. "How is your boy?" She rested her hands on her walking stick. "Is he with you today?"

"He is on my back." I shifted to ease my aching muscles. "Where is your Zachariah?"

"At home with my mother." Eden gave me a mischievous smile. "I can get more work done when she watches him."

"I wish my mother were here." I continued down the steps and lowered my jars into the pool. "Avidan says I must teach Seraiah to walk at my side. It is an effort to carry him *and* our water."

"Speaking of your husband"—Eden lowered her voice—"I have heard about the role he played in Stephen's arrest. His trial will be held today."

For an instant I thought she meant that Avidan would be on trial; then I realized she was speaking of the man my husband had been watching.

"Stephen stands before the Sanhedrin at midday," Eden said, her expression somber. "If he has not committed blasphemy, he has nothing to fear. But I find it hard to believe he would blaspheme HaShem."

I examined her face. "You speak as if you know this Stephen."

"I have heard him speak, so I know he is a good man," she said. "He has shown great respect for HaShem and great kindness to some of the Greek-speaking widows. How can a man like that be accused of blasphemy?"

"He will be judged by his words," I reminded her. "So, if he is innocent—"

"All will be well," she finished, but her distressed expression remained. "May HaShem's will be done."

Could Avidan have informed on an innocent man? Surely not. But Eden was right; if Stephen had done nothing wrong, he had no reason to fear.

I thanked her for the news but was so distraught I hurried home and left my jars at the pool.

TWENTY-SEVEN

Sha'ul

Avidan, who had been summoned as a witness, looked like a respectable, devout scholar as he stood before the assembled Sanhedrin. Though I tried to remain detached, I could not help but feel pleased with my brother-in-law. Today, if HaShem allowed, we would reap the benefit of our combined efforts.

"I have heard this man," Avidan began, his words echoing in the chamber, "speak blasphemous words against Moses and against God. He never stops speaking against the holy Temple and the Torah. I have heard him say that Yeshua ha-Natzrati will destroy this place and change the customs Moses handed down to us."

I glanced at the accused. Stephen stood alone, several paces away from Avidan and other witnesses who had been aroused by my brother-in-law's passion. Their eyes glittered, their fists were clenched, yet the accused did not seem anxious or fearful. He stood with his feet planted firmly on the floor, unmovable. With his hands clasped in front of him, he looked at nothing in particular, certainly not at the high priest or the other ruling elders. I expected him to appear gravely serious, given the reason for his arrest, but he seemed to pay little attention to the witnesses who were intent on destroying his credibility. Indeed, if I had to describe his appearance in one word, I would say he looked *confident.*

I had made inquiries into Stephen's background, and what I learned did not please me. Stephen was a Hellenist, a Greek-speaking Jew whose forefathers had most likely followed the Seleucids when they sought to outlaw the Torah during the time of the Maccabees. Like many Hellenists who sought to return to Torah, Stephen came to Jerusalem in search of knowledge and fell in with those who followed the Way. Because he was bright and articulate, he had become a leader among them.

When all the witnesses had finished their testimonies, Caiaphas stared at Stephen. "What do you say, then? Are these charges true?"

The man had the temerity to smile. "Brothers and fathers," he said, turning to address the entire body, "listen. The God of glory appeared to our father Abraham when he was in Mesopotamia, before he lived in Haran. He said to him, 'Leave your country and your relatives, and come here to the land I will show you.'"

Stephen proceeded to give a respectful history of our people, detailing the journeys of Abraham, Jacob, and Joseph. He gave an account of Moses, our greatest prophet. Then Stephen lowered his voice and spoke so quietly we strained to hear. "This is the Moses who said to *Bnei-Yisrael*, 'God will raise up for you a prophet like me from among your brothers.'"

He continued his recitation, recounting how our fathers disobeyed HaShem in the wilderness, how they worshiped a golden calf, and how God's glory dwelt in a Tabernacle made with human hands. He walked us through the time of Solomon, who built the first Temple.

"However," Stephen said, his voice rising in pitch and fervor,

"Elyon does not dwell in man-made houses. As the prophet says, 'Heaven is My throne, and the earth is the footstool of My feet. What kind of house will you build for Me, says Adonai, or what is the place of My rest? Did not My Hand make all these things?'

"Oh, you stiff-necked people! You uncircumcised of heart and ears! You always resist the Ruach HaKodesh; just as your fathers did, you do as well. Which of the prophets did your fathers not persecute? They killed the ones who foretold the coming of the Righteous One. Now you have become His betrayers and murderers—you who received the Torah by direction of angels and did not keep it!"

He had gone too far. First, he turned the hot light of scorn upon our fathers; now he turned it toward us, we who had spent our entire *lives* studying the Law and the prophets.

Cries erupted from the throats of every man in the assembly as my fellow scholars sprang from their seats. The high priest went red in the face, and his father, the esteemed Annas, flashed a smug smile: another blasphemer had been exposed, and more leaven would be removed from the righteous loaf. As one, the Sanhedrin surged forward, but we halted in mid-step when Stephen raised his eyes toward heaven and lifted his arms . . .

Was he going to beg for mercy? Would he call on Abraham? Would he renounce the false messiah who had troubled so many?

Silence fell over the room, a dense quiet like the expectant holding of breaths. "Look!" A smile curved the corners of Stephen's mouth. "I see the heavens opened and the Son of Man standing at the right hand of God!"

The men around me erupted in vehemence. Some of them moved toward the accused while others held their ears against further blasphemy. The men down front took hold of Stephen, grabbing his arms, legs, and shoulders, and dragged him out of the Chamber of Hewn Stone.

I stood and caught Caiaphas's eye. Without saying a word, I

lifted a brow, seeking permission, and Caiaphas nodded. Confident in what I was about to do, I descended the steps and followed the mob that had swept Stephen from the chamber.

I did not intend to take part in the execution but followed the crowd to make certain every requirement of the Law was satisfied.

The men who carried Stephen out of the chamber were determined to dispatch him as quickly as possible. Those who could not get a grip on the man's body followed closely, striving to land a blow whenever they could find an opening to strike. I walked behind the others, dodging curious onlookers who stopped to stare as the procession passed.

Finally, we carried him through the city gate. The Law forbade executions within Jerusalem, so the mob carried Stephen to one of the narrow pits outside the city walls. They threw him into the pit headfirst, then gathered around the edges to see if their prisoner had survived the fall.

I ventured closer so I could give an accurate account to the high priest. Peering into the pit, I saw Stephen bent and twisted, his robe torn and his head bloody. With an agonized effort he straightened his limbs, bracing himself on the side of the shaft as he stood. He looked up, but his gaze did not touch any individual, instead focusing on the heavens. Blood dripped from his scalp and an awkwardly bent arm while bruises darkened his cheek.

Then he smiled.

The sight of that smile sent fresh fury racing through my veins. "Witnesses!" I shouted, summoning those who had just given testimony. "You are required to cast the first stones."

Several of those who had supported Avidan picked up rocks and stepped forward, but I could not see my brother-in-law. He had organized the opposition, so why had he disappeared? I glanced around and spotted him near the city gate, standing in a shadow.

"Avidan!" My rebuke echoed in the stillness. "It is your duty to act according to your testimony."

Avidan wore a troubled expression as he trudged forward and slipped out of his mantle. He handed the garment to me, then silently picked up a rock and tossed it into the pit without waiting to see if it struck its target.

I could see he did not have the heart to carry out the execution, yet his gesture was enough to encourage the other witnesses. In a rush of exuberance, they shed their outer garments and dropped them at my feet, then hurried to throw stones into the pit. The onlookers cheered every blow, and when the witnesses had finished, others continued the onslaught, throwing stones at the man in the pit.

Amid the shouts for justice, we heard nothing from the condemned man. Then, in a surprisingly loud voice, he called, "Lord Yeshua! Lord Yeshua, receive my spirit!"

Curious to understand how he still possessed enough breath to speak, I moved closer to the pit. He was swaying on his feet, but while I watched, he fell to his knees. "Lord"—his eyes brimmed with tears—"do not hold this sin against them!"

Stephen slumped back and closed his eyes. The observers rained more stones upon him, but the man was dead.

I left the witnesses' garments in a heap and walked back into the city, unable to forget what I had seen and heard. Stephen had spoken the same words reportedly uttered by Yeshua when he hung on the execution stake. He, too, had forgiven those who carried out his death sentence.

But I did not need forgiveness. I had done what was necessary to safeguard the people of Israel, and if necessary I would do it again.

TWENTY-EIGHT

Sha'ul

When I visited the high priest's palace that evening, Caiaphas congratulated me on a job well done.

"But half done is not enough," I told him. "The sect continues to grow, and the leaders may redouble their efforts after this man's death. Stephen was considered godly, and it may be that his death—appropriate as it was—will be mourned while his blasphemy is overlooked."

Caiaphas stroked his beard. "Why do you say this group presents a problem? They are Jews. They still worship at the Temple and follow the traditions."

"They are a problem," I answered, "because their movement is imbued with power from the evil one. I have heard people speak foreign tongues they did not learn. I have seen a former cripple leap for joy. I watched that so-called messiah wreak havoc in the Temple courtyard, overturning tables and causing chaos during a holy festival. And I have listened to Yeshua's coarse, uneducated followers speak with authority and knowledge they could not have obtained after three years with an untrained Torah teacher from Nazareth."

"Three years is a long time," Caiaphas remarked.

"I have been a yeshiva student since the age of ten," I reminded him. "I have been ordained. Who examined Yeshua of Nazareth? Who was his teacher? Whom does he quote when giving his judgments, and upon whose authority does he rely?"

"They say," Caiaphas said, "he referred to his Father as his authority."

I scoffed. "Another blasphemy. The truth is that Yeshua had no teacher, or none we know of. He was cut from the same cloth as his kinsman John the Baptizer, another upstart from outside Jerusalem."

Caiaphas rested his elbows on the armrests of his chair. "So, Sha'ul—how would you curtail the growth of this sect?"

I lifted my chin, pleased with his confidence in me. "I would grant warrants for the arrest of anyone who follows the Way, and I would entrust the warrants to devout men who obey the holy Law. I would arrest these believers, punish them, and warn them of even worse consequences should they continue in their dangerous pursuit."

Caiaphas tented his hands. "So it shall be done, Sha'ul, and clearly you are the man to do it. If you are successful, we will allow you to extend your efforts beyond Judea and Galilee. Perhaps, with the blessing of HaShem, we will eradicate this threat."

The ruling council granted my request the next day. The successful action against Stephen invigorated the members who had been afraid to attack the cult growing among us. Gamaliel's words about patience were forgotten as Caiaphas granted permission for the Temple authorities to locate and imprison anyone who claimed to follow the Way.

To my ordination papers, which had read, "Let him teach; let him judge; let him decide on questions of firstborn; let him decide; let him judge!" were added these words: "Let him prosecute; let him imprison."

I bowed before Caiaphas and left the council with a light heart. But before returning to my own quiet house, I decided to visit Aya and Avidan. They needed to know the final results of my pursuit of Stephen, and I felt the need for amiable company.

TWENTY-NINE

Aya

I set out an extra plate when Sha'ul showed up for dinner, but as he began to recount the day's events, I barely noticed what my hands were doing. When he told me how boldly Avidan had denounced the blasphemous Stephen, and how my husband had been the first to drop a stone into the pit, an odd shudder overtook my heart. I was grateful Avidan had become more serious about his ambition, yet I had never imagined him with a stone in his hand.

I lowered my head, hoping Sha'ul would protect Avidan from unwise decisions. If he would encourage my husband more often, Avidan could become a leader in Jerusalem. My parents had been people of renown in Tarsus . . . perhaps we could achieve the same status in the Holy City.

"If all goes well," Sha'ul said as we ate, "I might ask Caiaphas for permission to arrest followers of the Way in other cities. I hear there is a man in Samaria who works miracles and proclaims Yeshua as Messiah."

"I have heard of him, as well," Avidan said. "He is called Philip."

225

"Be careful," I said, looking from Avidan to Sha'ul. "You must use caution when dealing with these people. You are members of the majority in Jerusalem, but in another city, those people might outnumber you, and they are zealous."

Avidan ignored my comment. "You must realize," he said, speaking to Sha'ul, "that if you persecute the Way in Jerusalem, many of them will leave and spread their Gospel elsewhere. Did you not notice Stephen's devotion? He did not recant, nor did he renounce his beliefs. His last words only reinforced his testimony."

"What did he say?" I looked from one man to the other, but neither seemed willing to tell me. "What were Stephen's last words?"

Avidan finally relented. "He forgave us," he said, hanging his head. "Though we had just thrown stones at him, he asked HaShem not to hold the sin against us."

I brought my hand to my lips as my thoughts tumbled in amazement. My parents had always protected me from gladiatorial contests and other sights of bloodshed, so I had never watched a man die. I had always assumed that most people resisted death, so why didn't Stephen?

My preconceived notions fell apart. "Did he not resist?" I asked. "Did he try to run?"

Avidan shook his head. "How could he? He was in a pit."

"Surely he tried to climb out. As you carried him away from the Temple, he must have struggled against you."

"He did not." Avidan's voice broke. "Could you"—he held out his cup—"pour more wine?"

I brought the wineskin and refilled the men's cups. My husband never drank two cups of wine at dinner. Either he was drinking to forget or he wanted me to think of something other than death . . . and his part in it.

Within hours, my brother had developed a plan for finding and capturing those who followed the teachings of Yeshua. As he explained his plan to Avidan, I realized that he had finally found a purpose for his ambition: no longer was he striving to be the best student or the best teacher; now he wanted to be the best defender of the Law. And, knowing Sha'ul, he would not rest until he had accomplished his goal.

Sha'ul and his cohorts began to linger outside any house where Yeshua's followers were rumored to meet. If they noticed people arriving on the first day of the week—the day Yeshua's followers usually met—he and his men waited until the foot traffic slowed, then they forced their way into the house and arrested every adult present. After several days in jail, the prisoners were brought before the Sanhedrin, where Sha'ul and others testified against them. When it came time to pass judgment, those arrested for the first time were warned and released. Those arrested a second time were flogged and released. Those arrested a third time were stoned.

After their first arrest, most believers went home, packed their belongings, and left Jerusalem.

Followers of the Way stopped meeting in Solomon's Colonnade, and Sha'ul took great pleasure in walking through that space without encountering anyone who proclaimed Yeshua as Messiah. The Pharisees who quietly believed in Yeshua—most notably, a Torah teacher called Nicodemus, and another known as Joseph of Arimathea—withdrew from Jerusalem and moved, albeit temporarily, to other cities.

But just as Avidan predicted, those who left Jerusalem did not slink away like defeated dogs—they took their bold testimonies with them. In new communities they spread the teachings of Yeshua and created new followers of the Way.

"They are like birds," Sha'ul groused. "They eat weeds and fly to a new area, where they alight on a branch and spread the seeds. Then new weeds sprout, and more birds eat them and carry the seeds to more distant places."

Avidan lifted his head. "You will want to know this: Peter and John have left Jerusalem."

"This information is from a reliable source?"

Avidan nodded. "But they were not running. Apparently, they received a summons from Samaria, so they have gone there to preach."

"Samaria." Sha'ul spat the word. "Why should we be surprised? The half-breeds of that region will believe anything."

"Philip the preacher resides there," Avidan said. "I would imagine many followers of the Way live in that area."

"I will not waste time with them," Sha'ul said, shaking his head. "The Samaritans have believed lies for years, so what does it matter if they believe in Yeshua?"

Several days later, Sha'ul returned, bringing gifts. "For my nephew," he said, placing a pair of wooden blocks in front of Seraiah. "I am going away, and I may not return for a while. I wanted to give him something to remind him of his uncle."

I looked up, surprised. "You sound as if you will be gone a long time."

"Who can say?" Sha'ul smiled. "I will not return to Jerusalem until Damascus is cleansed of all who follow the Way."

As Seraiah toddled toward Avidan, I caught my husband's gaze. We knew Damascus—the Syrian city that lay north of Jerusalem was an important trading post for Jews and Gentiles.

"How can you carry out your orders in Syria?" Avidan asked. "Our religious leaders have no authority there."

"We do now." Sha'ul's smile deepened. "Caiaphas has been in touch with the emperor. Rome has authorized extradition permits for our cause, so I have complete authority to arrest followers of the Way no matter where I find them. I am authorized to bring prisoners back to Jerusalem so they can be tried before the Great Sanhedrin."

Shadows appeared behind my husband's eyes. "You have been arresting men and women," he said, his gaze drifting toward our son. "You have dragged them from their homes, leaving their children helpless. What will happen to the children in Damascus? Families in Jerusalem have relatives to care for the little ones, but what of the Jewish children of Damascus? Who will care for them?"

"Their parents should have considered such consequences before following heresy." Sha'ul opened his arms to Seraiah. "Come, nephew, and give your uncle a kiss. I have to go, but I will have wonderful stories to tell you when I return. And I promise to bring gifts."

Tears flooded my eyes as Seraiah toddled toward his uncle. I blinked them away, unable to decide if my tears sprang from the sight of Sha'ul embracing Seraiah or the thought of my brother ripping parents from their children.

THIRTY

Aya

After months of training and rehearsal, Yosef announced that we were ready to sing. We would not sing in the sanctuary, but in the outer court, "where even Gentiles will hear us," Yosef said.

"We will sing," he announced, "on the first day of Tishri, Rosh Hashanah. The shofar will sound to begin the Feast of Trumpets, and we will let all who come to the Temple hear us sing praise to Adonai. And you, ladies, should wear white, in honor of the festival."

I smothered a smile. I knew he was trying to allay our disappointment at not singing in an actual service, yet I was grateful to use my voice again. I had not even minded the long rehearsals, because the act of joining the sound of pure voices had been a gift. Avidan did not understand the contentment that filled me after every rehearsal, but he did not mind my participation in the choir.

"When you finally sing for us," he said, "perhaps I will understand."

Yosef had taught us so much. We could now look at a scroll and identify the accents above certain words as the gestures Yosef used to indicate which pitch we should sing.

The day of our concert opened with brilliant sunshine that gilded the Temple stones and lightened my heart. In the center of the outer court, Yosef arranged us in three rows, then shaped the rows into a semicircle, just as we had rehearsed in the Chamber of Hewn Stone.

He stood before us, sang a simple pitch, and lifted his arms, our signal to sing.

As he directed, those with the lowest voices began the psalm:

> "Sing to Adonai a new song!
> Sing to Adonai, all the earth.
> Sing to Adonai, bless His Name."

They were joined by the highest voices, which echoed their melody:

> "Proclaim the good news of His salvation from day to
> day.
> Declare His glory among the nations,
> His marvelous deeds among all peoples."

The lowest voices kept repeating the refrain while the medium voices joined in:

> "For great is Adonai, and greatly to be praised.
> He is to be feared above all gods.
> For all the gods of the peoples are idols,
> But Adonai made the heavens."

Finally, all four groups sang together, each harmonizing with the others:

"Splendor and majesty are before Him.
Strength and beauty are in His Sanctuary.
Ascribe to Adonai, O families of peoples.
Ascribe to Adonai glory and strength.
Ascribe to Adonai the glory of His Name.
Bring an offering and come into His courts.
Bow down to Adonai in holy splendor.
Tremble before Him, all the earth.
Say among the nations: 'Adonai reigns!'"

When we finished, the entire Temple Mount resounded with enthusiastic amens. Men and women wiped tears from their eyes, and several of the priests wore approving smiles. Yosef himself looked pleased, as did all the women with me.

I closed my eyes and whispered a fervent prayer of thanks. "Even if it is only this once, I am honored to have been able to use my gift at your holy Temple."

Sha'ul had left Jerusalem in the hot month of Elul, and months passed without word from him. Avidan made inquiries as to Sha'ul's welfare, but no one at the Temple seemed to know anything. Avidan finally sent a letter to the high priest's house but received no reply.

"It is as if Caiaphas cannot be bothered to answer a man of my status," Avidan grumbled. "Either that or he is too busy celebrating Sha'ul's success."

Then one winter afternoon Avidan came home, locked the door, and closed the shutters. "I have news." He gripped my arm. "And this report terrifies me."

I bit my lip and struggled to remain calm, not wanting to frighten Seraiah. "What is this news?"

He pulled me onto the bed and knelt at my feet, clinging to my waist as if he were drowning. "I have heard the most unbelievable tale," he said, his words muffled by my tunic. "I could not believe it, but then I wondered if it explains why Caiaphas would not answer my letter. Why else would they pretend Sha'ul no longer exists? Why else would they blot his name from the records of the Sanhedrin?"

My mind spun with questions. "Tell me, what happened to my brother?"

Avidan regarded me with bleary eyes. "They say he is a follower of the Way."

Anger flared as I struggled to make sense of his words. "That is a lie. Someone is trying to ruin my brother's name."

"I didn't want to believe it, but the story is so detailed—"

"Forget the story—where is Sha'ul?"

"Still in Damascus, if the reports can be believed. They say he speaks in the synagogues and uses the Scriptures to prove that Yeshua is the promised Messiah."

I laughed aloud. "Avidan, you are a good man, but you are far too gullible. Perhaps you should ask Gamaliel if you can travel to Damascus and find Sha'ul yourself. Your status would rise if you can disprove this horrible rumor."

Avidan sat next to me and rested his elbows on his knees. "I am afraid of what I might find. They say Sha'ul was walking the road to Damascus when he was struck blind. He fell and heard a voice ask why Sha'ul was persecuting him. Sha'ul said, 'Who are you?' And the voice answered, 'I am Yeshua, whom you are persecuting. Now get up and go into the city.'"

Avidan's eyes met mine. "Do you see why I doubted the story?"

"That is impossible." I shook my head. "That sort of thing does not happen, especially to Sha'ul."

"But those traveling with him heard the voice," Avidan said. "They saw nothing but took Sha'ul to a home in Damascus. Sha'ul has been there ever since, living with the community of believers and preaching in the synagogues. He says—he *teaches*—that Yeshua was the son of HaShem. Could it be true?"

I opened my mouth to speak, but this time the word *impossible* would not come. *Could* such a story be true? How could a brilliant man of iron opinions and granite convictions crumble so easily?

We sat and pondered the inconceivable. Sha'ul . . . and Yeshua? My brother was the most resolute person I knew, and he had been determined to blot Yeshua's name from the history of our people. So how could he be preaching that a lowly man from Nazareth was HaShem's son?

"The story makes no sense." I placed my hand on my husband's arm. "I cannot believe it. I will not."

"Sha'ul has never been changeable in his affections," Avidan said. "I cannot understand how he could insist that HaShem has no son and then say that Yeshua was the son of HaShem."

"What shall we do?" I met Avidan's gaze. "Should we try to find him? Should we send a doctor to him? Perhaps he has gone mad. It can happen, particularly with much studying. We should send a message to the high priest—"

"We cannot afford to do those things," Avidan reminded me. "And the high priest does not know us. For now, all we can do is wait."

I thought of my parents, at home in Tarsus. They would be grief-stricken to learn that Sha'ul had deviated from the faith they had instilled in him. They would be mortified if the news reached their synagogue, and—

I gasped. "The Romans crucified Yeshua," I said. "The Roman governor of Tarsus holds my parents in high esteem. What will he do if he hears that Sha'ul supports the man who would have declared himself king instead of Caesar?"

"I do not know." Avidan slipped his arms around me and

lowered his forehead to mine. "I do not have any answers, but I will try to learn what I can."

———— • ————

Though Avidan and I anxiously awaited Sha'ul's return, months would pass before we received any new information about him.

We were not the only people interested in my brother. Avidan said the men at his yeshiva were shocked and angry when they heard that Sha'ul had converted to the Way. Nothing so scandalous had occurred in years, and never had a teacher as outspoken as Sha'ul changed his position so drastically.

"They refuse to even say his name," Avidan told me. "His students at the bet soper are forbidden to speak of him, and his name has been blotted out on every record, going back to when he first arrived in Jerusalem."

"Is it safe for him to return?" I asked. "Are they angry enough to stone him?"

The look in Avidan's eye gave me my answer.

"If they are ready to stone him," I asked, "are *you* safe?"

Avidan sighed. "Often, when I enter a room, everyone goes quiet. No one has accused me of anything, but I can feel them watching me." He patted my hand. "Do not worry, Aya. They will not move against me unless I do something to indicate my support for the Way. Until then, all they can do is watch."

One evening, just before sunset, I was clearing the table when we heard a voice from outside. When Avidan opened the door, I saw Yosef at our courtyard gate.

"Shalom," he called, a tide of red rising from his throat.

"Shalom aleichem," Avidan responded. "Would you like to come in?"

Yosef shook his head. "I have come—I am sorry." He looked past Avidan and gave me a sad smile. "I have been sent . . . to say you are no longer needed in the choir."

He turned and would have hurried down the street if Avidan had not caught his arm. "Who sent you?" he asked, his voice gruff. "And what reason did they give for this?"

As the old man trembled beneath Avidan's hot gaze, I almost felt sorry for him. "One of the high priest's men ordered me to come. They will not allow a blasphemer's sister to sing in the choir."

Avidan released the Levite, who ducked and scurried away.

My husband shook his head. "I am sorry, Aya. I know how much you loved the choir."

Somehow I managed to smile. "All of this is based on a rumor. When Sha'ul comes home, he will explain the truth, and everything will be set right. You will see."

But I could not believe my own words.

As the weeks passed, we began to hear other rumors. We heard that Sha'ul was living with a group of Yeshua's followers in Damascus and had risen to a position of leadership among them. That news did not surprise us, for Sha'ul would be likely to take charge of any group he joined. We heard he spoke frequently in the synagogues, opening the Scriptures every Shabbat and using the words of the prophets to prove that Yeshua was the Messiah.

Then the rumors changed. By the time Pesach arrived, we had heard that Sha'ul had left Damascus and gone to Arabia.

"Why would he go there?" I asked Avidan. "He knows no one in the desert."

Avidan's brow wrinkled. "HaShem led Moses into the desert. Elijah as well. Even Abraham. Perhaps HaShem chooses to train men in a place where they are alone and utterly dependent on Him."

"You think HaShem is in this?" I asked. "How can you think so?"

"I know Sha'ul," he said, "and both of us know he is not a fool. If he was ill or deluded when he first reached Damascus, he has had time to recover. But he continues to preach about Yeshua, and now he has gone into the desert." A smile crossed his face. "They say Yeshua went into the desert at the beginning of his ministry. Perhaps the desert is HaShem's training ground."

"Training for what?" I stared at my husband in disbelief, then shook my head and went to tend to Seraiah. I did not know what to think.

Since Sha'ul left Jerusalem, hundreds of Yeshua's followers had returned, though most of them met quietly in homes and out-of-the-way locations. Avidan and I often spotted them observing the festivals and prayers at the Temple, and though their eyes shone with a sort of mad joy, they did not speak publicly about Yeshua.

On the Feast of Firstfruits, I carried Seraiah into the Court of the Women and spotted Eden with her walking stick. I greeted her, and we waited for the morning prayers to begin.

I had just given Seraiah a piece of honeycomb to chew when four striking women entered through the southern gate. As the Levites led us in the *Shacharit*, the women knelt on the stone floor and began to pray in a manner I had never seen. They recited the prayer with flamboyant gestures and dazzling smiles, praising HaShem and lifting their eyes to heaven.

I did not know if they intended to draw attention to themselves, but they certainly did.

I glanced at Eden. Though blind, she had heard the women's upraised voices, and her wide eyes appeared at risk of falling out of her face. "Who are they?"

"I do not know," I whispered. "They are four women, and they look alike. They are tall, wearing colorful tunics and headscarves. They are also wearing bright jewelry."

"Ah. I have heard about these four," Eden said. "They are the unmarried daughters of a man called Philip, and they live in Samaria." She moved closer and lowered her voice. "They are prophetesses and followers of the Way."

I stared, unable to decide which bit of news astonished me most. I could not believe a father would allow his daughters to remain unmarried, and I could not understand why followers of the Way would draw attention to themselves, especially at the Temple.

The quartet would have stood out no matter how they prayed. All four were beautiful. Like their father, who had entered the sanctuary, they had lustrous dark hair. The women's hair was so long it hung like silky fringe beneath the lower edge of their head coverings.

"Do they have names?" I asked, unable to look away.

Eden chuckled. "I'm sure they do, but I have only heard them called 'the daughters of Philip.'"

"Many men are known as Philip—"

"This one is known as the proclaimer of good news."

"Which is?"

"The news that Yeshua is Messiah." Eden's brow furrowed. "Of course, Philip will not proclaim that news today. Not unless he wants to be flogged and imprisoned."

We waited until the morning prayers ended, then Eden took my arm and we turned to leave. But I could not resist taking one last look at the sisters and saw one of them staring at me.

"Aya of Tarsus," she called, her voice rising above the sound of the departing worshipers.

I froze. I wanted Eden to jerk me out of the dream I'd stumbled into, yet I could not speak because my tongue had suddenly grown heavy. The sights and sounds of the Temple faded, though I could still hear the woman's voice and see her shining eyes.

"Blessed are you, for one day you will meet Yeshua," the woman said. "And on that day your heart will open, and you will understand."

Understand . . . what? I stood perfectly still, my mind spinning in confusion, and only when Eden tugged on my arm could I move again. I took a step forward and glanced over my shoulder. The sisters had been swallowed up by the crowd.

———•———

I hurried home, eager to tell Avidan about my encounter with the prophetess, then remembered he was studying with members of his yeshiva. So I nursed Seraiah and put him down for a nap.

With the baby asleep, I sank onto a bench to think about what Philip's daughter had said. How could she be a true prophetess? She was a follower of the Way, and the Way had proven to be a dangerous movement that led many astray, including my brother.

The woman was also a stranger and did not know me. She could have made the same utterance to Eden, and we would have no way of proving her prophecy. I did not object to the idea of a woman as prophet. Moses' sister Miriam was a prophetess, and the Scriptures revealed several occasions of HaShem speaking to women. He had guided Deborah, an esteemed judge, and sent His angel to give a message to Samson's mother.

So I did not doubt that HaShem could speak to a woman, yet I yearned to know more about the daughters of Philip. Did HaShem speak to them frequently? Did they have actual conversations with Adonai, or did they only receive occasional messages from the Most High? Were their prophecies ever false? If they were, they should not call themselves prophetesses, because no one who spoke for HaShem could lie.

As to the prophecy itself—ha! The woman had overstepped credibility. I would see *Yeshua*? The Nazarene was dead and buried in some far-flung place. I would *never* see Yeshua, nor would I ever believe in him. I was the daughter of a Pharisee, the wife of a Pharisee, and sister to a man on the Sanhedrin. Furthermore, I had family and a husband to consider. I would never shame my parents or Avidan by professing belief in a false messiah.

When Seraiah woke from his nap, I picked him up and glanced out the window. The shadows had lengthened, so Avidan would soon be home. I needed to prepare a light supper, but first I had to nurse my son and change his tunic . . .

I watched Seraiah play with his blocks while I waited for Avidan. I kept revisiting the story of the prophetess, knowing Avidan would help me make sense of it. I felt positively pregnant with expectation, waiting to unburden myself by sharing with him.

I glanced out the window again. The shadows were long and blue, the sun about to set. What was keeping him? I paced through the house, then straightened one of Avidan's tunics that hung on a hook. His extra sandals sat by the door, so I straightened them, then moved to the table where he had left a half-eaten pomegranate in a bowl. Where was the man?

Seraiah had dropped into a light doze by the time I heard a knock on the door. Alarmed by the unexpected sound, I placed my sleepy son on a pillow and threw my headscarf over my hair. I opened the door and found two men from Avidan's yeshiva outside. Avidan had introduced me to one of them, Ezra, when we met outside the Temple.

I glanced from one man to the other, alarmed at their somber expressions. "Yes?"

"We come with distressing news," Ezra said. "Avidan is dead. His body will be arriving soon."

Confused by Ezra's nonsense, I turned to the stranger. "How can I help you?" I asked. "Avidan is not yet home, but—"

"He is coming," the second man said, beating his breast. "He was crossing the street when a runaway wagon—"

"—pulled by a horse," Ezra interrupted.

"—struck him," the other man finished. "Avidan did not look around the corner. An inexperienced youth was driving the wagon."

"Others have picked up the body." Ezra clasped his hands. "They are behind us and will arrive in a few moments."

The disjointed words came at me like enemy combatants, one after another, striking my head, my heart, my body. Paralysis invaded my limbs while confusion roared in my head.

By some miracle I managed to string words together: "I am sorry—did you say my husband is *dead*?"

The words had no sooner left my mouth than six men appeared in the street, carrying a man on a length of canvas. Avidan lay on that canvas, his eyes closed, a smear of blood across his forehead. A cloak lay over his body.

I folded at the knees, kneeling in my doorway as they laid my husband in our courtyard. I touched his skin, looked into his eyes, and saw that he was gone.

My husband . . . had left me. So had Sha'ul.

I was alone.

The realization struck with the force of a blow, but I could not let myself collapse. Other matters needed to be addressed, so I grasped the doorframe and pulled myself up, then stepped back and opened the door, allowing the men to bring Avidan into the house. They placed him on the table, where he could be prepared for burial.

"Thank you," I told the men who carried the body. They had paid a price for their kindness; they would be ceremonially unclean for seven days and unable to enter the Temple. "Thank you for this mitzvah," I whispered.

One of the men, an older fellow with a gray beard, stopped in the doorway. "Baruch dayan ha'emet." *Blessed be the true Judge . . .*

"Do you have someone to help you?" Ezra asked.

"I have a neighbor."

He shook his head. "Avidan was a good friend, so leave it to me. Do not be anxious. My wife and I will be sure you are looked after during this time. Baruch dayan ha'emet."

Without another word, the men departed, leaving me stunned, silent, and alone.

Widow

AD 35

THIRTY-ONE

Aya

I sat on a pillow in the house, my garment ripped at the neckline, and wondered why HaShem had abandoned me. He had removed me from my parents, then He had taken my brother and my husband. Even the choir, a joy that had been uniquely mine, had been ripped away.

Did Joseph feel like this when his brothers sold him to the slave traders? Did Job feel like this when HaShem took his health, his wealth, and his children?

Avidan and I had been cheated. HaShem had not given him an opportunity to state his last wishes or confess his sins. I did not sit by his bedside, hold his hand, and assure him of my love. I was not able to hear his last breath or place a feather on his lips.

Everyone had trials, but must all of them arrive at once? My brother should have been with me; he should have been comforting my fatherless boy. But Sha'ul was off in the desert, breaking bread with Gentiles and nattering about a false messiah. I could not even speak his name for fear it would leave a bad taste in my mouth. He would not know of Avidan's death for weeks, perhaps months.

"Baruch dayan ha'emet." Everyone who came to the house uttered these words. *Blessed be the true Judge. Everything from HaShem's hand is good.*

I could not accept it.

Several members of the hevra kadisha quietly went about the work of bathing and anointing Avidan for burial. Ezra, the man from the yeshiva, had summoned them for me. The women, most of whom were past childbearing age, murmured in low voices as they tenderly washed Avidan's broken body. One woman trimmed his hair and beard while another ran a twig under his fingernails and clipped his toenails.

The oldest woman sat next to me and quietly asked about Avidan's *kitel*, the white robe he wore on Shabbat and other holy days. I pointed to the chest where I kept it.

The women pulled a length of white linen from a basket. I watched as they gathered the seven parts of a man's burial garments: the linen face covering, pants, shirt, belt, the kitel, his prayer shawl, and the sheet. Because a shroud could have no seams, knots, or buttons, the belt was looped without knots. A corner of the fringe on his prayer shawl was cut off, deliberately rendering the shawl unfit for use, and the remnant placed in a fold, indicating that the bond of life had been severed.

A tear slipped from my eye as I watched. No longer would Avidan have to pray the morning, midday, and evening prayers. No longer would he have to observe all the commands in the Torah. No longer would he have to wash and tithe and do all the things a devout man spent his life doing.

But no longer would he come home and sweep me into his arms. No longer would he place his head in my lap and smile while he pretended to sleep. No longer would he kiss my forehead upon waking or trace the outline of my face just before he blew out the lamp and went to sleep.

I had not wanted to marry Avidan . . . and now I did not want to lose him. But HaShem did not give me a choice on either occasion.

The women worked swiftly because burial needed to take place on the morrow. The eldest woman sat beside me again and spoke in a firm, compassionate voice. "We will walk with you to the graveyard. We will grieve with you, so there is no need for you to hire mourners. We will call the flute players. We will make certain everything is done in accordance with the Law."

She gave me a sad smile. "We will remain with you through the seven days of mourning. Some of our members are preparing food, so you do not need to worry about feeding guests. All you need to do is take care of your baby and mourn your husband. We will do everything else."

I drew a deep breath, grateful she could not hear the thoughts in my head. I wanted to ask if she would spit on my brother for me. If she would curse him for abandoning us, for leaving his place in the Sanhedrin, and for following a false prophet. His betrayal had caused Avidan to feel the scorn of his fellow students. I had been forced out of the choir. Did Sha'ul not consider *us* when he decided to upend his life?

But this woman might not know anything about Sha'ul, so I thanked her for her kindness. "I am alone," I told her. "My husband and I came to Jerusalem so he could study under Gamaliel, and now I do not know what to do."

The woman took my hand. "You must ask HaShem for wisdom. You could go home to your parents. Or you could stay and raise your son in the Holy City. The Temple is wonderful, but you should find a synagogue. Become part of that family and allow the others to help you." Her voice softened. "Have you any way to earn a living? Do you sew or make cheese, or would you be willing to be a wet nurse? They are always in demand, and your son does not look old enough to be weaned."

I blinked, surprised by the idea. I had never considered

nursing another baby, but why not? I would not wean Seraiah for at least another year, so I could easily feed another child. Perhaps HaShem had extended a sliver of mercy to us by taking Avidan before I weaned my son.

"I have never considered it before, but I would be willing."

"You are fortunate." The woman released my hand. "As long as you have milk, you should be able to find employment. I will inquire among my friends. One of their daughters will likely need a wet nurse."

The woman looked around the house. "I do not know if being a wet nurse will provide enough to enable you to keep your home. How did your husband provide your living?"

My stomach dropped. Avidan's father had taken care of our financial needs, but would he continue to do so? Knowing Matan and Zara, they would want me to come back to Tarsus with their grandson. They would take over Seraiah's upbringing; they might even suggest that I return to my father's house and find another husband . . .

But going back to Tarsus would mean surrendering everything I had worked for: my home, my friends, my small status in this community. No, I realized, I could not return to the girl I used to be.

A sudden, fierce determination roared in my head. I would do almost anything to remain in this house. Avidan chose it, Seraiah was born in it, and I did not want to leave it. I had friends in Jerusalem. And though I would always love Tarsus, Avidan and I had created a new life in Jerusalem, and I would not abandon it.

I had been a mere child when I arrived in the Holy City. Now I was heartbroken and confused, though stronger than I had ever been.

I looked at the half-eaten pomegranate, the shoes by the door, the man-shaped tunics hanging on the wall. This was my home, mine and Seraiah's. I would do whatever I could to keep it.

I turned to the kind woman, who was waiting for an answer. "My husband's parents supported us," I said. "But I will pay the rent if I must. As long as HaShem is willing, I will find a way."

———•———

The answer came to me as my month of mourning ended. Sitting at my rickety table, I realized I had a skill that might allow me to earn a good living. I had used it once before, in Tarsus.

I could make my living with music.

I had learned much from Yosef, and singing in the Temple choir had strengthened my voice. Yosef used to remind us that the voice benefitted from regular exercise. The throat should be kept warm and lubricated with honey water, he insisted, and a singer should never shout or scream. *"Honor the gift HaShem gave you,"* he would say, pressing his hand to his chest. *"And treat it like the precious treasure it is."*

He had taught us how to do warm-up exercises—wordless melodies that rose and fell, skipping and jumping like a brook on its way to the sea. I began to sing the exercises as I cared for Seraiah and cleaned the house, even when I carried my water jars to the well. More than once I caught other women staring at me, but occasionally someone would smile and sing something in response, so I knew I was not the only woman who loved to make music.

I also began to *listen*. Eden offered to watch Seraiah whenever I needed help, so I would let him nap at her house so I could wander through the city streets. Whenever I heard the sound of a female singing, I would stop to listen. Many women were natural music makers. They sang lullabies to put their babies to sleep. They sang washing songs when they scrubbed laundry, and stomping songs for making wine. One woman sang a milking song every afternoon when she led her goat into her courtyard; another sang a gentle song as she embroidered garments for the marketplace. Women sang the psalms men sang at the Temple, and sometimes those songs sounded more beautiful when coming from a lamplit home.

After assuring myself that no one would think it shameful for a woman to sing or love music, I decided to make my availability known. I would teach music to children. I would also sing at banquets. Jerusalem was home to rich and poor, and the rich liked to entertain. I would need time to build a solid reputation, and I could work as a wet nurse until I needed to wean Seraiah. By that time, if HaShem willed, I would be available to sing more often.

I rested my head on my arms, grateful that I had found a way out of despair. I would revisit my childhood dream, only this time I would approach it more wisely. I would be circumspect in all things, I would sing only for devout Jews, and I would never mention my brother.

Perhaps, in time, I could crawl out from under the shadow Sha'ul had cast over our family.

I wrote my parents and Avidan's after his death, but two months passed before I received replies from Tarsus. The first letter came from my parents, who expressed their condolences about Avidan's passing and inquired about Seraiah's health. They did not mention coming to Jerusalem for the festivals, and I doubted their health would allow them to make the journey.

My father signed his letter with an assurance of his love, then reminded me that I could always bring Seraiah and live in Tarsus. "Our home will belong to Sha'ul one day," he wrote, "and I know he would be happy to let you live here. He certainly has no intention of settling in one place."

That was his only mention of my brother, and I wondered if he knew about Sha'ul's decision to join those who followed the Way. I had not been able to muster the courage to tell him of the rumors, but someone else might. While Tarsus might be far away, rumors had wings.

The second letter was from Matan, Avidan's father. The first paragraphs were a lament for a dearly loved and only begotten son, then the merchant shifted to a more practical tone.

"Zara and I long to see you and our grandson," he wrote, "but we also long to know that Seraiah will follow in his father's footsteps. We have decided to offer you a choice: you may return to Tarsus and live with us, where we will see to all the child's needs, or he may remain with you in Jerusalem on the condition that he enter Gamaliel's yeshiva at age ten. If you choose to remain in Jerusalem, we will continue to pay the expenses for your home. If Seraiah does not enter the yeshiva by the accepted time, or if you choose to remarry, we will cease to pay. We believe this is a fair arrangement. Please let us know your decision. Shalom and love to you and the boy."

I lowered the scroll, relieved that we could keep our house. But because Matan had provided far more than rent, I would be responsible for our food, clothing, and everything else.

At least we would not have to move. Agreeing to the bargain was easy—I felt certain Seraiah could enter Gamaliel's yeshiva at the appropriate time, and until then I would teach him the stories of the Tanakh and how to read and write. I would make certain Avidan's son was properly educated.

The corner of my mouth twisted when I considered Matan's stipulation about remarriage. I was barely twenty-one, young enough to remarry and have children, but would anyone even want me? If Sha'ul's betrayal was enough to have me removed from the women's choir, it would also be enough to keep any of my acquaintances from trying to match me with a suitable husband.

I took parchment and a quill from my trunk, then sat and dipped my quill in ink. I would write my father-in-law and accept his offer. I would assure him that Seraiah would be well educated at home and under Gamaliel, if HaShem willed.

HaShem had wounded me deeply, but I still lived. I had a son. I had a voice. And I had hope that one day I would understand what I was meant to do with my life.

Perhaps my purpose had little to do with Avidan or music but centered on my son. As a result of my teaching and devoted prayers, he might rise to be a great scholar, a Torah teacher, a high priest . . . or even the Messiah.

If that was HaShem's will, I could only beg Him to equip me for the task.

The old woman from the hevra kadisha had not forgotten me. Three months after Avidan's death, I received a message. "I have spoken to my daughter, Mayah," she wrote. "She has just given birth to a baby girl and desires a wet nurse, since she has five other children who occupy her time. She and her husband will bring the baby to your home with a contract. If all is agreeable, sign and be well. They will pay you handsomely, and this should ease some of your anxiety."

Since the woman had not specified when her daughter would arrive, I embarked on a flurry of housecleaning. I had never known a wet nurse and wasn't sure what would be expected of me. The contract, I presumed, would detail my responsibilities.

The next day, right after I put Seraiah down for a nap, someone hailed me from the courtyard gate. I opened the door and saw a man and woman with an infant. Their highly embroidered clothing assured me they were wealthy enough to afford a wet nurse.

"Mayah?" I asked.

The woman nodded. "This is Etan, my husband. Our baby is called Ionanna."

I invited them in and offered them a seat while I smiled and tried to look wholesome.

"My mother," Mayah began, "told me you would make an excellent wet nurse. If you are willing, I would have you nurse Ionanna for several months."

"I would be happy to."

Etan pulled a parchment from his robe. "Here is the contract. Read it over and let me know if it is agreeable to you."

I took the parchment and spread it on the table.

Aya, widow of Avidan, agrees that she will for eighteen months bring up and suckle in her own house in Jerusalem, with her own milk pure and uncontaminated, the infant daughter of Etan and Mayah. For this service to the child Ionanna, Aya will receive from Etan each month as payment for her milk and care, two silver shekels besides olive oil. Aya has duly received from Etan for the agreed eighteen months, wages for nine months adding up to eighteen shekels. If the child chances to die within this time and Mayah gives birth again, Aya will take up the other child and nurse it and suckle it, receiving no wages, since she has undertaken to nurse continually. She will provide her monthly care honestly and take fitting thought for the child, not damaging her milk, not lying with a man, not conceiving, and not taking another child to suckle apart from her own son.

I read the document twice, then looked at the couple. "Does this mean you will give me eighteen shekels today?"

Etan pulled a purse from his robe. "You will receive the balance at the end of eighteen months, if you return the child to us healthy and strong."

I studied the parchment again, almost unable to believe my good fortune. Eighteen shekels was the equivalent of seventy-two sheep or seventy-two days of labor. With that amount set aside, plus olive oil . . .

I glanced at Etan. "How much olive oil?"

He shrugged. "One hin every month?"

Mayah smiled. "My husband owns the olive press at Gethsemane."

I nodded. "I agree. Let me fetch the ink."

Etan stood while I brought a quill and ink from my trunk, then both of us signed our names.

"You may keep the document," Etan said, handing it to me. "Would you allow my wife to visit on occasion? She is fond of the child."

"Of course." I gave Mayah a reassuring smile. "You may come anytime."

Mayah stood. "My mother mentioned that you have a son."

"Seraiah." Smiling, I gestured to the spot where he slept. "He is eighteen months old."

"Well . . ." Mayah held out her arms, and I took the child. The pink-cheeked baby was sweet, and I wondered how Mayah could let her go. But some women had trouble nursing, and if that was the case, I understood why Mayah didn't want to speak of it. No woman wanted to admit she could not feed her child.

I nestled the little girl in my arms and crooned a line of a lullaby. "You sing well," Mayah said, her eyes filling with tears. "I am glad Ima told me about you."

"The praise goes to HaShem," I answered, meaning every word. "Your baby will be a blessing to me and my son."

THIRTY-TWO

Aya

On the second anniversary of my husband's death, I peered into the looking brass and wondered if Avidan would still recognize me. At twenty and three, I was not the girl I had been when we married, nor was I the naïve wife he had loved. I was a mother now, a widow, and a woman determined to persevere despite everything HaShem had thrown at me. Those roles had erased the softness around my eyes and tightened the lines at my mouth. Seraiah and I were surviving, and yet life was not easy.

My eighteen months as a wet nurse had been both a joy and a trial. Ionanna was a delight and grew into a sweet toddling child who loved to follow Seraiah and play with him in the courtyard. Her mother visited on the first day of every week, and whenever she left, I noted the pain of parting in her eyes and told myself I'd be feeling the same pain soon enough.

And I did. When the contract ended and Mayah and Etan came to pay the money they owed me, I gave their daughter back with great reluctance. Ionanna cried and reached for me.

I turned away, knowing she would take a little part of my heart as she went.

Seraiah cried, too. He didn't understand why she had to go, and I didn't know how to explain that she did not belong to us. Grateful that this particular chapter in my life had ended, I rocked him until he cried himself to sleep.

With no more babies to care for, I focused on becoming a music teacher. On the first day of every week, *Yom Rishon*, I taught a group of children, including three-year-old Seraiah, how to sing and play the harp. The next day, *Yom Sheni*, I taught a group of boys how to blow shofars. On *Yom Shlishi*, I directed a female choir; the ten women met in my house, and I did my best to teach them the notations in the psalms and the corresponding hand signals. Though we made no plans to perform, occasionally I looked out the window and saw that people had stopped on the street to listen.

Yom Rev'i brought the children who wanted to blow a trumpet or flute. Most of these were boys who hoped to play in the Temple, but several were girls who simply enjoyed making music. *Yom Chamishi* brought the percussionists—girls and boys who wanted to strike cymbals, bells, tambourines, or sistra. These were the most enthusiastic pupils, as anyone could strike or shake an instrument. The challenge lay in teaching them to strike or shake in *unison*.

I devoted the sixth day, *Yom Shishi*, to the harp, lute, and psaltery. This was the smallest class, and these instruments the most difficult to master. My students began with the harp, moved to the lute, and then attempted the psaltery with its twelve strings and quill. Even I struggled with the psaltery, and only one of my students felt inclined to attempt it.

On *Yom Shabbat*, Seraiah and I rested. After the string students left, we watched the sun set, and then I lit the Shabbat candles. We would eat the evening meal and go to bed, then wake to a sweet day of silence and rest. Sometimes Seraiah would recite the alphabet or retell a Bible story I'd taught him. I would tell him about Avidan and emphasize that he had been a gentle and gracious man and a doting father. I reminded Seraiah of how Avidan loved him, and that he would want Seraiah to study diligently, because Avidan knew no greater joy than studying the truths of HaShem.

I still mourned my husband, yet the wise ones were right—the pain *did* lessen as time passed. I missed watching him study, hearing his laughter, and watching him gaze at Seraiah, who had been cast in his image. I missed being enfolded in his arms and rubbing my cheek against his beard as I kissed him good morning.

But between teaching and caring for Seraiah, life was busy enough that I did not often reflect upon everything I missed.

Because Seraiah was young and had trouble standing still, when we visited the Temple Mount, I often took him by the hand and walked the length and breadth of the Court of the Women. Four small chambers had been built off the women's court, one in each corner. Levites often held meetings in these rooms, and several times I heard snippets of conversation as Seraiah and I walked by.

One morning, as we walked past the Chamber of Oils, I overheard someone say that Lucius Vitellius planned to depose Caiaphas and replace him with his brother Jonathan. I had no idea who Lucius Vitellius was, but the name was Roman. I smiled at the news because I had not forgiven Caiaphas for blotting Sha'ul's name from the records of the Sanhedrin.

On another occasion I overheard a conversation about the high priest's vestments. For years the Romans had maintained control over those sacred garments, locking them away in the Fortress Antonia, except for when they were needed for Yom Kippur. To win favor with the people, Vitellius was planning to return the sacred garments to the high priest.

Hearing about the Fortress Antonia made me think of

Claudius Lysias. Was he still in charge of the Fortress or had he been transferred to another post? I had no idea.

I learned many things while walking near those meeting rooms, and while such information proved interesting, it was not particularly useful. I no longer had a husband who might benefit from such knowledge, and my brother seemed to have forgotten about Jerusalem. My friends, all women, cared more about how to raise their children than hearing gossip about people in exalted positions.

In truth, I missed having men in my life. I missed reading the Torah to Avidan and discussing the Oral Torah with him. I missed arguing with Sha'ul. I missed his brilliance, his stubbornness, his boldness, and his overweening confidence. Despite the rumors, I missed almost everything about him.

He was my brother, and as far as I knew, he still lived. On many a sleepless night I went to the table and penned a letter to my absent sibling. I told him about my day, my work, and my rapidly growing son. I described how difficult life had become and confessed that I resented him for turning against his own people. "If Yeshua was the Messiah," I wrote, "then why are we not delivered from our enemies? Why do the Romans still patrol our streets and appoint our high priest?"

Many nights I poured out my heart, and many mornings I tossed my letter into the cook fire. After sunset, when the air cooled and my heart softened, it was easy to pretend that Sha'ul and I were not walking different paths. But in the hard light of day, when I hugged the little boy Sha'ul had vowed to protect, reality burst my dream like a bubble.

I never sent any of those letters . . . I never knew where to send them.

Truth be told, I missed my brother desperately. Not the new Sha'ul, not the one who ate with Gentiles and walked with followers of Yeshua, but the brother who had encouraged me with my music, the one who used to sit at my table and debate

Avidan over arcane aspects of the Law. I missed his snapping eyes and his way of weaseling through a crowd. I missed the way he talked to Seraiah, as if my son were an adult. I missed having him nearby, because for so many years life had kept us in separate cities. Most of all, I missed him because Sha'ul was one of the few men who actually *listened* to me.

But four years after Yeshua's execution, another Passover approached, and along with it, a new rumor: my brother had returned to Damascus and was planning to come to Jerusalem for the festival.

Eden brought me the news, and I listened to her report with mixed feelings. Would Sha'ul attempt to see me? If he knocked on our door, should I let him in?

I had already suffered on his account. If I welcomed him into my home, I could lose my music students.

"What will you do?" she asked, concern knitting her brow.

I shook my head. "I do not know, but one thing is certain: as a woman who owes her livelihood to Law-abiding Jews, I cannot seek him out."

THIRTY-THREE

Sha'ul

I entered Jerusalem alone and under cover of darkness, arriving just before the guards closed the mighty gates. I was fortunate to find a room at an inn, so I settled down without attracting attention.

The next morning, I broke my fast with bread and cheese, then sought the Spirit's guidance about what to do next. My feet itched to travel familiar streets and visit places I had not seen in years, but the saving grace of second thought constrained me. I knew too many people in Jerusalem, and too many people knew me. Travelers to Damascus had told me that those who followed Yeshua were still being persecuted in the Holy City, though not as ardently as before.

For that I had only myself to blame. If my love for HaShem had been as fervent as my love for the Law, I might not have made so many mistakes.

When I felt the gentle nudge of the Spirit, I threw my mantle over my shoulder and went outside, heading toward the Temple Mount. I did not know if any of Yeshua's disciples still preached in the outer courtyard, yet I hoped to see one of my old friends from the yeshiva. They might know where Yeshua's disciples could be found.

I entered the Court of the Gentiles and beheld the Holy Place towering above the Gate of Nicanor. My heart used to fill with pride whenever I glimpsed HaShem's dwelling place, but at that moment I felt a curious emptiness. HaShem no longer lived here, but in the hearts of men. The Shekinah glory departed generations ago, and all that remained were a series of sacrifices and prescribed festivals. Those rituals had painted a picture for Israel; they had pointed the way, but we had been so focused on the details that we failed to see the larger picture.

We failed to grasp the meaning behind the Scriptures we had been studying for years.

I crossed the Court of the Gentiles and entered through the Beautiful Gate, where I could see through the Court of the Women into the sanctuary. The priests were lighting the incense as a male choir sang a psalm of ascent.

Emptiness.

"'I hate, I despise your festivals!'" I whispered, quoting the prophet Amos. "'I take no delight in your sacred assemblies. Even if you offer me burnt offerings and your grain offerings, I will not accept them, nor will I look at peace offerings of your fattened animals. Take away from Me the noise of your songs! I will not listen to the melody of your harps . . .'"

I turned, and in that instant I saw Simon Peter, the man who had stood before the Sanhedrin. By an act of HaShem, he was walking alone, with no one to distract him.

I ran after him.

The Ruach HaKodesh must have prepared Peter for my appearance because he did not seem surprised to see me. "Sha'ul," he said, his brows lifting. "You are here."

"I would like to speak to you."

"And I you." He looked around for a moment, then smiled. "You have been preaching in Damascus?"

I laughed. "I barely escaped that city with my life. My enemies were watching the city gates to waylay and kill me, so friends lowered me in a basket through an opening in the wall."

Peter snorted. "You are fortunate! I would never fit into a basket." He clapped his hand on my shoulder. "My wife would be happy to prepare a meal for us, and we have a comfortable guest room. Please come. I would like to hear about your work in Damascus . . . and what did I hear about your time in Arabia?"

"Ah, that is quite a story." I went with him, walking double time to keep pace with his long stride.

THIRTY-FOUR

Aya

A man from Tarsus, visiting Jerusalem for Pesach, stopped by my house to present me with a letter. The message had been written in Matan's hand, so I suspected he was sending his regrets for not attending the festival.

Grief struck like a blow to the belly when I read his news:

Aya, Widow of Avidan, Jerusalem:

I am sorry to have to tell you that your beloved parents have passed away. Last month a strange and virulent fever raced through the Jewish sector, and many of our people were taken ill. The old and weak were stricken, and many of them, including your parents, succumbed quickly.

We buried them in accordance with the Law and closed up the house. The man who managed your father's business will continue his work until Sha'ul takes possession of the estate. I do not know where to reach your brother, but if you encounter him, or know where he can be reached, please share these sad tidings.

Shalom. Baruch dayan ha'emet.
This is also for the good.

> *Love to you and many*
> *blessings to Seraiah,*

> *Matan*

I sank to a bench as a new anguish seared my heart. Though I had not seen my parents in seven years, the many letters traveling from Tarsus to Jerusalem assured me they were still part of my life. I had always looked forward to Ima's news about the city of my youth, and I enjoyed responding with stories of Seraiah's first word, first step, and first prayer. In a city where I was one woman among thousands, their letters allowed me to rest in the knowledge that my parents still adored me.

Now they were no longer within my reach, and their house belonged to Sha'ul. I had no idea what he would do with the estate once he learned it was his.

Baruch dayan ha'emet, Matan had written. *Blessed be the true Judge.*

I would now begin my time of mourning. A week to sit shiva and eleven months to observe sheloshim, the mourning period for parents. As long as I mourned, I would not wear festive clothing, make music for my own pleasure, or go out for social visits. Instead, I would sit in my house, remember my parents, and weep, with no one but Seraiah for company.

THIRTY-FIVE

Sha'ul

I spent two weeks and a day with Simon Peter. I listened to his stories about walking and talking with Yeshua, and he asked many questions about my experience on the road to Damascus. Then he asked about my work in the Kingdom of Nabataea, also known as Provincia Arabia. Did I, he asked, require those who accepted Yeshua to be circumcised and follow the Law?

"No," I answered, "because the Law cannot save."

Peter did not dispute me, but pressed a finger to his lips. "The brothers have questions about this, and we are not sure what to do about the Gentiles."

"The Spirit will show us what should be done," I said. "But we must not let any disagreement stop us from spreading the Gospel. Did Yeshua not say we were to share the news in Judea, Samaria, and the uttermost parts of the earth?"

"He did." Peter smiled. "And I believe my wife has invited a special guest for dinner. Come, let us go into the dining hall."

We went into the next room, where the tables had been spread with eggs, cheese, roasted chicken, barley cakes, and stuffed grape leaves. Pitchers of honey water stood on trays, and a young girl stood ready to serve us.

"My daughter," Peter said, gesturing to the girl. "And my wife."

Another woman, who clearly resembled Peter's daughter, entered and gave me a hesitant smile.

"This is a feast," I said, nodding at Peter's wife. "Thank you for your hospitality."

I looked up when a stranger entered the room. He was not as tall as Peter but had dark hair, a beard, and tanned flesh. Yet there was something about the eyes . . . and an instant later I realized why they looked familiar. "You look like Him," I said, marveling. "You have His eyes."

"Sha'ul"—Peter gestured to the man—"meet James, Yeshua's younger brother. He is the leader of the *ecclēsia* in Jerusalem."

James held out his arms, and I stepped into them, grateful that HaShem had granted me the honor of meeting someone who had grown up with my Lord. Tears had filled my eyes by the time I stepped away. "I am happy to meet you, brother."

"And I you," he said, his voice reminding me of Yeshua again. "I have heard many things about your work. Your experience and faith have impressed many in Jerusalem."

"But not everyone, hmm?"

James smiled. "People have long memories. Some of them cannot forget that not so long ago you dragged many of our brothers and sisters to prison."

"I can only beg their forgiveness. Yeshua has forgiven me."

"They will, too, I am certain. But first they must be convinced of your sincerity."

We ate, talked, and shared our hopes for the continued spread of the Gospel. James told us about the new high priest and the relaxed attitude of Lucius Vitellius, the new Roman procurator. Peter discussed plans about an upcoming trip to

Lydda, where many believers had gone after the persecution in Jerusalem.

"What you did was part of HaShem's plan," Peter said, reclining on a dining couch. "Though many of our community fled during the persecution, many others heard the Gospel as believers settled in new cities."

James lifted his cup. "Tell me—you have a sister in Jerusalem, do you not?"

I lowered my head, embarrassed by my neglect. "Aya. She is married to a student at Gamaliel's yeshiva."

James shook his head. "I am sorry to share bad news, but she is now a widow. Her husband died almost three years ago."

My heart twisted. "And? What became of Aya and her son?"

"She lives in the same house," James said. "She teaches music to earn her living. Some of the brothers send their children to her."

I exhaled in relief that she had not left the city. "Has she remarried?"

"I do not believe so." The lines around James's eyes crinkled as he smiled. "You should go see her."

"I will, but I have not written her since leaving Jerusalem."

"You should go," James said, his expression turning serious. "Never forget, Yeshua loves your sister, too."

Because the Spirit had nudged me through James, I knew I had to make one more visit before I could leave Jerusalem.

I said farewell to Peter's family and stopped by the marketplace to buy something for Seraiah. I had no idea what he liked, but since he was nearly old enough for school, I bought him a wax tablet and stylus.

I walked to the lower city, where the stone-brick houses crowded together on the sloping street. My steps slowed when I passed the house I had shared with Bettina. The exterior had not changed, but through the open window I could see bread loaves on a table and a young boy writing on a pottery shard. I breathed a prayer of gratitude.

When I lived in that house, my feet had been mired in a rutted road of my own choosing, but HaShem lifted me out. I no longer had a wife, son, or home, but at least I knew what HaShem had called me to do.

I continued up the street, toward the house Aya had shared with Avidan. That building had not changed either, though the courtyard was filled with young boys, each holding a small ram's horn.

I should have known.

"Shalom." I nodded to the children, opened the gate, and knocked. I was grateful when Aya did not answer immediately—I needed a moment to arrange my face in placid lines so she would not see the yearning that had abruptly gripped me.

Odd that meeting my sister could make me more anxious than facing a hundred angry Jews. Did she hate me? Would she slam the door in my face? Had I lost the affection of my only sibling?

A wave of nostalgia rose within me, and all at once I felt the sting of losing Avidan. We had spent so many nights sharing a meal and studying Torah. Together, Avidan and I had explored the sacred traditions and hotly debated whether or not breaking a stalk of wheat with one hand on Shabbat was considered harvesting and therefore a violation of the Law. In this city, perhaps in homes not far from me, other young men were debating similar questions, focusing their energy on minuscule points of the Law while they missed the miracle of what HaShem had done through Yeshua.

What did such rules matter? My spirit groaned at the thought of Avidan dying without realizing how blind we had been. The prophets spoke of Yeshua so clearly; every writer of the Scriptures had pointed to Him. The truth had been revealed in patterns and parables, although in His unfathomable will, HaShem had hidden it from so many of us.

HaShem had also given me this opportunity to share the Gospel with Aya, so I would not squander it. I knocked again.

I heard the sound of movement within, then the door opened. I caught my breath—my sister had matured while I was away. Her eyes were sharper now, her lips fuller, her figure more rounded. Lines had appeared in her cheeks and forehead, and those lines deepened when she realized who had come to visit.

"Sha'ul." She did not sound especially pleased to see me.

I gestured to the tablet in my hand. "I have brought a gift for Seraiah."

She hesitated, then stepped back to let me enter.

The little boy at the table looked nothing like the baby I had known. He stared at me with Aya's dark eyes. His nose was Avidan's, while his lips appeared to be his own.

I smiled and offered him the wax tablet and stylus. "For you, Seraiah, from your uncle Sha'ul. For when you attend bet soper."

The boy looked at his mother, who nodded. He took the tablet, picked up the stylus, and drew a perfect *bet* on the wax.

"You have learned already." I smiled. "You are very bright, just like your ima and abba."

Aya gave me a tight smile. "Thank you for the gift." She moved toward the table. "Would you like something to drink?" Her voice was as cool as spring water.

"Yes, thank you."

I sat next to Seraiah at the table. "I am sorry I have been away so long," I said, folding my hands. "I was grieved to hear about Avidan. I know you miss him."

She kept her back to me as she poured water into two cups. "What brings you to Jerusalem?"

"The Ruach HaKodesh. I have seen the light, Aya. I have seen Yeshua."

She turned, showing her teeth in an expression that was not a smile. "I have heard many rumors about you, Sha'ul, and each of them pierced my heart like a blade. How could you turn your back upon all you have been taught? I can only hope our parents did not hear the rumors before they went to their graves."

I stared, stunned by the sudden flash of vehemence.

"Yes," she said, reading the astonishment on my face. "Two weeks ago I received a letter from my father-in-law. Our parents are dead, and the estate is yours."

I shook my head, stunned. "How?"

"A contagion. Apparently, it took the older people in great numbers."

I buried my face in my hands. I was hoping to preach the Gospel in Tarsus. I had wanted to tell my parents about Yeshua, about all that happened to convince me that HaShem had called me to be an emissary to the Gentiles . . .

"Baruch dayan ha'emet," Aya said, setting a cup of water before me. "This is also for the good."

"You mean—"

"It is a good thing our parents died before hearing about your betrayal. Matan did not mention it to me, so I do not think they knew."

I shook my head. "HaShem is the true Judge, but this is not what I would have wanted." I tore the neckline of my tunic. "Baruch dayan ha'emet."

"At least you have not forgotten everything you learned." Aya sat across from me, her eyes large and fierce, and for a long moment the only sounds came from the boys in the courtyard.

Then Aya flushed to the roots of her hair. "How could you, Sha'ul? How could you think only of yourself?"

I looked up, bewildered. "What?"

"Once the word of your betrayal reached Jerusalem, Avidan was scorned in his yeshiva. I was told to leave the choir. Several of our neighbors no longer speak to me—only Eden remains a friend."

"I-I am sorry," I stammered. "I did not realize . . ."

"Well." She looked away. "Now you know."

"But, Aya . . ." I prayed for wisdom, for words to reach my sister. "I know you must have been dumbfounded by the reports, but I came face-to-face with Yeshua! He is our Messiah, the only begotten of HaShem. He appeared to me on the way to Damascus. I was struck blind, made helpless, and forced to depend on the kindness of others. But He restored my sight, and I have committed my life to spreading the Good News. The Law should be our teacher, not our master—Yeshua is Lord! He lives, His Spirit guides and teaches us, and He has given us the gift of eternal life."

Unmoved, Aya sipped from her cup.

"Have you nothing to say?"

She heaved a sigh. "I met a prophetess," she said. "The woman said I would meet Yeshua. I do not know how that could be possible."

"Truly?"

Aya shrugged. "I do not believe her. Yeshua is as dead as Avidan, as dead as our parents. You may have seen something on that road, but it was probably because you had walked too long in the hot sun. You exchanged one obsession for another, Sha'ul, and now you are doing what you have always done—trying to be the best at your new endeavor."

"Aya, I—"

"It would have been better for us if on the road to Damascus you had died from sunstroke."

I stared wordlessly across the table, stunned by Aya's bluntness. She was no longer the soft, yielding sister who used to gaze at me with admiration. This was someone else altogether.

"Now," she said, standing, "I have students waiting. Thank you for coming, and do not forget us. Since he has no father,

I want Seraiah to know his uncle. As you leave, please tell the boys outside to come in."

I struggled to speak over the lump that had risen in my throat. "Do you need anything? Do you have enough to eat?"

"We need nothing from you," she said. "Thank you, and shalom."

Lord, what have I done?

I moved toward the door, then took another long look at my younger sister and nephew. When would I see them again? Only HaShem knew, but until that time I would diligently pray that they would be saved . . . and I would be forgiven.

THIRTY-SIX

Aya

I watched Sha'ul walk out of the house, then turned away as my students poured into the room. I needed a moment to sort through my thoughts. I needed a moment to grieve, think, and cry, but I could not take that moment now. I had students who wanted to learn, and I had to teach. But afterward, when the house was quiet and Seraiah slept, I would weep for my brother, for the relationship we once had and would never have again. His new mission would stand between us for the rest of our lives.

How could he have seen Yeshua? The experience he described had been simple sunstroke; I had seen men stricken by it before. They fell, light-headed and pale, they trembled, and sounds became amplified while the world turned into a white-hot blur.

I no longer considered my brother the most brilliant man in the world; he was the most foolish. After jailing so many Jewish followers of Yeshua, perhaps his conscience rebelled—what better way to absolve himself than by joining their movement? He might have adopted new beliefs, but he was still the over-achieving, confident, dominant man I had known all my life.

Now he would undoubtedly go to Tarsus to settle our parents' estate. Would he keep the house? Would he sell the business? I had no idea, and I did not care. A generous brother might offer me a share in the proceeds, but I would not expect a single farthing.

Then I would not be disappointed.

I pasted on a smile and turned to the boys, who had taken their places on the bench against the wall. "Who can play the three sounds of the shofar for me? Hosea? Are you ready?"

The youth lifted his horn, and I crossed my arms to listen.

* * *

One afternoon I stepped outside and saw Eden sitting in her courtyard, her face lifted toward the sun. Golden beams glimmered on her olive skin as her lips moved soundlessly. I knew she was praying when a tear slid from her closed eyes and trickled over her cheek.

I waited until she had finished her prayers, then called her name.

Her sightless eyes opened, and she turned toward me. "Shalom," she said, her voice brimming with warmth. "I was hoping to speak to you today."

I remembered her tears. "Is something wrong?"

She smiled. "Something is always wrong somewhere, but HaShem has provided an answer. And that is what I wanted to tell you."

Intrigued, I moved closer to the low wall that separated our courtyards. "I'm listening."

She drew a deep breath. "I understand now . . . and I, too, have become a follower of Yeshua. And though I cannot be dissuaded from my choice, I do not want this to come between us. You have already lost a brother. I do not want to lose a friend."

Shocked into speechlessness, I finally managed to find my tongue. "How could you?"

"I know," she said, smiling. "I was not expecting it, either. But I was talking to a woman at the pool, and she explained the Scriptures to me. Remember the story of Israel's first battle? Our forefathers had just left Egypt, and Amalek came against us."

"Of course I remember."

"I knew you would. Joshua led our fighters into battle while Moses climbed a hill. When he held up his hands, Israel prevailed. But when he wearied and his hands fell, the Amalekites prevailed."

"So Aaron and Hur went up to support Moses' hands," I finished. "But I do not understand how that has anything to do with Yeshua and—"

"Wait." A smile played around her lips. "The Hebrew says, 'So Moses' hands were *faith* until the sun went down.' His hands were truth, for those who believed."

I dropped onto the courtyard bench. "I do not see any connection."

Eden rested her arm on the wall between us. "Think about what the fighters must have seen when they looked toward that hill—even a blind woman knows they saw a man with his arms outstretched, like a man hanging on an execution stake."

I shook my head, still not understanding. "So?"

"It happened again when our people sinned and HaShem sent poisonous serpents among them. When the people begged for mercy, God told Moses to mount a snake upon a pole. Whoever was dying from snakebite had only to look at it and be healed. Again, our people were saved through faith as they looked at an execution stake."

I crossed my arms, bewildered and slightly irritated. I had heard these stories since childhood but could not understand why my friend had become enthralled by them. "I know the Scriptures, Eden, and—"

"One more thing," she interrupted. "When Yeshua lived

among us, Nicodemus, a member of the Sanhedrin, went to
visit him. Yeshua told him, 'Just as Moses lifted up the serpent
in the desert, so the Son of Man must be lifted up, so that whoever believes in Him may have eternal life.' Yeshua was lifted up,
too, Aya—on an execution stake. Ever since the days of Moses,
HaShem has been telling us to look at a cross . . . with faith."

She smiled at me, her unseeing eyes filled with hope, her
smile brimming with joy. But I could not see hope in a bloody
cross, nor did I want to build my life around an execution stake.

Yet I loved my friend and did not want to lose her.

"Believe what you will," I finally told her. "I will remain your
friend as long as you are willing to speak to me."

Days rolled into weeks, weeks into months, and months into
years. Seraiah entered his seventh year, and I continued teaching
him at home. I sent regular reports of his progress to Matan
so my father-in-law would know I was giving his grandson a
solid education.

My older students matured, and a few were employed at the
Temple as flautists or trumpeters. One young man, Alexander,
became proficient with the shofar. I stood in the Court of the
Women and basked in a glow of pleasure when he blew the
ram's horn for Yom Kippur.

Three years after my visit with Sha'ul, Jerusalem faced a
different nightmare, this time from Rome. The emperor, Gaius
Julius Caesar, more commonly known as Caligula, declared
himself a divine being. We were accustomed to Roman emper-
ors being worshiped after their deaths, but Caligula was the first
emperor to declare himself divine while living. Furthermore, he
ordered that a gilded statue of himself be placed in every house
of worship throughout the Empire, including synagogues and
the Jerusalem Temple.

Publius Petronius, the Roman governor of Syria, knew

we Jews would rather die than allow a pagan statue to defile our holy Temple. Petronius, aided by Herod Agrippa, began a quiet campaign to dissuade the emperor, but was unsuccessful.

That year we celebrated Hanukkah under a cloud of foreboding, because no one, not even Theophilus, the current high priest, had been able to convince Caligula to exclude the Jews from his edict.

Every day I heard rumors and reports on the dire situation. As I waited by the Pool of Siloam with my water jars, one woman proclaimed that the Roman army was already en route and had been ordered to kill any man, woman, or child who opposed the emperor's edict.

Another woman remarked that her husband was convinced HaShem would use the situation to reveal our Messiah, who would rise up and destroy Rome.

Eden quietly told me that believers in Yeshua were praying and fasting for the peace of Jerusalem. Because Caligula's actions mirrored those of Antiochus Epiphanes, who had desecrated the Temple during the time of the Maccabees, many of their leaders were convinced these events would bring about Yeshua's return and the end of days.

I did not know what to believe. Every night I prayed that Seraiah and I would be safe. As the days passed, I often climbed onto the roof and searched the western horizon for signs of an approaching army.

One day, after I finished the midday prayers, a sudden thought occurred: I knew an important Roman. When the emperor's legions arrived, Claudius Lysias would certainly play a pivotal role. Surely he knew how far the army had progressed on their march to Jerusalem. Messengers were always riding through the gates of the Fortress Antonia, so Claudius had to know when the Romans would arrive.

If I could find the courage to approach the Fortress, perhaps he would be willing to grant safe passage to me and Seraiah. Once we were safely out of the city, we could flee to Tarsus.

At first, the idea seemed crazy, even to me. No Jewish woman would seek an audience with a Roman official; the notion was unthinkable.

But if I did nothing to protect my son, who would? I had no husband. My bold brother, who would approach a monster without fear, was lost to me. My father, who had held some sway with the Roman officials in Tarsus, was dead.

So why not approach Claudius? I *knew* him. We were not exactly friends, but he had spoken kindly to me on two occasions and had never said or done anything to sully my reputation.

The idea niggled at my brain for a week. I listened intently to the rumors, hoping to hear that the Roman army had been diverted or that Petronius had persuaded the emperor to show mercy on Jerusalem, but the reports continued to be worrisome. Apparently, Herod Agrippa had nearly convinced Caligula to cancel his plans for the Temple, but then the emperor had a change of heart and ordered Petronius to do two things: install the statue in the Jewish Temple and then kill himself.

After hearing *that* report, I went to see Eden and asked what she thought about my plan to visit Claudius Lysias.

She gasped. "Why would you want to enter the Roman fortress?"

"Because I want my son to live." I clasped my hands. "Your son should live, too. Claudius will know what is happening with the Roman army, and he could get us out of the city before they barricade the gates."

She pressed her hand to her forehead. "And you *know* this man?"

"Not well," I admitted. "But I have met him twice. He has always been kind and respectful."

"But why would he speak to you? I have never heard a Roman officer speak kindly to any Jewish woman."

"I do not believe he thinks of me as a Jewish woman. He thinks of me as a singer . . . and he likes my music."

Her eyes widened. "Are you saying a Roman officer attended a Jewish banquet?"

"Not exactly. A Jewish woman sang for a Gentile banquet. In Tarsus, not Jerusalem."

She arched a brow. "You are full of secrets, my friend."

"But should I do it? And if I do, do you want me to include your family?"

Eden bit her lower lip, then nodded. "My husband would not like it, but when the Romans appear on the horizon, he may have a change of heart."

THIRTY-SEVEN

Aya

I dressed carefully for my meeting with the Roman, choosing my best tunic, a colorful mantle, and a modest head covering. I did not want him to see me as a widow looking for pity but as an acquaintance who needed help.

I left Seraiah at Eden's house and set out for the Fortress Antonia. The imposing structure had been built adjacent to the Temple—undoubtedly to intimidate us—and was rumored to hold one thousand legionaries. In times of peace, the soldiers seemed to enjoy our Holy City, but in times of strife, they looked at us as if we were vermin.

Most of the men at the Antonia were not Roman—they were auxiliaries, men from the region who agreed to fight for Rome in exchange for wages and Roman citizenship. I knew of no Jews who would willingly join the army that oppressed us with taxes, regulations, and forced servitude, but hundreds of Syrians and Nabateans enlisted. Auxiliaries, Avidan had once told me, offered Rome an advantage because they knew the land and its people better than nonnative soldiers did.

I approached the Fortress with my heart in my throat, then

stepped back as a pair of men on horseback cantered through the gate. When I was certain I would not be trampled, I pulled my head covering more tightly around my hair and walked over to the guards.

"Shalom," I said, offering them a polite smile. "I would like to speak to Claudius Lysias."

The tallest guard gaped at me. "And who are you?"

"I am called Aya . . . if he does not remember my name, mention that I am a singer."

The guard elbowed his companion. "Has the commander ever asked about a singer?"

"Not to my knowledge." The second man waved me away. "Be off, woman. The tribune is a busy man."

"Please. It is important that I speak to him. If you give him my name and mention Tarsus, I am sure he will agree to see me."

The guards looked at each other. "What do you think?"

The second man shrugged, then glared at me. "I'll go, but if he tells me he's never heard of you, you'll be doing our wash, you hear?"

I lifted my chin. "He will not say that."

The second guard ambled away, muttering under his breath. I retreated, trying to blend into the street traffic. The first guard turned his attention to others who were coming and going, so I smoothed my tunic and tried to be patient.

When the second guard returned, I stepped forward and waited until he spotted me. "Come on, then," he said, waving me forward. "The tribune will see you, but only for a moment."

I plunged ahead, following the guard through an open area. A columned portico ran around all four walls, and additional structures lay behind the portico. Conscious of several pairs of curious eyes on me, I did my best to keep up with the long-legged guard, who was clearly not happy to be escorting a woman.

We stepped into a hallway off the portico, then climbed a flight of stairs that opened into a reception area. The soldier snapped to attention. "Tribune! Your visitor has arrived."

Claudius Lysias entered through a doorway, drying his hands with a towel. "What a delightful surprise," he said, giving me a broad smile. "Aya! It is a pleasure to see you. Come." He nodded to the guard. "You may go."

I followed Claudius into a spacious chamber with a desk and several fine pieces of furniture. Claudius sat behind the desk and gestured to a cushioned chair. "Please, be seated and tell me how I can serve you."

"It is good to see you," I said as I sat, embarrassed by the quaver in my voice. "I am surprised you remembered me."

"How could I forget?" He leaned forward. "I told you I'd never heard anything like your song. That statement is still true."

"Thank you." I forced a smile. "I have come to ask—we have heard that Caligula is determined to destroy Jerusalem unless we allow a statue of him in our Temple. Is that true?"

The smile on Claudius's face evaporated. "That was true until a few days ago."

I blinked. "Has the emperor changed his mind?"

Though he did not smile, the eyes that returned my surprised look crinkled at the corners. "Caligula will never change his mind again. This morning I received a report from Rome: the emperor was murdered by his own Praetorians."

My mind refused to register his reply. "I don't care what happens in Rome. But my husband is dead, and I have a young son. If Jerusalem is to be attacked, I would—I beg you—" I halted, confused. "Wait, did you say . . . ?"

This time, the smile reached his lips. "The madman is dead. Petronius has already begun to march his legions back to Syria."

I slumped as all breath left my lungs. The threat was gone. Peace had been restored and not a single drop of Jewish blood had been spilled. A miracle that would be celebrated in every home once the news was made public.

"HaShem be praised," I whispered. "And who rules us now?"

Claudius clasped his hands. "The Senate is meeting to answer that very question. I expect we will hear their answer within a few days."

I straightened, abruptly realizing how completely I had debased myself. Like a selfish coward, I had begged not for my people but only for myself, my son, and my friend.

"I apologize," I said, bringing my hand to my head. "I have been utterly selfish. But my son and I have no one to defend us, and I let fear overtake me—"

"You do not have to be ashamed, and I am sorry to hear about your husband. Was he ill?"

"He had an accident, five years ago. It was . . . sudden."

"I am truly sorry. Have you been able to support yourself?"

"I teach music lessons. I have several students. It is not an easy life, but my son and I do not need much."

"Do you still sing?" He smiled, and something that looked like eagerness lit his eyes. "As tribune, I am often required to host banquets for visiting dignitaries. I have yet to find anyone who sings as beautifully as you do."

An unwelcome blush burned my cheeks. "You are too kind. But it wouldn't be proper for me to—"

"I assure you, Aya, I will make sure you remain safe. I would have a man escort you to and from the banquet location, and no one would bother you. Please—I desperately need a singer, and I'd like to help you . . . though it sounds as if you might not need my help."

I laughed. "I am not so successful that I could turn down a generous offer."

"Then you'll do it?"

I considered a moment. If anyone had seen me enter the Fortress, my reputation—or what was left of it after Sha'ul's betrayal—was already ruined. A lifetime of restraint fell away as I lifted my head. "I will."

"Good." He clapped, and a guard appeared.

Claudius stood. "Escort this lady to her home, make note of where it is, and report back to me. She will provide the musical entertainment for my next banquet."

"And when is that?" I asked.

"In two weeks," he answered. "Publius Petronius is coming to celebrate the rise of our new emperor. I think he will enjoy hearing a Jewish woman sing—and you might enjoy the evening yourself."

I returned Claudius's smile in full measure. "Petronius, the man who sought peace for Jerusalem? I am certain I will enjoy singing for him."

———————————— ● ————————————

I sang the songs of Zion for Publius Petronius, Claudius Lysias, and several of his centurions. Claudius hosted the event, and several women were among the guests. I did not know who they were, nor did I ask, as they did not appear to be Jewish or particularly well-mannered.

The tribune did his best to preserve my modesty and my reputation. He arranged the furnishings like a triclinium, with several dining couches in the center of the room. A stream of servants brought trays in and out, and leafy potted plants decorated the corners of the chamber. I was able to sing behind a wide bush, which protected my identity. I do not think anyone in the room recognized me *or* my songs, because I sang in Hebrew about Jerusalem, HaShem, and the delights of dwelling in the house of the Lord.

By the end of the evening, my initial nervousness had disappeared and I felt comfortable with my arrangement with the tribune. When I arrived home and opened the linen square that held my wages, I gasped at the amount inside—five denarii.

The amount was more than I earned in a month of teaching. If Claudius asked me to sing for at least one banquet a month, I would never need to worry about providing food for our table.

I thanked HaShem for His provision, but my euphoria did not last long. Eden reluctantly told me that someone in the neighborhood had seen me walking with my Roman escort, and the fact that I *willingly* walked with a Roman was enough to merit condemnation from most of my neighbors. The few who had not already ostracized me for having a blasphemous brother turned their backs when Seraiah and I approached the Pool of Siloam.

Their rejection hurt, for my heart was not made of stone. But for Seraiah's sake I put on a brave face. Instead of waiting in line to enter the pool via the stairs, I simply walked to the side and jumped in. Delighted by my bravado, Seraiah jumped in next to me, and together we splashed and noisily filled our water jars.

We walked home with wet tunics, but I did not care. Those women could turn their backs, gossip about me, and even spread lies, but as long as HaShem provided me with a way to take care of my son, I would survive.

None of my music students came to class the following week. The ladies of my choir decided to remain at home, so Seraiah and I had the house to ourselves. When he asked why our students failed to appear, I told them they had made other plans.

"Do not worry," I assured him. "HaShem will take care of us."

As I went through my day, filling unexpectedly empty hours with housework and teaching my son, I realized that what my neighbors considered an unpardonable sin would not be unusual if I were in Tarsus. My family had mingled with Gentiles every day but Shabbat. My father did business with Gentiles, my mother bargained and laughed with Gentile women in the marketplace, and even now my brother thought nothing of preaching to Gentiles and eating with them. Perhaps our tolerance for the outsiders had been foreordained, all part of HaShem's plan for our lives.

From reading to Avidan, I knew the Torah well enough to realize that HaShem never forbade us from mingling with Gentiles. We were forbidden from worshiping their idols or marrying them, but the Gentiles living among us were to be welcomed with kindness and never mistreated. God-fearing Gentiles who believed in HaShem, according to the Torah, should even be allowed to join in our worship, so why had I allowed myself to feel guilty for my innocent relationship with Claudius Lysias?

On Shabbat, as I stood inside my house and watched the rising sun push its rays through my shuttered window, I determined never to be embarrassed about my relationship with a Gentile. And though I still believed Sha'ul had grievously wronged us by following Yeshua, I could not fault him for mingling with non-Jews. I never would.

And the next time I saw Claudius Lysias, instead of shying away, I would smile.

For the next four years, I lived for my son, my music, and my Roman benefactor.

Seraiah grew from a boy to a youth, and every day he reminded me more of Avidan. He had my husband's gentleness, good humor, and height. When he walked next to Zachariah, Eden's son, Avidan stood a head taller. Both boys would soon be considered men, and already they were ready to begin their formal schooling.

Zachariah had enrolled in a Temple yeshiva, but Seraiah could not. He had no father to pave the way, and my reputation—or lack thereof—would work against him. The Temple authorities might have forgiven the fact that his uncle was an ardent proponent of the Way, but they could not forgive my involvement with the Romans. I knew this without asking, so I did not even attempt to enroll Seraiah in a Temple yeshiva. If I had dared take my son to Gamaliel or one of the other leading teachers, he would be scorned and humiliated.

I would not do that to my son.

My inability to enroll my son in a Temple yeshiva did not please Avidan's father. Matan wrote during Seraiah's tenth year and asked which yeshiva his grandson would attend. When I answered and said Seraiah would not be attending a yeshiva, the money for our rent stopped coming. If not for the kindness of Claudius Lysias, we would have lost our home, but the income I made from singing gave us security.

Sha'ul had not forgotten about Seraiah's education. A few months after my son's eleventh birthday, I received a letter from my brother. Sha'ul was not the most regular correspondent, but he wrote often, informing me of his work in Tarsus, other cities in Cilicia, and in Syria. He had spent several months in Antioch, where he joined an assembly of believers.

"I have met a knowledgeable physician," he wrote. "His name is Luke, and I think you would like him. He frequently asks questions about Yeshua and makes copious notes. So if you are concerned about my health, you have no need to worry. Luke takes good care of me."

In Antioch, Sha'ul wrote, while members of the ecclēsia were worshiping and fasting, the Ruach HaKodesh said, "Set apart for me Barnabas and Sha'ul for the work to which I have called them."

"Barnabas and I have had many adventures in the Lord since then," he wrote, "and if the Lord wills, I will share some of them with you when we meet again. But I am writing today because our Seraiah must surely be ready to begin his formal education. It has occurred to me that it may be difficult for you to find a suitable teacher. So I implore you to follow my suggestion in this matter: seek out a man called Nicodemus. He sat on the Sanhedrin with me and was greatly respected. I do not know what he is doing, or even if he still lives, but I pray he is well and willing to teach Seraiah. Find him, Aya, and beg him to educate our boy. You will not find anyone who loves HaShem more.

"I must be honest with you—Nicodemus is a follower of Yeshua. But since a teacher in a *bet midrash* teaches the prophets, the traditions, and the Torah, I can promise that Seraiah will learn all he should under Nicodemus.

"May the grace of the Lord Yeshua the Messiah be with your spirit, sister. Amen."

Torn between gratitude and irritation, I lowered Sha'ul's letter and considered his advice. I did not know anything about Nicodemus, and sending Seraiah to a follower of the Way would not be my first choice. But since my son had little chance of enrolling in another yeshiva, I would do what I could for my son.

But every day when he returned home, I would ask him to repeat his lesson so I could be alert for signs of blasphemy.

I called Seraiah to come in from the courtyard and tried to assume a pleasant expression. Despite my concerns, I could not let my boy know that his education might be provided by a man I distrusted.

The next morning, Seraiah and I dressed in our best tunics and went in search of the man Sha'ul had recommended. I began my search near the mikvahs outside the Temple, knowing that the Levites and priests would visit that area before entering the outer court. The first three men I approached lifted their hands to ward me off, but though I knew it was improper for a woman to speak to a man she did not know, I had no choice.

Finally I asked another man, and while a wary look crossed

his face when I approached, the sight of Seraiah must have allayed his concerns.

"Please," I said, stopping a respectable distance away. "My son and I are searching for a Torah teacher called Nicodemus. He used to be part of the Sanhedrin."

The man's gaze shifted to Seraiah, and his eyes softened. "Nicodemus lives in the upper city, not far from the home of the high priest. You will see a fig tree in his courtyard."

"Thank you." I bowed in gratitude. "May HaShem richly bless you."

I grasped Seraiah's hand and set out with a lighter step, convinced that Sha'ul had given us good advice.

———————●———————

The servant at the door did not want to let us in, but I heard a male voice from somewhere behind her: "Who is it, Beulah? I am expecting guests."

The servant gave me a pointed look. "Are you the guests?"

"I-I don't think so."

"Bring them in, Beulah."

The servant stepped back, allowing us passage. Seraiah and I walked into a small foyer, removed our shoes, and waited while the servant splashed the dust from our feet. Then she led the way into a spacious room, where a middle-aged man with a dark beard sat in a padded chair, his hands resting on his knees.

His eyes lit with interest when he saw us. "I am Nicodemus," he said. "And you are?"

"Shalom." I bowed in respect. "I am Aya of Tarsus, and this is my son, Seraiah. He is eleven, and I will not be able to find a place for him at the Temple yeshiva schools."

The man's bushy brows lifted. "Why will you not be able to enroll him?"

I considered hedging my answer, then decided to speak the truth. "My husband, of blessed memory, was a student of Gamaliel, but my brother is Sha'ul of Tarsus. I am not a follower of the Way, but I earn my living singing for banquets usually hosted by Claudius Lysias, commander of the Antonia. My reputation, and that of my brother, would not endear me to the Temple authorities."

A smile winked in and out of the man's beard. "You have your brother's gift for straight speech."

"You know Sha'ul?"

"I know of him, and I observed him in the Sanhedrin." He turned to Seraiah and leaned forward, his eyes narrowing. "Are you ready to study Torah, my son?"

Seraiah nodded.

"Have you learned to read and write? Have you memorized the books of Torah?"

Seraiah nodded again.

"That is good. Have you a voice? Can you recite the first book of Moses?"

Seraiah closed his eyes.

"In the beginning Elohim created *hashomayim* and *haaretz*.

    And the earth was *tohu vavohu*; and darkness was upon the face of the deep. And the *Ruach Elohim* was hovering upon the face of the waters.

    And Elohim said, Let there be light: and there was light.

    By the *Devar HaShem* were *Shomayim* made; and all the *tz'va* of them by the Ruach . . .

    And Elohim saw the light, that it was tov; and Elohim divided the *ohr* from the *choshech*.

    And Elohim called the light *Yom*, and the darkness He called *Lailah*. And the *erev* and the *boker* were *Yom Echad*."

Nicodemus lifted his hand. "That is enough, son. Thank you." He looked up at me. "I have not taught in many years, but during morning prayer I heard the Ruach say that I would soon receive visitors, and I should welcome them and grant their request. So yes, Seraiah, my home will become your bet midrash, and I will be your teacher."

I gasped, unable to believe that HaShem had provided so readily. "Thank you! My son will be a good student. We are so grateful for your kindness."

Nicodemus turned and regarded my son with a speculative gaze. "I wonder what HaShem has planned for you," he said, his dark eyes gleaming. "I cannot wait to see."

Sha'ul, a servant of Christ Jesus, called to be an apostle and set apart for the Gospel of HaShem—the Gospel He promised through His prophets in the Holy Scriptures regarding His Son: Yeshua the Messiah.

To my sister Aya in Jerusalem, who is loved by HaShem. Grace and peace to you from HaShem our Father.

I have so much to tell you, sister. I was comforted to hear that Nicodemus is teaching Seraiah, who will doubtless soak up the Word like his father before him. Give my love and regards to that venerable teacher when you see him again.

I have been laboring in Antioch four years now, and the community of believers is strong. Barnabas is here with me—he is a good man, full of the Ruach HaKodesh and faith. For the past year, we have been teaching great numbers of new converts, and those who do not understand have begun to call us Christians. They intend it as a term of derision, but to be described as a "little Christ" is an honor I will never deserve.

Some prophets from Jerusalem recently visited us. One of them, a brother called Agabus, predicted, through the Ruach, that a severe famine would soon spread over the Roman Empire. So our brothers gave an offering—each according to his ability—to help the believers in Judea.

They have entrusted Barnabas and me with the offering, so we will soon arrive in Jerusalem to distribute the money among the believers there.

I hope to see you and Seraiah when I come. I pray I will find you well and living in grace.

I also hope to meet with Yeshua's disciples. I do not know which emissaries are still in Jerusalem, but it would be a great encouragement to meet all of them and share our joy in the Lord.

This letter should reach you before I arrive, so look for me soon!

Now, to Him who is able to save you through His Gospel, to the only wise God be glory forever through Yeshua, His Son!

Sha'ul

I did not want Sha'ul to come to Jerusalem, not now. Perhaps he did not know that Herod, grandson of the bloodthirsty king who killed the babies of Bethlehem, had decided to boost his popularity among the Jewish authorities by persecuting believers in Yeshua.

The day before I received Sha'ul's letter, Nicodemus had pulled me aside and said that James, son of Zebedee and brother to the disciple John, had been beheaded. Seeing that this action pleased the religious leaders, Herod also arrested Simon Peter and intended to put him on trial after Passover.

"The believers," Nicodemus said, keeping his voice low, "have been praying urgently in small gatherings throughout the city. At this time, it is not safe for them to meet openly."

Yet another reason why it is foolish to believe in Yeshua.

I was not so rude as to speak my thought aloud, but I was concerned for the kind man who had taught Seraiah so much. "What about you?" I asked. "Are you safe?"

Nicodemus smiled. "I am a man of no consequence. I live a quiet life, doing what the Ruach leads me to do. But your brother and Simon Peter are leaders. To lose either of them would be a severe blow."

I had thanked him for the news and walked home with Seraiah, my thoughts heavy. And Sha'ul was planning on coming to Jerusalem?

Inside the house, I fell to my knees and prayed for my brother. Though he was a thorn in my side, I did not wish him ill. I certainly did not want him to be executed like James or imprisoned like Simon Peter.

The heaviness in my chest felt like a millstone as I listened to Seraiah repeat his daily lesson. "Today I learned that Israel is the firstborn of HaShem," Seraiah said, his eyes filled with wonder. "HaShem told Moses, 'Israel is My son, My firstborn.'"

I nodded.

"My teacher says that when we read about Abraham going out to slay Isaac, we see a father willing to sacrifice his son, and a son who was willing to climb onto the altar. My teacher asked, 'Who suffered most, the father or the son?'"

Seraiah tilted his head, expecting an answer, and I could not speak. I had never considered the question.

"I do not know," I admitted. "How did you answer?"

Seraiah's eyes glowed. "Moses wrote, 'The two of them walked on together.' Since they were both willing, I think they wept together over the sorrow to come."

"Ah." I nodded. "You are wise, son. I believe you are right."

"Likewise," Seraiah continued, "it is said that Yeshua wept over Jerusalem before he died, because they would not believe."

I blinked, surprised by the unexpected twist in the lesson. "Your teacher did not tell you about the ram in the bush?"

Seraiah shook his head. "Today's lesson was about love and pain. My teacher says HaShem does not lack emotion. He always loves what He loves, and He always hates what He hates.

But He loves Israel, His firstborn. And before he died, Yeshua looked out over the Holy City he loved and wept because of the sorrows that will come."

My forearms pebbled with gooseflesh. "Sorrows are coming?"

Seraiah nodded. "Much suffering. But that does not mean HaShem has stopped loving Israel. He always will."

I forced a smile. "You have learned well. I have fresh bread and figs on the table. You have filled your head, now fill your belly."

As he hurried away, his words remained with me. Sorrows were coming . . .

I did not believe in Yeshua, but I did not doubt those words. I had experienced enough soul-searing sorrow to know it did not end. As life ended in death, joy ended in pain. Life was a circle of sorrows.

And if Herod was still on a killing rampage when Sha'ul arrived in Jerusalem, I might soon experience sorrow again.

THIRTY-EIGHT

Sha'ul

We heard the news before we reached Jerusalem. A group of Passover pilgrims traveling home stopped at an inn where we were dining. When they realized we were believers, they shared their report with great joy.

"The angel of the Lord released Peter from jail," they told us, their eyes shining. "The chains fell off Peter's wrists, and the angel led him out of his cell, past the guards, and through the gate of the Antonia. The gate opened by itself, allowing him to walk into the city."

We had been praying for Peter as well but were astounded by the news.

The man telling the story pulled over a stool and joined us. "Peter went to the house of Mary, mother to John Mark," he said. "The servant who answered the door thought she was seeing Peter's ghost. Finally, she let him in, and he told the others how the Lord had brought him out of prison."

"All praise to HaShem!" Barnabas grinned at me. "Another miracle. How could we have doubted?"

"It is not doubt to admit we do not always know HaShem's

will," I pointed out. "We prayed for James, but he was not delivered."

We thanked the brothers for their news, prayed with them, and said our farewells.

As we continued to Jerusalem, I could not help but think about Nicodemus's influence on my sister and nephew. I did not doubt that young Seraiah would grasp the truth about Yeshua—after all, everyone from Moses to the prophets had written about the coming Messiah, so he was sure to see HaShem's plan. But Aya? Grief and hardship had hardened her heart. She did not always answer my letters—I could not blame her, as I rarely stayed in one place—but I knew the Ruach HaKodesh was working in her heart.

The night before we were to enter Jerusalem, we made camp by the side of the road. We spread our mantles and stretched out, staring at the stars as we waited for sleep.

"Tomorrow," I said, speaking to Barnabas, "we must find the disciples. Where should we look first?"

Barnabas yawned. "They will not advertise their location. You should visit your sister while I make inquiries."

"Surely we should inquire together. Two are better than one, because they can cover more ground."

Barnabas scoffed at my adaptation of the Scripture. "I have friends among the believing Levites. Let me go to them alone, then I will find you."

I sighed, knowing he was right. The man had been an encouraging friend from the beginning of our journey, but he was also intensely practical.

He was also right about my need to see Aya. We had been apart far too long.

⸻

When Aya opened the door, for an instant her face flooded with joy. Then she drew me into an embrace and began to scold.

"You should not have come," she said, pounding my back as I hugged her. "It is too dangerous for—what is the word? You who call yourselves *Christian*."

I released her and looked into the house, where I saw a boy nearly as tall as myself. "Seraiah! Come embrace your uncle. You have grown!"

The lad endured my affectionate greeting with good grace, then stood behind his mother.

"You might as well come in and eat." Aya opened the door wider and peered into the street. "Are you alone?"

"I am traveling with Barnabas, but he has gone to make inquiries." I looked at the generous spread on the table—she must have been expecting us, because she had prepared enough for half a dozen men. "Did you know we were coming?"

"No. But you always seem to show up when I would rather you did not." She was trying hard to work up a display of righteous indignation, yet she couldn't overcome her relief. She gestured to the food. "Eat. I made plenty."

I took a healthy helping of bread, cheese, and honeyed figs, then said the blessing. When I lifted my head, she was looking at me as if I might disappear before her eyes.

"Is all well with you?" I asked. "How are you earning your living?"

"You may not approve." She sat across the table and folded her hands. "I sing for my living. At weddings and funerals, but mostly at banquets."

"Why wouldn't I approve?" I swallowed a bite of fig. "I thought you were teaching students."

"I was, but my students abandoned me after I was seen walking with a Roman soldier. After that, no one wanted their children to sit under my teaching." Her mouth tightened. "Things were hard when you became a follower of the Way, but then I made things worse."

"I am sorry."

I reached for her hand, but she pulled away. "I have learned to adjust. Life is always changing, and I must change with it."

I broke off another bit of bread and dipped it in honey. "I do not understand. If the local families will not let you teach their children, why do they hire you to sing at their weddings and funerals?"

"They do not. Gentiles hire me. A few Romans, a few Greeks, occasionally other foreigners. They do not care that my brother follows Yeshua."

"Aya." I softened my tone. "More than anything, I wish I could help you see the truth."

"And have the city leaders reject my son as they rejected you?" She glanced at Seraiah, who sat reading in a corner, and lowered her voice. "I am going to make certain my son is educated and married to a girl from an upstanding family. I will not have him starving or working for Romans. He will be everything you were supposed to be."

I sighed. "Is he a good student? Does he enjoy learning?"

"Yes. Every afternoon he tells me what he has learned. And so far, he has only studied Hebrew Scriptures and the traditions, nothing more."

I wanted to reply that the Hebrew Scriptures pointed to Yeshua, but Aya's heart had not yet softened. Had Seraiah's?

"So." She lifted a brow. "What brings you to Jerusalem? You mentioned you were bringing a gift?"

I nodded. "A famine is coming. Save your money, and store as much food as you can. Next year's harvest will fail."

She crossed her arms, but she would heed my words. For although she might be stubborn, she would not risk her son's life.

"Is there anything else I should know? Will there be an earthquake or a fire?"

I shrugged. "Not to my knowledge—HaShem does not reveal all His will to us."

"All right." A smile flitted across her face. "I am sure you will leave soon. What other business do you have in Jerusalem?"

I swallowed the last of my bread. "Barnabas has gone in search of Yeshua's disciples so I can meet them before we return to Antioch. I am sure they are curious about my work with the Gentiles."

Aya snorted. "You and I are both working with Gentiles. Our parents would never have imagined this, would they?"

I chuckled. "Perhaps not. But HaShem is never surprised."

<hr />

Barnabas went around the circle, introducing me to the remaining eleven disciples. With great joy I embraced Peter; then I met Matthew; John, son of Zebedee; Philip; Thomas; Andrew; Matthias; Simon; Thaddaeus; James, son of Alphaeus; and Bartholomew.

"I was grieved to hear about James Zebedee," I told them. "And I rejoiced when we heard that the Lord had sent an angel to free Peter from prison."

A murmur of agreement passed through the group, but no one spoke. They had received me with pleasant smiles, though wariness filled their eyes, and I could not blame them for the cautious welcome. I had been too aggressive an opponent when I worked for the Temple authorities, and I was responsible for Stephen's death.

I had flogged too many Christian brothers and sisters to be welcomed with open arms.

But Barnabas, may HaShem bless him, was a true brother. He told them about my experience on the road to Damascus, and they stared in stunned disbelief when he said I ended up preaching there in Yeshua's name. He explained that the unbelieving Jews had forced me to leave Damascus, but I had gone to Arabia where the Spirit instructed me and revealed many things.

299

"Tell them," Peter said, folding his arms. "Tell them what the Ruach taught you while you were preaching to the Nabateans."

I drew a deep breath. "When I surrendered to Yeshua," I began, "I understood that He was the Messiah, the Son of Man described by Daniel, and the only begotten of the Father. I had studied Torah for years, so once I accepted that He could be both man and God, understanding came easily to me.

"But when HaShem called me to preach to the Gentiles, I faced a new challenge. The Gentiles have not studied Torah. They do not know the Law of Moses. They do not understand circumcision, nor do they grasp the significance of our festivals. They could not see that Yeshua came to be the Passover Lamb that saves us, or that HaShem gave His Son to be the eternal, blameless sacrifice for sin.

"So how could I teach them? How would they be saved? I had spoken to Peter"—I nodded to the former fisherman—"the first time I visited Jerusalem, and he told me about his encounter with Cornelius, the God-fearing Gentile in Caesarea. When Peter shared the Gospel with Cornelius, he explained that everyone who trusts Yeshua receives the forgiveness of sins through His name. And while Peter was speaking, the Ruach HaKodesh fell on all who heard the message."

I looked around the circle. These men had heard Peter's story and were patiently waiting for me to make my point.

"Those men had not been circumcised," I continued. "They did not know our Law. Yet HaShem, in His mercy, sent the Holy Spirit to baptize them into the body of believers. So two things are necessary for a Gentile to follow Yeshua: knowledge and faith. But how can they know unless they hear the Gospel? So that is what I have determined to do. With all my power, energy, and ability, I will preach the Good News of Yeshua wherever HaShem leads me."

When I finished, the disciples opened their arms and welcomed me in the name of Yeshua.

I spent the next several days working with them, preaching in synagogues and in homes, helping them spread the Gospel. Many times I was tempted to stop by Aya's house to see if her heart had softened, but each time I heard the Spirit say, *Not yet*.

My heart ached when the time came for us to leave Jerusalem. "I know," I told my newfound brothers, "that Peter was the first to share the Gospel with foreigners. But HaShem has appointed me as an emissary to the Gentiles. By the blood of the Messiah, we have become brothers with believing Gentiles. For He is our *shalom*, the One who demolished the wall of separation between us. He did this in order to create one body from two groups, and to reconcile us to God through the cross."

We prayed together and embraced again, then Barnabas and I departed for Antioch.

THIRTY-NINE

Aya

The famine Sha'ul warned about arrived a few months after his departure. The spring rains did not fall, and the crops did not grow. By the time summer arrived, the fields were either bare or filled with brown stubble, so it was difficult to celebrate Shavuot, which required two loaves of bread made from the harvest.

Grain was almost impossible to find, and when it could be found in the market, it was so expensive I could not afford to buy it. I thought of the money Sha'ul had brought to help the assemblies of believers—how were they faring? If we could not afford to eat, Seraiah and I might have to beg a Christian for food.

One morning, after offering our prayers at the Temple, Seraiah and I began to walk home. The crowded streets were filled with beggars—men and women holding out baskets, hoping for a coin, some figs, or a piece of bread. I averted my eyes because I had nothing to give them.

We were nearly home when a familiar figure caught my attention—I stared, certain my eyes were playing tricks on me.

"Seraiah, go on," I told him. "I will be along in a minute."

My son gave me a curious look, then continued down the street.

Claudius Lysias was standing in an alley, wearing a simple linen tunic and carrying a linen sack. He might have *thought* he looked like a common man, but he would never blend in. His shaved face immediately identified him as a Gentile, and his broad shoulders and erect bearing marked him as a man of authority.

I caught his eye and pointedly walked toward another alley. Once I entered it, I turned and waited.

He arrived a moment later, offering me a sheepish smile. "You are looking well, Aya. How is your son?"

"He is fine." I crossed my arms, unsettled by his unexpected appearance. "What brings you to my neighborhood—and why are you dressed like a farmer?"

"I did not want to draw attention."

I laughed. "How can I help you? Do you need a musician?"

"Not this week. I came because I was concerned about you and your boy. Have you been able to find food? Growing boys eat like locusts, or so my mother used to say."

I wanted to say we were fine, but a hungry woman could not afford to be proud. "We have very little," I admitted, lowering my gaze. "That is why I was hoping you wanted a singer . . . or you had news about a shipment of grain from Rome."

He crossed his arms. "I wish that were true, but Rome's grain comes from Egypt, and Egypt has been affected by flooding. The Nile rose higher than expected this year and drowned most of the wheat crop."

"So the entire world is suffering."

"Our part of it, at least. But this is for you." He dropped the linen sack at my feet. "I tried to find foods that would not violate your Law."

"What have you done?" I knelt and opened the sack—it held a bag of wheat, along with smaller bags of barley and rye. Figs and pomegranates and grapes . . .

"The Roman army is well provisioned," he said, his mouth twisting in a one-sided smile. "We have more than we need."

"Are you sure you want to do this? I'm grateful, but if it will cause a problem—"

"No one needs it more than you." He knelt in front of me, and his hand closed around my arm. "You are special, Aya. I do not want to see you suffer."

My throat went dry. No man, save Sha'ul and my son, had touched me in years. And while I had no trouble interpreting the look in Claudius's eye, this was not right—this was forbidden.

What had I done? I had determined to be friendly, to observe the Torah's command to be kind to the Gentiles among us, but clearly Claudius did not understand my intention.

"Tribune." I pulled my arm free and held out the sack. "I cannot accept this."

He stood, misery darkening his face. "I apologize. It will never happen again."

"It should not have happened this time."

"Forgive me, Aya. I meant nothing untoward . . . truly. But you are the only woman in Jerusalem who has demonstrated even a small bit of kindness. Surely you know that we are not allowed to marry while serving Rome, and sometimes a man can get lonely—"

I turned away, resisting the urge to clap my hands over my ears. "You should take this food and go. The streets are filled with hungry people, so give it to someone who needs it more than I."

"But you need it! You have a son, and you have no husband."

"If someone asks where it came from, how could I explain?"

"Tell them your God provided." He backed away, leaving the food on the ground. "If you cannot accept it, then give it to someone else. In return, I will arrange a banquet this week. I am sure I need to honor *someone* in this city."

Before I could protest again, he turned and strode away.

FORTY

Aya

Seraiah and I survived the famine, largely due to Claudius
Lysias's generous efforts to find work for me. Our last
conversation must have embarrassed him because he
did not seek me out but sent a slave with news of upcoming
banquets where I could sing. While I appreciated Claudius's
sensitivity to my position, I regretted not being able to speak
to him as a friend.

Seraiah praised HaShem for sustaining us through the famine. I did not dispute him, but quietly wondered why HaShem
insisted on putting His chosen people through such trials. If
He was all-powerful, why did He not send the rains and bless
Israel with food? If our crops flourished and Egypt's failed,
would that not demonstrate HaShem's love for His people?

Sha'ul continued to send letters, though I could never predict
when they would arrive. Seraiah enjoyed reading them, and
since I did not want to criticize his beloved uncle, I held my
tongue whenever Sha'ul mentioned Yeshua.

In Seraiah's sixteenth year, we received a letter with unexpected news: Sha'ul was returning to Jerusalem.

Sha'ul, an emissary of Messiah Yeshua through the will of God,

To Aya and Seraiah, my family.

Grace to you and shalom from God our Father and the Lord Yeshua the Messiah.

I wanted to write you about our visit to Lystra, a small town in the province of Galatia. As we approached the city, we saw a cripple sitting on the ground. When I looked more closely, I saw he had the faith to be healed. "Stand upright on your feet!" I told him, and he did.

But I did not anticipate the reaction of the people around us. "The gods have come down to us!" they shouted. They called Barnabas "Zeus"—because he is tall—and referred to me as "Hermes" because I did most of the talking.

The priest of Zeus, whose temple was by the city gate, brought bulls and garlands, preparing to make a sacrifice to us. When Barnabas and I realized what was happening, we tore off our coats and tunics so they could see we were mortal men. "We proclaim the Good News to you so you can turn from these worthless things to the living God," I told them.

They did not make their sacrifices, but neither did they accept Yeshua.

Barnabas and I stayed with a unique family—the husband was Greek, but the wife, Eunice, and her mother were Jewish. The women received the Gospel almost immediately, but their son, Timothy, was reluctant. He had been raised in the full knowledge of the Scriptures but had not been circumcised on account of his Gentile father.

While we were there, some Jews from Antioch and Iconium arrived. They told the people I was a false witness. With wily words, they convinced the crowd to pelt me with stones.

Barnabas dragged my lifeless body out of the city and sat outside the gate, praying. Within the walls, the believers prayed as well. After a short time, I opened my eyes and sat up. "How could I be dead," I asked Barnabas, "when the Lord still has work for me to do?"

That night Timothy and his mother came to check on us and found me alive. Timothy was amazed to see how his prayers had been answered and received the Lord Yeshua and the Ruach HaKodesh. I blessed him and sent him home, knowing I would see him again.

Barnabas and I left the next day for Derbe, where we preached and made many disciples.

We were greatly encouraged and returned to Antioch, but our happiness dimmed when we learned that believers from Jerusalem had been preaching in our absence— but they were preaching an altered Gospel. They insisted that all Gentile converts become Jews and keep the Law, including circumcision!

I know what you will say, sister—that it is not fair for the Gentiles to join us on such simple terms. The believers from Jerusalem would agree with you. "We have suffered all our lives on account of being Jews," they would say. "Why make it so easy for the Gentiles?"

So Barnabas and I are coming to the Holy City, where we will meet with Peter, James, and John of the ecclēsia in Jerusalem. We hope to settle these matters in order to have shalom among those who follow Yeshua.

I have learned, dear Aya, not to be discouraged, because God is over all. And even if this earthly tent is torn down, I have a home not made with human hands, eternal in the heavens. If I do not see you when I come, my constant prayer is that HaShem will soon open your heart so you will meet me in heaven.

Greet my nephew with a kiss. Barnabas sends his greet-

ings. The grace of the Lord Yeshua the Messiah and the love of God be with you both. Amen.

Sha'ul

"Will Uncle Sha'ul stay with us?" Seraiah asked after I read the letter. "I want to hear more of his stories."

"You shouldn't encourage him. He will keep you up all night."

Seraiah grinned. "I will talk to him after you are asleep."

I smiled, yet I was distressed by Sha'ul's letter. He had been *stoned*, but he didn't seem to think that remarkable. If Avidan had been stoned for teaching, I would have told him to stop teaching. How could a man teach or preach from the grave?

The visit to Jerusalem troubled me, as well. Though I did not agree with my brother's beliefs, I did not want him to be the center of another controversy. We had all suffered on his account, so why argue with others, especially if they were in leadership positions?

He was right about another thing—I *did* understand how the men from Jerusalem felt. Like me, they had probably been devout Jews since childhood. They had studied the Law, kept it, taught it to their children, worn it on their foreheads and arms. They had been circumcised; they ate only clean foods; they would not worship unless ritually pure. So why was so much required of them, and so little required of Gentiles?

I did not understand, but I feared my brother might soon experience a rude awakening.

After participating in the morning prayers, Eden started talking to a neighbor who had no use for me, so I slipped away and strolled through the Court of the Women.

Many concerns troubled my mind, so I was grateful for

solitude. I had no peace about Sha'ul coming to Jerusalem. Though I longed to see my brother, I dreaded hearing that he was in trouble yet again. Could he, I wondered, come to town only to see me and Seraiah?

I had grown concerned for my son. He was growing older, and within a few years he would need to consider marriage. Since he had no father to give him advice, I was hoping Sha'ul would talk to him . . . if I could convince my brother to stay in one place for more than one night.

As I walked through the court, I studied the worshiping women. I could not help myself—every time I visited the Temple, I searched for women in bright tunics or with unusually long hair.

"Aya?"

I turned. Eden had finished talking to the neighbor and was waiting for me. I crossed the court and tapped her shoulder, then extended my arm. "Are you ready to go?"

"Almost," she said. "Let us walk closer to the altar, so I can smell the incense."

I led her toward the Gate of Nicanor. Eden smiled as we walked through a cloud of incense, but her smile faded as I led her away. "What are you doing?"

"I am walking with you."

"You are doing more than that. You are looking at something, and you are distracted. You are often distracted when we are here. What is it that captures your attention?"

"You are more observant than most women. I cannot believe you are blind."

"You have not answered my question."

I sighed. "I'm not looking at anything—I'm searching for someone."

"Who?"

"One of the daughters of Philip."

She tilted her head and frowned. "Which one?"

"The one who prophesied about me. You must remember, you were there."

"I do remember. So why do you need to talk to her?"

"I want to understand what she meant when she said I would meet Yeshua. How could she know such a thing? How can I meet a man who has been dead for years?"

"That was not all she said," Eden added, her voice softening. "She also said your heart would open and you would understand."

"You see?" I smacked my forehead. "What does that mean? My heart is not closed. Am I not understanding? Do I not seek HaShem at every opportunity? Do I not love?"

Eden did not answer but smiled and drew me toward the outer court.

I once considered asking Nicodemus what the woman could have meant but did not want to appear ignorant in front of him. The Christians I knew seemed so certain about their conviction that I felt insecure in comparison. While I did not lack confidence in my beliefs, I could not understand how any devout Jew could accept what the Sanhedrin had declared blatantly unacceptable.

Even Seraiah . . . I sighed. Despite my best intentions, I had seen a change in him and realized that he had become a believer in Yeshua. He did not speak of the Nazarene in my presence, yet his eyes lit up when he read certain portions of the Scriptures.

One night, while reading a passage in Job, a wide smile overtook his features. "'Yet I know,'" he read, "'that my Redeemer lives, and in the end He will stand on earth. Even after my skin has been destroyed, yet in my flesh I will see God.'" He lowered the scroll. "How is that possible, Ima?"

I knew what he was doing—I had used the same approach when I was the teacher and he the student.

"How is *what* possible?"

"How can a dead man see HaShem in his flesh? How can any man see God, who is Spirit?"

I sighed. "Suppose you tell me."

"Well . . . Job may be speaking of the world to come. 'Then we will see the One Daniel spoke of, the Son of Man who approached the Ancient of Days and was given authority, glory, and sovereign power, so all people, nations, and men of every language worshiped Him.'"

"And who might that be?"

"I believe it *must* be Yeshua."

I closed my eyes, not wanting him to see my weariness. I had resigned myself to the knowledge that Seraiah believed; how could he help it? But as long as he kept the Law and did not anger the Temple authorities, I could tolerate his belief.

As long as he did not regularly risk his life like Sha'ul was doing.

"Seraiah?" I lifted my head. "What does it mean to know Yeshua?"

He gave me a startled look, then smiled. "I suppose it means you have met Him."

"How can I meet a dead Torah teacher?"

"Oh, Ima." His eyes softened. "Uncle Sha'ul did. And I have."

I blew out a breath. "I know you count yourself among his followers; I am resigned to it. But I cannot understand how you could possibly have met him."

"One day, you may. But Yeshua himself said no one could come to Him unless His Father drew them first." He leaned forward and kissed my forehead. "I pray, Ima, that HaShem will soon open your heart."

FORTY-ONE

Aya

Sha'ul came to Jerusalem, participated in a reportedly dramatic meeting among the Christian leaders, and left without visiting us. He sent us a long letter afterward, apologizing for his absence and explaining what took place in his meeting.

Sha'ul, an emissary of Messiah Yeshua through the will of God,

> *To Aya, beloved sister, and Seraiah, beloved nephew.*
> *Grace to you and shalom from God our Father and the Lord Yeshua the Messiah.*

I was exceedingly sorrowful when I was not able to visit when in Jerusalem. My meeting with the leaders of the ecclēsia went well, even though false brothers had attempted to bring us into bondage. But from those who seemed to be influential (whatever they were makes no difference to me; God shows no partiality)—well, they saw that I had been entrusted with the Good News for the uncircumcised just as Peter was for the circumcised. Realizing the favor that had been given to me, Peter, John, and James, the Lord's brother—who are the recognized pillars—shook hands in partnership with Barnabas and me, agreeing that we would go to the Gentiles and they to the Jews.

And now I write to you, Aya and Seraiah, because of the great love I have for you. Since we were all born Jews and taught to follow the Law of Moses from childhood, I understand how difficult it must be for you to grasp the freedom of faith. But faith is what HaShem required of Noah, Abraham, Jacob, Moses, Rahab, and all the prophets. No matter what your deeds, without faith, it is impossible to please HaShem.

A person is set right not by deeds based on Torah, but through putting trust in Yeshua. No human will ever be justified by human deeds. If righteousness comes through Torah, then Messiah died for no reason.

Aya, I know you cannot understand why HaShem asks us to endure suffering. Perhaps this story will make things clear: The year Seraiah was born, just before Pesach, a man named Lazarus became sick. He lived with his sisters in Bethany, and he was Yeshua's friend. When he fell ill, his sisters sent a message to Yeshua and said, "Master, the one you love is sick." When Yeshua heard this, He said, "This sickness will not end in death. It is for God's glory, so that the Son of God may be glorified through it."

Even though Yeshua loved Martha, Mary, and Lazarus, He remained where He was for two more days before traveling to Bethany. He told His disciples, "Lazarus is dead. I'm glad for your sake I wasn't there so that you may believe."

They went to Bethany, and when Yeshua saw Lazarus's sisters weeping with the mourners, He wept as well. After that, he commanded those who were there to remove the stone from the tomb's entrance. One of the sisters protested on account of the stench, but Yeshua replied, "Didn't I tell you that if you believed, you would see the glory of God?"

Before he commanded the dead man, He prayed: "Father, I thank you that you have heard Me. I know that You always hear Me; but because of this crowd I said it, so that they may believe You sent Me." Then he commanded the dead man to come out of the tomb, and he did.

I am writing you not to prove that Yeshua could work miracles of life and death (because clearly, if He could resurrect himself, raising a man from death is not beyond His authority), but to point out that He waited. He wept. And Lazarus's suffering had purpose.

Lazarus did not suffer and die because he sinned; he suffered for the sake of those who would see his resurrection and believe. Many times, Aya, you have asked why Israel suffers, why you suffer, why HaShem allows our family to suffer. I could ask the same question: Why do I face opposition at every turn? Why have I been in danger countless times? Why was I stoned in Lystra?

Many times the answer lies not in us but in HaShem's sovereign will. He has a purpose. I suffer so I will rely upon HaShem's strength and not my own. Not so long ago, a thorn in the flesh was given to me so I would not exalt myself. Three times I pleaded with the Lord, begging that it might leave me. But He said, "My grace is sufficient for you, for power is made perfect in weakness." Therefore, I will boast all the more gladly in my weaknesses, so the power of Messiah may dwell in me. For Yeshua's sake, I delight in weaknesses, insults, distresses, persecutions, and calamities. For when I am weak, then I am strong.

As to Israel, she is like Job and Lazarus. HaShem did

not prevent His only begotten Son from suffering, so why do we expect Him to prevent Israel's affliction? Israel is HaShem's firstborn, and just as Isaac was bound over for sacrifice, Israel has been bound over so the Gentiles could receive life.

You may object to the Good News, sister, but you are loved on account of Abraham, Isaac, and Jacob, for the gifts and the calling of God are irrevocable. If all the Jews had accepted Yeshua when He came, how would the Gentiles be added in? But because many, like you, did not accept Him, the Gentiles have been shown mercy. And because of the mercy shown to the Gentiles, in like manner shall mercy be shown to you. For God has shut up all of us in disobedience, so He might show mercy to all.

My heart longs for your salvation, Aya, but I do not despair. As Joseph waited on his brothers to see the truth, as Yeshua waited before going to Lazarus, and as Job waited, enduring the misguided solace of his friends, so I will wait.

O the depth of the riches, both of the wisdom and knowledge of God! How unsearchable are His judgments and how incomprehensible His ways! Grace and shalom to you, beloved sister and nephew, until I see you again!

Sha'ul

After reading the letter, I rolled up the scroll and set it aside. I looked at Seraiah, who was studying me as if he thought I might suddenly burst into tears.

But Sha'ul was not going to make me cry. I did not cry when he caused me to be removed from the choir. I did not cry when Avidan was scorned by his fellow students. I did not cry when Sha'ul did not come to the house, even though HaShem knew I desperately wanted him to counsel Seraiah.

I tapped the scroll on the desk. "I will leave this here if you want to read it again. As for me, I will not."

"Ima, Uncle Sha'ul loves you—"

"You do not understand how it is between us," I said, lowering my voice. "He has always been the flamboyant, driven one; I have always been steady. I will follow the Law and traditions of my mother and father; Sha'ul will flit about and shout from the rooftops. He has his way; I have mine. Besides"—I wiped a traitorous tear from my eye—"your father dedicated his life to studying Torah, and I will die believing what he believed."

Seraiah pressed his lips together, then picked up the scroll. "May I show this to Nicodemus? I am sure he would like to read it."

"Be my guest." I blew out the lamp. "Good night, my son. Would you say the bedtime Shema?"

In the darkness, my son repeated the traditional prayer: "'Master of the universe, I hereby forgive anyone who angered or antagonized me or sinned against me—whether against my body, my property, my honor, or against anything of mine; whether he did so accidentally, willfully, carelessly, or purposely . . .'"

As he spoke, I tented my fingers and hoped Seraiah was not thinking of me as he prayed.

FORTY-TWO

Aya

For the next two years, life continued as it always had, with growth, change, and maturity. I sang for banquets and was occasionally employed to play the harp for weddings and funerals. I worked solely for Gentiles until Eden's unmarried brother died unexpectedly. Despite her grief, she thought of me and shocked the neighborhood by hiring me to play the harp for his procession and funeral.

Her act of love broke through the barriers that had constrained me. Other Jews began to ask me to provide funeral music, and I eagerly accepted. The money was not abundant, but being accepted by my fellow Jews made my efforts worthwhile.

One day, as I reentered my house after singing at a Jewish wedding, I hung up my headscarf and blinked in a sudden epiphany: I was living the life I had dreamed of as a girl. I made my living by singing for Jews and Gentiles. I had done what I set out to do so long ago . . . but what had it brought me?

The music I had so passionately loved so much now seemed ordinary. I still enjoyed using my gifts, but excitement no longer kept me awake the night before an engagement, and my pleasure at a job well done faded after a few moments.

In truth, the role of *singer* was not as fulfilling as the role of *wife*. Or *mother*. But though I would always be my son's mother, he no longer needed me to guide him.

Seraiah continued his Torah studies with Nicodemus until the time came for his ordination. I doubted the examination committee would approve him, especially if they asked for his views about the Messiah.

I was not allowed in the examination chamber, but afterward Nicodemus told me that Seraiah answered their questions easily, always quoting the appropriate Scripture as his authority.

Still, the council did not approve him, and I struggled to hold my tongue when I heard the news from Nicodemus. I thought Seraiah would be upset. Instead, he entered the house in his usual good humor and went straight to the table, where I had set out comforting foods.

"Are you all right?" I asked, going to him.

He smiled. "The council did not ordain me."

"I heard." I studied him more closely. "Are you upset? Will you try again?"

"No." He rapped his knuckles on the table. "I wanted to stand before them to see how I would fare under their questioning. I did not falter, and I do not believe they could find fault with any of my answers."

"That is good."

"They did not ordain me because I said Yeshua was ben-Elohim, the Son of God. They might have thrown me out of the chamber if Nicodemus were not standing behind me. But when they finished deliberating, they came back into the room and said they would not give me papers. Nicodemus and I thanked them and departed, and I doubt we will ever go back."

I sank onto the bench. "Then what purpose did your years of study serve? Why did you work so hard?"

"To understand, Ima." He leaned toward me, his eyes glowing. "To understand HaShem, to see the thread of redemption running through all the sacred writings, and to know I can give an answer to any man, woman, or child who asks why I follow Yeshua. I do not need to be ordained by the council. I can be examined by the elders at the Jerusalem ecclēsia. If they agree, I can be ordained by them."

"I must admit," I said, "I did not think you would be ordained, but I do not understand why you are so happy about it."

"I'm not happy about their rejection," he answered, blushing. "I'm happy because today I met my master's granddaughter. She is from Galilee."

My pulse quickened. I had wondered what Seraiah would do when the time came to negotiate a betrothal. Sha'ul was not likely to be available, but perhaps Nicodemus would be willing, especially if the situation involved someone in his family.

"Does this girl have a name?"

"Lilith," he said, staring past me at something I could only imagine. "She is beautiful and gentle."

"Does she live in—" I struggled to think of Galilean towns— "Capernaum?"

"Nazareth," he said, his gaze coming to rest on me. He chuckled. "She actually lives near the house where Yeshua grew up."

"Interesting," I murmured, but Seraiah was no longer listening. If his expression could be trusted, he was lost in his dreams of the beautiful, gentle girl who had stolen his heart.

———————— • ————————

One year later, Seraiah married Lilith in Jerusalem. At their wedding feast, I gave Lilith the same gift I had received from my mother.

"It is simple," I said, handing her the platter. "But it has always been precious to me."

She read the inscription:

> May this home have light and gladness,
> Shalom and companionship.
> Bestow abundant blessings and holiness in every room
> And love in every corner.
> May the windows be illuminated by Your
> Holy Torah and Your commandments.

"Thank you." She kissed my cheek. "But the best thing about our windows is that I can look through them and see your house."

Their small house was but ten paces away, and whenever I felt lonely, I had only to look out my crooked window and feel my heart lighten.

Though my little house seemed smaller without Seraiah, I continued singing and playing, happy to count some Jews among my regular clients. I was not sure why they no longer rebuffed me—Eden's endorsement had helped, but time had probably eased my stigma, as well. I did not earn as much from weddings and funerals as I had from Roman banquets, yet I had enough to eat, keep my house, and save a little for the grandchildren I hoped to have one day.

One afternoon, while Eden and I were discussing grandchildren, she asked if I had ever thought about marrying again. I laughed. "Who would have me?"

"Seriously," she said. "Your brother has been away for years, so few people make the connection between you. And when is the last time you were publicly seen with a Roman?"

I shook my head. "I can't remember."

"You should think about marriage," Eden insisted. "HaShem did not create us to be alone."

"I care more about ensuring Seraiah and Lilith's happiness," I told her. "And I am forty. A man wants a woman who can give him children. I am not so young anymore."

"Sarah was ninety when she conceived Isaac," Eden said, teasing. "HaShem can do anything."

"I am not Sarah."

What I did not tell her was a simpler truth: when I crawled into bed and closed my eyes, Avidan's was the face I saw. I still loved him, dreamed of him, and missed him. I could not imagine myself living with another man.

Though my life did not remarkably change, the world outside Jerusalem roiled with trouble. The persecution of Christians continued, but Jews were being persecuted, too. In the year Seraiah and Lilith married, the emperor Claudius expelled all Jews from Rome. Apparently, orthodox Jews were having heated public debates with Jews who believed in Yeshua. The emperor did not realize that a chasm had formed between the two groups, and so to keep the peace, he banned all Jews from the imperial city.

In one of his letters, Sha'ul mentioned that he had befriended a married couple, Aquilla and Priscilla, who had to leave Rome. Like our father, they were tentmakers, so the three of them were earning a living making tents while they preached and taught about Yeshua.

Seraiah, meanwhile, seemed destined to follow in his uncle's footsteps. A few months after being denied by the council of rulers at the Temple, he went before Peter, James, and John. After questioning him about Torah and the teachings of Yeshua, they laid hands on him and prayed, setting him apart for ministry to the ecclēsia.

I did not attend the ceremony. Though I loved my son dearly and wanted him to succeed, I could not endorse something that went against everything I had been taught. I tried to explain this to Eden, but she only shook her head.

"One day you will be sorry you missed it," she said. "I know you would have been greatly pleased to see him being dedicated to HaShem's service."

"Yeshua's service," I corrected her. "And that does not bring me joy."

Though we could not agree about Yeshua, Seraiah and I remained on good terms—we simply did not discuss Yeshua or his work with the ecclēsia.

Lilith proved to be a wonderful daughter-in-law, who visited frequently and invited me to every Shabbat dinner. Since a Shabbat dinner for one is a lonely event indeed, I was always happy to accept.

The week Lilith bore my third grandchild—a boy, to keep his two older sisters company—I received a disturbing letter.

Sha'ul, a slave to Yeshua the Messiah,
To Aya, beloved sister, Seraiah and Lilith.

I hope this missive finds you well. I am writing from Caesarea, the house of Philip the evangelist. Luke and I have been enjoying his hospitality—and that of his four daughters—for several days.

My throat went dry. He was with the four prophetesses! I had never ceased to search for them at the Temple, but Sha'ul had found them without even trying.

Yesterday, a prophet named Agabus came from Judea to meet us. (You may recall that he prophesied about the recent famine.) Coming over to us, he took my girdle, tied his hands and feet with it, and said, "The Ruach HaKodesh says this: 'In this way shall the Jewish people in Jerusalem bind the man who owns this belt and deliver him into the hands of the Gentiles.'"

After hearing the prophecy, everyone begged me not to go to Jerusalem, but who am I to protest the Lord's will? "Why are you weeping?" I asked them. "For I am ready not only to be bound but to die for the name of the Lord Yeshua."

So I am coming to Jerusalem and hope to see you and our beloved Seraiah and Lilith.

And now I urge you, dear sister, through the love of HaShem, to daily pray to God on my behalf. Pray that my service for Jerusalem might be acceptable to HaShem, and that I will be rescued from the unbelieving Judeans. Then, God willing, we can rejoice and enjoy our family together.

Sha'ul

Several days passed, and I heard nothing from or about Sha'ul. Then one afternoon Seraiah burst into the house.

"Uncle Sha'ul has arrived," he said, breathless as he dropped onto a bench. "I saw him when he went to see James and the elders of the ecclēsia. Uncle Sha'ul reported everything HaShem has done among the Gentiles."

"Did he greet you?" I asked.

"Of course."

"And how did the elders receive his news?"

"They were pleased, but one thing disturbed them: they had heard that Sha'ul teaches the Jews who live among Gentiles to turn away from Moses and not circumcise their children or live according to the other customs. The elders do not expect Gentile converts to live as Jews, but they do not believe Sha'ul should be telling Jews to renounce the Law."

I frowned. I had never heard Sha'ul say anything to suggest that Jews should not live according to the Law, but perhaps his thinking had changed. I sighed. At least the Temple rulers had not arrested him.

"What was the outcome of the meeting?" I asked. "Is Sha'ul at peace with the elders?"

Seraiah nodded. "The elders suggested that he take a vow along with four others of their assembly and join their purification ceremony. Everyone will see Uncle Sha'ul living as a Jew, according to the Law. That should settle the question."

I nodded slowly. Men underwent a purification ceremony whenever they wished to separate themselves in order to fully focus on God. During the time of separation, which could range from a week to a lifetime, the participant forsook wine, did not allow a razor to cut his hair, and could not touch a dead body. Their unkempt hair was a public sign of piety, the refusal to touch a dead body kept the participant ready for divine service at any moment, and the avoidance of wine kept the mind sober.

"How long will Sha'ul be set apart?"

"Seven days. After that, he is to make an offering for himself and the other men, demonstrating his generosity toward his fellow Jews. Then he will have his head shaved and all should be well."

"Thank you, son." I patted his hand. "Keep me informed, please."

"Will you try to see him during the week of purification?"

I shook my head. "I will not let anyone criticize him for consorting with a woman who consorts with Gentiles. I will wait until the seven days have passed."

"Sha'ul is traveling with Gentiles," Seraiah remarked, standing. "I believe the men are Greeks."

I smiled. "I am not at all surprised."

FORTY-THREE

Shaʾul

Everything had gone according to plan. The elders of the Jerusalem ecclēsia were pleased with my willingness to demonstrate my adherence to the Law, and I was happy to make peace with the brothers. As the sun rose on the fourth day of my purification, I said the morning prayers, dressed quickly, and met my brothers outside the house. Together the five of us walked to the Temple.

We knelt in the sanctuary and lifted our thoughts toward HaShem. I closed my eyes to calm my spirit and reviewed the steps I would need to take when this week of purification ended. On the eighth day, we would each bring the prescribed offerings to the priest, and I would pay for my brothers' sacrifices. The priest would offer the sacrifices to the Lord, then he would shave our heads. When the ceremony was complete, we would be free to go our way.

Surely my shaved head would assure the doubters that I still followed the Law! But even though I had agreed to do this, I could not forget Agabus's prophecy—I would be bound and delivered to Gentiles.

Lord Yeshua, do with me as you will.

"HaShem, I heard what you made me hear and I was frightened. I raise my eyes to the mountains: whence will come my help? My help is from HaShem, Maker of heaven and earth."

My voice stilled as I fell into a trance. In it I saw the Lord Yeshua, and His eyes were dark with urgency . . .

Hurry! Get out of Jerusalem quickly, because they will not accept your witness about me.

But, Lord, they themselves know that in one synagogue after another, I was imprisoning and beating those who trusted in you. Even when the blood of Stephen was spilled, I stood by and approved—

Go! For I will send you far away to the Gentiles.

I blinked as the world came back into focus, and immediately I became aware of agitated voices in the distance. "Men of Israel, help!" One voice rose above the others. "This is the man who is teaching against our people and the Torah and this place. He has even brought Greeks into the Temple and defiled the Holy Place!"

Whom was he talking about?

I turned and saw a crowd of pilgrims—from their clothing, I assumed they were Jews from Asia. Clearly, they had heard of my journeys to spread the Gospel and now they intended to spread the lies they had heard.

I stood and motioned for quiet, but they would not stop yelling. Other men, distracted from their prayers, turned in our direction. My four brothers, who did not want to be the center of attention, quietly slipped away.

"May I speak?" I asked, only to be shouted down. Particularly alarming was the men's insistence that I had brought Greeks into the Temple. Everyone in Jerusalem knew that escorting a Gentile past the Court of the Gentiles was punishable by death.

The day before I had walked through Jerusalem with Trophimus the Ephesian, but he had not come with me to the Temple. He had not even ventured onto the Temple Mount.

"May I speak?" I said again, but the mob would not hear me. As the shouts grew louder, hysteria seemed to crackle in the air. The mob surged forward, fastening their hands on me, and I could not move. My accusers grabbed my arms and shoulders, dragging me from the sanctuary and through the outer courts. Once we passed the gates, the Temple guards closed them—after doing nothing to help me.

I had seen mobs before, and I knew what would happen next. Unless HaShem intervened, this mob would carry me outside the city walls. I would be dropped into a pit and stoned without a trial or even a formal accusation.

Agabus had prophesied that I would be bound and handed over to Gentiles. These men were not Gentiles, so this was not the end.

I closed my eyes and surrendered to the mob. I trusted in the Lord's words, but if this was what HaShem planned for me, I would not complain. I had been the accuser when Stephen was stoned. I had been the leader of a similar crowd, and I had been just as convinced that he was trying to destroy everything we lived for. I would have carried him through the gates of the city myself if I'd had the strength.

While those intent on stoning me attempted to drag me away, others took advantage of the opportunity to beat me. I felt several blows from a shepherd's staff, a whip cut my cheek, and innumerable fists pummeled my head, shoulders, belly, and limbs. I breathed in the odor of sweat and fury and could see nothing through the haze of violence around me.

But HaShem had other plans. We had not yet reached the city walls when I heard the sound of hoofbeats. Other voices joined the cacophony, and when the dust cleared, I saw Roman soldiers, led by a stern-faced man with a plumed helmet—the Fortress commander.

The mounted Romans circled the mob, and the rain of blows ceased. The commander's voice rang out over the crowd. "What is this?" he shouted in Aramaic. "Who dares disturb the peace of this city?"

My accusers had not given up. "Away with him! You must not stop us from guarding our sacred Temple!"

The commander gave an order, and two legionaries dismounted, each carrying a chain. These were fastened to my wrists and ankles.

"What has this man done?" the commander asked, surveying the crowd.

"He has defiled our Temple!"

"He has brought Gentiles into the Holy Place!"

"He is a traitor to Israel!"

Through bleary eyes, one of which had nearly swollen shut, I studied the exasperated commander. Lines of frustration marked his face, and I knew he was considering his choices: should he submit to the crowd and keep the Jews happy, or should he maintain Roman control? If he gave in to the mob this time, they would expect him to do it again.

"Take this man to the Fortress," he barked. "Then we will see if we can determine what the problem is."

The soldiers led me toward the Fortress Antonia, which stood north of the Temple Mount. I walked as best I could, but the crowd followed closely, shouting with every step, throwing stones and curses. When we reached the steps of the Antonia, the mob surged forward, but the tribune ordered his men to pick me up and carry me inside.

While they lifted me, the crowd intensified their shouts: "Away with him!"

The commander dismounted, handed his reins to a slave, and walked toward me, distrust and dislike in his eyes. "Move him into the barracks," he ordered one of his men. "Secure him until I arrive."

"Wait." I caught the commander's eye. Speaking Greek, I said, "May I say something to you?"

The man's brows lifted. "You know Greek? So you're not the Egyptian who stirred up a rebellion and led four thousand assassins into the desert?"

"I am a Jewish man from Tarsus in Cilicia, a citizen of no insignificant city. I beg you, let me speak to these people."

The commander gave me a skeptical look, then jerked his chin upward. The two guards holding my chains led me out to the top of the stone staircase where I could survey every fevered face.

"Brothers and fathers," I called, "listen to my defense."

When the mob heard me speak in Aramaic, their protests quieted, and several men appeared confused. Apparently, some of them had heard I was a Gentile who had invaded the Temple.

"I am a Jewish man," I went on, "born in Tarsus of Cilicia but brought up in this city at the feet of Gamaliel, trained strictly according to the Torah of our fathers, being zealous for God just as all of you are today. I persecuted followers of the Way to the death, arresting both men and women and throwing them in prison—as the *cohen gadol* and the council of elders can testify. I also received orders from them, and I went to Damascus to bring followers of Yeshua back to Jerusalem in chains to be punished."

I continued, telling the story of the great light and the voice from heaven. I told them that Yeshua himself spoke to me and sent me to Damascus, where I met with Ananias, a devout Jew, who explained that I would bear witness of what I had seen and heard to all people.

I told them of the vision I had just seen in the Temple, and of the Lord's promise to send me to the Gentiles. Until I uttered that last word, they listened. But when they heard *Gentiles*, they raised their fists, screaming, "Away from the earth with this fellow! He's not fit to live!"

As they shouted, tossing their cloaks and flinging dust into the air, the commander repeated his order that I be taken to the barracks. Then he told a centurion to flog me and question me about why I had disturbed the peace.

Inside the Antonia, as a legionary strapped my wrists to a post, I calmly asked the supervising centurion if it was legal to flog a Roman citizen who had not been found guilty of a crime.

The man went pale and slapped the legionary's arm. "Wait." Then he walked away.

A few moments later, the commander appeared, trailed by the centurion. "Release him," the man ordered. When the legionary had done so, the commander stepped closer. "Are you truly a Roman citizen?"

"I am."

The commander drew a deep breath. "I had to pay a big price for my citizenship."

"I was born a citizen."

The soldiers who were preparing to question me immediately stepped away. The commander made an abrupt gesture, and two more legionaries strode forward to remove my chains.

"I will give you a room and have food sent to you," the commander said. "I will also send a slave to tend your wounds."

"And after that?"

"I will send you to your own people." He crossed his arms. "I will let the chief priests and the Sanhedrin decide your fate."

I had stood before the Great Sanhedrin on two other occasions, once at my ordination, and again when I received my orders to ferret out Christians in Damascus.

During those events, I would never have believed that one day I would stand before my peers as a follower and slave of Yeshua.

The commander and two centurions escorted me from the Antonia to the Chamber of Hewn Stone. The full Sanhedrin had assembled, and I could feel the pressure of their stares as the Romans brought me into the vaulted chamber.

With chains on my ankles and wrists, I moved to the space between the two clerks' tables and looked up.

"My brothers," I began, "I have lived my life in all good conscience for HaShem up to this day."

A man at the end of a row ordered one of the clerks to slap my mouth.

My anger flared. "God is going to strike you on the mouth, you whitewashed wall!" I pinned the man with a hot look. "Do you sit judging me according to the Torah, yet in violation of the Torah you order me to be struck?"

Several members gasped, and one of the clerks hissed at me, "Would you insult God's high priest?"

I lifted my hand. It was an honest mistake, for the man who spoke had not been high priest when I last visited Jerusalem, and he was not sitting in the high priest's chair.

"I didn't know, brothers, that he is the high priest. And yes, it is written, 'You shall not speak evil of a ruler of your people.'"

I took a moment to look around and see what else had changed. As usual, the Pharisees sat on one side of the chamber and the Sadducees on the other, but the balance had shifted. From their garb I could see that the Sadducees no longer held the majority.

"Brothers"—I turned toward the Pharisees—"I am a Pharisee, a son of Pharisees! I am on trial because of the hope of the resurrection of the dead!"

Almost immediately, an argument broke out between the two factions, as I had hoped it would. The Sadducees, who did not believe in the afterlife, angels, or spirits, vehemently voiced their objections, while the Pharisees affirmed my statement. Several of the Torah teachers stood and proclaimed, "We find nothing wrong with this man! What if a spirit or angel has spoken to him?"

The uproar increased, the furor becoming as hot as it was the day they dragged Stephen outside the city.

I shot the commander a warning look. He was astute, that one, and he immediately ordered the centurions to return me to the Antonia.

I knew he would. Yeshua had promised that I would be sent to the Gentiles.

FORTY-FOUR

Aya

I was practicing a new song on the lute when Seraiah ran
into the house, his forehead beaded with perspiration.
"Ima—"

"Pour yourself some honey water," I interrupted. "You
should not get so worked up in this heat."

"Ima, Uncle Sha'ul is being held at the Antonia!"

My mind went blank with shock. "Sha'ul?" The name came
out as a croak. "At the Fortress?"

Seraiah sank to a stool near my feet. "Did you hear about
the riot at the Temple? Apparently, it started because men accused Uncle Sha'ul of bringing Gentiles into the sanctuary. The
crowd nearly tore him apart, but the commander pulled him out
of the fray and arranged for him to speak to the Sanhedrin."

My heart, which had stopped beating for a moment, began
to thump heavily. "That is good, so everything must be settled.
We must learn where he is staying and have Sha'ul join us for
dinner—"

"Ima, do you not understand? The meeting before the court

dissolved in an uproar, so Uncle Sha'ul was taken back to the Antonia. He is still a prisoner there."

I blinked. "For what crime is he being held?"

"I do not know."

I bowed my head. My brother was with Claudius Lysias, so I should not worry. But Claudius did not known Sha'ul was my brother, and Sha'ul did not know Claudius was—or used to be—a friend.

"Ima—"

"Quiet, Seraiah, I need to think."

I pressed my hand to my forehead and turned away. Why was Claudius holding Sha'ul at the barracks? Probably because the legionaries were charged with keeping the peace in Jerusalem. Claudius must have feared that Sha'ul would start a riot . . . or cause one.

"Go back to the Temple Mount," I told my son. "Wear a cloak, cover your face, and walk through the area near the Chamber of Hewn Stone. Listen for rumors and reports. If you hear a single word concerning Sha'ul's fate, come tell me at once."

"Surely he is in no danger, not from his own people."

"Sha'ul is no longer counted among his own people," I reminded my son. "Many of the chief priests are aligned against him. So be careful, mind your step, and listen well."

———————•———————

I waited for hours but heard nothing from Seraiah. So as the sun dropped toward the west, I pulled on my cloak and stepped into the gathering darkness. I could not approach the Fortress in daylight, but perhaps I could travel unnoticed in the gloom of early evening.

I was not certain what I could do for my brother, yet I would offer to do whatever I could. I could go to Nicodemus and ask him to intervene with the Sanhedrin on Sha'ul's behalf. Or perhaps I could go to the leaders of the believing community—if others had lowered Sha'ul over a city wall in a basket, perhaps the leaders in Jerusalem could help him escape the Antonia.

I strode quickly through the residential streets, skirted the Temple Mount, and approached the Roman fort. At the gate to the only entrance, six guards stood beneath a pair of burning torches, but I could not see any Jews.

Praying for courage, I walked toward the gate, remembering the last time I had walked toward these guards. How long had it been? Seventeen years. I had trembled in every limb on that former occasion, but this time I could not afford to be afraid. Sha'ul's life was at stake.

I walked up to the tallest guard and looked directly into his eyes. "My name is Aya and I would like to see a prisoner, Sha'ul of Tarsus."

The guard narrowed his eyes. "Our prisoners aren't allowed women. Go ply your trade elsewhere."

"I am not plying a trade. That man is my brother."

The guard squinted, then glanced at his indifferent companions. "This woman says she's sister to the prisoner called Sha'ul."

"So?"

"I have not seen him in years," I added. "If he is at risk of losing his life, I would like to see him before it is too late."

The guard shook his head. "No one gets in without permission from the commander."

"Would that be Tribune Claudius Lysias? If so, we are acquainted. I do not wish to bother him, but I need to see my brother. Please ask if I may visit Sha'ul of Tarsus for at least a few moments."

The guard studied my face more intently. "What was your name?"

"Aya of Tarsus. If the commander does not recognize my name, remind him that I am a musician."

The guard grunted. "Wait here."

I stepped into a pool of shadow and waited for what felt like an eternity. I hoped my message would not bring Claudius out—I did not want these guards to assume the worst about my relationship with the Roman, nor did I want to disturb him.

But I could not let this opportunity slip away.

◆

"Come, woman." The guard opened the small door in the gatekeeper's lodge, then led me through the large courtyard at the center of the Antonia. The place had not changed since my last visit.

Even now, the memory of that visit had the power to make me flush with shame. Why did I think I deserved to escape the fate that would have befallen everyone in the city? I must have been half mad with fear in those days.

I shook my head, grateful that HaShem had shown mercy to Jerusalem. Now, if He would only do the same for my brother . . .

The guard led me beneath the columned portico, then opened a locked door. I saw a hallway with iron bars at regular intervals. Prison cells, for those Rome deemed a threat to the peace of Jerusalem.

"You'll find your brother back there." The guard pointed to a cell at the end of the hallway. "Say what you must and return to this door, and I'll walk you out."

I nodded and moved forward, keeping my eyes on the stone floor until I heard the sound of Sha'ul's anguished voice.

"I am ready to go," he was saying, his voice rent by tears, "and will do your will, but I beg you to consider my nephew and sister. I love them and wanted to see them while I was in Jerusalem."

He was praying, but this was no liturgical prayer. I quickened my step, then stopped when I realized he was not alone—

another man stood beside him, a man who had placed his hand on Sha'ul's shoulder as my brother knelt at the man's feet.

"Take courage," the man said, his voice barely reaching my ear. "Just as you have testified about me in Jerusalem, so you must also testify in Rome."

And then, while Sha'ul murmured something in response, the man turned his head and I recognized him: Yeshua—the Galilean I had seen in the Temple courtyard—stood next to Sha'ul, supporting and comforting him. But he was *seeing me*. I stood there, amazed and trembling, and then I turned and ran.

<hr />

I did not stop gasping until after I ran into my house and barred the door. Sha'ul was right. The prophetess had spoken the truth. I had met Yeshua and could no longer deny that he lived.

I lunged for the table, gripped the edge, and released a hysterical laugh. At least I no longer had reason to doubt Sha'ul's sanity. Somehow—perhaps through a miracle—Yeshua had survived his crucifixion. He had looked at me with piercing eyes, and my startled and confused mind could not make sense of who he was or how he came to be in that prison cell.

But that did not mean he was the son of HaShem. That did not mean my life had to change as Sha'ul's had. I still had real problems to face, and the man I saw with Sha'ul had done nothing to get my brother out of prison.

I hung my head covering on a hook, then smoothed my tunic and tried to calm my heightened nerves. I ought to practice my new song but could not concentrate on fingerings and strings while my heart fluttered. I picked up a cloth and scrubbed at a stubborn stain on the table, then gave up.

The hour was late, and I needed to sleep. I had no idea what the morrow would bring, and I should get some rest.

But I could not sleep, so I sat at the table with a Torah scroll open to the first book of Moses, Bereshit. I read the story of Abraham's trek with Isaac, the son of promise, and remembered the night Avidan and I had read the same passage at the beginning of his yeshiva study. I had moved my finger over each individual letter: *"God will provide himself a lamb for the burnt offering. God will provide himself a lamb in His son."*

Those words were a mystery when Avidan and I first considered them. But now I *knew* what they meant. The journey to Mount Moriah was a picture of the time when HaShem and Yeshua would walk together, each sorrowful, yet each fully willing to *provide Himself a lamb in His son.*

I could almost hear Sha'ul's voice: *See, Aya? The truth has always been in the Torah.*

I stood, turning away from the scroll as my heart pounded painfully in my chest. Would I ever see my brother again? I walked from one side of the house to the other, wringing my hands. Why had Sha'ul fallen under the spell of Yeshua? His conversion had brought nothing but suffering and pain. As a Pharisee, he had been respected and successful. He could have worked his way up the hierarchy; he could have become wealthy through his connections with other Pharisees. He could have married again and had children. He could have taken a seat on the religious council and, if he worked his way into the good graces of the Roman procurator, he could have been appointed high priest.

But after one day in the sun, he had thrown every possibility away. Since declaring himself a follower of Yeshua, he had been stoned, starved, mocked, beaten, accused, misunderstood, and imprisoned. He had probably suffered far worse, but never shared those misadventures with me.

I had frequently complained that Seraiah and I suffered on Sha'ul's account, but in truth, he suffered worse for Yeshua. Why? Why didn't he stop believing?

I loved my brother, but I had grown weary of worrying about

him. He needed to stop his foolish preaching. He had converted; now he needed to recant his testimony and beg the Sanhedrin's pardon. He needed to reclaim what he could from his old life.

I no longer cared about being right. I only wanted my brother to survive.

I blew out the lamp and slipped out of my outer garment. I eased into bed and stared into darkness as my thoughts gradually quieted.

A noise from outside the house brought me fully awake, so I went to the window and opened the shutter. I saw no movement on the silvered street, so the noise must have been caused by a rat or some other animal. I fastened the shutter and returned to bed.

But when I touched my pillow, I felt *wetness*. I pulled my hand back and looked up at the ceiling, expecting to see a crack in the plaster, but we had not received rain. I had not spilled any water near the bed, and I had not wept as I lay in the darkness . . .

I weep with you.

The voice was not audible, but I heard it nonetheless. And with the voice came a flood of other memories: Yeshua weeping because his friend Lazarus had suffered and died. Joseph weeping when he recognized his brothers. Abraham weeping when he lifted the knife to slay his son. Sha'ul weeping in his prison cell because he wanted to be more about his Lord . . .

Your heart will open, and you will understand.

The tears on my pillow had come from Yeshua.

FORTY-FIVE

Aya

I woke to the sound of someone pounding on the barred door. I rolled out of bed and lifted the latch, then stepped aside as Seraiah entered, his face flushed. "There is a plot," he said, not bothering with the usual pleasantries. "Some of the Jews have bound themselves with an oath not to eat or drink until they have killed Uncle Sha'ul."

My heart nearly stopped. "What?"

"They have sent a message to the commander at the Antonia, saying the Sanhedrin wants to ask Sha'ul for more information. It is a ploy, Ima—they plan to kill him tomorrow morning as he is transported to the Chamber of Hewn Stone."

I pressed my hand to my mouth, overcome by the news. What could I do? If Yeshua were the savior Sha'ul believed he was, he should have helped Sha'ul escape. He should have gone to the leaders at the ecclēsia, and they should have marshaled forces or enlisted a few Zealots to get Sha'ul out of prison . . .

But he hadn't. So Sha'ul had only me and Seraiah for help, and we had nothing but determination . . . and a friend at the

Antonia. Claudius Lysias had allowed me to enter last night, and perhaps he would be willing to help us today.

I grabbed my son's hand. "I cannot go back there today— the guards barely allowed me entrance last night. But you can go, Seraiah. Wait."

I took a sheet of parchment from my trunk and wrote a note in Greek, then pressed it into Seraiah's hand. "You must take this note to your uncle. And you must be quick."

"What if they don't let me in? Why would they?"

"If they question you, tell them Aya of Tarsus, who was allowed to enter last night, sends you to visit Sha'ul. Why wouldn't a young man want to visit his uncle?"

Seraiah took the note, but before he left, I embraced and kissed him as if I might never see him again. "Go!"

I stood at the door and watched Seraiah climb the hill with long strides. Few of my neighbors would dare to send their son to the Roman fortress. The very thought was enough to send a wave of gooseflesh rippling over a mother's arms. Anything could happen in that godless place, anything at all.

Yet I had no choice. Entering those gates had been difficult for me, but fear for my family had driven me forward each time I approached the Fortress. I would have done it again, but I knew the guards would laugh at me. Asking to see my brother *again*? They wouldn't have believed me.

I sank to the floor as panic made my knees weak. Was there a prayer for blind terror? I could not think of one, so I said the first words that came to mind: "Have mercy, HaShem, on your servant and her son and brother. Have mercy and spare them, have mercy on us for your name's sake."

Still on my knees, I lowered my head to the bench. I had no more strength, no will to fight. I could no longer refuse to admit what I had seen when I entered the Fortress and saw Sha'ul in his jail cell.

I had seen my brother with Yeshua, and the Nazarene had

seen me. His eyes, at once powerful and gentle, seemed to see everything in my heart and mind, including my doubts and defenses, my stubbornness and my arguments, my loves and my hates. He saw my past and present, good and bad, yet in his eyes I saw forgiveness and patience and longing . . . as if he had been waiting years for me to walk down that hallway and see him as Messiah and King, not only for Israel, but for Sha'ul's frightened sister . . .

And he had wept for me.

My face twisted, my eyes clamped tight to stop a rush of tears, but finally I surrendered and let them fall.

"Forgive me, Yeshua. My son knows and trusts you, as does my brother. Wise Nicodemus has known you for years, and all the while I doubted because . . ."

Why? Because I could not believe that a man could rise from the tomb. Because I could not accept that a man could be both human and divine. Because I wanted to follow the example of my parents and my husband, and at least partly because I did not want to admit my brilliant brother was right . . . as always.

"Forgive this stubborn, prideful woman." I tried to control myself, but my chin wobbled, and my voice trembled despite my efforts. "I have been so foolish, so ridiculously stubborn . . . I am amazed that you would even look at a woman like me. But you did. You saw me. And what did I do? I ran. I denied. But I can deny the truth no longer."

All the years I spent in ignorance . . . why? Why did Abraham have to wait so long for Isaac's arrival? Why did Joseph have to wait for his wayward brothers to appear in Egypt? Why did Yeshua tarry while his friend Lazarus sickened and died? Why did Sha'ul have to wait so long for me to accept the truth?

For God's glory, so the Son of God may be glorified.

Who was I to question HaShem? His reasons and thoughts were beyond my imagining.

I would trust that everything in my life, even the suffering and waiting, was for God's glory. So others might believe.

———————•———————

When Seraiah returned and told me what happened at the Fortress, I understood everything.

I understood why HaShem led me to meet Claudius Lysias in Tarsus. I understood why I had been given an independent spirit and a love for music. I understood why my life had been a tapestry of events and desires and situations that worked together to help save my brother's life. Because Sha'ul of Tarsus was the man HaShem would use to present salvation through Yeshua to the world outside Jerusalem.

Seraiah could not wait to tell me what happened. After returning to my house, he sank to a stool and told me that he had been allowed to visit Sha'ul. Once inside the cell, Seraiah described the plot he had overheard. Sha'ul alerted the centurion, who went to Claudius Lysias and informed him about the conspiracy.

Claudius sent for Seraiah, and after interviewing him and learning that he was my son, Claudius warned Seraiah not to speak of the plot to anyone else. He summoned centurions and had them prepare a detachment of two hundred soldiers, seventy horsemen, and two hundred spearmen.

Then he sat and wrote a letter, speaking aloud as he wrote:

Claudius Lysias,
   To His Excellency, Governor Felix: Greetings.

This man was seized by the Judean leaders and was about to be killed by them. I came on the scene with soldiers and rescued him, having learned that he is a Roman citizen. Desiring to know the charge of which they were accusing him, I brought him down to their Sanhedrin. I found that he was accused concerning issues of their law but charged with nothing worthy of death or imprisonment. When I was informed about a plot against the man, I sent him to you immediately. I will order his accusers to state before you what they have against him.

"He sealed the letter and handed it to one of the centurions," Seraiah finished. "I asked when Uncle Sha'ul would leave, and the tribune said they would depart immediately."

Together Seraiah and I prayed and thanked God that Sha'ul had been saved from those who plotted against his life.

When we lifted our heads, Seraiah looked at me and smiled. "Ima," he said, his eyes brightening, "you have met Yeshua."

I put out my arms and drew him close. "Thank you," I whispered in his ear. "For being patient with your mother. I am sorry it took me so long to realize the truth."

"Peter says a day is like a thousand years to the Lord, and a thousand years is like a day," Seraiah said when I released him. "Do not worry, Ima—the Lord does not reckon time like we do."

The next day we learned that Sha'ul had been safely escorted to Caesarea. We also learned that the chief priests and elders were enraged by my brother's escape and were making plans to travel to Caesarea with a lawyer, Tertullus, where they would present their case before Governor Felix.

Before meeting Yeshua, I would have been worried about Sha'ul's fate, but I knew he would not die in Caesarea. I did not know how long he would remain with Governor Felix, but he was destined for Rome, where he would testify of Yeshua to people in high places.

I could rest in that knowledge.

Two days after Sha'ul's departure for Caesarea, I picked up my water jugs and went to the Pool of Siloam. The usual group of neighborhood faces was there, but several unfamiliar women stood in the shade, drinking from clay cups and talking with one another. I couldn't help but notice them—four were strikingly alike, each of them tall, slender, and with hair so long that not even a head covering could disguise it.

Philip's daughters had come to Jerusalem.

I left my jars by the stairs and walked toward them, my heart lifting. As I approached, one of the women gave me a noncommittal smile, then a flash of recognition lit her eyes.

"Aya," she said when I drew closer. "You have met Yeshua."

"I have." My smile broadened. "How can you tell?"

She chuckled. "The Spirit. He dwells in you, too."

"The Spirit . . . is in us?"

She nodded. "The Ruach HaKodesh dwells in all who know Yeshua. It's how we recognize another believer—we look for the fruit of the Spirit. Not everyone who claims to be a follower of the Way truly knows Yeshua, as your brother will surely tell you."

"How is my brother?" I asked. "Can you see him?"

She shook her head. "The Spirit cannot be commanded, Aya. Sometimes He whispers to me, but most of the time I simply let Him bear His fruit. Joy, for instance. I saw it in you when you approached the pool."

I felt my cheeks heat. "Love? That's what I saw when I saw Yeshua. He was comforting Sha'ul."

The woman nodded. "Shalom is another fruit you will see in believers. And the goodness of a Father. The gentleness of a shepherd. And patience, because the Spirit gives us time to learn." She smiled. "You will learn many things as you live for Yeshua. We all do."

My heart felt as full as the pool. "When I met you the first time," I said, struggling to offer the right words, "I was confused about the purpose of my life. Over the years I have thought I was meant to be many things—a singer, a wife, a mother, a widow—"

"None of us is ever only one thing. Consider Yeshua—He was a teacher, a carpenter, a son, a ruler, a servant, Messiah and King. No one could ever name all the things He is . . . and it will be the same with you." She leaned closer. "All you have to be is Yeshua's follower. All you have to do is live for Him."

"How?"

"The Spirit will show you . . . in His time. Until then, listen for His voice and learn from those who knew Him."

"I was thinking . . ." I bit my lip. "I was thinking I should go to Caesarea and help my brother. I know the Roman tribune, and he might help me arrange the journey."

The woman put her hand on my shoulder and smiled. "Don't rush ahead of the Spirit, Aya. You have waited all these years. You can wait until you hear His voice."

I did not have to go to the Antonia. After returning from the Pool of Siloam, a centurion knocked on my door with a message from the tribune. He was preparing to depart for Caesarea, to testify before Governor Felix. Would I be interested in traveling to see my brother?

"Oh, yes!" I told the centurion. "When should I be ready?"

"By tomorrow morning," he answered. "And the tribune wants you to know that you will travel in a private coach, so you will be undisturbed."

I thanked the man, then hurried next door to ask Eden to pray about my visit with Sha'ul.

The next morning, I packed a bag with my best tunic and himation, then walked to the Antonia. The guards at the gate let me pass without a word, and Claudius acknowledged me with a sharp nod. "There," he said, pointing to a closed carriage in a line of horses and chariots. "You will ride in there."

I smiled, not at all offended by his brusque manner. He was doing his best to preserve my reputation and his authority, so

I understood. I walked to the carriage, where a soldier opened the door and helped me climb in.

Once we were under way, I opened the shuttered window for fresh air, but passed most of the hours praying from my heart, not my prayer book. Often I could not find words to express my feelings, so I used that rocking carriage as a holy place, offering my wounded heart to HaShem, and asking Him to use it to help Sha'ul.

When we stopped for the last time, I remained in the carriage until Claudius Lysias came to the door and helped me disembark. "There is a bath," he said, pointing into the darkness, "where you can wash and take care of your needs. After that, I will have a man take you to see your brother."

"Tonight? The hour is so late."

"Better tonight when everyone else is abed. We will return to Jerusalem tomorrow, right after I have testified before the governor. So tonight, after you have seen Sha'ul, return to the carriage and sleep there. Then you will not attract any undue attention."

His eyes gentled. "I apologize for the rough conditions. You deserve better, but your visit has not—let us say it has not been officially sanctioned."

"I would sleep on the ground if necessary," I told him. "Thank you. May HaShem bless you for this."

His mouth twisted in what might have been a smile. I clutched my bag. I was about to stride toward the baths, then stopped. "Claudius Lysias," I said, strangely aware that I would never speak to him again, "you have been a true friend to me. Thank you. You may not believe in HaShem, but He has used you to bless me and my family. I will be praying that you find Him, and that He opens your heart to the truth about His Son Yeshua."

While the Roman stammered in the darkness, I turned and headed toward the baths.

———————•———————

After I had washed and changed my tunic, I lingered outside the baths until a soldier with a torch appeared. "Aya, sister of Sha'ul?"

"Yes."

"Come."

Though it was difficult to see anything in the darkness, he led me away from an imposing palace toward a smaller building surrounded by a stone wall. A guard allowed us to pass through a gate, then we walked through a graveled courtyard not unlike the one at the Antonia. Finally we entered the stone structure and came to the prison cells.

The man unlocked the heavy wooden door, and I stepped through the opening.

Sha'ul lay on a cot, illuminated only by the torch the soldier was fitting into a socket. As the golden light set shadows to dancing on the walls, Sha'ul propped himself on an elbow and squinted at me. "Aya?"

I nodded.

Sha'ul's mouth spread in a lopsided smile. "Am I dreaming, or is this a vision from the Lord?"

"It is I," I said, dropping onto his cot. I squeezed his foot through the thin blanket. "The tribune was kind enough to sneak me into the governor's palace."

"All praise to our Lord Yeshua!" He sat up and studied my face. "You are here—and you are now my sister not only by blood, but by the Spirit." Grinning like a simpleton, he kicked off the blanket and planted his feet on the floor. "My sister: singer, wife, believer. In His mercy, HaShem has opened your heart to receive the Gospel."

I nodded as tears blurred my vision. "It is true. And I am sorry I took so long to understand."

Sha'ul shook his head. "You have believed, and that is all that matters. So why have you come all this way?"

"I have come because . . ." My throat clotted with emotion. "Because I know I will not see you again. I don't know how I know, but I feel it here." I tapped the space above my breastbone. "I know you will be sent to the Gentiles, and you will appear before powerful men. Some of your words will bear fruit, some will fall by the wayside. But you, Sha'ul, were fashioned by HaShem to be a light to the world outside Jerusalem, and a teacher to the assemblies that will carry the Gospel beyond your reach. And when the end comes"—though tears flowed down my cheeks and my ragged voice faltered, I persevered, uttering words that had been given to me—"you will finish the course and receive a crown of righteousness."

Sha'ul stood, held out his arms, and I stepped into them. Neither of us had any more words, yet a new bond existed between us, a bond that would not be severed by distance or time, emperor or governor, life or death.

When the guard in the doorway cleared his throat, I reluctantly released my brother and stepped back. "Write me," I said, wiping tears from my face. "And I will write you."

"Pray for me," he said, a catch in his voice. "And I will continue to pray for you."

As the guard removed the torch from its socket, I stepped forward one last time, kissed Sha'ul on both cheeks, and somehow managed to smile.

"Go in grace." I pressed my hand to his bearded cheek. "With my love, and for the glory of HaShem."

FORTY-SIX

Aya

Two months after my return from Caesarea, I received a letter. I went across the street to share it with Seraiah and Lilith.

Sha'ul, called as an emissary of Messiah Yeshua by the will of God,
To Aya, my beloved sister, and Seraiah and Lilith, my beloved children in the Lord.

Grace to you and shalom from God our Father, and the Lord Yeshua the Messiah!
I always thank my God for you because of God's grace that was given to you in Messiah Yeshua. The Ruach Ha-Kodesh has let me know that He dwells in each of you, and that our family has been made complete in Yeshua. My heart rejoices to know the Spirit is working in you.
I know, Aya, that you are anxious to learn what has happened since I last saw you. The high priest Ananias came with some of the elders and an attorney named

Tertullus. *They brought formal charges against me before the governor. When I was escorted into the chamber, I heard Tertullus heaping praise upon the governor's head, calling him "most excellent" and congratulating him on his foresight and knowledge.*

He then accused me of being a pest who stirred up riots among the Jewish people throughout the world, and a "ringleader" of the sect of the Natzratim. He said I tried to defile the Temple! The Judean leaders joined in, saying these things were true.

When the governor allowed me to speak, I said, "It is no more than twelve days since I went up to Jerusalem to worship. They did not find me arguing with anyone or inciting a riot—not in the Temple or in the synagogues or anywhere else in the city. Nor can they prove to you the charges they now bring against me.

"But this I confess to you, that according to the Way— which they call a sect—I worship the God of our fathers, believing everything written in the Torah and the Prophets." I went on, relating events with which you are familiar, and Felix decided to defer his decision. Then he had me imprisoned, but I am allowed visitors, and these friends have seen to my needs.

A few days later, Felix came with his wife, Drusilla, who is Jewish. He asked me to speak about faith in Messiah Yeshua, and I did. But as I spoke about righteousness, self-control, and the coming judgment, Felix grew afraid and sent me away. I do believe my words had an effect on the governor and his wife because God's Word never fails.

I do not know how long I will remain here, Aya, and I know you have been worried about my health. But the physician Luke is with me as well as other friends, so I am in good hands.

Though you may want to join me, you are needed in

Jerusalem. Seraiah needs you now. As one who serves the ecclēsia in Jerusalem, he will need your support, as will his wife and children. Remain in Jerusalem, dear sister, where you have friends and more influence than you know. The women who spurned you when you dared to sing for Gentiles will be watching you as you walk in the light of Messiah Yeshua.

Grace, peace, and love to all of you.

Sha'ul

I did as Sha'ul recommended. I remained in Jerusalem and prayed in Yeshua's name, asking HaShem to reveal His will for the rest of my life. He did not write on the wall for me as He did for Belshazzar, but I felt a strong impression to remain in the Holy City and start another choir for women. We began to meet in my home, and within a few weeks we were making joyful, beautiful praise to HaShem our Father and Yeshua our Messiah.

We did not sing on the Temple Mount, but in the Xystus, the same open area where Peter gave his sermon at Pentecost. The women stood in a semicircle as I directed, and we sang a song of salvation from the prophet Isaiah. The song just happened to be filled with Yeshua's name.

> Hinei, El is my Yeshuah;
> I will trust, and not be afraid;
> for HaShem is my strength and my zemirah;
> He also has become my Yeshuah.
> Therefore with sasson shall ye draw mayim
> out of the wells of Yeshuah.
>
> Behold, God is my salvation!
> I will trust and will not be afraid.
> For the Lord Adonai is my strength
> and my song.

He also has become my salvation.
With joy you will draw water
from the wells of salvation.

After we finished, our singers dispersed into the crowd that had gathered to listen. A man and woman approached me, and for a moment I did not recognize either of them. Then I realized who he was—Avidan's friend from the yeshiva.

"Ezra!" I gave him a broad smile. "Shalom! I hope you are well."

"My wife and I are very well, thank you." He nodded, then gestured to the place where we had sung. "You were singing of Yeshua."

"Yes." I smiled at his wife, barely able to contain my joy. "I have become a believer."

"Ah." He bit his lip. "I have wanted to tell you something for many years, but never found the courage."

"What is that?"

"It is about Avidan. About the day he died." His eyes softened. "He would have been late coming home because we had been engaged in a heated debate at the yeshiva."

I gave him a noncommittal nod. "I seem to remember hearing something—but I remember very little of that day, other than grief."

"I am not surprised." He glanced at his wife. "I would have told you sooner, but thought the news might upset you."

"Told me what?" I looked from Ezra to his wife, who seemed to know what he was about to say. "Something about Avidan?"

Ezra cleared his throat. "Avidan and I were studying the prophet Isaiah, the passage about the suffering servant. I insisted the passage was about Israel because we have certainly suffered, but Avidan became convinced the Scripture was about Yeshua. Before we left the yeshiva, Avidan proclaimed himself a believer. He could not wait to get home to tell you, which is probably why he hurried around the corner without looking."

Shock siphoned the words from my mouth. I stared at him, amazed, as a whirlwind of thoughts and feelings rushed through my soul. Avidan . . . had believed. He had read the Torah and seen Yeshua in its pages, in the word pictures, in the patterns. He saw what I had finally seen, but he saw the truth long before I did . . . because HaShem opened his heart.

I gaped at Ezra, then laughed aloud. "He believed! Praise HaShem, he believed!"

Ezra nodded, his eyes wide, as I ignored every prohibition against touching and shook his hand. "Thank you for sharing this news! I cannot wait to tell my son and daughter-in-law. And the children. They will be so happy to know that Avidan is with the Lord, waiting for them."

Ezra and his wife stared as I shook their hands again, then whirled and ran home to tell my loved ones.

Author's Note

Thank you for joining me in this fourth book of the JERUSALEM ROAD series. Many readers are interested in knowing how much of a historical novel is based on fact, and how much is a creation of my imagination, so I'm happy to explain the choices I made in this novel.

Q. Is Paul's sister a biblical character? What about her son?

A. Both Paul's sister and nephew are mentioned in the Bible. We are not told their names or their circumstances, but they are both living in Jerusalem at the time of Sha'ul's arrest (AD 57). Acts 23:16 says, "But the son of Paul's sister heard of their ambush. He went into the [Roman] headquarters and told Paul."

Q. Is Claudius Lysias a biblical character?

A. Yes. His name is given and his role explained in Acts 23. Josephus, the Jewish historian, also mentioned him and confirmed Luke's account.

Q. Do you really think Paul was once married?

A. Yes. In 1 Corinthians 7:8, Paul wrote, "But I say to the unmarried and to widows that it is good for them to remain as I am," so we know he was unmarried when he wrote the first letter to the Corinthians.

The Greek word for "unmarried" is *agamos*, and in the verse above, it refers to an unmarried man whether bachelor or widower. Paul also uses this term to refer to those who were *once married* but are no longer married: 1 Corinthians 7:10–11 says, "But to the married I command—not I, but the Lord—a wife is not to be separated from her husband (but if she gets separated, let her remain *unmarried* or else be reconciled to her husband), and the husband is not to divorce his wife."

In 1 Corinthians 7:34, Paul compares an "unmarried" (agamos) woman with a "virgin"—someone who has never been married: "The unmarried woman, as well as the virgin, cares about the things of the Lord, so that she may be holy both in body and in spirit."

Since Paul considers himself *agamos*, like the people in 1 Corinthians 7:8, it is likely he was once married.

Another reason to believe Paul was married is his status as a Pharisee and a member of the Sanhedrin. Someone who considered himself a Pharisee to the highest degree could not ignore the command to marry and bear children.

So it is likely Paul married and his wife died. But God gave him the gift of self-control so he was able to remain unmarried: "But I say to the unmarried and to widows that it is good for them to remain as I am. But if they do not have self-control, let them marry. For it is better to marry than to burn with desire" (1 Corinthians 7:8).

Q. I have always understood that the apostle was known as Sha'ul (or Saul) before his conversion and was afterward

called Paul. So why do you refer to him as Sha'ul throughout the novel?

A. Sha'ul is the apostle's actual Hebrew name, so in Jew-
ish circles he was called Sha'ul throughout his life.
Messianic Jews today still call him Sha'ul, pronounced
"Sha-UL."

His sister would have always called him Sha'ul. *Paulos* was the Latin name he used while speaking Greek
among Gentiles, and he may have been known as Paulos
while in Tarsus. But since he is primarily known as the
"apostle to the Gentiles," we know him best as Paulos.
When transliterated into English, *Sha'ul* and *Paulos* become *Saul* and *Paul*.

Luke himself writes, "But Saul, who is also Paul,
filled with the Ruach HaKodesh, fixed his gaze on
him . . ." (Acts 13:9).

Q. Did Jesus really appear to Paul while he was being held in the Antonia Fortress?

A. Acts 23:11: "The following night the Lord *stood beside
Paul* and said, 'Take courage! For just as you have testified about Me in Jerusalem, so you must also testify
in Rome!'" (italics mine). I suppose it is possible that
"stood beside Paul" could be meant metaphorically, but
in every translation I read, Yeshua was standing by or
near Paul, so why not take it literally?

Q. Do we have evidence that Paul witnessed the trial of Jesus?

A. Not to my knowledge. He may have, if he had been
elevated to a position on the Sanhedrin by the time of
Jesus' trial, but since he does not mention the experience in his many letters, I doubt he did.

Q. Did the Temple really have choirs? How did the singers read the music?

A. Scripture describes orchestras and choirs of male and female singers, but those seem to have existed only in Solomon's Temple. According to the *Mishna*, those early musicians trained for an average of five years. Professional male and female singers were employed (Ecclesiastes 2:8), and some scholars believe the prophet Samuel organized a school for Levites, with music and prophecy as part of the curriculum (1 Samuel 10:5; 2 Samuel 6:5; 1 Chronicles 15:16; 25:1–6).

By the second Temple period, Herod's Temple, the choirs were exclusively male. Apparently, the orchestras no longer existed, though gongs, trumpets, flutes (on special occasions), and shofars were used, serving more as "signals" than musical accompaniment.

How did people learn music? The art of chironomy, developed in ancient Egypt, was a system of hand signals that helped singers and instrumentalists follow a director. In my days as a music major, I realized that teaching an unfamiliar song to people who don't read music was easier if I used one hand to keep the beat and the other to move up or down along with the melody. Chironomy must have been similar.

Ancient musicians may have had an even more sophisticated method of musical notation. In the oldest existing example of a Hebrew Bible, the Aleppo Codex (Masoretic Text), accents known as *te amim* are depicted above certain words and letters. The exact meaning of those accents has often been debated, but Suzanne Haik Vantoura, a twentieth-century organist and musicologist, was convinced they are a method of indicating melody. Her work is too involved to explain in detail, but if you search for her on the internet, you can find recordings of the ancient psalms, "translated" according to the accents. You may find yourself listening to Psalm 23 just as David sang it!

Q. Did women really hand their babies off to wet nurses for long periods of time?

A. Yes, though I don't believe the practice was common. The agreement Aya signs was adapted from an actual contract written in 13 BC. That original contract was given to a woman from a man who had custody of an infant born into slavery. He hired a wet nurse to feed the child until the baby was old enough to be weaned.

Q. Could women read and write? I thought most people were illiterate in those days, especially if they were poor.

A. Not at all! The Jews are known for being "People of the Book," and even the poorest villages had synagogue schools where very young boys and girls were taught to read and write the Hebrew alphabet. Salome Alexandria, queen of Jerusalem from 75 BC until her death in 57 BC, established a system of education for girls in Jerusalem so they could read and write as well as the boys.

Q. Are we sure Nicodemus became a Christian?

A. To my knowledge, no historical documents record his conversion. I would like to think he did believe, however, because he sought Yeshua privately and helped with His burial. We do know he remained an active part of the Jerusalem council for several years after Christ's resurrection.

We also know what happened to him a few years later.

Around AD 67, before the Temple was destroyed, the Zealots wrested control of Jerusalem from the Romans. They took control of the Fortress Antonia, assassinated the high priest, and murdered the Jewish elites who had cooperated with Rome. They also burned three granaries belonging to wealthy patricians, and one of those belonged to Nicodemus. He died several months later—probably from hunger or illness—in the resulting war that saw the destruction of the Temple and the death or enslavement of thousands of Jews.

Q. Several times you mention the Oral Torah, but I've never heard of it. What is it?

A. I had never heard of it until I began to study this period. My explanation will be more helpful if we review a few basics: The *Tanakh* is the Hebrew Bible, or what Christians would call the Old Testament. It is divided into three sections: The Law, the Prophets, and Collected Writings (everything else).

The first five books of the Hebrew Bible are the *Torah*, also known as the Pentateuch. These books—Genesis, Exodus, Leviticus, Numbers, and Deuteronomy—were written by Moses and detailed the Law the Jews were to observe after their exodus from Egypt. Most of the Law had to do with the Tabernacle and the Temple, detailing the festivals, sacrifices, and the priestly system.

By the time Yeshua was born, the rabbis had also developed what they called the "Oral Torah" or "the traditions." These teachings do not claim to be inspired Scripture, but came from rabbis who wanted to explain, illustrate, clarify, or expound on the Torah. These were passed orally from teacher to student and memorized.

The daily Scripture readings, the liturgy of the daily prayers, and the order of Shabbat services all came from the Oral Torah. When Yeshua attended a synagogue (Mark 6) and read the Scripture portion of the day, He was following a tradition from the Oral Torah.

After Sha'ul became a believer, he continued to observe the Jewish traditions. "I am a Pharisee," he told the Sanhedrin in Acts 23:6. He *didn't* say, "I used to be a Pharisee."

Jesus told the people, "The Torah scholars and Pharisees sit on the seat of Moses. So whatever they tell you, *do and observe*. But don't do what they do; for what they say, they do not do." In other words, the Torah scholars and Pharisees were teaching biblical principles, but they weren't practicing what they preached. Jesus didn't condemn what the Pharisees were teaching, but the way they sought to glorify themselves instead of God.

The Mosaic covenant, which God established with Israel after the exodus, is found in the Torah. Yeshua (who knew the Temple would soon be destroyed) said He had come to give the Jews a *new* covenant, which would be written on their hearts (Jeremiah 31:33; Hebrews 8:10; Luke 22:20).

The rabbis taught that after God gave Moses the written Law on Mount Sinai, He also gave instructions that were not written. These instructions were supposedly passed down from generation to generation until the Pharisees began to compile them in the second century. The *Mishna* (AD 200–220) and the *Gemara* were combined into the *Talmud*, which exists in two versions. The Jerusalem Talmud (AD 300–350) was written in Galilee, and the larger Babylonian Talmud (AD 450–500) was written in Babylon.

Yet the Talmud/Oral Torah have not been universally accepted. The Sadducees in Jesus' day rejected it and so do the modern Karaite Jews. Why?

Exodus 24:4 says, "Moses wrote down *all* the words of Adonai . . ." If the Oral Torah was given to clarify the Law, one has to wonder why Moses had to consult the Lord when the Jews came to him with a problem. During the time of the Tabernacle, the *Urim* and the *Thummin* of the high priest also clarified the Lord's position (Numbers 27:21).

In 2 Kings 22, we read about a priest who found a Torah scroll during the time of King Josiah. During the reign of the previous kings, the Law had been completely forgotten. When Josiah heard the words of the Law, he tore his clothes and vowed to renew Israel's covenant with God, keep His Law, and celebrate the Passover, which had not been observed since the time of the judges. If the Oral Torah was being passed from generation to generation, why did no one know the Law during the years between the judges and Josiah?

Personally, I do not believe God gave Moses oral instructions that were not written down. I do believe that men of God began to teach younger men, and the traditions were developed as far back as the Hasmonean (intertestamental) period.

Yeshua observed the traditions, and so did His disciples. Sha'ul did, both before and after his conversion.

In the Oral Torah, a reader can find beauty, history, and godly principles. Many Oral Torah passages amplify the Scriptures and provide fascinating insights. (The midwife's description of Aya's embryo comes directly from the Talmud, Niddah 25b). The traditions, especially in the Seder, establish elements of Jewish holidays that picture the death and resurrection of Ye-shua.

Rabbi John Fischer wrote, "The stirring images and striking pictures which richly reflect Yeshua would be lost to us apart from the 'traditional' Seder. The traditions give us the afikomen (the broken matzah used for dessert) and the three pieces of matzah, the cup of redemption, Elijah's cup, and more."[1]

Yet the Oral Torah also contains ideas that have nothing to do with the God of Israel.

When the Temple was destroyed in AD 70, the rabbis who did not accept Yeshua had to adapt the form of Judaism because the Temple no longer existed. So they began to record the Oral Torah and over the years they added to it. I am no expert on the Talmud, but what I have learned leads me to believe that the rabbinical writings of the Oral Torah became less trustworthy as the years progressed.

In some passages, the Oral Torah contradicts science. It claims, among other things, that bats lay eggs, mermaids exist, and thunder is produced when clouds rub against the stars.[2]

The Oral Torah does not always reflect the ethics of the Bible. Portions of the Oral Torah says women are enslaved to their husbands and may be beaten with a rod if they do not do their work. It also says a man can do anything he likes with his wife, for she is his property. The Oral Torah says Jews should never befriend a

1. Fischer, John. "The Place of Rabbinic Tradition in a Messianic Jewish Lifestyle." *The Enduring Paradox: Exploratory Essays in Messianic Judaism.* Baltimore, MD: Messianic Jewish Publishers, 2000.

2. First Ever Orthodox vs. Messianic Debate—in Hebrew! April 28, 2021, One for Israel, https://www.oneforisrael.org/apologetics/rabbinic/first-ever-orthodox-vs-messianic-debate-in-hebrew/, accessed July 15, 2021.

Gentile, for Gentiles are like donkeys, without a spirit or soul. "Even the most righteous Gentile deserves to be killed," according to a portion of the Oral Torah.[3]

The Oral Torah is undoubtedly a man-made work. According to Rabbi John Fischer, "The focus of Messianic Judaism must remain squarely on Yeshua, and this does not mean setting aside the traditions. Further, the traditions are not authoritative, as is only the Bible. However, the prayers and teachings of 'the Rabbis' are valid and helpful *as they reflect and do not contradict scripture* . . . God used these very traditions to preserve our people through the centuries"[4] (italics added).

Christian religious leaders have also added to God's Word over the years.

A saying exists among writers: "No urge is as strong as the urge to edit someone else's prose." While that adage makes us smile, the "urge to tweak" is endemic to mankind. Thinking *we* know best, we want to add our own requirements and embellishments to God's Word. "Yes," we may say, "the Bible says *this*, but I think (or 'our church says') you must *also* do this and this and this . . ."

While religious writings (including historical fiction!) may hold and teach spiritual truths, they are no substitute for the Word of God. Take what is good and true and biblical from the former, but cling to the latter.

God's truth lies in the words God gave to Moses, Yeshua, His prophets and apostles. As Sha'ul wrote to Timothy, "All Scripture is God-breathed and is valuable for teaching the truth, convicting of sin, correct-

---

3. Major Rabbi Says Non-Jews Are Donkeys, Created to Serve Jews, October 18, 2010, http://www.thepeoplesvoice.org/TPV3/Voices.php/2010/10/18/major-rabbi-says-non-jews-are-donkeys, accessed December 13, 2021.

4. Fischer, Ibid.

ing faults and training in right living; thus anyone who belongs to God may be fully equipped for every good work" (2 Timothy 3:16–17).

The Bible—Old Testament and New—contains *all* you need to know to find salvation and live a life that pleases God.

References

Achtemeier, Paul J. *Harper's Bible Dictionary*. Harper & Row and Society of Biblical Literature. 1985.

Barclay, William, ed. *The Acts of the Apostles*. Philadelphia, PA: The Westminster John Knox Press, 1976.

Barton, Bruce B., David Veerman, and Neil S. Wilson. *1 Timothy, 2 Timothy, Titus*. Wheaton, IL: Tyndale House Publishers, 1993.

Beasley-Murray, George R. *Word Biblical Commentary*. "John." Vol. 36. Dallas: Word, Inc., 1999.

Beck, John A. *The Baker Book of Bible Charts, Maps, and Timelines*. Grand Rapids, MI: Baker Books, 2016.

Bock, Darrell L. "Luke." *Holman Concise Bible Commentary*. Ed. David S. Dockery. Nashville, TN: Broadman & Holman Publishers, 1998.

Blum, Julia. *As Though Hiding His Face*. USA: My Zion LLC, 2017.

Borchert, Gerald L. *The New American Commentary*. John 1–11. Vol. 25A. Nashville, TN: Broadman & Holman Publishers, 1996.

Brenton, Lancelot Charles Lee. *The Septuagint Version of the Old Testament: English Translation*. London: Samuel Bagster and Sons, 1870.

Burk, Denny. "Was the Apostle Paul Married?" August 30, 2011, http://www.dennyburk.com/was-the-apostle-paul-married/, accessed November 24, 2017.

Byfield, Ted, ed. "The Veil Is Torn." *The Christians: Their First Two*

Thousand Years. Canada: Christian Millennial History Project, 2002.

Dean, Robert J. "Sanhedrin." Ed. Chad Brand et al. *Holman Illustrated Bible Dictionary.* Nashville, TN: Broadman & Holman Publishers, 2003.

Easley, Kendell H. *Holman QuickSource Guide to Understanding the Bible.* Nashville, TN: Broadman & Holman Publishers, 2002.

Edersheim, Alfred. *The Life and Times of Jesus the Messiah.* Vol. 1. New York: Longmans, Green, and Co., 1896.

———. *The Temple: Its Ministry and Services as They Were at the Time of Jesus Christ.* Mount Pleasant, SC: Arcadia Press, 2017.

———. *Sketches of Jewish Social Life in the Days of Christ, Revised and Illustrated.* Clearwater, FL: Hunt Haven Press, 2019.

Edwards, Douglas R. "Dress and Ornamentation." Ed. David Noel Freedman. *The Anchor Yale Bible Dictionary,* 1992.

Eisenberg, Joyce, and Ellen Scolnic. *The JPS Dictionary of Jewish Words.* Philadelphia: The Jewish Publication Society, 2001.

Eisenberg, Ronald L. *The JPS Guide to Jewish Traditions.* Philadelphia: The Jewish Publication Society, 2004.

Elwell, Walter A., and Philip Wesley Comfort. *Tyndale Bible Dictionary.* Elgin, IL: Tyndale House Publishers, 2001.

Elwell, Walter A., and Barry J. Beitzel. *The Baker Encyclopedia of the Bible.* Grand Rapids, MI: Baker Books, 1988.

Fischer, John. "The Place of Rabbinic Tradition in a Messianic Jewish Lifestyle." *The Enduring Paradox: Exploratory Essays in Messianic Judaism.* Baltimore, MD: Messianic Jewish Publishers, 2000.

Flusser, David. "Character Profiles: Gamaliel and Nicodemus," https://www.jerusalemperspective.com/11476, accessed May 18, 2021.

Fruchtenbaum, Arnold G. "Foreword." *Discovering the Mystery of the Unity of God: A Theological Study on the Plurality and Tri-Unity of God in the Hebrew Scriptures.* San Antonio, TX: Ariel Ministries, 2010.

———. *The Messianic Bible Study Collection.* Vol. 22–23. Tustin, CA: Ariel Ministries, 1983.

Gapp, Kenneth Sperber. "The Universal Famine under Claudius." Cambridge University Press, October 5, 2011, https://www.cam-

bridge.org/core/journals/harvard-theological-review/article/abs
/universal-famine-under-claudius/, accessed June 24, 2021.

Gasque, W. Ward. "Tarsus (Place)." Ed. David Noel Freedman. *The Anchor Yale Bible Dictionary*. 1992.

Gillman, Rabbi Neil. *The Jewish Approach to God: A Brief Introduction for Christians*. Woodstock, Vermont: Jewish Lights Publishing, 2003.

Guthrie, Donald. *New Testament Introduction*. 4th rev. ed. Downers Grove, IL: InterVarsity Press, 1996.

Hayford, Jack W., and Joseph Snider. *Kingdom Power: Receiving the Power of the Promise, A Study in the Book of Acts*. Nashville, TN: Thomas Nelson Publishers, 1993.

Hensley, Carl Wayne. "Golgotha." *The Baker Encyclopedia of the Bible*. Grand Rapids, MI: Baker Books, 1988.

Josephus, Flavius, and William Whiston. *The Works of Josephus: Complete and Unabridged*. Peabody, MA: Hendrickson Publishers, 1987.

Kasdan, Barney. *Matthew Presents Yeshua, King Messiah: A Messianic Commentary*. Clarksville, MD: Messianic Jewish Publishers, 2011.

Levertoff, Paul. "Sanhedrin." Ed. James Orr et al. *The International Standard Bible Encyclopedia*. Grand Rapids, MI: William B. Eerdmans, 1915.

Lumbroso, Patrick Gabriel. *Under the Vine: Messianic Thought through the Hebrew Calendar*. Clarksville, MD: Messianic Jewish Publishers, 2013.

Lunceford, Joe E. "Congregation." Ed. Chad Brand et al. *Holman Illustrated Bible Dictionary*. Nashville, TN: Broadman & Holman Publishers, 2003.

Manser, Martin H. *Dictionary of Bible Themes: The Accessible and Comprehensive Tool for Topical Studies*. London: Martin Manser, 2009.

Martin, D. Michael. "1, 2 Thessalonians." *The New American Commentary*. Vol. 33. Nashville, TN: Broadman & Holman Publishers, 1995.

McArthur, Harvey. *Celibacy in Judaism at the Time of Christian Beginnings*. Berrien Springs, MI: Andrews University Press, 1987.

McGee, J. Vernon. *Thru the Bible Commentary*. Vol. 5. Nashville: Thomas Nelson Publishers, 1997.

Meldau, Fred John. *The Prophets Still Speak: Messiah in Both Testaments*. Bellmawr, NJ: Friends of Israel Gospel Ministry, 1988.

Ogilvie, Lloyd J. *Acts*. Vol. 28. Nashville, TN: Thomas Nelson Publishers, 1983.

One for Israel Ministry. "First Ever Orthodox vs Messianic Debate in Hebrew! With English subs," https://www.youtube.com/, July 14, 2021, accessed July 15, 2021.

———. "The Talmud (rabbinic tradition) vs. The New Testament," https://www.youtube.com/watch, March 14, 2018, accessed July 25, 2021.

O'Toole, Robert F. "Paul's Nephew." Ed. David Noel Freedman. *The Anchor Yale Bible Dictionary*. 1992.

Packer, J. I., Merrill Chapin Tenney, and William White Jr. *Nelson's Illustrated Manners and Customs of the Bible*. Nashville, TN: Thomas Nelson Publishers, 1997.

Pelser, G. M. M. "Governing Authorities in Jewish National Life in Palestine in New Testament Times." *The New Testament Milieu*. Ed. A. B. du Toit. Vol. 2. Halfway House: Orion Publishers, 1998.

Polhill, John B. "Acts." *The New American Commentary*. Vol. 26. Nashville, TN: Broadman & Holman Publishers, 1992.

Saldarini, Anthony J. "Sanhedrin." Ed. David Noel Freedman. *The Anchor Yale Bible Dictionary*, 1992.

Simmons, William A. *Peoples of the New Testament World: An Illustrated Guide*. Peabody, MA: Hendrickson Publishers, 2008.

Steinsaltz, Adin. *The Essential Talmud*. New York: Basic Books, 1976.

Stern, David H. *Jewish New Testament: A Translation of the New Testament That Expresses Its Jewishness*. 1st ed. Jerusalem, Israel; Clarksville, MD, USA: Jewish New Testament Publications, 1989.

———. *Jewish New Testament Commentary: A Companion Volume to the Jewish New Testament*. Clarksdale, MD: Jewish New Testament Publications, 1992.

Strange, James F. "Sepphoris." Ed. David Noel Freedman. New Haven, CT: *The Anchor Yale Bible Dictionary*, 1992.

Taitz, Emily, Sondra Henry, and Cheryl Tallan. *The JPS Guide to Jew-*

ish Women: 600 BCE–1900 CE. Philadelphia: The Jewish Publication Society, 2003.

Tasker, R. V. G. "Matthew, Gospel of." Ed. D. R. W. Wood et al. *New Bible Dictionary.* Downers Grove, IL: InterVarsity Press, 1996.

Thompson, J. A. "Sanhedrin." Ed. D. R. W. Wood et al. *New Bible Dictionary.* Downers Grove, IL: InterVarsity Press, 1996.

Townsend, John T. "Education: Greco-Roman Period." Ed. David Noel Freedman. *The Anchor Yale Bible Dictionary,* 1992.

Vamosh, Miriam Feinberg. *Food at the Time of the Bible: From Adam's Apple to the Last Supper.* Herzlia, Israel: Palphot Ltd., 2007.

Vos, Howard Frederic. *Nelson's New Illustrated Bible Manners & Customs: How the People of the Bible Really Lived.* Nashville, TN: Thomas Nelson Publishers, 1999.

Watson, JoAnn Ford. "Claudius Lysias (Person)." Ed. David Noel Freedman. *The Anchor Yale Bible Dictionary,* 1992.

Young, Robert. *Young's Literal Translation.* Bellingham, WA: Logos Bible Software, 1997.

Youngblood, Ronald F., F. F. Bruce, and R. K. Harrison, eds. *Nelson's New Illustrated Bible Dictionary.* Nashville, TN: Thomas Nelson Publishers, 1995.

Angela Hunt has published more than 150 books, with sales exceeding five million copies worldwide. She's the *New York Times* bestselling author of *The Tale of Three Trees*, *The Note*, and *The Nativity Story*. Angela's novels have won or been nominated for several prestigious industry awards, such as the RITA Award, the Christy Award, the ECPA Christian Book Award, and the HOLT Medallion Award. Romantic Times Book Club presented her with a Lifetime Achievement Award in 2006. She holds both a doctorate in Biblical Studies and a Th.D. degree. Angela and her husband live in Florida, along with their mastiffs and chickens. For a complete list of the author's books, visit angelahuntbooks.com.

Sign Up for Angela's Newsletter

Keep up to date with Angela's news on book releases and events by signing up for her email list at angelahuntbooks.com.

More from Angela Hunt

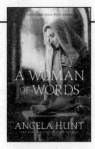

Asked by Mary to record stories of Yeshua while the eyewitnesses are still alive, Matthew, a disciple, reluctantly agrees. But the longer they work together, the more difficult their task becomes as they face threats and opposition. And when Matthew works to save his people, he realizes that the job he hesitantly accepted may be his God-given destiny.

A Woman of Words
JERUSALEM ROAD #3

You May Also Like . . .

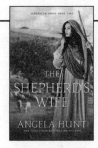

When her husband is thrown into debtor's prison, Pheodora—sister of Yeshua of Nazareth—pins her hopes on the birth of two spotless goats to sell for the upcoming Yom Kippur sacrifice so that she can provide for her daughters and survive. Calling on her wits, her family, and her God, can she trust that He will hear and help a lowly shepherd's wife?

The Shepherd's Wife by Angela Hunt
JERUSALEM ROAD #2
angelahuntbooks.com

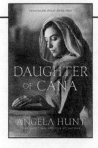

When a wedding guest tells Tasmin to have the servants fill the pitchers with water, she reluctantly obeys and is amazed when it turns into the finest wine ever tasted in Cana. But when her twin brother, Thomas, impulsively chooses to follow the Teacher from Nazareth, she decides to follow the group and do whatever she must to bring her brother home.

Daughter of Cana by Angela Hunt
JERUSALEM ROAD #1
angelahuntbooks.com

Two women occupy a place in Herod's court: the king's only sister, Salome, a resentful woman who has been told she is from an inferior race, and her lowly handmaid, Zara, who sees the hurt in those around her. Both women struggle to reach their goals and survive in Herod the Great's tumultuous court, where no one is trustworthy and no one is safe.

King's Shadow by Angela Hunt
THE SILENT YEARS
angelahuntbooks.com

⊘ BETHANYHOUSE

More from Bethany House

Natalia Blackstone relies on Count Dimitri Sokolov to oversee the construction of the Trans-Siberian Railway. Dimitri loses everything after witnessing a deadly tragedy and its cover-up, but he has an asset the czar knows nothing about: Natalia. Together they fight to save the railroad while exposing the truth, but can their love survive the ordeal?

Written on the Wind by Elizabeth Camden
THE BLACKSTONE LEGACY #2
elizabethcamden.com

Allie Massey's dream to use her grandparents' estate for equine therapy is crushed when she discovers the property has been sold to a contractor. With weeks until demolition, Allie unearths some of Nana Dale's best-kept secrets—including her champion filly, a handsome man, and one fateful night during WWII—and perhaps a clue to keep her own dream alive.

By Way of the Moonlight by Elizabeth Musser
elizabethmusser.com

Del Nielsen's teaching job in town offers hope, not only to support her three sisters but also to better her students' lives. When their brother visits with his war-wounded friend RJ, Del finds RJ barely polite and wants nothing to do with him. But despite the sisters' best-laid plans, the future—and RJ—might surprise them all.

A Time to Bloom by Lauraine Snelling
LEAH'S GARDEN #2
laurainesnelling.com

BETHANYHOUSE